Carl,
All the best to you. Thank you for
your many years of support!!

Dan Mallach

Gravity Divided

By
David A. Mallach

FIRST EDITION

Library of Congress

ISBN 978-0-9860458-1-3

Website: dmallach.com

Penhurst Books

Printed in the United States of America
Bookmaster Book Printing

Dedicated

To

Dr. Jack Hawkins
Chancellor

For Making Troy University
A Great Educational Institution

From the Author

This book is a work of fiction. Therefore, it should not be assumed by any reader that any specific investment or investment strategy made reference to in this book will be either profitable or equal to historical or anticipated performance levels. It should also not be assumed that the performance of any specific investment style or sector will be either profitable or equal to its corresponding historical index benchmark. Finally, different types of investments involve varying degrees of risk, and there can be no assurance that any specific investment or investment strategy made reference to in this book will be suitable or otherwise appropriate for an individual's investment portfolio. To the extent that readers have any questions regarding the suitability of any specific investment or investment strategy made reference to in this book for their individual investment(s) or financial situation, they are encouraged to consult with the investment professional of their choosing.

About the Author

David Mallach is a Managing Director of Investments for one of the world's largest investment firms where he has spent his entire professional career since 1973. He resides in the greater Philadelphia area. He is the author of *Dancing With The Analysts, Walking With The Analysts, Running With The Analysts, Myth, The Trillion Dollar Sure Thing, Turning Final and Angle of Attack.*

David is a selected member of *Registered Representative Magazine's* Outstanding Advisor of the Year and *Research Magazine's* Hall of Fame. In 2010, 2011 and 2012, he was selected as one of the top 1,000 advisors in America by *Barron's Magazine*. David serves on the Board of Trustees for Gwynedd Mercy University and the Troy University Foundation. David is the proud father of five children, an accomplished saxophone player, and a registered private pilot.

Preface

Leigh Brackett, the heralded Queen of Space Opera who penned *The Empire Strikes Back* series among many other scripts and novels, says this: "Plot is people. Human emotions and desires founded on the realities of life, working across purposes, getting hotter and fiercer as they strike against each other until finally there's an explosion – that's Plot." Indeed, lurking just beneath the surface of a good story is a seething, primal mass of humanity threatening to burst forth and form new life. In this regard, the art of the novel is the art of creation, and plot a sort of Big Bang exploding forth in each new work.

Prior to embarking upon the fantastic journey that unfolds in the story that follows, I wrote a trilogy exploring a collective human reality in which we readily accept in our chosen male leaders' behaviors and attitudes that we would otherwise find reprehensible. I took great pains to craft a world as ironic and paradoxical as the one in which we wake up every day. And yet, we largely sleepwalk through the many decades of our fleeting human existence. I set out to create a character powerful enough to resonate and reverberate like a massive bell striking midnight and shattering our collective Jungian somnambulance.

Camille O'Keefe was born. As *The Trillion Dollar Sure Thing* grew into *Turning Final*, and then into *Angle of Attack*, this powerful female protagonist became something special. She became the herald of a new spirit of change and voice of alterity. She became a symbol of power from outside the system.

Camille O'Keefe is now the lifeblood running through a series of books. Like Leigh Brackett, I seek to drive characters together, then sit back and watch as they "grow hotter and fiercer as they strike against each other until finally there's an explosion." Again, plot is like the Big Bang. After the cataclysmic explosion, we're left with a new universe of wonderful possibilities replete with hopes, aspirations, and the potential for transcendence.

The tremendous possibilities of *Gravity Divided* (the title itself suggesting an upheaval in the order of things) are the possibilities of human ingenuity stunted only by fear and ego. Where there is hope for the many, there is also the concentrated will to power. Where there are new life forms and new bodies, there are also reactionary forces and mass-produced yesteryears. Gravity symbolizes both a force from above pulling us away and a force from below pulling us down. Physics tells us massive size always wins this existential tug of war. But what if we shifted the paradigm?

Gravity Divided is the space between us where the paradigm is reformulated and the future is remade.

This is the eighth book I've written. Each time I embark upon a new book, it seems I have more to say than I have pages on which to write. More stories must be written. This novel only works because of my twenty-year working relationship with Todd Napolitano. Todd and I have developed a collaborative partnership that, at times, comes to life like a symphony. Together we build worlds and birth characters that amount to much more than the sum of our two minds. That's the beauty of our collaboration – energy, intellect, and passion all coming together to form something truly wonderful. I am pleased to offer *Gravity Divided* as the most recent generation in this distinguished lineage.

I am also deeply indebted to the following people:

Jeanette Freudiger, to whom once again I owe special thanks
  for her long-term work so closely related to this novel
  and my previous works. She was always ready with
  her wit, help, and advice to insure that this novel was
  designed in the most thorough and entertaining fashion;
Sharon Cromwell, my editor who made this manuscript and
  all my books readable novels;
Stephanie Heckman, for her tireless editing of this novel;
John Mallach, for his time and help in editing this novel;
Kyle Mallach, for his time and help in editing this novel;
Patrick Hoffman, for his support and editing skills;
John Sasso, my longtime friend and editing professional;
Bob Wagner, my Costa Rican advisor whose Internet skills
  are equal to his generosity;
Lastly, I thank all the wonderful investors I have known,
  who in their quest for growth chose to honor me with
  their trust.

Chapter 1

Achère, France, April 29, 1899

Twenty-five kilometers outside of Paris, a warm breeze hints at spring's arrival. Scores of mockingbirds, robins, and thrushes dart and dance overhead as they make their yearly migration toward Schaerbeek, Belgium. A young Belgian man named Cam Jenatzi climbs into his vehicle. He is unassuming and rather inconspicuous; his car, however, is not. Atop those four wheels is a missile-shaped vehicle made from lightweight metals. The tubular body, painted a glossy, gunmetal gray, sits on a bright-red wooden chassis like the kind on a child's wagon. It looks more like a teetering torpedo on a weapons dolly than a futuristic, state-of-the-art race car.

Jenatzi looks up and takes note of the birds passing overhead. They swarm and look like pulsing clouds. He grew up with these birds. He knows them intimately because his hometown of Schaerbeek is famous for them. He reflects on the moment... here he is in France, having come from Belgium while those birds are headed to his hometown back in Belgium. Things are transitory, he thinks to himself. He will make history here today. That's what he thinks.

Is it any wonder that he named a strange-looking race car, which he designed and built himself, *La Jamais Contente*, The Never Satisfied?

He climbs into *La Jamais Contente*. There is no safety harness to fasten. It's the oddest-looking thing because over half his body remains outside the vehicle as if he is sitting on a saddle. He looks hilariously like Slim Pickens riding that missile in *Dr. Strangelove*. As far as Cam Jenatzi is concerned, though, everything is firmly planted on the ground. It's this moment in history that he hopes will launch him to fame.

He presses the ignition switch, then revs the engine once… twice… three times. The tachometer jumps to life each time, but there is barely a sound. It's virtually silent, a far cry from the pits of NASCAR we associate with racing today. Why? Because *La Jamais Contente*, The Never Satisfied, is completely electric. That's right, the year is 1899, and Cam Jenatzi is about to break the land speed record, a blistering 62 miles per hour, in a car that is 100 percent electric.

He takes several deep breaths. He's confident, having crafted every inch of the car from one conical end to the other. For him, it's more than just a machine. It has a life force running through it, his life force. For him, the car is part machine and part human. He feels what is about to happen. This moment is crystallizing for him into the manifestation of his dream since he was a child. On April 29, 1899, Cam Jenatzi will try to make his dreams real. He will never be satisfied with anything less.

As he eases the torpedo-car to the start line, Jenatzi allows himself a moment to reminisce. When he was a young boy, he used to bolt from his mother during their walks in Josaphat Park off the *Boulevard Lambermont*. Dust and gravel would kick up under his heels. He moved fast, bobbing through the many pedestrians casually strolling toward the *Laiterie* for an ice cream. His white twill baker-boy hat would fly off without fail. His white knickerbockers were always the worse for wear.

He fancied himself as a cheetah or a horse tearing around the well-manicured gravel pathways. Always, he was some sort of animal in his mind's eye, fast but never furious. Always, he was faster than anything. That's how the boy saw himself back then; that's how the man sees himself now.

There was something special about Cam Jenatzi, something timeless that defied limitation, something transcendent that marked him for potential greatness. An intangible force existed around him that others couldn't see as surely as there was the omnipresent force of gravity. Great innovators like Cam Jenatzi will always move us forward. Jenatzi and his completely electric racing torpedo represented the indomitable spirit of the entrepreneurial required to propel the world forward.

Required now, as ever, are those who can make dreams real.

And yet, despite his dreams, the world opted to go another way. An electric world or a petroleum world? Jenatzi went one way, the world went another. Petroleum won, electricity lost. It was really just a matter of timing. Jenatzi was bold enough to glimpse the future and put forth a great new world of possibilities. Unfortunately for him, he could not make his dreams a reality. They flamed out quite unceremoniously before being relegated to history's mountainous trash heap. Who knows what other dreams are piled there? The Fountain of Youth or the cure for cancer may be buried there a hundred times over.

So much for Cam Jenatzi, a man who could not make dreams real. Onto the heap with him.

Philadelphia, PA, July 4, 1976

We jump to 1976, Philadelphia, the American Bicentennial. Birthplace of the Constitution, home of the Liberty Bell, epicenter of American independence, the City of Brotherly Love has been hopping all week. Tall ships, masts majestically reaching into the sky, stand anchored along the Delaware River stretching two miles up to the Benjamin Franklin Bridge. Old City is the Bicentennial nucleus. The neighborhood is imbued with history, a living, breathing monument to America's forefathers. The entire historic district is a national park, a thriving, bustling testament to a group of men who fought for an ideal and forged a great nation out of the raw material of pure dreams.

The country is caught in the swells of patriotic celebration. Even so, Philadelphia has a special vibe this evening. Thousands of people have gathered to watch a spectacular fireworks show in honor of their proud but pimply and pubescent country. They stand among the ghosts of great men, the founding fathers... George Washington, Benjamin Franklin, Alexander Hamilton, and James Madison.

As if drawing energy from this intangible supply of energy, a young boy agilely weaves through the throng of people amassed in Liberty Bell Park. The knees of his white pants are soiled irrevocably.

His matching white baker-boy hat flies off and lands in a dirty puddle. He stops, retrieves it, and flops it back on his sweaty head. Somewhere his mother is calling after him frantically.

The great men of America's birth are gone, but their legacy flows like lifeblood through the veins of American democracy. They were, all of them, men who made dreams real. The boy is filled with their spirit. Mostly, he is driven to overcome ghosts like the indefatigable General Washington and compelled to invent like the pragmatic Ben Franklin. The boy's nature is thus composed, domineering but practical above all.

Only ten years old, this boy is already destined for greatness. Like Cam Jenatzi, this boy in Philadelphia is one of the never satisfied. But unlike Jenatzi, this boy is capable of making dreams real. That's where Jenatzi was never able to make the rubber meet the road. It will not be so with this boy.

He hears his mother calling out as she searches frantically through the crowd. Her voice has the shrill urgency that only a parent looking for a lost child can have. It's dark out. They do not know the city. She is worried about her son. Worse yet, if Eagles fans are any indication, her darling boy could be torn limb from limb.

"Rickey! Rickey, where are you? Rickey Ormand answer me this minute!"

Ten-year-old Rickey Ormand doesn't hear her. Or if he does, he pays her no mind. He is unconcerned both for the mass of people pressing ever closer upon him and his mother's desperation. His concerns lie elsewhere. He looks into the evening sky, rockets bursting in air. The crowd, pressing closer still, grows more and more energized with every luminescent burst and thunderous explosion. But young Rickey Ormand barely notices. His interest lies elsewhere, beyond even the apex of the fireworks exploding overhead that are enthralling the crowd more and more with every volley.

High in the sky, off to one side, a full moon stands proud, aloof, as if to say, "Here is the real show, people." At least that's what the moon says to Rickey Ormand. The boy is fixated on the glowing ball of celestial grandeur. The gray pockmarks remind him that there are forces at work around him that are far greater and more ancient than anything two hundred years can encompass. With fireworks exploding overhead, the entranced crowd cheering, Rickey Ormand closes his eyes and breaks away from everyone. In that crystalline moment – a moment he will never forget – he realizes that one day he will turn science fiction into science fact. He imagines a world where people can fly as easily as they walk, a world filled with excitement like in the *Star Trek* episodes his father lets him watch every night after dinner.

Yes, the boy has spent hours imagining himself in a gigantic spaceship zooming from galaxy to galaxy faster than light itself. In his mind's eye, he exists as both person and machine, a mischievous boy and a blurry mass of particles defying every law of physics known to mankind. Someday, he thinks, he will be like Mr. Spock, and Scotty, and even Captain Kirk, all rolled into one. Ah, the invincible Kirk is irresistible to even green alien females. Someday, he thinks, he will sit in the Captain's chair and have a half-naked, green girlfriend from another galaxy. He smiles when he thinks about it… someday, even William Shatner will want to shake *my* hand. Imagine that?

Then, out of nowhere, he feels an excruciating sharp pain. His scream is cut short by a second bolt of pain. His reverie is terminated abruptly, a dreadful reminder that even particle boys must eventually pay the piper and answer to the laws of men and mothers. Having located her boy at last using little more than her maternal radar and the extra set of eyes that she has in the back of her head, Mrs. Ormand has firmly secured her meandering boy by the ear. She is "pissed off to no end," as she likes to say, and proceeds to drag his disobedient butt back through the crowd from whence she emerged like a spectre.

"Rickey Francis Ormand, you're in for one heck of a grounding. Someone could have kidnapped you. God only knows how many of those Eagles fans are here."

Little Rickey howls in pain. His ear feels like it's being pulled off, but this is a tough town. It's Philly, it's the Seventies... nobody cares, boyo. Nobody's calling Child Services. Nobody's batting an eye in this town until a limb comes off, and then they expect it to be used as a bludgeon lest they lose interest. Little Rickey knows his goose is cooked. He caught it clear as day. In addressing him by his full name – "Rickey Francis Ormand" – his mother sent him a clear message that leniency would not fall within the scope of discipline on this given day.

Three names… three names could mean only one thing – the spoon. The spoon meant a wooden spoon over the head. His mother intends it as a stern lesson. The place is packed, on the verge of chaos, strangers in a strange land and all that jazz. But it never occurs to the kid that harm may have befallen him in a crowd of strangers. Why would it? There is none of that in his dreams of space and exploration. In his dreams of fame, he is as invincible as Kirk.

He winces and whines as he tries to keep up with his furious mother, who still has a hold of his ear. He is sure it will look like cauliflower tomorrow. She maneuvers him through the sardine-packed crowd, deftly turning his body to and fro like he's a trailer hitch as she wends her way back to Chestnut Street. Somehow, she knows these streets like the back of her hand. How does she do that?

When at last their feet hit the cobblestone on the Old City street, Mrs. Ormand swings her son around by the earlobe, which, thankfully, has the elasticity of youth. Once again, she reminds him of what lies in store.

"Rickey Francis Ormand, your father is going to be very angry. I don't think you'll be leaving your room until you're old enough to drive."

She clenches her teeth and grunts. If they only made a holster for wooden spoons....

Never mind his dad, Rickey thinks. He has bigger problems. Three names. She called him by his three names again. That makes twice in the span of minutes. Forget about grounding. A rendezvous with the spoon is a certainty now. He notes to himself that their efficiency hotel room has a kitchenette. He's sure he saw his mother scrambling eggs for breakfast that very morning using... a wooden spoon supplied by the hotel. If she broke one on his head, they could have a million more.

He resolves to accept his punishment like a man. Someday, he thinks, his parents will be reading about him. That's right, someday everyone will know his name. That's what he tells himself. And anyway, the spoon doesn't really hurt. Most of the time, the thin handle breaks, prompting his mother to say the same thing every time…. "You're hard headed like your father, Rickey Francis Ormand."

Decades later, the very same Rickey Francis Ormand will be recognized as America's most innovative entrepreneur, a trendsetter and a world changer. He will stand before the president, the Congress, and the entire nation, and announce that humanity is about to catapult forward thanks to him.

"I have turned the world of make-believe into the world of make real," he will tell them. "I have transcended convention and constraint. I have harnessed the most powerful force in the universe. I have changed the world forever."

Like Cam Jenatzi, Rickey Ormand embodies the great spirit of invention and the mind to envision the most daring undertakings. He has the iron determination to move humanity forward, even if he has to push this giant rock called Earth up that damned hill himself. Both men share the entrepreneurial spirit, the great force that propels the world forward. But Ormand possesses something Jenatzi did not, something that will immortalize him whereas his predecessor was relegated to the trash heap. This particular quality is uncommon, intangible, and illusory. It is a force unto itself. It is the ability to create fact from fiction, make science from fantasy, and make dreams real.

Like an alchemist, Rickey Ormand has the rare ability to turn nothing into something of incredible value and do it over and over again. He creates life-changing machines from pure ideas. Where Jenatzi failed, Ormand succeeds. Convention holds no sway over the symphonic score of possibilities resonating inside Rickey Ormand's head. Convention is but a target for this man who has believed since he was a child that he would someday transcend time and space as easily as snapping his fingers.

For whatever reason, the world around him fits together like a jigsaw puzzle. Perhaps it's intuition? Perhaps it's some ethereal connection with the cosmos? Whatever the wellspring of his brilliance, he is able to tap it in such a way that the most fantastic ideas become material realities. He brings to fruition what others can only conceptualize. He is part man, part enigma. He refuses to settle. He will not be stopped. He is a force unto himself willing to fight anyone and anything standing in his way.

He is Rickey Francis Ormand, founder of Liquid Sky, the man who is about to change the world.

Chapter 2

The woman is beautiful but clearly worn out. Perhaps frazzled is a better description. She is probably both. She is tall, but not too tall, thin but not too thin. She has fire in her eyes. She drains the highball glass effortlessly and slams it down on the bar. Ice – offered by request only – rattles like dice in a tumbler. It's her way of getting the bartender's attention.

"*Yapa, porfa,*" she blurts out. Another, please.

They all know her at the Fallout Shelter. It's her favorite bar. It's a hip, American, urban-style joint. Think street art meets hyper graphic design. Whatever it is, it seems as out of place in Lake Titicaca as she does.

"Yeah, yeah, *cholita,*" replies the bartender. He refers to her as mixed-blood. What he means is that she isn't exactly from around there. She's an outsider, a well-to-do, single American woman living in Lake Titicaca, Peru, for the last two years. That makes her a *cholita*, but a good *cholita* because she seems to have an endless supply of U.S. dollars. Stranger still, this woman is a theoretical physicist, but there's something about her, something scrappy that suggests there's much more to her than meets the eye.

Her I.Q. may be 153, but she can bust balls as easily as cracking walnuts. Case in point, the bartender's name is Rodrigo, but she prefers to call him as *huevón*, meaning dude. As she is well aware, it also means asshole. She's smart like that. She can master local *idomas* as easily as running an acceleration problem in her head, which she was doing at the age of thirteen.

The *cholita* and *huevón* are both cool with it, though. They're in the Fallout Shelter after all. The place is like a time warp. It seems more like a joint on the Upper East Side than a Peruvian watering hole set against the backdrop of the ancient and mysterious Lake Titicaca. Rodrigo, aka *huevón*, hails from Bolivia on the other side of Lake Titicaca, but he lived in New York City for seven years. He looks like he soaked it in pretty good, too. His gleaming pompadour, his Ed Hardy graphic T-shirt, sleeveless to show off his tattoos on each arm, his tight, ass-gripping Levi's and worn motorcycle boots would fit in anywhere in Hell's Kitchen or Alphabet City, post gentrification, of course.

The woman, the *cholita*, her name is Parker Fitzgerald, Ph.D., in theoretical physics. She can calculate equations about black holes and dark matter that require forty feet of white board, but she's never seen *Star Wars*, and she's just fine with that. She doesn't give a crap about Wookies or tiny-ass Hobbits for that matter. As hot as she is with her tussled, bookish look – and she does clean up nice – no one dials her digits for a late-night booty call. Nobody sends her flowers or anything like that. Why bother? She's smarter than any three men put together around there, and a night of drinking always ends up with her outwitting the entire room. It was very "erection negative," as she admitted.

But people back in the States sure as hell call her for answers to questions nobody else can answer. And they send her equations nobody else can solve. Parker Fitzgerald was only completely unobtainable outside the realm of physics. It made her magic. It made her even hotter.

Sitting there on a worn, red leather bar stool in her white Señor Frogs tank, cowboy boots, ripped jeans, and a well-worn Red Sox baseball hat covering a thick head of bobbed blonde hair, she seems as alien as the bar itself, not to mention the guy tending it. She is clearly American but seems completely unconcerned about it. The way she raps her fist on the bar when her refill is too slow in coming says one thing. The way she casually weaves together sentences with strands of Spanish, English, and local Peruvian idioms says she also has enough respect for local culture to earn her a bit of respect from the locals in return.

How did the Fallout Shelter come to be in this land of Inca temples? For that matter, what about Rock-n-Rolla, Pacha Mixology, Positive Rock Reggae, and the slew of other trendy American-style bars dotting Lake Titicaca? How did they take root in this ancient soil? How did Rodrigo and this American woman from MIT find their way to the Andes mountains and the highest lake in the world, home to llamas and indigenous people carrying out customs and traditions dating back over a thousand years?

Answer: Time, space, and culture have a different interplay in this place.

Rodrigo swaps the empty highball glass with a full one like he is capturing a chess piece from his opponent. "Here you go, *cholita*," he says. "One more Launch Pad that makes *tres* for you. You are hella crazy, stone *loca* from your titties up."

He holds up three fingers with his left hand.

She snorts and dismisses him with a curt retort. "I've got just one finger to hold up for you, *broco*," she says, suggesting he prefers the pleasures of his own gender.

He pulls a lighter out of his skin-tight jeans in order to ignite the drink.

She waves him off. "No fire. Seriously? Do I look like a tourist to you?"

Rodrigo shrugs off her earlier remark about his sexual preference. "I can only imagine who taught you that word *broco*, *cholita*."

Believing that scientists ought to use their talents to enhance and verify all facets of life, she holds the full highball glass up to one of the light fixtures to assess its opacity and, therefore, its alcohol content. The fixtures hanging over the bar consist of a single bulb on a black wire set inside an empty Patron tequila bottle. There are almost two dozen of them hanging across the full length of the long bar constructed from a translucent teal resin and lit from within to make it glow.

"Don't worry," says Rodrigo. "It will knock your panties off."

Fitzgerald tilts her head from side to side and purses her lips as if scrutinizing a test sample rather than a cocktail. "I don't wear any," she says in a completely flat tone.

Rodrigo just smiles and delicately prods his pompadour lovingly.

Satisfied with her visual assessment, Fitzgerald swivels back toward the bar and raises her glass as if to toast. "Behold, the infamous Launch Pad, the beverage of choice for real atomic aficionados."

Matter-of-factly, she drains half the glass and sets it down on the bar with little more than the slightest quiver while the potent concoction passes over her lips and assaults her insides.

Rodrigo raises an eyebrow. American women drink too much. Seven years in NYC taught him that. And this is not some fruity, frou-frou, chick drink. This is her third Launch Pad before lunchtime, and she's only had a couple of the empanadas for breakfast. That's saying something. A Rodrigo Launch Pad was no joke, man. A curious combination of pisco sour, *caipirinha*, tequila, 151 rum, and fresh mint, the Launch Pad (or LP as real Shelterites call it) is six ounces of distilled neurotoxin with just enough sweetness and fresh mint to bypass the human species' instincts for self-preservation. As any legit Shelterite will tell you, the unique combination makes the whole far more lethal than the sum of its parts. Consumed at over 12,000 feet above sea level, the Andean altitude of Lake Titicaca, she's one bad mamma jamma.

Pisco is innocuous enough. Pisco brandy is to Peru what apple pie is to America, and drinking pisco sours almost constitutes a national pastime. Suggest to a Peruvian that adding egg whites, lime, and simple syrup to pisco was the Chilean's idea, and they may stab you. Parker Fitzgerald learned this the hard way her first week in the country when she found herself squaring off with some old woman, a local alpaca farmer. Judging from the leather she called skin, the woman had to be eighty years old if she was a day but was said to have straight-up coldcocked more than a dozen unruly alpacas over the years.

The *caipirinha* is Brazilian rum. But it is not really rum. It's straight-up jet fuel, almost as flammable, and capable of launching a flaming human liver clear across the room. It is rumored that *caipirinha* is directly linked to the North Korean missile program as well as the spontaneous combustion of several of Kim Jong Un's generals who fell out of favor with their temperamental leader. The Supreme Leader himself is also said to fancy a quaff from time to time, which accounts for his haircut... and calling himself Supreme Leader.

The fabled drink master who created the Launch Pad was a cheeky *cabon* with a green Mohawk they called Macho Nacho. Mach Nacho believed that creating a signature cocktail required one thing above all. "If you want to put this place on the map," he used to say, "you need the danger factor."

The mere presence of Brazilian jet fuel being deemed not quite toxic enough, tequila was added for the "danger factor." Tequila... to-kill-ya... it's what the Americans like to drink when they're heading toward a terrible idea, and what people trying to act like Americans heading toward a terrible idea like to drink, as well. Nothing sells like tequila when you want to take off the training wheels... or the wheels off the train entirely. Toss it in for good measure, why don't we? It was an executive decision by Macho Nacho himself.

Adding a 151 rum was a no-brainer for a man like Macho Nacho. With almost twice the alcohol content of the booze sensible humans consume, 151 comes in handy should a patron require anesthesia in the absence of a doctor... or a hospital... or antibiotics. It also comes in handy if no gasoline is available to make a firebomb. Point blank though, Macho Nacho knew that any truly dangerous drink – a drink that would put the Fallout Shelter on the map – had to be flammable. What could be more fitting in a place like Lake Titicaca, known throughout the world for its serenity and cosmic connectedness?

"Light it and they will come," Macho Nacho used to say. It was actually one of the last things he said, as he met his early demise skydiving. It is widely believed that he had a few too many Launch Pads and packed his shoot incorrectly. To this day, witnesses claim there was, in fact, no canopy at all in his pack. As they say now about the great mixologist, "He had plenty of launch, just not enough pad."

And so there you have it. The Launch Pad.

Rodrigo looks at the big Elvis clock hanging on the wall. The King's hips and legs hang down like a pendulum and appear to swivel. It's barely noon.

"Remember Macho Nacho," he cautions.

Fitzgerald raises her glass once more. "Don't worry about me. No *estoy huasca*," she clarifies for the record. She nods assertively. It takes more than that to get her drunk.

Rodrigo nods back. In point of fact, he has never seen the brilliant physicist drunk. "How come you're not working today? They say you work around the clock up there in that fancy lab of yours."

She bottoms out the drink, spits an ice cube back in the glass, and smiles coquettishly back at him. "Oh, yeah? Who's 'they?'"

Rodrigo shrugs as he dries a glass with a white towel that glows in the black light from the specials board behind him. "Oh... people. *La gente*... you know. They talk. You live and work up in that fancy, secret building overlooking the lake... people wonder what goes on... what you do. Your place looks like a spaceship. And everyone has heard of your boss."

She shakes her head as if amazed, but she is not amazed. After all, her lab is owned by Liquid Sky and was designed by Silicon Valley superstar CEO Rickey Ormand himself. She clicks her tongue. Even the folks around Lake Titicaca know Rickey Ormand.

"Yeah," she admits. "I have some pretty cool toys up there." That's a gross understatement, and she knows it. Her lab, which has doubled as her temporary home these last two years, is a state-of-the-art facility, among the most top secret at Liquid Sky, and filled to the brim with the most sophisticated instrumentation in the world for simulating, collecting, and analyzing seismic and electromagnetic phenomena. Add to that the thirteenth most powerful supercomputer in the world, and you have a powerful nexus for scientific exploration, to say the least.

Rodrigo's been around. He knows bullshit when he hears it. "Oh, come on. You told me yourself that you work for Liquid Sky. Man, your boss, he doesn't fool around."

Another gross understatement.

"I lived in New York City for seven years, *cholita*."

"So, you remind me every time I'm here."

He puts the glass and towel down. He's done cleaning for a while. He eyes her instead. "Rickey Ormand is no *figureti*."

She laughs, although it comes off as sardonic. "No, he's no poser. You're right about that. He can be demanding, though. He gets so excited, you know? Certain things grab him, and he's, like, on top of you for days. He has these tremendous bursts of energy. It's hard to keep up with him sometimes."

She thinks before continuing. "He can be a complete asshole sometimes. Not pleasant. I wouldn't put anything past him."

She should not have said that last bit. She wonders if the booze isn't getting to her a bit? She glances at her phone again. Nothing. That's good. A few moments of peace without Rickey Ormand up her ass is a nice change.

Rodrigo pops the last little bit of caipirinha in the bottle over the ice remaining in her glass. He tosses the bottle into the garbage with a clang. "Una *yapa* for the *cholita*."

The *yapa*, the last bit of the bottle. It's good luck. She winks. She'll take it.

"Thanks," she says. "So anyway, my famous boss has taken a keen interest in my project lately. We've been going at it around the clock for days." She leans back and stretches her arms over her head. "And now I'm taking a much-needed break, thank you very much."

"*Paja, paja*, cool. Americans work too much. Better you drink a few LP's now and again. You lose your liver, but at least you keep your sanity."

In unison, their attention turns to the television. Rodrigo has CNN on. He feels American news is the most despicable and adds to the mystique of the place.

"Wolf Blitzer," he says with awe. "I love this guy, you know? Wolf... *El Lobo*. I don't believe a word he says, but I *want to*, you know? That's the important thing." He winks at her. "I have a saying, you know. Lie to me all you want so long as it makes me happy."

Fitzgerald holds up her hand to silence the chatty bartender. He returns his attention to *El Lobo*. There has been an earthquake in Sumatra, Indonesia, and Malaysia... all hit hard again. Those poor people, thinks Fitzgerald. Again... thousands expected dead. There is video showing many of the tallest skyscrapers in Jakarta's Golden Triangle swaying visibly. Other footage depicts the towering Petronas Towers in Kuala Lumpur vibrating and swaying, as well.

Parker Fitzgerald is not a seismologist, but her expertise in electromagnetic phenomena makes any tectonic event interesting. "8.5," she says.

"That's a big bastard," opines Rodrigo from a less scientific perspective.

Next, *El Lobo* draws their attention to California, where a much smaller quake is hitting as they speak. It's enough to cause damage to buildings. Video footage of San Francisco depicts the Golden Gate Bridge rocking.

Wait... there's something far greater going on. She can feel it. She squints as she takes in the scroll running across the bottom of the screen.

"Apparently, there is some sort of unprecedented seismic shift going on," she reads aloud. "Quakes are also being reported in Japan." She jumps to her feet and tosses a neatly folded wad of Soles on the bar to cover her tab and tip.

"Where are you going?" asks Rodrigo.

"I picked the wrong damned day to take off."

She knew it was coming. She could feel it. No sooner had she put on her sunglasses and her phone began to ring. She didn't have to look at the screen to know it was a shaker of another kind. Rickey Ormand was calling.

She answers, making her way toward her green Range Rover.

"Hello, Fitzy," he says.

She opens the car door and climbs in. "Hey, Rickey. What's up?" she replies, trying to sound cool and collected. She starts the engine and jams the shifter into gear.

"You tell me. Are you seeing these earthquakes?"

"I am," she says. "Quite an anomaly for sure."

"Shit, yeah," he says. "Listen...."

"Yes?" she replies. She hates it when he starts a conversation like this. It always means the same thing. He wants the world. And when he gets something like that fixed in his head, he would rather die than let go. He could be a real pain in the ass. And he could be a real mean son-of-a-bitch, too. She learned both the hard way. She didn't need repeat lessons.

She can feel the manic pitch of his voice. He loved to tell people in California about how his mother used to hit him over the head with a wooden spoon or some shit like that. He liked telling it because it horrified people from California, who couldn't imagine using a pussy willow to discipline their delicate offspring, let alone a cooking utensil. Right now, Parker Fitzgerald wished Ormand's mother was sneaking up behind him with one of those giant, wall-sized wooden spoons raised high like she's a Samurai warrior.

Ormand's voice cracks a bit. "So, I am about to jump on the corporate jet and head to Las Vegas. Tomorrow, I'm announcing the next Propel Challenge, and I'm hoping you've got something spectacular for me to announce that blows the roof off the joint. You've been up in those mountains for two years, Fitzy. You gotta gimme something here. The stuffed shirts on the board keep hassling me about expenses like they know the first thing about anything we do."

She whips the Range Rover hard around a tight turn. Gravel flies up. She's sure now that the third Launch Pad hit her harder than she thought.

The event Ormand is referring to is Liquid Sky's yearly Propel Challenge. The premise is simple but ingenious nonetheless. Being far shrewder than he appears, Rickey Ormand likes getting his hands-on great ideas for a fraction of what the intellectual property is worth should it come to market. The concept of exploitation doesn't really factor in his world. In his mind, basking in the radiant glow of his genius and magnificence ought to be reward enough. Salaries, bonuses, and the like he pays generously at times. But he considers it more of a gift than earned remuneration. Salary and bonus is his gift to his employees because there would be nothing without him. If he had it his way, people would pay him for the right to work at Liquid Sky. To Rickey Ormand, the "company store" concept is grossly underrated.

Always on the hunt for a bargain, Ormand puts out to the scientific world at large a massive call for ideas on a given subject. Ideas flood in from every nook and cranny of the scientific establishment. The vast majority Ormand considers to be "on par with the thought of a worm." A distinguished bunch earn the title of "modern-day troglodyte." Only a handful of the world's most brilliant papers make the short list. The winner of the yearly contest is immediately elevated above "trog" to find themselves in rarefied air. Their elite status earns them a Liquid Sky experimental program based on the proposal they submitted.

It's ingenious if not a bit dehumanizing. Sensitive scientists are an oxymoron to Ormand, so he doesn't care what a few offended, outraged, or otherwise disgruntled hacks write about him in some column of a newspaper or magazine. Nobody really reads anymore anyway.

Parker Fitzgerald is well aware of how high-profile the Challenge is. Racing back to her mountain lair, she begins to feel the stress of whatever is coming.

"Listen Fitzy," says Ormand. "I have my speech and topic for the Challenge kickoff, but I'm hoping you have something about electromagnetic propulsion I can use instead. It's your reason for being."

His voice seems booming through the truck's Bose sound system linked to her phone. She inhales deeply and speeds up a winding road toward her lab. "I've been running a completely new set of parameters."

"And?" He sounds hopeful but equally unimpressed.

She grimaces. "Nothing." She pushes the truck harder up the mountain.

There is silence for a moment. "Well, keep me posted. Let me know if any lightbulbs go off with all these earthquakes and stuff."

She tries to manage his expectations. She knows he has lofty ideas and even loftier expectations when one of them grabs his imagination. "It's not that easy, Rickey." "That's why I hired you, Fitzy. You're the best with this magnetic stuff. I have every faith in you."

Here it comes. Wait for it.

"But... Fitzy... I would really love something for this next Challenge. I don't give my speech until tomorrow. Keep me posted."

She feels pressure. She isn't really good with this whole public announcement stuff. There's no rushing the science.

Ormand hangs up before she can respond. It was just his way. She's sure he is already dialing the number of another one of his top-secret researchers with the very same request.

Chapter 3

Parker Fitzgerald drives the Range Rover hard the rest of the way. Even after two years traversing these winding, poorly maintained roads, a curve or two can still take her by surprise. As she has often remarked, calling this a road is hyperbole bordering on absurdity. It's more of a rural thoroughfare, for lack of a better word, mostly dirt and gravel with occasional patches of broken blacktop the first few miles only. And about halfway up to the lab, a $75 llama or alpaca might fare far better than a $210,000 SUV.

She knows a mistake at this speed could be the end of her. God knows she's heard enough stories in the Fallout Shelter. One mishap... by the time her truck stopped tumbling and careening down the side of the mountain, she would be barely recognizable as Parker Fitzgerald, the beautiful brainiac running the Liquid Sky magneto-thrust research program. She would resemble beets and chopped meat, barely distinguishable from the mangled machine she was driving.

She prefers keeping her organs on the inside where they belong, and melding with a machine is hardly what she calls life fulfillment. Prudent and (mostly) law abiding by nature, Fitzgerald ordinarily takes the treacherous road slowly. Today is different. Ormand is up her ass like a drunk proctologist. Got the whole fist up there, doc? And besides, this global string of seismic activity is a huge window of opportunity. So much is at stake.

Like those tectonic plates shifting, she feels the pressure mounting and needs to release it. Ormand has been pressing her more and more lately. He's getting to be a real dick about it, too. She can't really blame him. Her operation is damned expensive and running on two years now without any tangible return on investment. Sooner or later, he will have to cut her program unless she delivers results they can use to build out a magnetic drive. When not cursing him, she has to admire the guy. Were she in his position, she would be far less tolerant than Ormand. Sooner or later, that will come to an abrupt end. She knows that.

How much more is Ormand willing to spend? That's the question she keeps asking herself. He could kill her program with a single phone call. Just like that, she would be dead, defunct, out of business. Then what? Would he find another role for her, or would he toss her away like an old, windup toy robot? She wouldn't put anything past the guy.

This run of quakes hitting one after the other... this could be the big break she needs to save her skin. She needs desperately to get back to the lab and reset the parameters on her equipment to ensure she captures exactly what she needs. She loses herself in her own theorizing, in the remarkable world of "What If's" that she can conjure up like nobody else in her field. Her mind is racing faster even than her truck. So many ideas are flying through her head... new ideas, brilliant ideas. She may never witness conditions like this again, certainly not in her current research position.

As the mountaintop lab comes into view, its many windows scintillating in the bright sunlight, she pushes the truck just a little too much. As she hits the big s-curve about a mile before the lab, she overcuts the wheel. Ripped from her world of ideas, Fitzgerald suddenly finds herself in very real, very dire circumstances. Instantly alert, she doesn't need to look out her window to know that the driver's side rear wheel has slipped completely off the edge. Pebbles and chunks of dirt fly off the cliff as part of the rear bottoms out on the ledge. She is completely out of phase with the circumstances of the great lake around her.

Dumbass. That's what she thinks in that first split-second of recognition that seems to stand still.

As a matter of sheer luck and Ormand's generous budget, the Range Rover she's driving has a supercharged, 557 horse-powered V-8 and a "smart" all-wheel-drive transmission system that is so smart, the $210,000 vehicle senses in milliseconds what's happening. Switching instantaneously to front-wheel-drive-only mode, the SUV's self-driving mechanism takes control of the steering and the drive-by-wire throttle controls. The advanced LIDAR sensors detect that there is nothing but vast emptiness and an abrupt termination of services a mere ten inches to the left. The steering wheel turns automatically, cutting the vehicle hard to the right and away from the cliff. As if one with her truck, Parker Fitzgerald loosens her white-knuckled grip allowing the computer to turn the wheel freely in her hands.

With a sudden jolt, the auto drive puts the whip to its 557 horses, and the truck bolts forward, pinning Fitzgerald back in her seat as the front-wheel drive pulls the left rear tire back onto solid earth. But she's not out of danger. The road is narrow. While the cliff to the left poses a catastrophic threat, the mountain wall bordering the road on the right presents its own set of perils. No sooner has the auto drive successfully navigated the cliff that it brings the SUV back to the left, centering in the narrow road, recoils Fitzgerald's fastened seatbelt pulling her into her seat back and hits the brakes.

With a screech of tires, the Range Rover stops on a dime, its engine quietly idling like it's just sitting in a driveway. As if some sort of parental consternation was programmed into the system, the auto drive switches off the radio just to remind Fitzgerald who's really in control. There is silence now, although the drama of what just happened still resonates in Fitzgerald's head. She sits motionless, sweat now beading on her forehead. She rolls her eyes left... then right... then up and down. What just happened?

Unlike Macho Nacho, Parker Fitzgerald has more pad than launch today.

She takes a deep breath. She realizes that her foot has been hard on the brake the entire time. Luckily for her, the Range Rover had a mind of its own. She smiles ever so slightly. Just as quickly, her smile is gone. Had she erred just a bit more, the little cloud of dust rising behind her would be all that remained of Liquid Sky's most promising theoretical physicist.

She refocuses herself. Her body seems to have processed out the three Launch Pads, including the *yapa* top off, and replaced it with adrenaline. Her eyes are wide open again. She remembers the historic tectonic events taking place half a world away. As a theoretical physicist searching for electromagnetic anomalies and trying to discover a source of magnetic propulsion, she lives for moments like this. She can feel a breakthrough coming. She can sense something hanging out there in the universe for her to pluck off and bring back to Rickey Ormand. She is determined to change the future. She senses success sitting right there at the apex of her reach. It excites her like nothing else.

Be that as it may, Lake Titicaca does not give up its secrets easily. It is an ancient place and stingy in doling out its wisdom accumulated over the millennia. Life up the mountain is inverted for Fitzgerald. The higher into the clouds Fitzgerald ascends, the more she must reckon with universal forces that make cool bars and hip fashion trends seem like a piece of lint on a pair of cosmic trousers. Indeed, it almost swallowed her whole a moment ago. And as surely as it let her go, it could snatch her back again.

Lake Titicaca is a special place, a powerful place. Sitting 12,500 feet atop the Andes, Lake Titicaca is the highest navigable lake in the world. It is a profound place. Thirty-five million years ago, the lake was violently carved out by an earthquake and volcanic eruption. Tectonic cataclysm has continued shaping and reshaping this great, aqueous wonder ever since. Its depth is almost one-thousand feet, but the energy of this special place runs much deeper than that.

The history of the world can be found in this place. The geology reads like a reference book on the forces of nature that have shaped our planet. The sociology is equally compelling. Ancient ruins thought to be more than 1,500 years old rest beneath these powerful, sacred waters. Small islands dot the lake, home to some 10,000 people. The Quechua, the Uru, the Taquileños, and Tiwanaku people… they trace their lineage back to the Incas and still see the lake as a conduit to the universe.

There is intense energy here, an ethereal force flowing through this place that people have worshipped for the last two thousand years. For as long as there have been people inhabiting the region, there have been those who believe Titicaca is a vortex portal, a prevailing source of anionic energy traversing time and space. An ethereal, luminescent salt-field is said to be the source of this tremendous energy. It is very real and actually protected by the United Nations.

Lake Titicaca captures the imagination. It is a special realm where science and speculation, past and present, dream and reality intertwine endlessly. It is a fecund world unto itself, a world full of possibilities, pathways, and endless convergences. It's a perfect spot for a guy like Rickey Ormand to set up shop and search for some cosmic clue. It is here, too, that one of the greatest scientific discoveries of the modern age is about to occur entirely by accident.

As predicted, the series of earthquakes continues rocking continent after continent for hours. Also, as predicted, the event marks an historical series of geological anomalies. And yet, for all her zeal, Parker Fitzgerald is more frustrated than anything else. It's been hours since she almost bought the farm. Data is flowing in from all over the world, but none of it jumps out at her. The riddle of magnetic power still evades her.

She gently lobs her mechanical pencil at a wireless keyboard sitting on the huge desk in front of her. She makes a throaty, explosive noise like an aerial bomb exploding upon impact. Running her right hand through her hair, letting thick rows gather between her fingers before yanking them painfully.

"You win again, you bastard," she grumbles through clenched teeth.

"I ask that you refrain from calling me vulgar names, Dr. Fitzgerald." The voice is soft but measured, almost mechanical.

Fitzgerald rubs her temples. "My deepest apologies, Max. I promise it won't happen again."

"According to my audio records, it has happened 763 times in the last three months alone. The probability of it happening again are exactly–"

"Pause," she orders. Max stops speaking immediately. She rolls her eyes in relief. If only it were that easy with men, she thinks.

Max is not a man. He is one of the most powerful supercomputers in the world. Mounted on the wall across the room from her is a ninety-inch flat screen. It is her slick interface with Max. Max runs an ingenious hybrid operating system marrying two entirely different types of computers – the NASA Pleiades supercomputer and the Orion 8Pack, a $30,000 mega-gaming computer designed by Overclockers UK. The synergies between the number-crunching supercomputer and the freewheeling, interactive, scenario-based super-gamer make Max the most dynamic computer in the world.

The rest of Max, a room full of black cabinet processing towers, hums quietly on the other side of the wall. Like the great lake which Fitzgerald's lab overlooks, Max possesses tremendous power beneath the surface. Where a typical laptop runs one quad-core for efficient, everyday personal computing, Max has 206,000 cores, a 3-petaflop monster capable of processing 3 quadrillion mathematical operations per second. As he reminds Fitzgerald regularly, it is one of Ormand's crown jewels and an invaluable resource.

As far as the folks at the Fallout Shelter are concerned, Fitzgerald is the queen bee, "the zazaza," as Rodrigo likes to say. In truth, she is one of ten theoretical physicists working for Liquid Sky in a remote, top-secret facility. The experimental program is called Liquid-Drive. Ormand set up Lake Titicaca and the other nine Process labs in order to probe the world and push the envelope for new ideas. Fitzgerald's mountain lair is by far the most "out there" lab of the group, reflecting

Ormand's personal interest in Tesla's work on Scalar energy and Jung's theory of the collective unconscious.

When he created the lab at Lake Titicaca, his senior executives thought he was crazy. They challenged his judgment. Did he really expect to make the next great discovery in propulsion technology trying to tap the universe with some lab in the clouds? They wondered if perhaps his head was too far in the clouds. Why not a location more logistically tenable like Nevada? That's where Elon Musk set up shop.

None of it bothered the Chief Executive Dreamer, though. My name is Rickey Ormand, not Elon Musk, he told the board. The world has enough conventional boxes containing conventional thinking put forth by perfectly sane, rational people. He created Liquid Sky in the first place for the sole purpose of thinking outside that box. The faint of heart and the weak of spirit need not apply. What was really required, he told them, was a bit of the irrational, something called inspiration that they probably knew little about.

According to Ormand's plan, not the board's, all ten Liquid-Drive labs are located near some fabled source of cosmic energy. Ormand's looking for something radically different, a paradigm shift, looking for some sort of wellspring from which he would draw the next world-changing technology. It's no different than scouring the rainforests for new pharmaceutical ideas. What Rickey Ormand wants most of all is a new power source capable of breaking the world away from oil and coal. He wants more than that, though. He wants to usher in a new world order with Liquid Sky at the epicenter.

To do this, he has selected Process locations known to be either geologically active, known for strong magnetic fields, or spiritually energized. Lake Titicaca is the trifecta. Perched high in the Andes, this fabled region is a gateway through which all three forces – geological, magnetic, and spiritual – come together. The implications boggle the mind and rupture the walls of conventional thinking. Fitzgerald's Process lab and the lake in general represent everything the Liquid Sky board resents about Rickey Ormand, whom they see as a dreamer and a rambunctious child in need of a stern governess.

Parker Fitzgerald bought into it from the get-go. She has been going at it for almost two years now. Her last great cheeseburger is but a distant memory… Boston, a little joint outside Fenway she used to hit up before Sox games when she was getting her doctoral degree at MIT. That's where Ormand found her, fresh out of her oral defense. Literally, she had just left the Green Center cutting across Eastman Court, when she saw some guy wearing a NASA JPL hoodie running after her. He was even calling her by name. It kind of freaked her out.

She was thinking stalker, especially since the dude ran right up to her and starting gesticulating all over the place. It was a wonder she didn't mace his ass.

"Blown away" was what the guy said. He was "blown away" by her dissertation on geomagnetic storms. Had she ever thought about magnetic energy replacing the gas engine? That's what he wanted to know. She simply had to come work for him, had to. No question about it. He was very famous, didn't she know? He could make her famous, too.

When she thought about it, he did look kind of familiar. No sooner did he introduce himself as Rickey Ormand, founder and CEO of Liquid Sky, then she was reaching for his hand to seal the deal. Ten minutes of unemployment was enough for Parker Fitzgerald, now Dr. Parker Fitzgerald. Liquid Sky, she knew, was the top of the top. Fresh out of graduate school, joining a team like this was a dream come true. And to do so minutes after earning her Ph.D. was more than she could have asked.

Now, this 2,500 square-foot facility has been her temporary home for two years. It's not for everybody. Isolation, loneliness, frustration, and failure got the best of several Liquid-Drive scientists, including one suicide. Ormand knows this. So, what he did was hand her the keys to a state-of-the-art facility that included a slew of creature comforts to keep his prized scientist feeling more like a wealthy explorer than a neurotic recluse. Gourmet kitchen, gym, sauna, state-of-the art entertainment system, UV-blocking solarium providing breath-taking panoramic views, even a heated dipping pool… Ormand built it as if he was going to live there himself.

Of course, her equipment and other technical resources were second to none, culminating in Max. Having a supercomputer like Max at her disposal allows Fitzgerald to run wild through every conceivable scenario, every possibility her brilliant mind can possibly come up with. Still… no breakthroughs in magnetic power have come her way.

She picks up the mechanical pencil she just lobbed on the keyboard and twists it between her thumb and forefinger. Parker Fitzgerald is no stranger to adversity. But she is unaccustomed to failure, and the stress is getting to her. Her temporary assignment is starting to feel less temporary now. Work from home is one thing; work as home is quite another. Lately, her mind has been straying, wondering what life would be like had she not accepted Ormand's proposal without seeing what else was out there for her. With increasing frequency, she's been imaging herself walking the streets of Boston again, maybe catching a Sox game or, God forbid, going on a date. One thing's for sure – her future did not include alpacas or barbecued guinea pig, or anybody named Max, male, female, or supercomputer.

She has been running simulated geomagnetic storms, using the unique conditions that exist nowhere else in the world outside of the Titicaca region. But so far, the naysayers are right… nothing has come to fruition despite the millions and millions of dollars Ormand has invested in the project. She tosses the mechanical pencil more assertively this time, inhales deeply and squints. She does this whenever she is trying too hard to come up with an idea that's too intangible.

She abruptly stands up, walks deliberately into the adjoining kitchen, and grabs another bottle of Club-Mate. The magnum-powered energy drink reminds her of the year she spent in Berlin before starting grad school. She has it shipped in by the case. It's almost comfort food for her. Throw in a nice, big wiener, and she'd be in heaven. Sighing, she resigns herself to working through another beautiful, star-laden night, the kind she used to find mesmerizing. Not anymore. Nowadays, she barely finds anything enjoyable, not even a Launch Pad.

She twists off the top of the Club-Mate, tosses it into one half of the double sink, and swigs. There are times when she feels the drink is her only friend. Next stop will be four a.m... She takes off her light-blue Puma zip-up she put on when she got home and tosses it on one of the kitchen chairs. She realizes she's been wearing the same tight Señor Frogs tank for two days. She can thank the Club-Mate for that. She takes a whiff of each armpit. Damn, she can thank Launch Pads for that. Standing on one leg and then the other, she pulls off her cowboy boots with the balance of a gymnast and replaces them with a worn pair of pink sneaks. She tosses the boots in the corner next to the chair and breathes a sigh of relief.

"Max," she says as she strides back into the lab.

"Yes, Dr. Fitzgerald?"

"I have something for you."

"I can hardly wait, Dr."

She walks over to a small air intake near the huge flat screen. It's Max's electronic nose, the sort used in food, flavor, and fragrance testing. It's one of 42 environmental, biometric, and organoleptic sensors operating pervasively in every room of the facility. Fitzgerald also has a sensor/transmitter about the size of a bottle cap implanted in her side, transmitting a continuous stream of biometric information back to Max. Although Rickey Ormand would love to have conceived it, it was Fitzgerald who came up with the idea for both the ambient and implanted sensor systems.

At first, she thought implanting a piece of robotics inside her body would be weird, even outlandish. Where does a person draw the line? She could easily imagine a day when everything from cell phones to virtual-reality receptors would be implanted right into peoples' brains. Why would she want to be part robot?

After using Max's Liquid-Link, however, she totally changed her mind. She loved the seamless interface between her mind and the world around her. The idea that people could one day interconnect like that is something she thinks could be very interesting indeed. With Max, she feels she has to push the envelope, too. She needs to be interconnected to Max even if that makes her a bit robotic.

The constant flow of environmental and personal data back to Max allows the supercomputer to "know" – that is, to process and correlate – what is going on in the facility as well as with Parker Fitzgerald. It has worked brilliantly from day one. She and Max have what can only be called "a relationship" that can extend to any aspect of her life so long as there is response data.

Admittedly, it's emotionally one-sided and overly logical. "I imagine this is what it's like to be a football widow," she once told Ormand. "Or married to Spock."

Still, it's been a long two years, and Fitzgerald needs to get her kicks where she can. So, she leans in closer to Max's electronic nose and wafts her armpit toward it.

Max processes the sensory data instantaneously. "Dr. Fitzgerald, I believe a small animal has died in the vicinity of my olfactory sensor."

It's come to this. She must amuse herself with potty humor and wisecracks from a supercomputer. She takes another swig of Club-Mate.

"I'm smelling a little ripe," she says.

"I don't mind so long as you keep my nose turned off. Otherwise, a shower might be in order."

Fitzgerald takes a pair of stylish glasses from one of the cargo pockets in her green camo pants, puts them on, and sits back at her desk. She quickly reviews some printouts and tosses them on top of a mounting pile of similar reports before continuing.

"I want you to rerun the last simulation."

"What parameters, Dr?"

"Use the 1859 Carrington Event," she instructs, referring to the greatest geomagnetic storm ever recorded. "Only this time, I want you bounce the coronal mass ejection into the earth's magnetosphere as it would exist if the earth's rotation were three percent faster."

"Confirmed," replies Max. "I am calculating using a rotation speed of one-thousand thirty miles per hour."

Dr. Fitzgerald shrugs. Ormand built the lab at Lake Titicaca for a reason. There is something very special about the region, something very powerful that spans the millennia. Adding thirty miles per hour to the planet's rotation speed is yet another shot in the dark. But that's her job, she reasons. As a theoretical physicist, she must incorporate both halves of her mind. She's there to run as many variables as possible. She can do this like few others. This is what makes her unique, differentiating her from all the rest, even at MIT, Cal Tech, or Cambridge. Redefining the laws governing time, space, the entire universe... this takes someone very special, indeed. Like Einstein, Hawking, or Hubble, Parker Fitzgerald must search for the meaning of life with artistry and aplomb. The math alone is enough to dim even the brightest intellect. Add to that the great leaps of creativity required to reimagine universal laws, and the task is nothing short of Herculean.

"Confirmed," replies Max again. "Establishing test conditions." A moment later, Max reports that "all test parameters have been set."

Fitzgerald smiles. Even after two years, the speed with which Max crunches massive amounts of data amazes her. She clucks her tongue.

She looks over to the test chamber spanning the wall to her far right. Standing roughly eight feet high, twelve feet long, and six feet deep, the chamber is loaded with innumerable mechanisms for creating, recreating, and otherwise controlling the conditions inside. The base and top of the apparatus, as well as the clear poly "glass" on all four sides, have been crafted from LI-900 silica like that used to make the space-shuttle heat shield and a unique poly material developed by Liquid Sky that acts as an RF shield but also reroutes any magnetic flux back into the chamber rather than directly at Parker Fitzgerald's brain. Blocking out brain fry, this is a good thing.

With Max as her source of power, Parker Fitzgerald can formulate any test environment she desires. It is the single greatest tool a theoretical physicist could ever have. With it, Fitzgerald can create her own world in which time, space, matter, and every other scientific precept are hers to govern. Dozens of meters and sensors are hooked up to the chamber, some visible, some encased or otherwise obscured, so that Max can measure and record any conceivable data Fitzgerald wishes to gather from the Lake Titicaca region. The amount of data she can collect is astronomical.

At the same time, thanks to sharing arrangements set up through Liquid Sky, Max is capable of tapping into a vast array of information systems. As the global earthquake event unfolds, Max is not only able to capture massive amounts of data from monitoring networks all over the world, the supercomputer is also able to incorporate that same data, real time, into any theoretical scenarios Fitzgerald can conjure up.

As Rickey Ormand once said, "Fitzy, the chamber is your personal universe for you to play God. Old Testament, New Testament... I don't care which. Just make something new run that turbine."

The turbine... that's what it all comes down to. It sits in the middle of the test chamber. Fitzgerald is staring at it as she issues her new parameters. It's her job to find a way to power it up using nothing but magnetic energy for power. The way she's eyeballing it, it's clear she and the turbine have had their moments. It's got all kinds of receptors, convertors, and fancy doodads that only she and a couple of Liquid Sky engineers understand. That damned turbine. Maybe the Launch Pads are re-emerging from her liver. Whatever it is, she can feel something coming.

"Max," she commands.

"Yes, Dr. Fitzgerald."

"I've got a good one for you to wrap your processors around. I want to add some more parameters."

"What are your instructions, Dr. Fitzgerald?"

"Use the average electromagnetic, gravitational, and atmospheric conditions from each of the recent earthquake sites. Crunch 'em all," she instructs. "Make that turbine whine like a spoiled little bitch, Max."

"Processing the data," says Max.

She looks at her watch and thinks about Ormand. He's undoubtedly in Vegas by now doing God knows what. He'll probably stay up all night working on some project. He has such huge bursts of energy, she reminds herself. She had a few friends like that back at MIT. They were hard to keep up with. Running one of Liquid Sky's top-secret programs doesn't help matters.

"Initiate test protocol," she tells Max. She raps her knuckles against her wooden desk for luck. "Come on, Maxie. Mamma needs a new pair of boots."

Max begins accumulating seismological and other related data from scores of networks worldwide. As the voluminous amount of information comes in, Max plugs it all into the 1859 Carrington Event model and also postulates the implications of speeding the earth's rotation as Fitzgerald instructed. Using incredibly advanced algorithms, Max is able to run millions of scenario permutations and categorize them according to their potential for follow-up.

Fitzgerald clicks through with her mouse, scanning the 3-D models, trying to find something, anything in one of the models that she can report back to Ormand. Wouldn't that be amazing? She allows herself one brief moment to bask in thought before returning her attention to Max's output. Always, her gaze returns to that damned turbine. It remains still, inactive… failure.

Max interrupts her concentration. "Dr. Fitzgerald, I have an urgent warning. My deep-earth sensors and USGA earthquake early-warning system are picking up a significant seismic activity building force."

Fitzgerald stops what she's doing and purses her lips. "Explain."

"There is a high probability of a plate subluxation—"

She cuts Max off. "Where?" A plate subluxation caused the tsunami that rocked Thailand in 2004, she reminds herself. The motion is like snapping two fingers. The only thing is, in this case each finger is a tectonic plate that can be as large as 100,000,000 square kilometers. The force is exponentially large.

Max specifies. "The epicenter is along the Nazca and South America plates approximately 300 miles south of Lima."

For what seems like an eternity, Parker Fitzgerald's brain freezes. It's a strange sensation. Rarely does this happen. In actuality, only a couple of seconds pass before she is wrenched back before all hell breaks loose. She realizes the epicenter of the quake that is about to hit is only 200 miles due east of her position. This constitutes a potentially catastrophic situation as the lab is a single-story building full of ultra-sensitive, super expensive equipment perched precariously atop a mountain peak some 12,000 feet high.

"Brace for impact… brace for impact." Max's monotone voice is now female and strident, part of his emergency-warning-system protocol modelled after the Nagging Nora voice used in fighter jets to prompt better human response in stressful conditions.

"Jesus Christ," yells Fitzgerald.

And then she feels it. The vibration mounts, increasing steadily until the entire place is shaking. A sound like a long roll of thunder fills Fitzgerald's head. Several ceiling tiles fall and wiring of different colors hangs out of the openings. Even so, she can hear plates and glasses dislodging and shattering in the kitchen. She's a Bostonian. She's never been in an earthquake. Not sure what to do, she hits the deck and crawls under her desk, where she remains on all fours taking in the awesome display of nature's ferocious power.

Through the one large window in the lab area, Fitzgerald watches the two giant antennae from the roof fall to the ground and land in a twisted heap. The sound of wrenching metal is terrifying. At an altitude of over 12,000 feet, one might think the foliage would be sparse. This is hardly the case. Lake Titicaca boasts dense crops of trees in certain areas such as on *Isla del Sol*. Although not abundant, there are several large trees on the laboratory property. And right now, Parker Fitzgerald eyes them with trepidation.

One tree falls… then another. The second tree takes out the power lines feeding juice to the building. The wires spark and flare as they dance menacingly on the rumbling earth. Because the building is equipped with a Liquid Sky solar mega-battery pack that runs in the background continuously, there is no power loss. This is critical because all systems, including Max, remain running uninterrupted without requiring a reboot. Ormand insisted on this during the planning stage, and now his foresight is paying off. He looks like a clairvoyant right about now.

Seconds later, the huge diesel generator kicks in. The power transfer executed without a hitch. Fitzgerald closes her eyes in humble thanksgiving. She knows down in town, they will likely be without power for days if not weeks. And where her building is over-engineered in its construction design, she knows that many of the homes and businesses in the lake region are probably collapsing and trapping or killing many of the people inside.

She thinks of Rodrigo behind the bar at the Fallout Shelter. The place is built with spit and stones. She wonders if he has been crushed under tons of rubble. He's a tough *cabron*, she assures herself. She sends him a thought… you'd better be alive. Fight, *huevón*.

Fitzgerald has little time to think. A brief respite to think about others is all nature allows her. Over the thunderous rumbling of the earth and the sound of the large generator, she hears a chilling sound… something really big is cracking. Her first thought is that the building is giving way. Then, through the window, she sees it. A third tree, by far the largest on the property, approximately fifty feet tall starts to move. The violent shaking uproots part of the tree. Fitzgerald watches in awe as the hefty evergreen splits about midway up. The cracking sound reverberates. It lands directly on the building with a crippling impact, crushing the eave above the large window and taking out the entire long pane of glass in the process. Shards of glass fly toward Fitzgerald, landing in a blast pattern all over the floor. She lowers her head and screams.

At that velocity, the shards are like razorblade shrapnel. A long, triangular piece about four inches long rips into her left forearm and buries itself in her flesh about two inches deep. Fitzgerald drops an F bomb almost as loud as the rumbling of the quake. She's angry enough now that the pain is inconsequential. Keeping her wits about her, she leaves the shard in her arm, fearful that the resulting bleeding would be far worse at that moment. For a second or two, she wishes she could take a selfie because she would look like one tough bitch.

As the quake continues running its course, Fitzgerald sees something that worries her far more than the piece of glass in her arm. She watches in horror as two of the walls begin to crack like a zipper opening. The brackets supporting the large flat-screen she uses to interface with Max give way as the surrounding wallboard crumbles. The screen crashes to the floor. It suddenly occurs to Fitzgerald that she is really screwed. Should a load-bearing section of wall give way, she could be crushed by the roof on which is mounted all sorts of equipment that has not yet blown off like the two antennae.

She takes a deep breath and rises off her knees like a sprinter in the blocks as she prepares to make a run for the bathroom and the safety of the bathtub, minimal as it is. That's when she sees it. Actually, she hears it first... an intense whine growing in pitch. She is frozen in her place. What the hell was that noise? And then, my God... it's the turbine inside the test chamber. Jesus Christ, the turbine is alive.

Fitzgerald is stunned. The immediate threat of this large quake vanishes from her consciousness. All she can think about is that turbine... the damned thing is powered up. Seconds later, the earth quiets and the tremors subside. All is quiet except for the turbine which is screaming with intensity now. The machine begins to shake. Smoke rises from its vents as more and more power pulses through it. Ten seconds later, having surpassed its maximum tolerances in a frenzied pitch, the turbine explodes. Pieces of metal hit the side of the test chamber, but the three-inch poly holds. No more shrapnel is headed for Fitzgerald today.

A bit of contained smoke and silence is all that remains now. Fitzgerald crawls out from under her desk and stands up. She casts a glance toward the flat-screen monitor lying in a broken heap. First things first, she runs to the bathroom closet and grabs some alcohol and gauze. She pulls the glass projectile from her forearm and slides it into her pocket for a souvenir. She pours alcohol over the wound and again lets fly with a string of obscenities before wrapping the gauze thickly and tightly around her forearm. She figures that ought to do it for now.

More important is the turbine. Oh, how she loves that little machine right now. She heads toward the test chamber.

"Max, do you still have audio?"

Max's voice has returned to its usual, non-emergency mode. That strikes Fitzgerald as odd. She assumed the supercomputer would still be in emergency mode.

"Hello," says Max flatly.

She smiles. Despite the scare this could be the moment she's been waiting for. This could be the big breakthrough. "Run damage assessment," she instructs.

A few seconds pass without response from the supercomputer.

"Damn," says Fitzgerald, sensing something isn't quite right. "Max?"

"Hello," is the only response.

Torn between the potential of what just happened in the test chamber and the possibility that her all-knowing supercomputer may have been damaged by the quake, Fitzgerald bites her nails.

"Don't do this to me," she mutters to herself. "Don't do this to me, Max." She runs her hand through her hair and instructs Max to run "self-diagnostic alpha."

In the meantime, she places her palm against the chamber and closes her eyes. She is barely aware of the cool air blowing through the broken window on the other wall where the tree landed. Instead, she is totally focused on isolating the source of energy that powered up the turbine, a source so great, it blew it to shit. Was it electromagnetic? Did it have to do with the parameters she instructed Max to input? Did it have something to do with the actual conditions at the lab itself when the earthquake hit, or was it something else entirely? The one thing she knows for sure is that finding answers to these questions will require Max's help.

What she hears next causes her stomach to bottom out. It's Max. He's speaking gibberish. "Purple story board is confined to the Roman Empire."

Fitzgerald can't believe what she's hearing as Max begins calculating *Pi* out to a hundred decimal digits.

"Pause," orders Fitzgerald, not knowing what else to do. "Pause, Max. Stop right now." She stares at the chamber and the pieces of exploded turbine. She runs her hands through her hair in exasperation again. She looks at the broken flat screen lying defunct on the floor. It's symbolic for her, like looking at the gravestone of a recently departed loved one. She is close to tears, but they are tears of anger. She is one pissed-off bitch right now.

Max is silent for a moment and then begins spewing out seemingly-random information. "The coronal mass ejection introduced a significant release of plasma. This transition state of matter does not otherwise exist on earth. It created a temporary magnetic field related to the flaring solar corona. Heterolytic fission occurred...." At this point, the supercomputer breaks off into some complex formulation about cleaving hydrogen atoms as typically occurs in fission.

Fitzgerald wipes tears from her eyes with the back of her clenched fist. She can barely contain the wave of intense frustration that is working its way through her body from head to toe. Instead of providing deep algorithmic analyses during an unprecedented seismic event, she recognized immediately that Max was simply providing a rudimentary overview of the Carrington Event she requested him to include in the test parameters. It was beginners' stuff.

She exhales deliberately. She has to keep it together. She's put too much into this to crumble now. That's not how she was raised. She shakes off the brain fog and refocuses. The first thing she needs to do is collect the pieces of the fragged turbine and get them to the mat-sci lab in New Mexico. They can perform forensic work to fill in some of the pieces to this puzzle. Yes, she assures herself, that's what I should do straightaway.

Still a bit frazzled, she pats her pockets and looks around quickly. Where'd she put those damned keys to the test chamber? She turns to check her desk when Max suddenly comes to life again.

"This solar event also created a significant magnetic field producing a significant gravitational anomaly generating 431 kilojoules of energy. "

Parker Fitzgerald stops dead in her tracks. What the hell did Max just say? "Significant gravitational anomaly?" she repeats out loud. She runs a quick calculation in her head. 431 kilojoules... she figures that's more or less the energy release in, say, a typical grenade explosion. It's amazing. Where did that energy come from?

It hits her like a ton of bricks. Max said *gravitational anomaly*. Yeah, that's what he said. "Holy shit," she spurts. "There was a gravitational anomaly that generated a shit-ton of energy."

Instantly, her mood changes. It has nothing to do with magnetic energy at all. The answer is *gravity*. She laughs. "Damn… we've been asking the wrong question all this time," she says.

This is it, she thinks to herself. This is the big breakthrough. Ormand will be ecstatic. She pulls her cell phone from her pocket. No reception. Of course not. What is she thinking? The quake would have knocked out service.

She snaps her fingers and runs to her bedroom. Stepping over a variety of broken objects that were dislodged from the wall during the quake, she runs into her bedroom, tears open a dresser drawer, and pulls out the satellite phone that's linked through one of two Liquid Sky satellites orbiting the earth. She dials Ormand's number. She looks at her watch. There's still time before Ormand gives his presentation at the Propel Challenge. Ormand's phone rings a few times and then goes to voice mail.

"Come on, come on," she says while disconnecting. "Answer the phone, you scrawny bastard."

She hits redial. The phone rings. This time, Ormand answers. She pumps her fist and heads back to the lab.

Rickey Ormand is sitting at a table having a pre-speech dinner with Alexa Manheim, the CEO of Q-Speed. Noah, a stick-thin waiter with a protruding Adam's apple, sad-looking eyes, and shoulder-length hair punctuated with a tousled man bun, is standing next to Rickey. When Fitzgerald's call came in, Noah was offering Ormand some sort of vegan curry dish. Ormand grimaces and waves it away in annoyance as if the waiter was asking him to smell an old gym shoe. He thinks to himself, "The place may be numero uno on Anthony Bourdain's "Best Hip Eats in Vegas" episode, but who the hell goes out for vegan food in the middle of Las Vegas?"

Anyway, Fitzgerald's call is far more important than whatever Noah is sticking in his face. "Fitzy, Jesus. Are you okay? I'm hearing from all over the place that there was an earthquake and the lab was damaged. I've been trying to call you. I thought you were buried under a pile of rubble or something. Jesus…."

Fitzgerald walks back into the lab, over to her desk, and pulls her laptop from the dock. The computer screen comes to life. She sets to work immediately.

"I'm fine, I'm fine," she says excitedly. "We took some significant damage. And Max is screwed up. And I had, like, a huge piece of glass sticking out of my arm." She laughs. The adrenaline makes it funny for now.

"What?" asks Ormand? "How badly?"

She looks down at her gauze-wrapped forearm. "I'll be okay. I may need a few stitches—"

Ormand cuts her off. "No, no. The computer... Max... how badly is he damaged?"

Fitzgerald purses her lips. "Your concern is overwhelming, Rickey. Thanks. As for Max, I'm not sure," she says. With the satellite phone pinned between her head and shoulder, her fingers fly furiously over her keyboard. "But listen, Rickey...."

"Go on," he says.

"I got some unbelievable data. I mean... I don't even know where to begin, let alone what it means. And for me to say that, it's... it's crazy."

Ormand sits bolt upright when he hears this. With a couple of hand gestures, he excuses himself from the table and moves onto the restaurant's main floor. "Jesus, Fitzy. Back up that data. For God's sake, please make sure you back it up."

She blows strands of blonde hair out of her face. "Again, your concern for my well-being is overwhelming. But don't worry, Rickey. I'm backing it up as we speak," she says sardonically, her fingers still moving deftly around the keyboard.

She leans in toward the screen and squints. "The amount of data is huge," she says. "But I'll be damned if it's not all here. I can't believe it. I think we hit the mother lode, Rickey."

Rickey Ormand likes what he's hearing and strokes his earlobe. He is thinking. Ordinarily, he wouldn't do something like this. But this is clearly a special situation. Yes, he thinks, this is very special, indeed. "Okay, pay close attention, Fitzy. I will tell you exactly what I want you to do."

Parker Fitzgerald laughs. It's so like him to hire her for her incredible intellect and still think she can't do something basic like back up her data. "I know how to back up my data, Rickey. Really?"

Noah, the waiter, returns. Ignoring the fact that Ormand is standing away from the table and otherwise extremely preoccupied, the sensitive young server walks over to Ormand and proudly displays a platter of assorted non-dairy, non-animal-exploitative nut "cheeses" and some sort of tofu-and-eggplant spread seasoned with turmeric and sweet chili paste. Ormand grimaces and stares at the young man clad in gray skinny pants and a crisp, white button down with just enough billow to seem hip.

But Ormand is too serious right now to waste time messing with some waiter. He's got no time for breads and spreads. He gestures menacingly for the kid to go away. Noah is clearly pained by the snub and sulks over to the table where he places the tray before Alexa Manheim.

"Listen to me, Parker," Rickey Ormand implores. "We cannot lose that data; do you hear me? I don't give a crap about Max now. He did his job. I can always buy another supercomputer. But we cannot –absolutely *cannot* – lose that data. Not if it's as significant as you say it is. Do you understand what I am telling you, Parker?"

She nods with some annoyance. "Yeah, yeah. My fingers are moving as fast as they can," she says, now cursing herself for downing that third Launch Pad. "It looks like Max is pretty screwed up. I'm not making any guarantees."

"I don't give a crap about the damned computer," says Ormand, trying to muffle his voice. "We need that data. Screw the computer." He can feel the other patrons of the upscale vegan eatery starting to take note of his carnivorous behavior. They can smell the stink of meat on him.

Fitzgerald seems satisfied with what she's seeing on her screen. "Okay, the download's gonna take some time. Like I said, it's a shit-ton of data, and I am using my laptop. It's not exactly a supercomputer, you know what I mean?"

"Can you send it to me instead? I know it's large, but you have enough bandwidth up there to choke Godzilla."

"No can do," she says. "The quake knocked out all connectivity. We have generator power, but even the two antennae on the roof are toast. I only have this satellite phone."

Ormand is conspicuously quiet again. He knows she's not going to like what's coming next. He knew she resented intrusions into her personal life. But to him, she, along with every other Liquid Sky employee, forfeited their right to privacy when they cashed their first paycheck.

"What?" She asks. "Whenever you stop talking like that, something's up."

Ormand clears his throat. "Well… we don't need conventional telecom. We'll just come directly in from Liquid Sky and grab it."

Fitzgerald stops typing again. "How's that, Rickey? Coms are down except for this sat—" She stops herself in mid-sentence. She gets it now. "Except for this satellite," she says.

"Exactly," says Ormand, trying to put lipstick on this pig. "We can tap directly into your data center via our satellite. We can pull the data that way. We do it all the time with you."

He bites his lip as soon as those unfortunate words pass his lips. He could punch himself in the balls for letting that last bit slip. Jesus, he is an idiot.

Fitzgerald is amazed. Why should she be, though? She knows he's capable of anything. That's what she reminds herself. "Really?" she says. "So, you just come and go with my work as you please, sharing my research with God knows who over there at Liquid Sky? You, like, virtually trespass whenever the mood strikes you? You need to keep an eye on me or something, Rickey?"

"Trespass?" he wants to ask. How is it trespassing when I own everything? That's what he wants to say. But he doesn't. Instead, he figures he might as well tell her more softly although he has a good mind to put the bitch in her place lest she forget who's the boss.

"That's not what I mean," he replies in a calm voice. "Look, Fitzy, there are certain... precautions, let's say, certain precautions that I take with vital data. So, okay, we set up a backdoor that allows me to access your entire system whenever I want. You know... to keep an eye on things. We can come right in and grab everything from Liquid Sky right now. Honestly, that's all that matters right now. I'm sorry if that offends you, but this is my company, and this is how I want things set up. I need to keep an eye on my data and my people."

Jesus Christ, he did it again. He bit his lip. Why can't I just shut up, he wonders.

Fitzgerald abruptly stops typing. "Excuse me?" Her nimble mind begins running through the scenarios. Did he say he likes to keep an eye on his people? Is he watching her, too? Shit, how many times was she pulling an all-nighter wearing nothing but her panties and a tank? Was he, like, watching her through her web-cam?

"What, are you spying on me, Rickey? Do you have, like, hidden cameras too?"

In point of fact, he has Max. Max, in turn, knows all, sees all. And so, Ormand knows all and sees all, as well. So yes, he thinks to himself, I can watch you via the camera eye on your laptop or via any of Max's camera eyes dispersed throughout the facility for that matter. Yes, he thinks, I have seen you naked. Eh... not bad. Not quite Playboy grotto material like the girls he dates, but pretty damned nice for a brainy chick. The uppity-bitch act he could do without for sure.

For the most part, though, Rickey Ormand has no interest in petty voyeurism. He can have a room filled with nude California beauties faster than he can insert a Viagra suppository (pills make him gag). He's got little time for spying on Parker Fitzgerald or anybody else. All he cares about is the project. If that means keeping a close eye on things, so be it. Personal liberties and private space only go so far in a company like Liquid Sky, where the intellectual property is among the most valuable in the world.

Of course, Rickey Ormand mentions none of this to Parker Fitzgerald. He doesn't have to. She's too smart. She gets it already. He knows this, so why poke the beast?

Her lips are tight as she returns to her assault upon her keyboard. "I see. You have Max. If you have Max, you have everything. It's funny," she quips. "It never occurred to me that Max could be used for surveillance. How naïve am I? Okay, the joke's on me. Parker's the dumb one."

Ormand tries to redirect her to what he considers the more important issue. "Hey, let's not lose sight of the task at hand. We can discuss this later. It's far more important to get your data backed up."

"Yeah, yeah," she says, leaning in toward her screen. "Let's just hope you don't lose your prized company someday like Steve Jobs did. What on earth would you do then?"

Ormand takes a deep breath and pretends he didn't hear what she said. He would kill everyone on the board before he let them take his company away. "Calm down and listen. We can tap right into your laptop and bridge into Max that way… just as if I were sitting in your seat."

She grunts gruffly. No other response forthcoming.

"Look, Fitzy. Everybody – I mean everybody – knows you're one of the best minds in the world. We're all happy to have you on our side, you know? Let's not worry about this shit right now. I'll make it up to you. I promise."

She grunts louder this time.

Ormand feels a headache coming on. It's just beginning to pop in his temple. Time… time is of the essence. He continues on about how much she means to Liquid Sky while, with his other hand, he removes a second cell phone from his hip pocket and deftly texts his IT manager.

Shortly thereafter, Fitzgerald's laptop beeps several times. She sits back and wonders what's going on. The screen flashes twice. The pointer begins moving around the screen seemingly on its own. Liquid Sky now has control of her computer. She watches in astonishment as powers unseen open a hidden application folder she never even knew existed.

"Bastards," she says to herself, albeit loud enough for her to know Ormand can hear it.

"It's okay, Fitzy," says Ormand reassuringly. "We'll take it from here."

"We?" she says sardonically. "I thought we were all on the same team?"

"*Touché*," he says.

She thinks for a second. "What's next? The Land Rover, my cell phone? I assume you can track my ass wherever I go?"

Ormand sighs. He uses that calm, nerdy tone of his that's peppered with just a bit of condescension. "Of course, but it's for your own safety, Fitzy. I can't afford to lose you."

That's a funny one. She laughs dismissively. "Sure, right... sounds like it's control you can't live without. Like I said, I hope you don't lose your precious company someday."

"Stop," he says. "You are vital to this company."

This seems to placate her for the time being at least. His concern seems genuine enough, she figures. Working for Rickey Ormand is never easy. But it takes more than some intrusive boss to rattle the youngest and only girl in an Irish family of six kids. She's taken as many jabs as jibes from her brothers growing up. Besides, he pays her exorbitantly and sure as hell provides all the creature comforts. That much she has to admit.

Thousands of scientists would make a deal with the devil to take her place high atop that mountain. She knows this. So what if he keeps tabs on her? She might do the exact same thing were she in his place. She came to this remote Inca mountain on a mission, and she'd be damned if she lost two years of her life with what could be the greatest scientific discovery in history over some foibles about personal freedom.

With that in mind, she puts her feet up on the desk and watches the ghost in the machine move through several more screens. Shortly thereafter, the data packet that will change the world begins transmitting via the Liquid Sky satellite connection.

Like flipping a switch, she becomes the quirky, brilliant scientist she was a few minutes earlier. She'd always had this ability. Her mother always said it was a survival mechanism growing up with five Irish brutes for brothers. If she didn't feel like swinging back, she could always charm those boys into a corner. She was quick to stand her ground, draw a line, and remind people in no uncertain terms of her true value. Then, she was more likely to shift gears, become a real charmer. And she wasn't afraid to adopt the same approach with Rickey Ormand.

"I'm fine, Rickey," she assures him in her best raspy voice.

"That's a relief," he says. He means it. He doesn't like problems, especially people problems.

She continues. "I was just... cracking the whip a little. Surely, you wouldn't begrudge a girl her fun, now would you, Rickey?"

"Of course not, Fitzy. You're the best I have, and you know it."

She leans in toward her desk and checks on the progress of the satellite upload. She looks at her watch. "Slow as balls," she mutters to herself.

"I can feel the love," she says, mocking him. "Anyway, I have something far more important to report. I mean, like, big... really big."

Ormand nods and smiles. "Excellent. That's what I like to hear from my prized physicist. Let's stick to the good stuff. That's what matters. We can talk about that other crap after we get you the hell out of there. What else do I need to know?"

Fitzgerald sits back and relishes the fact that she may have just made the most important discovery of the modern era. "Are you sitting down?"

Ormand raises a brow. "Actually, I'm standing in the middle of some restaurant. A bunch of vegans. I feel like a lion around a watering hole, you know." He laughs at his own joke.

"Well, make sure they're not too anemic to pick you up off the floor after you hear this. Because...." She pauses for dramatic effect. "I figured it out, Rickey!"

Chapter 4

At first, Ormand doesn't get her drift let alone the magnitude of what Fitzgerald is about to tell him. "Figured what out? The uplink is already under way."

Fitzgerald rolls her eyes. "Umm... I can see that, Rickey. By the way, I could die of old age before this thing finishes. But I'm talking about the project itself, harnessing magnetic energy for propulsion. Forget about all that. Think bigger. Isn't that what you always tell us?"

Ormand is floored. He feels his legs become a little gelatinous. He lowers his voice and spits into the phone now. "Forget about it? The entire concept? I mean... Fitzy, I know I always encourage my people to think outside the box, but come on. I've got two years and millions of dollars sunk into your lab."

He pulls the phone down and looks around him. He's getting a bit too loud to be standing in the middle of a restaurant. He realizes he needs to tone it down a bit. "What do you mean?" he prompts in a more restrained voice, albeit still full of urgency. "You're making me nervous. I know you're probably freaked out by the earthquake. But I wasn't expecting an aftershock like this, know what I mean?" He laughs at his own pun.

Parker Fitzgerald grunts. She's getting a bit impatient with her boss and annoyed how slow on the uptake Ormand is right now.

"You're not getting it." She grits her teeth, one elbow resting on her thigh. "Listen to me. We've been looking in the wrong place this whole time," she explains. "Do you hear what I'm saying, Rickey? We've been looking in the wrong place."

Ormand covers his mouth with his free hand to muffle his voice. "I hear what you're saying. I just don't understand what the hell you're talking about. What happened? Tell me."

Off the bit, Fitzgerald is getting excited now. "I don't know exactly," she says. "But something happened during the earthquake, something big... really big. Huge... historical."

She pauses to take a breath while Ormand hangs on her next words.

"All this time," she continues, "I've been crunching scenarios involving electromagnetic power."

"Right," says Ormand. "That's been the goal of this whole thing for the last two years."

"Obviously, that's what I thought, too. But now I see it," she clarifies. "I just fried a turbine. I mean, like, burnt to a crisp by a serious energy surge. And if the turbine fried for the reason I think it did, we've been asking the wrong question all along, Rickey. Follow me?"

Although he doesn't quit, her zeal seizes his full attention. "Go on," says Ormand, now in full CEO mode.

The earthquake is all but forgotten at this point. Despite their quibbling from time to time, they are more similar than different. They mostly click. Fitzgerald speaks passionately, with almost religious fervor. "The question we should be asking is not 'How do we harness magnetic energy?' That's totally wrong, a dead end."

Ormand doesn't know whether to laugh or cry. Two years... almost sixty million in. "Two years, Fitzy. Two years and sixty million dollars later and—"

Parker Fitzgerald barely acknowledges her boss's pain. "It's never about the money. That's what you said from the very beginning. It's never about the money, and you know it. Even if it is, something like this could prove to be the most valuable discovery ever. If nothing else, that's gotta excite you, Rickey."

Ormand can feel the acute pain in his right temple spreading into his temporal lobe as he recollects all the times he spouted off so cavalierly about "progress at any cost." That may have been fine before Liquid Sky went public. But now Liquid Sky has shareholders, a board of directors, earnings reports, a stadium of accountants, auditors, and other assorted bean counters multiplying like rabbits.

"Progress at any cost,'" she regurgitates back to him. She chuckles imagining the great Rickey Ormand standing in the middle of some restaurant pressing his temple. How many times has she seen him do that before? It's almost worth the price of his surveillance.

The knife blade of stress plunges deeper now, wrapping around into Ormand's occipital lobe. He thinks he just may need a bunch of these anemic vegans to carry him to the hospital when he stops breathing altogether.

"Rickey, that's a drop in the bucket, right?"

Ormand can barely get a word out. "Okay," he says. It more closely resembles a faint squeak.

Fitzgerald presses on enthusiastically. "Based on what happened today, magnetic energy is irrelevant. The question we should be asking is, 'How do we generate power from *gravity*? Gravity, Rickey. That's the missing link. Gravity."

Ormand's jaw drops. "Did you say gravity?" he asks.

Back at the table, Alexa Manheim, the CEO of Q-Speed and vegan foodie with whom he's dining, puts down her onion and cashew "cheese" and strains to hear Ormand's end of the conversation some twelve feet away.

"Gravity," Fitzgerald reiterates.

"Gravity?" repeats Ormand. "So that should be the new theme for this year's Propel Challenge? Is that what you're telling me?"

Fitzgerald laughs. How can a business guru like Rickey Ormand suddenly become a complete dolt? "Propel Challenge?" she retorts a bit too snidely. "Gravity power should be the focus of everything

Liquid Sky does going forward. You're getting it. If this pans out, the world as we know it is about to change in the blink of an eye. And Rickey Ormand will be standing in the middle of it all."

No response.

"Are you not understanding how huge this is, Rickey?"

He nibbles on two of his fingernails; the others are already nubbed. "I'm thinking."

"That's what I like to hear," she urges. "Because I'm not sure exactly what happened here during that quake. But I can tell you for certain, something monumental occurred. Gigantic, vast, unprecedented. The freakin' turbine exploded, Rickey. It blew like it was a lawnmower engine in a race car. Pieces everywhere. I'm telling you, this is it. This is the big one, man."

Ormand presses the phone against his ear with intensity. "What else can you tell me? Quickly. There's a lot of ears around here." He feels his dinner companion listening a bit too intently. "Never mind. We're coming to get you the hell out of there as soon as possible. I'll get a freakin' cavalcade of Sherpas and llamas if I have to."

She smiles. It's so like him. "You're really mixing metaphors there, boss man. Sherpas are half a world away."

"Whatever, you get my point. Don't you worry. But, listen...."

"Yes?"

"Whatever you do, just make sure the entire data upload goes through. Do you understand what I'm saying? The data upload, Fitzy. Speaking of which, how's it coming?"

Fitzgerald massages her left forearm near where the glass cut her. Her crystalline-blue eyes are like two tiny pools of liquid sky, fixated on the download progress bar. "Sure, you love me now," she mutters to herself.

"Hello?" prompts Ormand.

"It's coming," she reports back. "About fifty percent complete. But it's slow as balls."

Ormand scratches his cheek. "You've become terribly spoiled working with Max. It's moving pretty fast, all things considered. Still, I can't believe what we've stumbled upon," says Ormand.

She thinks about how close she came to dying today... twice. "Yeah, right," she mumbles to herself. "You mean what I've stumbled upon."

Ormand glances back at his table. He feels like Alexa Manheim has a wiretap in his brain. "I can't discuss this anymore right now, Fitzy. But listen, once the upload is complete, there is something else I need you to do. It's mission critical, do you understand?"

She has no idea what he could be getting at now. "Yeah... go on."

"Okay, listen. After the upload is complete, you need to pull all Max's hard drives."

"Are you serious? Why?"

"Two reasons. Think about it. Who knows who's going to be rooting around your lab after we pull you out of there? We can't risk this data getting out. I've got to be in control."

Fitzgerald is not pleased. "So, let me get this straight, Rickey. You want me to go back into that server room? Man, it's virtually hanging off the side of a mountain, and the foundation of this building is shot to shit. Besides, I don't even know what I'm fiddling around with. Hard drives? Where the hell do I even find them?"

Silence. No response.

Fitzgerald shakes her head. "Yeah, um... the last time I checked, Max has, like, 150 racks, 900 terabytes of memory integrated with some ridiculous number of Pflops, Tflops, nodes, peak clusters... hundreds of them. I don't know what any of that even means. It takes up an entire room the size of the house I grew up in. And again, that room is, like, virtually hanging off the mountain. Are you feeling me?"

"Not a problem," Ormand replies. "If you have to, call the emergency IT hotline. Use employee ID code seventy-six, Bravo, Bravo, Zulu, seventy-six. That's my personal pin. That will route you directly to the cell of the head of IT. Tell him I instructed you to call, and you need to pull Max's hard drives."

Fitzgerald is still resisting. "Dude, for all I know, the entire room will slide down the mountain the second I step foot in it. I'm not trying to be Wile E. Coyote here."

"Fine, never mind, Fitzy," says Ormand, annoyed but trying desperately to wrap up the call. "Forget about the hard drives, alright? I'll fly down there myself tonight after my speech at the Propel Challenge. I just have to figure out where the hell we can land. Maybe Bolivia... or Brazil?" he ponders aloud. "We have a lab in the Amazon with a landing strip. Anyway, hang in there, Fitzy. We're coming for ya. Now get back to that download. It's critical."

"Thank you," she blurts back. "See you soon, I hope."

Rickey reassures. "Relax. Everything's great. Believe me."

Ormand returns to his table and takes his seat across from Alexa Manheim, who is just chomping at the bit to catch any hint of what's got the great Rickey Ormand as giddy as a child on Christmas morning. The two power brokers exchange glances. Manheim arches a brow. Ormand does the same in return.

Noah, the waiter, interrupts the friendly stalemate when he returns, proffering a thick, green drink called the Roto-Rooter. The young man with the frizzy soul patch revels the secret blend. "I'm not supposed to tell anyone, but our secret blend contains celery, beet, flax, chlorophyll and Cascara Sagrada." He winks. "My kind of dessert. Best colon cleanse in the world."

Rickey Ormand, the most famous Silicon Valley CEO in the world, looks at him in complete disbelief. He looks at Alexa Manheim. She gives him the thumbs up. Apparently, she, too, admires a super-clean colon. Unbelievable.

Parker Fitzgerald tosses the satellite phone on the desk, stands up, and stretches her arms over her head. That was an odd way to finish the call, she thinks. See you soon, I hope? She sighs and chalks it up to getting older. She runs it through in her head a few times. It seems so.... she can't find the right word. Heavy... laden... ominous, maybe?

Anyway, enough about that, she thinks and pumps her fists in the air. "You did it, Fitzgerald. You did it," she calls out loud. "Booyah, baby!"

A woman, she thinks... a woman is going to reshape the world for a change. It's about damned time, too. If she could only develop a male mute button next, that would really be something. And some sort of penis lock to keep it in its pants. Who knows what would follow from that? Maybe an end to war?

She laughs to herself and takes a quick status check on the data upload. There's less than twenty percent remaining. Hands on hips now, she looks around and takes inventory of the lab. Not great, but it could be a hell of a lot worse. She decides she might as well drop a little Cuervo into her Club-Mate. What the hell, she figures. It's not every day a girl almost dies twice. And it's certainly not every day a woman makes the most significant scientific discovery since electricity, which she often jokes was really developed by men so women could keep doing housework at night.

She makes her way to the den, which has a nice teak bar against one of the walls. The den, itself, is decorated with ultra-modern Italian furniture of black, white, or gray leather and poly materials. Accenting the room are striking *object d'art*, hand-picked by Ormand himself, much of which lies in broken heaps on the tile floor. She blurts out a little cry of dismay when she sees that all three shelves of glassware and liquor bottles lie smashed on the tile floor. She peers over the bar and sighs. Looking around the room, she notices a seven-foot crack running from the top left diagonally down to the right at roughly a forty-five-degree angle.

"Jesus, that was some quake," she notes.

The three vibrant oil paintings that once adorned the cracked wall are lying face-down on the floor amid the shattered remains of two gorgeous Murano Venetian glass vases that fell from their wall shelves. The flat-screen T.V. is also destroyed completely and lies amid two piles of books that once occupied the inset bookshelves on either side of the screen. She also sees water flowing freely from under a closet door. She figures correctly that the exposed water pipe running through the top of the closet must have ruptured for sure.

"Shit," she says. Now that the excitement of the turbine explosion is subsiding, the severity of the damage is beginning to hit her. As if sensing a disturbance in the energy of the place, she turns to the long window that constitutes the entire wall opposite her. It affords her not only a phenomenal view of Lake Titicaca, but also some of the houses and businesses like the Fallout Shelter below, where she hangs out on occasions. She's way too high above to make out details, but she can clearly see the ominous glow of several fires burning freely. For a moment, she's embarrassed. She knows all those people down there can look up and see her place standing tall and lit up like a Christmas tree while their town burns.

She thinks about Ormand. He's certain to bring a small army to rescue her, or, rather, to rescue his data and her if convenient. She has no illusions about that, nor does she begrudge him for it. But she'll look like an even bigger elitist ass when Liquid Sky choppers and all sorts of land vehicles descend on the area en route to her lofty castle in the sky.

"Double shit," she says. "I must look like a total American prick."

She takes several deep yoga breaths, holds up her hands, and reminds herself out loud to "keep it together. Unfocus and let the superficial dissolve."

She clucks her tongue. She was never very good at meditation. It's nearly impossible to quell the unbelievable events of the day when they are running like the bulls of Pamplona through her head. "I can really use that drink," she says, again lamenting the pile of broken liquor bottles lining the floor behind the bar.

She snaps her fingers suddenly. She almost forgot. There's a bottle of citron vodka in the freezer. She's about to make for the kitchen when she remembers something important. Perhaps there's something to this yoga thing after all, she thinks.

Turning back toward the panoramic window, she sees the fires again. Even though she's been sequestered up in her aerial lab for the last two years, she has ventured to town enough to know that defenseless people have fallen prey not to an act of nature, which can happen to anyone anytime, but to a natural predator she will never worry about herself – poverty. She is at the top of the socioeconomic food chain; most everybody around her is not.

Parker Fitzgerald thinks again how her building must appear to all those people down below who are undoubtedly struggling with the quake's aftermath.

"You know what," she says aloud. "How about a little respect for the good people?"

And with that, she turns out the lights in the den out of solidarity with the people trying to survive in darkness below. Inside that brilliant head of hers, though, still burns the white-hot light of optimism, the luminescence of her discovery and what it will mean for the future of women in science.

Despite the tragic loss of life and property down below, another door is opening. The paradox can't be denied. Sometimes she feels like history's great advances often came at a tremendous cost born largely by the world's unfortunate, the dispossessed who, ironically, will never enjoy the benefits of the advances. Apolitical by nature, Parker Fitzgerald could still see the obvious for what it was... stagnation and complacency had to be fought on all fronts. She worked tirelessly in a never-ending pursuit of fulfilling this mantra.

Progress and profit as ends unto themselves never fully motivated her. Instead, she seeks progress and profits to drive something much larger, something global and beneficial to all humankind. Rickey Ormand calls her naive all the time. Lately, she's been thinking that's just fine with her.

She sighs in the still darkness that envelopes her. This is the moment she reminds herself, with crystalline lucidity, that the fame about to rain down on her is part of a greater social process. For the first time in a long time, Parker Fitzgerald feels that she is actually driving something much bigger than even the discovery of gravity power, assuming that is, in fact, where this is all heading.

Standing there alone and in darkness while the townsfolk below are suffering, Parker Fitzgerald understands for the first time how making a name for herself will clear the way for God knows how many other brilliant women who are this day still nameless, who are this day still faceless. She dares to think, if only for a moment, that she is more than a woman but something much different from a data-processing machine like Max, no matter how sophisticated that machine may be. After all, she muses, who played a bigger role in the events of the day, Max or that mute and mindless turbine?

She breathes deeply. Her lungs fill with ambient Andean air blowing in through the shattered windows. It is rich with fabled magic and mysticism. Her heart beats out the steady rhythm of the ancient lake's liquid percussion. But her head, her head is filled with trepidation. The really hard work, the work of one woman changing the world as we she knows it, is yet to come. At this singular moment, a first in her pedigreed life, Parker Fitzgerald wears her solidarity like ceremonial tribal garb.

Chapter 5

Fitzgerald flips off the hallway lights and heads for the kitchen. There lies that tasty bottle of almost-frozen citron vodka in the stainless-steel Viking freezer. In the kitchen, she picks up a toppled chair and contemplates sweeping up the broken plates and glasses. She dismisses the idea entirely. She has no doubt that Rickey Ormand and a small incursion force will be there sooner rather than later, so why bother? It's his problem now.

The only thing that matters is the critical upload. That's what he really cares about. She gets it. Cleaning up broken glass won't put her in the history books, but the data sure as hell will. She opens the freezer, and there it is. Yes, a frosty bottle of lemony liquor. She grabs it, closes the freezer, twists off the silver cap, and hoists the bottle up.

"Here's to you, Parker Fitzgerald. Now who's the crazy one, huh? Haters...." She takes a healthy swig without so much as a facial tic. It is not exactly a Launch Pad, but it serves its purpose. Her mood improves instantly. Maybe things aren't so bad after all, she assures herself.

She hoists the bottle again. "And here's to you, Rickey Ormand, you crazy son-of-a-bitch. Here's to your vision... and your money."

Another swig, longer this time.

"And here's to my brain, and all the women who are ready to pick up wherever I happen to leave off."

She twists the cap back on and puts the bottle on the table. Nudging aside a couple of broken scented jar candles with her pink-sneakered foot, she walks over to the walk-in pantry and hauls out a case of twelve new candle jars and vanilla pound cake, her favorite. She tears open the box and quickly lays the candles out around the kitchen. She opens a drawer and takes out a lighter. She proceeds to light all twelve candles and then flips off the lights in the kitchen. All the electric lights are off now. The kitchen is bathed in a soft, soothing candlelight that masks most of the debris, despite the mess. She inhales deeply. The scent is magnificent, re-energizing.

Fitzgerald pulls up a chair, sits down at the table with her bottle of vodka, and takes it all in. She takes a swig and issues another toast, this time to the lab itself. "In a weird way, I'm gonna miss this shit."

The candlelight dances off the eight-burner, stainless-steel Viking range. It's going to be hard for her to live without all these amenities. She certainly won't be able to afford all the lavish gadgets when it comes time to get her own place back in the real world. Perhaps more than anything else, Ormand is ingenious, a great problem solver. Better put, he has a great eye for finding ingenious people to work for him. He doesn't miss a trick, that Rickey Ormand.

Her Liquid-Drive lab was the pinnacle of that. For example, the satellite phone and the com link would save the data. There was no way he could have foreseen the disaster when he designed the place, but he demanded the utmost in preparation, nonetheless. Another good example is her gas supply. Having no way to run natural gas up the mountain, Ormand had a propane tank installed to supply gas to the lab using yellow flex hose running through several of the walls. The tank was enormous and lasted several months between refills.

How the hell is she going to find a landlord like Ormand? No way, Jose. More likely, it will be some douche canoe Silicon Valley entrepreneur buying up rental properties with the surplus millions he finds under his couch cushions. He'll probably be a bigger, creepier voyeur than Ormand.

Her dystopian musing is interrupted by a loud series of sounds from her laptop in the other room. She then hears some snarky bastard from Liquid Sky announce right through her computer…

"Upload complete. Thanks for the data, kitten. Don't forget to wear something nice when the boys come save your ass."

Some other dork emits a gangly, pubescent laugh… or was it a squeal? Either way… "Hey, bite me," she yells toward the other room. That is the vodka speaking. Or maybe it is her newfound sense of female righteousness? Anyway, it falls on deaf ears. The sharp, staccato crackle tells her the satellite uplink has been terminated.

She imagines them sitting around making lewd jokes about all the things they would do to get it up. It pisses her off because whoever those dweebs are, she's sure they don't have the balls to say stuff like that to her face. The double standard also pisses her off. She can't even imagine what would happen to their fragile nerd egos if the women at Liquid Sky spoke to them like that.

Fitzgerald chalks it up to the ignorance of the lesser sex and is determined not to let those numbskulls ruin her celebration, however ignominious given the destruction down in town. The house is mostly dark now except for the yellow glow of candlelight there in the kitchen. Fitzgerald takes another drink, licks her lips, and burps dramatically, the sort of primitive communication those two morons would understand.

She lets out a long, pronounced moan of relief. The upload is done. By modern standards, it was pretty damned slow. In the end, though, it really wasn't that long considering the damage caused by the quake to the region as a whole. She has no doubt that daylight will reveal nothing less than a disaster in a part of the world that, as rich as it is in both spirit and history, simply doesn't have the resources to throw at a full-tilt recovery and rebuild. For that matter, of the four regional so-called "hospitals," three looked as if they would crumble with the slightest gale storm while the largest, Carlos Monge Medrano, resembled an American middle school more than a trauma center capable of handling a natural disaster of this magnitude.

Preferring the brighter side, Fitzgerald notes to herself that, despite the shit storm that Mother Nature unleashed around her, at least Ormand let her off the hook for salvaging Max. She's relieved. Pulling all those freaking hard drives. Was he insane? What did he think she was, a robot? She's sure he had no idea of the actual force of the quake or the resulting damage. He had to be completely out of his gourd to think that she was going to root around in an unsecured, structurally compromised wing of the building just because he said so.

Fat chance, Rickey. That's what she thought when he first mentioned it, and it's what she's thinking right now. She was a lot of things, but crazy wasn't one of them... not today, at least. No, she has every intention of making it back to Fenway, that first taste of a piping-hot, sausage-and-peppers grinder, watching her boys beat the hell out of the Yankees. Can't get enough of that.

Oh man, she can almost taste that grinder chased down with a watery but ice-cold beer. Sure, that cup of suds costs as much as a six-pack at a packy, but man does she hate those chuckleheads from the Bronx.

Chapter 6

That's when she feels it happening again… the rumbling… growing in intensity. It's growing quickly now, very quickly. The building starts shaking violently. It's much, much stronger than before.

"Holy shit," exclaims Fitzgerald as the bottle of vodka tips and rolls off the table.

Anything left hanging on a wall or sitting on a shelf after the first jolt now plunges to the ground. She realizes in horror that the first quake was really just a foreshock. She hears decorations and furniture crashing. The intensity is so much greater now, this must be the main shock. She'd heard about quake patterns like this before. Now here it is, and it's going to be a son-of-a-bitch.

"Damn it," she yells in frustration as much as in fear.

Dust is falling from the corners of the kitchen now. It's like the room is coming apart at its seams. A large crack appears on the wall where the big Viking range is located. Fitzgerald is frozen in panic. The only thing she can think about is her laptop. What if there was some sort of problem with the satellite upload? With Max down, the only data repository she was sure of was on her laptop where she saved the data during the uplink.

She wants to scramble into the lab and grab the laptop, but she can't. She's frozen with fear. A major seismic event rocks every major fault line every 150 years or so. It's been about that long since a 9.0 quake along the Peru-Chile trench killed over 25,000 people. It's a numbers game really. Today, the number for the Nazca-Pacific fault line has come up.

It happens so fast... a tremendous cracking noise. Fitzgerald might as well be living in a house built of match sticks. The wall behind the range gives way first. The others start cracking, too. Realizing that the entire kitchen may crumble, she finally springs to action. She jumps to her feet, but she's too slow. A large piece of the ceiling collapses on top of her.

Because Rickey Ormand had the place built to such high standards, the weight of the materials raining down on Fitzgerald is significant. For extra support, there are rows of concrete-filled cinder blocks spaced every eight feet in the plenum between the ceiling and above her. When a section of the ceiling gives out, several of the blocks come down with it. One strikes her on the head. It's a glancing blow, but it's enough to knock her out cold.

Parker Fitzgerald lies unconscious on the floor like another broken *object d'art*. A magnitude 9.0 earthquake up there on top of that mountain... it's nothing she could have foreseen. She's at the mercy of nature. There's not a damned thing she can do about it. Right now, she's as helpless as the poorest villager in Lake Titicaca.

Fitzgerald is unconscious but still alive. The catastrophic main shock subsides less than sixty seconds later. When Fitzgerald comes to, the first thing she feels is a headache like lightning splitting her skull. She gingerly touches her head. She licks her fingers and tastes blood. She's very woozy and feels like she is going to pass out again.

She can't see much, especially in her state. If she could, she would see that much of the kitchen is still intact. Other than the section that landed on her, the remainder of the ceiling is cracked but intact. The walls are cracked, too, especially the wall where the range is. But none of the walls collapsed. That's why she's still alive.

She is faintly aware of a gushing noise coming from the hallway. Barely conscious, she can do little more than guess it's the sound of outside air rushing in through some large, gaping hole. Somehow, she manages to remember her laptop. Is the laboratory and computer room still attached, or has it broken off and tumbled down the mountain like a pile of sticks? She tries to move, she tries to get to all fours, but collapses, dizzy and in pain.

She knows she is about to lose consciousness again but doesn't know if she is dying or just passing out. As she struggles to stay conscious, an odd thought formulates in her boggled mind. The candles... many are still lit. The light comforts her. It's a miracle, she thinks. Then she smells it... unmistakable... gas... no, propane. The flex hose must have torn loose from the Viking range. Tears begin rolling down her cheeks, leaving tracks in the dirt that covers her face. She breathes deeply. The smell is unmistakable. It's propane. It's filling the room. Candles are still lit. Vanilla pound cake, her favorite.

The anguish of what's about to happen is incredible. Parker Fitzgerald knows now. This is the end. Thirty minutes later, an explosion decimates the Liquid Sky building perched so high atop that mountain. The loss is total... the facility, Max, the laptop, and Dr. Parker Fitzgerald... they are all vaporized instantly.

Chapter 7

Four thousand, five hundred miles away, Rickey Ormand is about to deliver his speech at the Propel Challenge. He stands off in the wings, stage right, as he is introduced with a waterfall of accolades detailing how great a man he is. His phone starts vibrating furiously in his Tufts hoodie. Part of him is immediately annoyed at the interruption and tempted to ignore the texts flowing in. He reaches into the pocket and pulls out his cell. A puff of breath that sounds like a short "woof" involuntarily bursts forth as he gets the news of the massive primary quake that rocked Lake Titicaca mere minutes after he hung up with Parker Fitzgerald.

His fingers fire away furiously as he texts back and forth with his top people at Liquid Sky. He has only a couple of questions, but he demands exact answers. The news is very bad… and very good. It all depends on the point of view. His people are flummoxed. Ormand is vexed. He feels powerless.

Ormand hears his name announced, followed by a wave of applause, and snaps to attention. It's showtime. He sends a final text and hands his phone to his personal assistant, a taught, almost genderless young man in a blue Armani suit that melds to him like a second skin. He's good at his job. He exudes absolute competence and a penchant for detail.

"Everything okay?" the assistant asks.

Ormand pauses for a second. The question catches him off guard. "Umm… yeah." But it's as if he has to think about it. Reaffirmed, he nods. "Yeah… yeah. Everything is gonna be great."

Ormand can cauterize his emotions like hot iron on an open wound. He slaps his assistant on his shoulder, pivots, and hits the stage exactly on cue like a seasoned actor.

Standing before the huge crowd now, Rickey Ormand takes a deep breath. It's barely perceptible behind his broad, toothy smile. He's such a performer, this man who makes dreams real like nobody else in the modern era. In a rare break from character, he pauses mid-sentence as he remembers that startling last text informing him that the uplink satellite detected a sizeable explosion. GPS pinpointed the epicenter as Fitzgerald's Drive lab. A sharp pang sweeps through his trim body. He sniffs once… twice… wipes his brow. He never does that. He reminds himself of the single most important fact – the data upload was completed prior to the explosion.

He clears his throat, and the red-light player re-emerges in complete control of the moment once again. "Ladies and gentlemen," he says. "Let's face facts. The list of world-changing discoveries is pretty damned short. The discovery of fire, the discovery of electricity, splitting the atom… these things have shaped our world. They've changed who we are."

Applause. Cheers. Much love for the man.

He waits for quiet before continuing. "I mean… there have been a million great ideas throughout history. But when it comes right down to it, the only thing that matters is turning a brilliant idea into reality. For example, what good is electricity without lightbulbs? That's where I come in. I take the impossible and make it a reality. I take dreams and make them real. That's what Liquid Sky is all about."

More applause. More cheers. Even more love for the man.

"And tonight, as you know, I am here to announce this year's Liquid Sky Propel Challenge. I am here to find that rare individual somewhere in the world to join us in moving the world forward."

This time, he holds his index finger up to silence the audience's enthusiastic support. Immediately they are quiet, hanging on his next words. They can sense the big reveal coming.

"Gravity," Ormand says, pausing heavily for effect and still holding that index finger in the air.

"I believe the time has come to move society forward. I dream of a world beyond fossil fuels. Gravity will be the world's next power source. And I promise you this. I will make that dream a reality because I am Rickey Ormand, my company is Liquid Sky, and this is the greatest challenge mankind has ever seen."

Ormand has at his fingertips the capacity to make gravity power a reality. With Rickey Ormand out front, a revolution is coming. The way we live, the way we travel, the limits of our collective experience, are about to burst forth into a totally new dimension driven by gravity power. Silent, safe, and efficient, capable of unfathomable force, gravity engines will supplant the putt-putt relics of yesteryear on which the world has relied. This is Rickey Ormand's vision of the future. Move over, Captain Kirk. Rickey Ormand's coming through.

Then again, maybe not. Ormand's hubris makes him vulnerable. As much as he wants to believe that gravity power will be his to roll out, there are powerful players dug in to grab this technology for themselves. They will stop at nothing to possess the power of gravity because an innovation as radical as this means toppling the world's most cherished institutions. Nothing will be safe from Fitzgerald's discovery or from whatever Liquid Sky does with it. Partitions will fall, hierarchies will crumble, and oligarchy will stagger, heave, and collapse, asphyxiating on its own vomit.

Rickey Ormand believes he will simply control the source of power on which the entire world will depend. Standing here in Las Vegas before thousands of adoring fans, he doesn't understand his rivals are willing to scorch the earth. Everything close dies.

Chapter 8

Black Rock Desert, Nevada.

Two years have passed since that dreadful day in the Andes. The name Parker Fitzgerald has been forgotten, buried under the rubble along with the woman herself. Outside of a terse press release confirming that Liquid Sky lost an unmanned weather station near the epicenter, little else was mentioned. The entirety of the media coverage focused on the death toll and the devastation suffered by the local inhabitants, which was something Fitzgerald would have appreciated.

Ormand revealed next to nothing about Parker Fitzgerald. He kept her and her work under tight wraps. Even if some shrewd reporter found their way to the Fallout Shelter, what was there to hear? Some fantastical talk about a glass and steel castle in the sky? From whom? Ormand paid off Rodrigo with the stipulation the bartender sign a non-disclosure agreement and relocate back to New York, a *nouveau-riche* millionaire. Rodrigo was just fine with that. Ormand also went to great lengths to sanitize the site. He ordered everything short of firebombing the site to ensure no physical evidence remained.

Back home, Ormand established a zero-tolerance gag order. He even instituted a gag order on the gag order. The few people who knew what really happened were restricted from even admitting they couldn't discuss it because "it" never happened in the first place. As far as Liquid Sky was concerned, nothing happened, none of it existed – the Liquid-Drive lab, Parker Fitzgerald, the gag order, witnesses... everything vanished behind the veil of Liquid Sky information control.

The hefty bonuses he laid on the few of his people who knew came with a caveat – any mention of the secret facility or what was discovered would result in termination and an ongoing bombardment of litigation guaranteed to bankrupt and blacklist the traitor. As Ormand reminded them, he controlled everything they did because everything they did was somehow vulnerable to network incursion. In other words, he threatened, he could tap a couple of very nasty hackers who could make Mother Theresa look like a gun runner, a Madam, and a dope trafficker with but a few clicks of the mouse.

The data he salvaged from Max was so valuable, he never once considered limiting the depth of his intimidation and, if necessary, retribution. There was way too much at stake. Every one of his competitors would pay a fortune to get their hands on the data, and Ormand felt he had no choice but to suspect each and every one of his people of corporate espionage. It was the only safe approach.

The people at Liquid Sky who knew about Parker Fitzgerald could be a golden goose if bought out by a competitor. So, Ormand put it to them bluntly. "Each of your bonuses has enough zeros tacked on that you will be able to retire. Screw with me on this, and I will destroy you, I will destroy your families, I will poison anything you've ever loved. We're dealing with a new world. I have no problem protecting that world by any means necessary."

As with Rodrigo, the bartender at the Fallout Shelter, that was pretty much all Rickey Ormand had to do or say. Who knew? Who remembered? Cash the check and carry on, carry on. News cycles came and went with the depth and complexity of a flash card. No news was good news as far as Ormand was concerned. And if some pain in the ass in the media tried to light a fire of speculation, it wouldn't have enough kindling to ignite.

As far as the world was concerned, Dr. Parker Fitzgerald was dead and gone. A real tragedy. The sudden disappearance of Parker Fitzgerald was quintessential to his two-year plan. There was too much riding on it. Now, two years later, the time had finally arrived for Ormand's two great announcements. The spectacle would be nothing short of spectacular. First, the truth about Parker Fitzgerald, his new creation. That will blow their minds. Then, he will introduce the Liquid-Drive gravity box itself. The world will change in a split second once he fires it up in public.

Ormand chose Burning Man to deliver his monumental address. It was the perfect pairing, like a vintage Screaming Eagle cabernet to accompany a Wagyu Pittsburgh ribeye. Like a cornucopia brimming over with rich, luscious delicacies, there was something for everyone at Burning Man. In the center of it all would be Rickey Ormand's Liquid Revolution stage. The throng of people were always energized at Burning Man. It was a mega-event, perfect for Ormand's mega-announcement. Burning Man was the fabled, grandiose cavalcade of iconoclasts and those who know better than everyone else, "the one percent," as they said. Burning Man was not an event; it was a happening.

Every year like clockwork, a temporary town called Black Rock City is erected soup to nuts. A who's who of the world's tech elite – the self-appointed "one percent" – and about 70,000 self-stylized pilgrims of assorted make and model shell out their $500 a ticket and undertake their holy passage to Nevada's Black Rock Desert, where they participate in a smorgasbord of communal activities, mindfulness exercises, and self-excoriations.

There are two primary elements at Burning Man. The elite consist of the one percent who have already connected to the Source or already tapped into the great wellspring of universal being where their silicon dreams are born. Such is their conjecture, for this is the camp of the "mindful intuitives." These folks live beyond human facts, above the messy mass of small-minded, low-vibrating, third-dimensioners who are responsible for global warming, overpopulation, poverty, sexism, hetero-sexism, homophobia, phobias in general, and, most egregiously, Donald Trump.

These exquisite beings of light and technological wisdom do not find affinity with human beings as much as they do with dolphins, the Dalai Lama, and his homeboy Richard Gere. Each of these delicate souls has long ago found their sacred shaman spirit masquerading as fire and shadow blithely dancing as shadow across the selenite. For the MI – the Mindful Intuitive – the only facts that really exist are generated by algorithms born of intricate motherboards. Human facts are fabricated lies created by Rush Limbaugh and Sean Hannity to puppeteer the ignorant masses of patriots and white men who seem to be only wife beaters. Like all things 3-D, they believe human facts are basic untruths worshipped by lower-functioning humans to reconcile their fear of wielding the tremendous power of the Source.

True devotees of Burning Man refer to themselves as "the one percent," but they still need people to foot the bill. That's where the other 99 percent come in. They range from activists, to hacktivists, to slick SVVC's (that's Silicon Valley Venture Capitalists to those in the know). They've been coming to Burning Man in record numbers. Now, they're coming to see one man, Rickey Ormand, answer one prevailing question – what will change the world?

Ormand has big plans. He intends to turn the festival into a frenzy. He knows he can do it easily. This is Burning Man. It's ritualistic. It's tribal. There's no deodorant or dad jeans. Rickey Ormand knows he can drop his bomb in the middle of this crowd, and it will send shock waves across the world like a tsunami. That's why he coined the catch phrase in the first place "In the wake of the quake."

It was the only reference to Peru he permitted, and it had to come from him directly and be ensconced in rhetoric of renewal and rebirth. In the months leading up to the event, he relentlessly pumped out provocative comments to the media without giving away his secrets in order to ferment both interest and disdain.

"In the wake of the quake, I feel a moral obligation to cut through red tape and smooth out the road to a bright, new world."

"In the wake of the quake, universal will work for us instead of against us."

"In the wake of the quake, Liquid Sky will set the world on fire."

"In the wake of the quake, I will reinvent human existence."

"In the wake of the quake, you must all journey to Burning Man. In the desert, you will see what the new world has to offer."

Going in to Burning Man, Rickey Ormand deftly raised the masses to a fevered pitch. As for the one percent, they loathed him so much, they had to hear his speech in person. Before anyone knew what was happening, Burning Man became synonymous with Liquid Sky as Ormand turned the event into his own private platform.

Come one, come all in the wake of the quake.

And now, at last, the time has come. Thanks to Rickey Ormand, there are more pilgrims amassed at Burning Man than ever before. It bothers the crap out of the one percent. Ormand is too populist and too popular. In his glossy event guide, he claims to have discovered a "radical new future inconceivable to the usual Silicon Valley elite." The one percent resent being eclipsed by a man who claims he "discovered a new mode of being that made algorithms and Artificial Intelligence look like long division and Atari."

It's clear to everyone that Rickey Ormand delights in pulling the tablecloth out from under the one percent elite just to see their finest china come crashing down. What outrages them even more is that he could have been one of them if only he followed the divine path of information technology by embracing the art of corralling personal data. Instead, he has chosen to blaze a path of his own and try to take their audience with him.

Turning his back on IT is heresy enough. But the real threat Ormand poses is financial, and everybody in Silicon Valley knows it. Only the one percent choose to deny it. Ormand has proclaimed an end to the old guard in Silicon Valley and in corporate America as a whole. Undoubtedly, the money – all that money, so much money – will leave them and follow him instead.

Showtime comes, and Ormand doesn't disappoint. The Liquid Sky Revolution stage is everything Ormand's fans expect and no less what his adversaries dread. Huge and back-lit in shifting shades of purple, orange, red, and magenta, the scene looks like an extension of the desert while also distinguishing the moment as something transcendental, something prodigious as if to say there is all this magic around us, but only Liquid Sky can make it real.

The sun dips below the horizon, casting the Black Rock desert in a mix of light and shadow. The crowd appears to stretch on endlessly. Ormand's stage director had the brilliant idea of providing over two thousand sofas, palor chairs, and cocktail tables. The feel is eclectic, even *avant-garde*. The vintage-style furniture is set about the main-stage arena that extends well beyond the perimeter of the area he's been allotted. Nobody but the one percent cares. But now that Ormand is about to take the stage, these amenities are little more than step stools for those trying to catch a better glimpse of the man they call the Liquid Messiah. Most in the audience are too far from the stage to see Ormand himself, but the massive video screens give them everything they could want.

Suddenly, the stage goes dark. Deep, penetrating synthesizer chords vibrate through the chest of each man, woman, and child. Even a dolphin would be impressed by the sonic appeal. Thirty seconds later, there is abrupt silence followed by an eerie sort of nursery-rhyme music. The juxtaposition is breathtaking.

The tune is familiar, but the words are new. "Hush little baby, don't say a word. Rickey Ormand is building a brand-new world. And if that brand-new world doesn't shine, Rickey will change it another time."

The one percent are appalled. They are offended. It's a damned outrage. How did this happen? How can people allow this man to slide into bed with them? They vow to resist Ormand's onslaught and attempts to usurp their capital. They will organize. They will rally. They will demand to know how many transgender employees work for Liquid Sky. And just what does Ormand mean by "control time?" Didn't Al Gore invent time? What the hell is happening?

The other 99 percent − from the weed shop owners to the six people who dared to smoke in L.A., from the venture capitalists to the pilots who choppered them in − are transfixed with awe and anticipation. Who needs a seven-shot mocha-choca-latté-yaya when just one drop of Liquid Sky can turn gravity into fuel? Sorry, Lady Marmalade.

The lulla-by-Ormand fades now. The stage goes dark and silent, but only for a moment. A thunderous cannon blast shatters the desert solace. The stage erupts with bright, white light as rap music bombards the crowd. *From Oakland to Sac-Town, the Bay area and back down, from Diego to the bay...* Dr. Dre, they all knew the song. Then Old School, LL Cool J... *Mama Said Knock You Out.*

Larger than life, LL Cool J walks out stage right. The crowd goes wild. Sporting his iconic Kangol, he's decked out like he cracked Zsa Zsa Gabor's safe. Caught up in the moment and the music, even some of the one percent are bobbing back and forth with their hands in the air like they just don't care. And the hip Venture Capitalists who wear Allbirds with tuxedos and sleep on mattresses full of hondos have candy in their heels.

This is Liquid Sky at Burning Man, an event without equal in the wake of the quake.

Don't call it a comeback
I've been here for years
I'm rocking my peers
Puttin' suckers in fear

Ormand is definitely sending a message, choosing LL Cool J, as his opener. The debonair rapper is not just dishing his most popular song, he's actually rapping about the Liquid Messiah himself, touting the man's prowess, warning all who stand in his way. When the song comes to an end LL Cool J drops the mic. Another cannon shot explodes, and the stage goes dark and silent for a second time. The soul-shaking synthesizer returns.

When the back-lighting begins to glow again, Rickey Ormand, the Liquid Messiah, is standing center stage wearing a white Kangol and a Liquid Sky hoodie. He looks like a kid wearing grown-up street clothes more than the CEO of a powerful company. He holds one hand up in the air to hush the boisterous audience. In his other hand, he has a golden microphone. He got the idea from Rush Limbaugh. It glistens as the main stage lights come up, bathing the Liquid Messiah in a pool of radiant white light that makes him appear as holy as his moniker.

He has a huge smile on his face.

"That's right," he says. "Don't call it a comeback. Liquid Sky has been blowing away the competition for years. And after you hear what I have to say this evening, you'll realize there really is no competition. Everything else is just a toy."

He's trying to act street tough. "Yeah, yeah… that will bother some people, I know." He begins walking across the stage. "Well, I've got news for those folks. What's that news, you ask? Well… simply this. The world is led from the middle."

Big smile… big smile.

"Yup, Liquid Sky serves you, the people of this world, by creating real things to improve your lives. Liquid Sky is worldwide. Liquid Sky is global. Liquid Sky is changing the world."

He holds up his hand to silence the applause. It takes a good fifteen seconds for them to settle down.

"Now… now," he beckons. "I have read a few articles – not a lot, mind you – but a few. One in particular by someone I've never heard of opining in the loftiest of tones that the terrible tragedy in Lake Titicaca marks the beginning of a precipitous decline for Liquid Sky and, by extension, one Rickey Ormand. I guess he means me."

Pause. Laughter. Smiles.

"I think you know both are equally untrue," he concludes.

Smiles. Cheers.

Although he refrains from naming names, everyone knows Ormand is referring to an op-ed in the *Times* that raised a personal attack to a new level, especially for a paper of this caliber.

"This so-called 'industry expert'… yeah, I know, right? So, this guy claims the terrible tragedy in Peru two years ago marks some sort of industry shift that will start a death spiral for Liquid Sky. And believe me, it was really terrible, alright? Horrible for those people, okay? But you know what really bothered me about that article? I mean really bothered me?"

Pause.

"I tell you what's worse. This so-called 'expert' I've never heard of writes that I was talking out my ass when I claimed I've discovered a radical new energy source unlike anything we have ever imagined possible. He writes about losing Dr. Parker Fitzgerald as if he actually knew her. Then I started thinking he was gloating or something, rubbing it in my face. He wrote something like, 'She's gone, and with it anything she might have discovered,' or some crap like that."

Shaking his head, he begins to laugh. The effect is almost eerie, this desert oasis filled with more billionaires than Davos during the World Economic Forum set against a backdrop of expansive night sky.

Ormand takes off his Kangol and frisbees it into the crowd. He's self-aware. He knows how to use props.

"Well, let me set the record straight for all you good people kind enough to schlep out to the desert to see me."

Ormand scans the crowd from left to right then back again. Nobody dares stir. Nobody dares utter a sound. It's all according to plan... all according to plan.

When he feels the stage is set just right, he continues. "You all know they call me the Liquid Messiah, right? But I can't walk on water... at least not yet. However, I can resurrect the dead. So why don't we let Dr. Fitzgerald tell you about what really happened up there on that mountain?"

A shockwave blows through the massive crowd, giving rise to a single collective thought. Can it really be?

The soul-shaking introduction to *2001: A Space Odyssey* explodes from the massive sound system, passing through the audience and out into the desert wilderness. The bass is ass clenching. Each down stroke of the pounding timpani hits like a slug to the chest. This moment, this music, is the manifestation of the raw energy, the unbridled power that has surrounded Rickey Ormand since the Bicentennial in Philadelphia. The force of his genius now rises up from the desert sands like the spirits of the ancient Pharaohs.

The music ends with one final, reverberating climax and then... awed silence.

Ormand allows the moment to make its full impact before continuing.

"Ladies and gentlemen," he announces. "Dr. Parker Fitzgerald is not dead. She is very much alive and an integral part of Liquid Sky. And she's here with us tonight."

The energy level rises precipitously. Ormand feeds off it.

"Good people of Burning Man, it is my great pleasure to introduce the one, the only, the very much alive, Dr. Parker Fitzgerald. Come on out here, Fitzy."

At first, nobody knows how to respond. Is this guy for real? Is Parker Fitzgerald really alive? Soon enough, their question is answered.

Emerging from the shadows stage left is a figure surely conjured from the distant future. It's her. It's Dr. Parker Fitzgerald sure enough. She is sporting her favorite Red Sox hat which, much like her, embodies the spirit of resilience. She is wearing a simple white T-shirt, and her torso appears lean and mean. Her shoulders and traps are as pronounced as her arms. Her long arms, visibly muscular, punctuate each stride with confidence, even attitude. The cutesy, professional bob is gone. Her blonde hair is long now. Her profile is more beautiful than ever.

But there is something else, something that immediately stifles the raucous applause. Is this Parker Fitzgerald or... or someone... something else?

From the waist up, Parker Fitzgerald has the body of a goddess. She is lean, muscular, proportioned, a vision of herself at twenty-five. But from the waist down, Parker Fitzgerald is completely gone. There is neither bone nor flesh remaining. Instead, a gleaming set of purple robotic legs extend down from her waist which is, apparently, also robotic. The mechanism looks nothing like the customary prosthetics one sees nowadays, even in the Olympics. To the contrary, Fitzgerald's "legs" are rather shapely. Her stride is really natural looking, as in a well-animated film, although there's a slight stiffness in her gait. To punctuate the look, she's wearing a totally cute pair of pink running shoes.

Fitzgerald looks totally badass as she strides over to Rickey Ormand with determination but also a fair degree of nonchalance, all things considered. It doesn't take long for the stunned crowd to figure out that her lower half is completely synthetic. They're right. By the time the Liquid Sky rescue team reached her, she was barely alive by some strange act of God. Her lower half was completely crushed and mangled. She would have quickly bled to death were it not for the tremendous weight of the debris pressing on her femoral artery. Her devastating mishap was softened by a bit of good fortune.

All eyes are on Fitzgerald as she strides across the stage. When she reaches Rickey Ormand, she turns to face the audience. A collective gasp is audible even to Fitzgerald up on stage. She winces a bit. It's an automatic response she can't control, no different from fight or flight. She feels awkward and self-conscious at times. She may be metal below the waist, but the courageous heart beating in her womanly chest still feels the pain and anguish of what happened to her in Peru. She's alive for all to see, but she feels like a part of her died on the mountain.

Fitzgerald says nothing. She just stands there smiling. Predictably, Ormand speaks first. "There but for the grace of God go you and I," he says. "It could have been any one of us working at Lake Titicaca. Lord knows we get enough applications. But I dare say, not many of us, myself included, could have survived the ordeal. The woman you see standing here is a survivor. She overcame tremendous adversity and transcended to a world of ordinary human beings. She's no longer simply Parker Fitzgerald, Ph.D. No sir, this person is someone – and something – very, very different. She's part woman, part genius, and part science fiction. Ladies and gentlemen of Burning Man, I give you the fascinating woman I now call the Phoenix."

There is a spattering of applause. Mostly there is utter confusion. Parker Fitzgerald is supposed to be dead. Fitzgerald opens a door in her right thigh and takes out a golden microphone just like Ormand's. She flexes both arms in triumph. Her biceps, forearms, and shoulders are pronounced. She's clearly been hitting the weights hard. This sign of strength sets the audience off. Now they are going crazy for the Phoenix. This is every bit the show they came to see and so, so much more.

"Hello, Burning Man!" she prompts like a seasoned MC. "Don't call it a comeback!"

The crowd goes wild. Now… now they understand Ormand's theme and why he opened with LL Cool J. She's about to speak again but holds up a finger pretending an idea just came to her. She hands her mic to Ormand, reaches into a similar storage area in her other thigh, pulls out a flask, takes a swig, returns it to her thigh, and takes her mic back.

"Ah," she says. "Much better, I'll have you know," she says. "That was my best Dean Martin impression." The bit goes over like she's been playing the circuit for years.

Not one for being upstaged, Ormand chimes in. "Yeah, Dean Martin meets the Terminator."

Eh, they may have come to see Rickey Ormand, but now everybody in the audience wants to see the Phoenix fire.

When she has the crowd's attention again, Fitzgerald continues. "You know," she gestures to her legs. "This was bad. I'll admit it. I don't remember very much from that night. But I do remember waking up in some hospital paralyzed from the waist down. Little did I know that there was nothing left from the waist down. I remember being furious at Rickey for saving me. I remember thinking he should have let me die. There was nothing below my waist. A total void."

No music or fancy light show is playing now. It's just the Fitzgerald and her audience, all of whom are hanging on her every word.

"That's pretty cliché, I know. Like some sort of war movie or something. Except that when it happens to you, you don't think about things like clichés and movies. You think about the future, your future, and how completely shitty it's going to be. I have to be honest. I felt like a freak, and I didn't want any part of it."

She paces a bit. Her pathos seems genuine. There's real pain there.

r   s

"That's how I was for a few weeks. I was too busy feeling sorry for myself to think about much else, let alone my recovery. Then Rickey told me Liquid Sky had a secret robotics lab where they were completely reinventing the idea of melding man and machine. He told me that I could be the first real-life test of the technology. It was propulsion technology, just different from how we might define it, right? Moving things, moving people, moving things merged with people. That's Liquid Sky."

She pauses to take it all in. She's been through so much these last two years. It's all flooding back now. She struggles to keep it together. Massive applause and adoration fill the gap between her and her fans. It grounds and refocuses her.

"And, it's not my intention to be, like, some sort of shill for my company, any more than it's my intention to live the rest of my life as some sort of sideshow freak."

Rickey Ormand feels the need to reassert himself again. "As a matter of fact, we have skin covering for her legs. I call it skin because it's actually an organic, living thing. The Phoenix decided not to wear her Liquid-Skin tonight, but were she wearing it, you would never, ever in a million years know her lower half is completely robotic."

Fitzgerald laughs. "Thank you for that fine sponsored message, Mr. Ormand. I think you've just made Liquid-Skin a household word."

Solid laughter. It makes her feel good.

"Also," she continues, "let me say that tonight is the last time you will hear me referred to as the Phoenix. That horrible nickname is going to end right here in the desert."

More laughter.

"Let me tell you all something else. I represent the future, that's true. But it's not about my legs. No, the future I represent will change the world as we know it today. It's been said that the earthquake marked the beginning of the end for Liquid Sky. But here I stand, tall and proud, telling you that Liquid Sky is about to define the future, not lag behind it."

The stage goes dark. Orchestral music returns. This time, it's Wagner's *Flight of the Valkyries*, the song made famous in the movie

Apocalypse Now. Parker scurries off in the dark for a quick wardrobe change. When she retakes her position, bright lights illuminate her. She's stunning. She is now wearing a sleek, black dress, sleeveless with a half-turtle, cut mid-thigh. It is Givenchy's best work of the year. Her robotic legs are now covered with the engineered skin Ormand boasted of earlier.

She is breathtakingly beautiful and from out of this world to boot.

"Gravity," she says, gesturing to all about. "It surrounds us, a constant field of energy exercising its power over everything. Gravity is ceaseless and possesses tremendous power. We see this in the ebb and wane of the tides which it governs. For the most part, though, we never notice it. An apple falls, and we pick it up. We throw a ball, it goes only so far before hitting the ground. Babe Ruth never hit a home run that went 20 miles. Our children swoosh down slides or trip on their shoelaces. We applaud or console them without much root cause analysis. We assume the tequila the bartender is about to pour out will flow down into the glass and not hover in globules near the top like something out of *The Matrix*. Similarly, when we step out of the house in the morning, we expect to remain standing on *terra firma* instead of floating up into space."

Wild images, conceptual contradictions, and bizarre juxtapositions play out on the gigantic back-lit screen behind her that, until now, was limited to a gentle panoply of soothing colors. The effect is startling. It's as if Parker Fitzgerald is taking the crowd through a brief history of time. Only what she's saying has never been said before. History is in the making here. This time, it's her-story, not his.

"Take a good look at me," she says. "If I didn't walk out here without my skin pants on, you would never have known that my lower half is 100 percent, state-of-the-art robotics. The technology is so lifelike, it blurs the lines between woman and machine."

There is a burst of frenzied applause.

"By the way," she quips, "Rickey hates it when I call it skin pants, but I hate it when he calls me the Phoenix, so we're even, right?"

The crowd eats it up.

Fitzgerald is enjoying herself now. God knows she's earned it. "Had I walked out on stage dressed like this, you would think I was just another woman. But that would be an illusion, wouldn't it? It would be an illusion based on the observation of apparent facts, but still a faulty assumption based on your assumptions of normality rather than the facts of the matter."

She smiles. "Ready to have your mind blown?" she says and holds her mic out to the fervent crowd. The roar is more like the Romans at the Coliseum.

The next thing Fitzgerald does can only be described as performance porn in the 22nd Century. She lifts up her Givenchy dress and pulls the waistline of her skin pants forward and back, forward and back as if it's Spandex. She's teasing and taunting the spellbound. She brings them to a climactic groan when she lets the Liquid-Skin snap back against her alloy pelvis like she's snapping a latex glove against her wrist. The abrupt pop hits the crowd like a slap in the face.

"See," she says. "Appearances *are* always deceiving. That's the difference between appearances and facts. Believe me, I know. I'm a scientist. It's the cornerstone of who I am. What really matters," she continues, "is everything we *don't* see. Returning to gravity, we never see it, do we? But it governs everything... simply everything. Gravity affects and controls our entire world and everything we do. It impacts everything while we humans think nothing of it. We take it for granted like a husband takes his wife on football Sundays."

She pauses to allow the joke to settle in. "Okay, okay. That was a cheap shot," she admits. "Men are equally bad with golf."

She gets a good, positive round of laughter. It's all in good fun, they know that.

"Yeah," she continues. "Stand up isn't exactly my thing. I'm better with Schrödinger's cat and stuff like that, as if anybody really cares. And I'm really good at disappearing, right? You all know that. But I bet you don't know that I lived sequestered on the top of a mountain for two years with no family or friends. I almost died there... twice. I also bet you don't know that immediately following my recovery,

I worked under top-secret conditions along with two other scientists. We're not even allowed to be in the same room together. But now, after four long years, two brushes with death, a pair of robotic legs with which I can crush a walnut between my thighs, I still can't get a date and I stand here before you ready to make the reveal."

The crowd chants her name, urging her on.

"Tonight," says Fitzgerald, "I'm here to deliver a message from the future, a message from another world even. What's that message? Simply this: We assume things are the way they are just because the limits of human understanding can't yet envision something beyond it. We came to depend on fossil fuels because they met our needs at the time. It was convenient and it worked. Electric cars? We've had that technology for almost two hundred years. In fact, the first all-electric car, a race car to be exact, set the land-speed record over 150 years ago. Some guy name Jenatzi. Do we know him today? Is 'Jenatzi' a household name?"

"No? Really? But the guy invented a fully electric car almost two centuries before Elon Musk. Wrong place, wrong time for poor Jenatzi."

She turns to the screens running along the back of the stage. Pictures of Cam Jenatzi and his electric torpedo car *La Jamais Contente* fill the massive space.

The audience finds it funny.

"Sure, we laugh. But think about it. That guy had special vision and saw past the limits of knowledge. Eh... nobody cared. Oil and gas were more convenient at the time. Now that everybody is freaking out over global warming, the electric car seems like the greatest invention ever. We still have no idea about this guy named Jenatzi, but everybody in Silicon Valley would kill to get in with Elon Musk. Millions of people know Tesla, the car company. But how many people know who Nikola Tesla is? Meh... nobody cares"

Cheers rise up from the crowd.

Fitzgerald laughs. "Yes, well, I'm sure all of you know who Nikola Tesla is. But, I'm sorry to say... all you Silicon Valley VC's, all you folks on the wait list for a shiny new Tesla that Elon Musk has to bolt together himself to meet quota... sorry. I'm sorry to tell you that electric power is not the future. I mean, where do we get electricity from anyway? We get it from coal. No, electric power is not the future."

Fitzgerald strolls around the stage. "I got some more news for ya. Magnetic power is not the future, either. Believe me, I tried like hell. For two damned years I lived on the top of a giant rock working on magnetic power, asking myself how can we harness it?

"Did I tell you I spent two years holed up on some mountain top in Peru searching for the answer? I did? Did I tell you I got blown up there, too? I did? Oh, sorry."

She laughs to herself. It's clear there are some challenging memories running through her head right now. "You see, during the earthquake, something magnificent revealed itself. Sometimes that's what happens during times of great upheaval. Something strange and wonderful happened in my lab while it was being destroyed. It seems the universe took one thing but also gave back something far greater in return. The experiment I was running when the quake hit went totally awry. But in the process, a new day for humankind was born. According to the data that I managed to upload to Liquid Sky just before I went lights out, a brand-new energy source revealed itself."

She is interrupted by a young man wearing stylishly torn jeans and a long, white linen shirt. His long, curly brown hair dances on his shoulders as he sprints toward the stage. Two tremendous security guards with thighs for biceps intercept the man just shy of center stage, which is, anyway, too high for him to reach.

"It's okay," says Fitzgerald. "This is Burning Man. He's trying to impress a girl. Let him speak."

He starts talking zealously. She strains to hear him.

"Can somebody please throw him a box?" she demands.

One of the tech crew tosses the man a "box," a padded cube inside of which is a mic. It's the sort of gadget you have at corporate events and such where audience participation is encouraged.

The young man with the wild hair, blazing eyes, and trimmed scruff reaches up and promptly drops the box that was thrown to him.

"Well, we know he's in IT," quips Fitzgerald.

The man seems not to care. He is humble. He rotates the box. His voice is soft. "Dr.Fitzgerald, I don't care what you've discovered. You're an amazing woman. You're beautiful."

Fitzgerald smiles. It's thin, a façade. She wishes she could agree with him. She doesn't. She can't. Not now. Maybe not ever. She nods to security, and they respectfully guide him back in the direction from which he came.

"You're gorgeous," the young man yells over his shoulder.

Fitzgerald snorts out a laugh. "And you, my dear friend, are a bit too high. I'll tell ya," she says. "Show a man a robotic pelvis, and he'll say anything. I say 'pelvis,' but you know what body part I'm really referring to, right ladies?"

The women in the audience hoot and holler.

"Where was I?" Fitzgerald wonders aloud. "Oh, yeah. So, I got hit on the head with a chunk of ceiling and then I got blown up. But the data — that marvellous, wondrous, world-changing data — was saved. That was a good thing because, um, when you get rocked like I did, you can't remember shit. After the quake, after I was rebuilt into whatever it is I am now – which, I am happy to say, includes a robo-pelvis young men find sexy — I finally got the chance to review the data.

"And I'll be damned if we didn't make a huge breakthrough when the experiment went bonkers. The quake caused something unprecedented. It caused some sort of rift in the gravitational field around ground zero, which just happened to be very near my lab. I suddenly realized we had been asking the wrong question the whole damned time."

The applause is raucous.

Fitzgerald looks over toward Ormand. "Rickey, come out here a sec."

She waves him over to her. "Just so you know," she says. "I'm totally off script. You might recognize the look of horror on Rickey's face right now. The man time blocks his bowel movements, okay?"

Willing to play the straight man, Ormand glides over. The sexy cyborg and the hoodie billionaire stand face-to-face.

"Rickey," she says.

Ormand replies in a sheepish tone. "Um, yes Dr. Fitzgerald?"

She holds her mic up closer. "You were asking the wrong question. Do you know that?"

"I'm sorry, Dr. Fitzgerald. My dog ate my homework, and I just made it up."

Fitzgerald wags her finger at her boss. "The question, 'How do we generate magnetic power?' was all wrong, Mr. Rickey Ormand. The question we needed to ask was this: How do we generate power from *gravity*. Now go to your room."

Playing his role perfectly, Ormand slinks off.

Returning her attention to the crowd, Fitzgerald continues with her explanation. "As I said earlier, we barely realize that gravity is present. It's unconscious. In reality, gravity is ubiquitous energy, massive in potential, dynamic in kinetic expression. Gravity is everywhere and everywhere exerting itself on a massive scale. Gravity spins this giant planet at a little over 1,000 miles per hour. And yet, paradoxically, gravity waves are very weak, so weak that we barely know they're there. Think about the energy that requires. And yet, gravity waves are so diffuse, we could barely detect them let alone harness them for energy… until now."

Rickey Ormand returns to the stage. This time, he is accompanied by two young men, both of whom are wide eyed and look stimulated to the point of bewilderment. They are both wearing khaki pants and V-neck sweaters, one red, the other sage. They both have brown leather messenger bags slung around their shoulders. One man is Rohit Gupta, the other is Bai "Bobby" Wei. They look more or less like your typical Liquid Sky employees. Except they're not. They are very, very special. Along with Parker Fitzgerald, they are going to change the world.

Rickey Ormand raises his hand to silence the crowd. "Ladies and gentlemen of Burning Man. It is my great pleasure to introduce to the public for the very first time since their hire almost two years ago, Rohit Gupta and Bobby Wei. With their help, Liquid Sky is going to redefine everything about the world as you know it today. Take one last look around, folks. Tomorrow, you won't recognize it."

It's just too much. The audience can't believe the stream of thrills pouring forth these last forty minutes.

Ormand gestures to Rohit and Bobby, who are waving to the joyous crowd like pie-eyed pageant winners. "When the quake hit," explains Ormand, "I was scheduled to announce the Propel Challenge that very night. Perhaps some of you out there even submitted proposals."

A few cheers roll out.

Ormand continues. "I don't even remember what the original topic was. Who cares? The only thing that matters now is that I made an executive decision on the spur of the moment. I pivoted and made gravity power the focus of the Propel Challenge two years ago. Being a great leader requires a sixth sense for recognizing opportunity in its most abstract form."

He laughs coyly. "Yeah, that's how Rickey rolls."

He laughs again, wishing he had his white Kangol. "It's been a wild adventure ever since. Not a day passed that we didn't laugh, cry, scream, and pout. What I received from these two guys standing next to me was nothing short of mind blowing. And now, in only two short years, I'm here talking about the real thing, a gravity engine called Liquid-Drive."

Smiling broadly, Rohit Gupta and Bobby Wei are once more waving to the cheering crowd.

Ormand laughs. "Look at these two. Who would have guessed, am I right? Amazing. Now, you might not know it to look at them. But these two guys are staggeringly brilliant. They both submitted proposals for the Propel Challenge that knocked my socks off. So, I announced them both co-winners immediately, hopped onto a Liquid Sky jet, and flew halfway around the world to pay them a visit in person. I hooked them up with Parker Fitzgerald when she recovered, and we never looked back."

Fitzgerald squirms a bit at Ormand's hubris. One thing they have never discussed is the way he buried her for the last two years. They each went about their work as if nothing happened. Fitzgerald got it. She and Ormand weren't in an intimate relationship. They weren't married. Theirs was a working relationship, plain and simple. As such, there were certain things better left unsaid.

Today, she knows it's her job to make Ormand look like a savior. That's part of her role. That's why he has her at his side. His hubris today is a bit heavy, though. She cringed a couple of times. Ormand loves himself so much. It's hard for her sometimes not to bring his fragile ego crashing down. But where would that get her? Plus, she doesn't trust Rohit Gupta or Bai Wei. She feels like she has to keep an eye on these two. She senses their greed and their willingness to do anything it takes to get ahead of her.

She sees the day as an opportunity to ingratiate herself, to stay in Ormand's best graces, and keep a step or two ahead of Gupta and Wei. What better way to do that, she thinks, than by going off script and singing Ormand's praises.

"Rickey always has something nice to say about his people. I think that often gets lost in the media fracas," she lies. "He cares about the world tremendously," she continues, pouring it on real thick now. "First, look at me. Rickey Ormand saved my life. Had he not done everything in his power, committing the full resources of Liquid Sky, I would have been dead for real. Also, I know some people are going to try and ruin the moment by blaming him for keeping me a secret these last two years. But when the world sees what we've discovered, I think there will be unanimous praise for the man.

"Suffice it to say, it was vitally important to keep our work absolutely secret. We're talking about changing the world overnight. This new technology had to be protected from just about everyone you can imagine. Remember, when you have the power to change life with the flick of a switch, there's no predicting who your friends, allies, and enemies are. As I've come to learn, everybody is a unique combination of all three."

She finishes and nods in satisfaction. She's said her piece. Rickey is thrilled. He winks at Fitzgerald. She winks back. They connect. Her supremacy is re-established. She looks at Gupta and Wai. The relative newbies are still around the large stage, oblivious to the politics she's laying down.

Fitzgerald smiles. As usual, it's so much easier than she imagines. Ormand returns the favor. "Isn't she amazing, folks? That's our selfless Phoenix."

His tone turns weightier now. "She's right, you know. With one flip of the switch, the world will change forever. Gravity power... it's bound to make the powerful paranoid, the fair-minded conniving, the satisfied greedy, and the greedy violent. I have no doubt there are people in this world who would do anything to seize hold of the power I am about to demonstrate. So, buckle up and hold onto your hats because for the next few years, you're going to be like infants opening your eyes for the first time."

Ormand motions to Parker Fitzgerald, Rohit Gupta, and Bobby Wei to join him in the middle of the stage. He nods to Gupta and Wei. Each man reaches into the leather courier bags slung over their shoulders and pulls out a black box, rectangular and a little larger than a hand. With all rounded edges and a bit of chrome detail, the device looks very futuristic. The plastic casing is opaque. The box glows blue from the neon light inside. The electronics and wiring inside are visible as well.

A hand-held cameraman is right there to make sure the box is visible on the big screens. Rohit and Bai hold their glowing boxes up in the air. As choreographed, Fitzgerald pops open one of her leg-storage compartments and takes out her futuristic pieces of glowing equipment as well. Her piece is larger than the others and has a big red button in the middle. She passes it over to Gupta. The pieces fit together like a puzzle. He slides his piece into a grove on one side of Fitzgerald's and passes the partial assembly to Wei who adds his piece to the other side and passes the assembly back to Fitzgerald.

She holds up the fully-assembled box like a talisman. It is aglow in her hand.

"Behold!" cries Fitzgerald. "The key to the future."

The stage plunges into darkness. The star-laden sky above hints at the magnitude of the occasion. The only thing visible up on stage is that glowing box in Fitzgerald's hand.

It's Rickey Ormand's turn to speak again. The sound techs make his whiney voice sound like God's now. "The scientific world is trapped, held hostage by Einstein's supposition that energy is neither created nor destroyed. Thus, the energy generated by an object falling due to gravity is offset by the energy required to raise it back up. This amounts to a zero-sum gain. End of story. That's where the gasoline engine seized. It's where the electric battery dies. It's where the rocket ships of our youthful dreams fall out of orbit in a glowing fireball. He was a smart guy. But his theoretical universe of zero-sum energy gets us nowhere."

More than a few jeers and boos go up, but it's unclear whether they're intended for Einstein or Ormand. If he's trying to grab as may headlines as possible, comparing himself to Einstein ought to grab the media's attention.

Ormand works his way around the stage. "The limits of fossil fuels are now plainly evident. But I'm not here to attack Big Oil. Their days are numbered."

This time there are no doubts the cheers are for him. Crowds are fickle that way.

Ormand shrugs. "Oil is not commensurate with the needs of the future. To the contrary, it gums everything up, it gives the illusion of propulsion while, in reality, it has caused stagnation. Look, rocket fuel won't get us to Mars. And it sure won't get us to another universe. The simple fact is this – oil won't propel us into the future. That much, I assure you. There was a time and a place for oil, but that time has come and gone."

The crowd is fully behind him now. He's positioned them masterfully. Now, he feels confident laying it all out for them. The word will spread like wildfire from there.

"Parker Fitzgerald is a hero," he proclaims. "With total disregard for her own safety, she discovered the magnificent anomaly she spoke of earlier. Again, because of her selfless bravery, we were able to save a massive amount of data proving that gravity is not only tremendous in its potential energy, it is something we can harness and put to work as well.

"While Parker was recuperating, these two guys, Rohit Gupta and Bai Wei, set to work tirelessly. One of them focused on capturing gravity power, and the other focused on converting it into useable energy… the capture and the conversion. Together, we've created something revolutionary. Together, we are the future. Together, we are Liquid Sky."

The lights return. Rickey Ormand now has the captivating box in his hand.

"Good people of Burning Man, we have done it. We have made gravity power a reality."

He holds the glowing box high in the air.

"I hold in my hand the ignition switch that will fire up the engine of a bold new era, a new world like nothing we've seen since the lightbulb. I say the lightbulb and not electricity because really, what good is electricity without a bulb? Am I right? It's the lightbulb, not electricity that changed the world."

He waves the ignition box over his head. "And it is the ability to harness and convert gravity into a useable form of energy that matters now. And this little box does just that."

His words blow through the crowd like a sandstorm. They can hardly believe what they're hearing. Can Ormand be serious? Is it some kind of publicity stunt? It's Rickey Ormand. Who knows what he's up to?

He hushes the crowd. "Here we go," he exclaims.

Ormand holds the box out to Fitzgerald. She sees in his eyes how much it pains him to do so. It was one of the few deal breakers she insisted upon. He is not going to steal her thunder. Neither will Rohit Gupta or Bai Wei. She figures she's earned it. She has an alloy vagina, for Christ's sake.

She snatches the ignition box from Ormand and holds it in the air for herself like a prize-fighter raising the championship belt. The roar of the crowd travels through her. She's never felt power like this before. There are so many emotions flowing through her right now. It's all welling up, from the quake, to her robotic legs, the gravity drive, Rickey Ormand, Burning Man, everything.

There she stands, the exalted Phoenix, before her adoring crowd. "People," she yells. "Say hello to Liquid-Drive."

She pushes the big red button on the ignition box. There is a deafening boom.

Fitzgerald pumps her fist. "Yeah, man! Can you feel it?"

Rohit Gupta and Bai Wei are jumping up and down. It isn't exactly a display of athleticism, especially when Gupta turns his ankle and stumbles. But the smile never leaves his face as he gets back up and hobbles around as best he can. As long as his mouse finger is safe, he's all good.

The realization spreads from person to person. Moving in slowly overhead is a huge, disk-like object, metallic and ominous against the expansive desert nightscape. The words "Liquid-Disk" are written in bright lights on the underside of the thing... whatever it is.

The Liquid-Disk might as well be a UFO. The audience stands gawking up at the intimidating object as it continues moving over their heads toward the stage. The disk stops, hovering about 100 feet above the stage. A beam of radiant bright light beams down on Rickey Ormand. He gave Fitzgerald the spotlight to fire the thing up. Now, it's his turn.

Surprising everyone, he turns to shtick. He is smiling broadly but keeps glancing up in trepidation at the big disk hovering 100 feet over the stage.

Fitzgerald takes her cue. "What is it, Rickey? Why do you keep looking up?"

"Um... like," he replies sheepishly. "Is this thing, like, gonna fall on us?"

It's working great. The audience eats it up.

"Don't worry about it," says Fitzgerald. "We'll just give you a robotic pelvis, too. With one of those babies, you finally will be able to get a date." She knocks on her pelvis to drive the point home.

"Rickey," she says. "We did it."

He turns off the shtick and turns on the salesman. "The giant object you see hovering overhead is powered by 100 percent gravity power. That's right, 100 percent gravity power. You are the very first people outside Liquid Sky to witness this marvel. Do you feel that? The world just changed. Almost everything in the world is now obsolete, courtesy of Liquid Sky."

Virtually everyone in the crowd was recording the spectacle on their cell phones. It was exactly what Ormand planned... going viral.

"Listen," he beckons. "You hear nothing. It's silent."

"Smell," he instructs. "No carbon footprint... absolutely clean energy, renewable, and... get this... infinite, inexhaustible. You never need to pull up to a pump and fill up your tank with gravity because Liquid-Drive pulls it from everywhere."

He knows this is a lie. He would never give anything away. His plan is for a monthly service linked to a payment source. According to his estimates, three-quarters of the world will be paying him monthly for the right to use Liquid-Drive.

Ormand is grinning broadly. "Sure, a company called Tesla has an electric car on the market that does zero to sixty in 2.8 seconds," he says. "But compared to a vehicle powered by Liquid-Drive, the most amazing invention of all time, his car is not much more than a snail racing a ray of light across the universe."

By now, the crowd has moved forward and is standing in a large mass close to the stage as they stare up in awe.

"Now watch this," he says. "Watch the power."

He snaps his fingers, and Fitzgerald obediently hands him the ignition box. It's off script, and she glares at him for demeaning her like that. He blows her a little kiss to let her know that he's the boss, he owns everything, and he'll patronize her whenever he damned well pleases.

Ormand slides his forefinger across a finger pad on the ignition pad, which, apparently, also serves as a controller. The big disk rockets straight up into the air. It's made of aluminium and is very light. It rises so quickly, only a few seconds pass before it isn't much more than a distant speck in the sky. It's stunning. In those few seconds, the world has entirely changed.

"Let's see a Tesla do that," he exclaims.

The crowd cheers riotously.

Ormand slides his finger around the pad some more. The lightning-fast Liquid-Disk is still high in the evening sky, but with its bright lights, everyone can see it move around under Ormand's control. He zooms it higher, out of sight now. In his mind's eye, he pilots the magnificent vehicle behind the audience, drops it back down to about 100 feet off the deck, and bolts it over the crowd. Running silent, nobody hears it until it rests hovering above the stage once more.

Ormand lets fly with a robust laugh of sheer delight. The dreamer, the boy from Philadelphia, has returned. He's playing with his magic flying machine. He is controlling not just his world but *the* world as a whole.

"Can a Tesla do that?" he shouts.

Parker Fitzgerald, Rohit Gupta, and Bobby Wei move in close to him. The three colleagues are now standing next to one of the greatest visionaries in the history of human civilization. Just like that, they have become the most popular scientists in the world.

The crowd is cheering so loudly, Ormand can barely hear himself speak. "We are true revolutionaries. Tomorrow morning, every history book will have to be rewritten. The moment I pressed that button, everything became obsolete instantly. Let me repeat that. Everything… every aspect of our lives… is now obsolete, no better than a caveman's club."

He points to the silent, hovering disk. "Look up. Leave Burning Man and be my apostles. Tell everyone you meet that this is not just some magical flying machine. It is the future, a marvellous, fantastic, wonderful future, led by Liquid Sky. I don't know where this will take us, but I can't wait to get there. Big Oil, Big Auto, Big Finance, Big everything, the omnipresent Military Industrial Complex, not to mention OPEC and the balance of power in the Middle East, China, and Russia. The list goes on across the globe. Everything in business, life, and politics will be upended. Everyone will feel threatened."

He looks at Parker Fitzgerald. For days leading up to the event, she begged him to cut these last few lines. He wouldn't even consider it. It was one of his deal breakers.

"What I am calling progress tonight translates into tremendous uncertainty in just about every major industry in the world and even the total collapse of certain sectors like energy. I know that. I also know that people will stop at nothing to get their hands on this technology. I know I would."

Fitzgerald bites her lip. She considers this next bit really unfortunate.

"But I say defiantly to the world now that you have no choice but to listen... nothing will stand in my way. When I pushed that button activating Liquid-Drive, I became the most powerful man in the world. And I will soon become the richest. As for governments, militaries, corporations... try to take me down."

He pauses now before uttering his final words of the presentation.

"Who's to say I don't have a gravity bomb?"

Mic drop, and he is gone. The silent disk bolts straight upward until it is out of site.

At this moment, Rickey Ormand is a God, and he knows it. He needs it. He has taken a fantastic dream and made it real. Tonight, in the temporary town called Black Rock City, he is staging his greatest performance ever. Liquid Sky may be poised to usher in a world-changing technology, but there are forces fighting to both protect the old guard and destroy it. Parker Fitzgerald was exactly right. The war is about to start, and there will be casualties.

Chapter 9

While Parker Fitzgerald is making history in the desert, another woman contemplates doing the same. She is gentle, beautiful, and demure. At the same time, she is a spiritual warrior to be reckoned with. The President of the United States, Harry Pierson, likes to call her the Red Dragon Lady. Her real name is Camille O'Keefe. She loves her fiery, red hair and her guardian angels. She hates the nickname Red Dragon Lady.

As Parker Fitzgerald traipses her robotic ass up and down the stage at Burning Man, Camille O'Keefe sits quietly meditating in her candle-lit den. She is trying to clear the noise in her head in order to create a still moment of reflection. Being a former First Lady and modern-day Joan of Arc, she finds quelling the din in her head can be a challenge.

Camille asks a lot of herself. She is quiet by nature, preferring the hypnotic chant of Buddhist monks to the disconcerting glamour of D.C. life. She seeks peace and harmony. She resists Beltway politics and the Machiavellian nature of it all. This is a problem for her because she has carried a karmic burden from incarnation to incarnation for two thousand years.

Camille O'Keefe feels obligated to speak for the downtrodden of the world. This puts her at odds with herself because in order to give voice to the disenfranchised, she must enter the political arena. She reckons the noise in her head is nothing in comparison to living in dire poverty with disease and death just outside the door waiting to come inside. She loathes politics and yet she must join the fray in order to speak for the women and children who cannot.

She breaks her silent meditation by repeating her intentions for the day.

"I will help the world by changing the world," she says in the calm, balanced voice of a seasoned yoga practitioner.

"I will empower poor women by empowering myself."

"I will save lives the way that I have saved my own."

This last intention gives her pause. She hadn't intended to say that. It just sort of came out. She breathes deeply with focus. Yes, she thinks, that must mean something. She unfolds her legs from a tight lotus position and stands up in a smooth, effortless motion. She heads into the bathroom and washes her face. She stares at herself in the mirror, droplets of water still beading on her pale skin.

The memories flood back. Meeting Becket Rosemore before he became president, becoming First Lady, divorcing him. That would be overwhelming enough for most people. Camille endured far more. A serious car accident... it may have been an attempt to kill her. She'll never know for sure. After she recovered, she found herself in the middle of a terrorist plot and a military rescue mission to save 5,000 women and girls from the clutches of *Boko Haram*. She shivers as the memories move through her.

Needless to say, a lot changed very quickly for Camille O'Keefe. And now, she's agreed to run for vice president.

From the hallowed halls of Capitol Hill to the slimiest back alleys of Europe, from the institutions propping Islamic terrorism to the dirt trails in Africa which are used to traffic sex slaves, Camille O'Keefe, the Red Dragon Lady, fights the many manifestations of hatred and greed. Her goal – save lives. This has been her purpose from the beginning, and she cannot deny her fate simply because she dislikes politics.

When Camille first hit the scene, she took the world by storm. A light seeker, she believes the physical world is "boot camp" where people must prove themselves capable of putting love in motion with so much inertia that the power of light builds critical mass and simply overwhelms the world of shadow. She knows the world needs her now more than ever. It's hard for her to imagine polishing up a world as tarnished, bleak, and depraved as this in order to reveal something precious beneath the grime. But she knows she must. Steadfast perseverance is Camille O'Keefe's greatest gift.

A renowned past-life regressionist, medium, and spiritual advisor, Camille O'Keefe keeps constant communication with ethereal energies. She connects to a multitude of planes. She understands intuitively that we are all energy, and so we must all interconnect if we are to raise ourselves up and out of the muck and mire. She knows human behavior most often boils down to self-interest. At the same time, she believes in the fundamental good of all people.

She's known the president, Harry Pierson, for years. Pierson was not elected president. He took over for Becket Rosemore. Rosemore had three claims to fame. He was Camille's husband. He divorced her while he was president. And he was the only U.S. president to commit suicide while in office. When the bullet hit Becket's brain, Harry Pierson found himself president of the United States, the most powerful man in the world.

"Ours is a marriage made in Hell," she wrote in her tell-all biography. Mesmerizing as she was, her cute laugh and gleaming smile were never enough to completely hide the winces of pain. Thus was the Red Dragon Lady forged.

Long before she met the junior senator from North Carolina named Becket Rosemore, Camille O'Keefe was known around D.C. as the intriguing medium with the wild red hair.

She always started her sessions with the same three words: "Okay, tell me."

It was short and sweet, but it always got them talking. She had quite a few political fat cats among her clients, although few would admit it. When she met Becket Rosemore – then a fortune-seeking, first-year senator – her life gained momentum quickly, although not necessarily in a direction that was good for her. Camille knew intuitively that she and Beck had history together, having shared many past lives. The law of eternal return governed their karmic history together and connected them like fuel to a fire.

When she first met Beck, she believed it was her karmic obligation to help him fulfil his immense potential. She pledged her life, her love, and her soul to him. As a result, she was inclined to follow him where he chose rather than blaze a trail of her own. Beck repaid her with a long string of affairs, laying women like a mason building a wall. Camille had her suspicions. At the time, she felt it more important – universally important – that she remain by Beck's side as he made a name for himself. She believed his potential to change the world superseded her own happiness.

She was right… at least about his potential. Before long, Becket Rosemore was synonymous with peace in the Middle East, bringing American troops home, and even building unprecedented political alliances with China. The way was clear for him to make his run for the White House. As a past-life regression therapist, Camille recognized the pattern of their many previous lives together. Every time, she was the passive receptacle for Beck's will. She had a funny knack for ending up dead every time

Beck loathed Camille's "New Age bullshit" and "spiritual mumbo jumbo," as he called it. She was a "pain in the ass," a "psy-chick," little more than a good lay back in the day. Ironically, that's what attracted him to her in the first place. He found her strangeness hot. For a man who sampled women like items on a buffet, he refused to settle for a single entree. There were just so many delicacies for him to sample as his appetite demanded. Why should he be expected to diet?

Beck was a serial cheater, sleeping with a different woman almost everywhere he ventured. Becket Rosemore considered his own power and privilege of the highest order. He organized his life accordingly. He needed sexual conquest to prop up his manhood, and he made little attempt to cover his tracks. He felt he was above the requirements of decency and respect that governed the throng of idiots he considered "the masses." Those rules didn't apply to him, or so he thought.

Camille, on the other hand, remained dutiful and faithful. "I must be paying the price for my history with Beck in past lives," she writes in her biography. In truth, the First Lady rarely came "first" in anything where her personal needs were concerned.

"It's just my lot in life," she continues. "It's all part of the pre-life plan I agreed to before coming down to this third-world existence."

She can hide behind the printed page in her writing, but she often fails to mask her pain in person. When Beck was in office, Camille did her best to keep up the appearance of a content First Lady. That was her primary job – make her husband, the president, look good no matter what. That's why Beck seduced her in the first place. She was perfect for the role. She weathered the humiliation and deep emotional pain caused by Beck's philandering as best she could. She desperately created for herself the role as Beck's spiritual chaperone even though he kept spiking the punch at the dance. They were both stuck.

For most of their time together, she believed in him. She loved him, too.

"I really believed in Beck," she confessed to Harry Pierson the day he was sworn in as president. "For a long time, I really loved him, too. I guess I had a lot to learn about faith and love."

All Pierson could muster as a response was a shrug and a terse response. "Too bad he didn't love you back, Red. By the way, you do know it's my inauguration, right? I'm a little busy here."

Harry Pierson was right, of course. Beck did not love Camille. He was incapable of loving people. He loved ideas, provided they concerned himself. At first, maybe, he felt something like very strong lust for Camille. In his defense, that was about as close to intimacy as he was capable of giving.

Like Camille, Beck also confided in Harry Pierson from time to time regarding his spouse. "The crazy, redheaded bitch drives me nuts," he would complain when he felt particularly put upon. "It's not like I haven't handed her everything, including the damned White House. And now I'm stuck with her. The president can't get a divorce. Even the Clintons stayed together."

Too smart to answer honestly, Harry Pierson usually responded with something flip yet noncommittal. "Maybe she doesn't like white?" or something to that effect.

What could Harry Pierson really say? Everyone knew Becket Rosemore married Camille O'Keefe out of pragmatism born of ambition. First of all, she was pregnant. There was no question the baby was his. Beck had little choice. If he left her in the lurch, how would that look? His opponent would have a field day, and his run for the White House would have ended then and there.

He needed a way out that would not blow up his reputation. He needed a way to terminate her pregnancy rather than his candidacy.

"It's a damned trap," he told himself over and over again. "The redheaded bitch is trying to trap me. She needs to be stopped."

It was the easiest way to justify to himself what he knew had to be done. A friend in the Indian consulate put him onto an abortion technique commonly used in Southeast Asia. Not another living soul knew about it. Camille never found out that her husband was slipping Black Cohash into her food until the deed was done. It worked like a charm. She lost the baby in a clumpy mass according to Beck's plan. Beck was off the hook.

Ever the opportunist, Beck's plans were far too grand to be jeopardized by some unwanted fetus. When Camille miscarried, Beck's people were ready to turn the thing into a media event, portraying Beck and Camille as two passionate lovers vowing to overcome the "staggering blow fate had dealt them." This, they advertised, reflected the sort of man the country needed to restore America's greatness. Camille opted to go with the flow. She had yet to experience her awakening and subsequent rebirth. She had yet to step onto the global stage, yet to enlist Harry Pierson's help in saving over 5,000 female refugees from certain demise at the hands of *Boko Haram*. Where her husband aborted her pregnancy without her knowledge, Camille O'Keefe saved thousands of women from slaughter and thousands of girls from being sold into sex slavery. One of them was the sort of person the country needed at the helm. The problem was, the wrong person was running for office.

A clairvoyant, Camille O'Keefe should have had intuitive insight into the loss of her baby. She didn't. On this matter, her vision was blocked, stunted. Her intuitive myopia stemmed from losing herself as well as her baby. She had yet to learn that. Even after the miscarriage, she propped Beck up, bolstering his massive ego and continuing to turn a blind eye to his infidelities no matter how much he reeked of other women every time he returned from a trip. The burden of obligation pricked her head like a crown of thorns. She subordinated herself to his needs to the point of despair, to the point where the beautiful, sagacious woman she once was vanished into thin air. In her place appeared a pod from which emerged an automaton to be used by Beck and his people to advance his cause.

Camille had her faults like anyone, but she charmed America from the beginning. She was strikingly beautiful, blazing red hair and eyes that held within their phosphorescent emerald depths the secrets of the cosmos. People loved her mysteriousness, too. There was a tantalizing rumor of a huge tattoo on her torso... a Japanese red dragon koi representing transition and spiritual growth. Few people other than Beck and the tattoo artist in Japan had ever seen it. She had a powerful charisma bordering on cult personality. And yet, she possessed the humility and innocence of an *ingénue*. Indeed, this was the second reason Beck married her... to win the female vote. And it worked. From that moment on, her life would never be the same.

Eventually, Camille suspected that Beck was just using her as a sort of muse or maybe a resource for softer ideas than his own. She confronted him on this a few times.

"You're using me, Beck," she told him a few months after they moved into the White House. "I feel like you drag me around like some sort of prop or something like that... you know, as eye candy and also to take my ideas so women will respect you. Sure, women like you for your money and power. But do they respect you? Well, now you use me like a membership card to make people think you're caring and sensitive."

It was the one and only time she mentioned it to him, in part because of his response.

"It took you this long to figure that out, Camille? When did I ever tell you otherwise? In case you haven't noticed, I made you the First Lady. You're married to the most powerful man in the world. That would be me, by the way, you're welcome."

That was his only comment on the issue. He knew she was right. With Camille in his corner, Beck was an unstoppable force. She stood behind his unprecedented achievements in China and the Middle East forged when he was an up-and-coming rookie senator from North Carolina. All the while, he paid lip service to Camille's refreshing belief in goodness and light.

Camille did not fare as well. As First Lady, she was completely out of her realm, preferring to conjoin with crystalline spirits of light rather than shadowy, self-serving politicians looking to promote their personal agendas of power and greed. She found most foreign dignitaries inconsequential. She considered the world of male ego and power impotent in the face of divine universal law, and openly criticized as insane the idea that war could actually bring peace. As a wife, she was left behind like an old suitcase as often as possible in favor of something newer and chicer. She tried desperately to bury the recurring realization that stabbed at her soul… there was a cavalcade of women across the globe smelling like her husband's cologne.

It was pretty straightforward. Gone were Camille O'Keefe the woman, and the things she once held sacred. Like so many women she once counseled as a medium, Camille found her life totally defined by her man's needs, wants, and desires. What Becket Rosemore needed was power. What he wanted was the presidency. What he desired was the sexual conquest of women. At the same time, she simply couldn't ignore the massive weight of her karma as it kept pulling her toward Beck, or so she thought.

All the while, Camille knew it amounted to just one basic drive. She termed it, "Beck's need to feed his bestial ego in order to hide his small, limp self-esteem." She wrote that in her diary. She kept the diary hidden and animosity buried deep. She covered it up like a shameful scar.

Then, one day, she'd had enough. Alone as usual – although in this case, alone meant home at the White House – she rang up one of the few friends she was permitted to have.

"I can't do this anymore," she said. "I can't live with myself now that I am beginning to see how much denial has clouded my vision."

"I'm not sure I'm getting you," replied her friend. "The last time I checked, you were the First Lady of the United States, you call the White House home, you're surrounded by servants, and you are in the papers every day. The world loves you, Camille. So what if your husband doesn't?"

Camille felt like crying and would have if she had the energy. "I just thought… is it too much to ask to be happy with my life partner?"

Her friend had no stomach for it. "Yeah, welcome to the real world, honey. Considering everything else you have, I'd say you're doing pretty damned well. Anytime you want to trade, let me know. I can wear a red wig."

Sensing her friend was commenting more from her own personal frustration, Camille tried to change the subject. Her friend, however, was intent to have the last word.

"I mean really, Camille. What more do you want? Let me guess. You want everything to feel good all the time. Well, honey, good luck with that. Be prepared for a lot of disappointment if you're going to use your feelings to measure happiness. I mean really, men have the emotional intelligence of a boulder. So, why are you surprised?"

"That's not entirely true," replied Camille. "Not every man is a dumb walking penis."

After a few seconds of uncomfortable silence, her friend said, "Wait a minute, Camille. You're not thinking about doing something stupid, are you?"

Camille did not answer. She was, in fact, planning to do something, something huge. Her spirit revolted with the force of the millennia to which she was inextricably connected. She finally realized that the hideous lack was not hers. The depravity was not hers. The defect was not hers. More importantly, her husband's life was not hers. The awakening occurred the moment she reconnected with the universe and discovered that her destiny did not run through a man but rather passed through her by necessity. The path to her own fulfilment had to run through her. She must become her own conduit for transcendence.

The automation short-circuited right there. Camille O'Keefe was born anew. Somehow, she managed to ride it out all the way to the White House. Then, with her new-found power as First Lady, she wrote her tell-all biography, *This Soul's Journey through the Eye of the Storm*. She made her stand. In the White House Rose Garden, of all places, she announced that she was leaving the president, revealed her forthcoming book, and pondered at length why we tolerate such deplorable behavior from men in whom we invest so much power and authority. She also humiliated Beck when she claimed to be throwing him out of the White House and having his things sent over to the Watergate Hotel.

"Those of you looking for the president, try the Watergate Hotel. That's where I sent his stuff. Just follow the trail of panties."

Of course, she knew it was a staged rebellion, but only where throwing Beck out was concerned. Otherwise, she was making a huge statement and backing it up with action in the form of a first-ever presidential divorce and tell-all book. Kidding aside, her message was surprisingly well-received. Camille O'Keefe became an overnight sensation, taking the world by storm. In a lightning flash, Camille became a role model, a paradigm of personal fortitude and self-determination, a voice of strength and virtue in a time of disintegration, fragmentation, and moral decay. The world viewed her as an amalgam of female power... the grace and beauty of Jackie O., the fortitude of Margaret Thatcher, the conviction of Eleanor Roosevelt. Unlike Hillary Clinton before her, even female Millennials gravitated to her.

What she had yet to achieve, however, was effecting real change for the masses of impoverished, abused, and victimized women and girls struggling and dying in the mindless, man-driven power machines of the Third World. That would come a bit later when she would find at last an angle of attack that fit both her political and spiritual demands.

Soon, it would be a woman's chance to change the world.

"All things in their time," she used to say. "All things in their time."

She was on the rise.

In stark contrast, Becket Rosemore's struggles were just beginning. He fell as precipitously as he rose. Both trajectories were self-directed. His meteoric rise to power began with an historical shift of power in the Middle East. He brokered a deal with the Chinese that allowed America to withdraw from the Middle East while the Chinese filled the void. In exchange, the manufacturing megalith would police the region while also providing a significant socioeconomic infrastructure that reclaimed the disenfranchised and destitute. Along the way, Beck also conquered a group known as Allah's Fortune, a new sort of organization attempting to wage "war" through economic terrorism and global destabilization.

Camille had always recognized Beck's great potential to move the world forward. It was the basis of their destiny intertwined. But Beck never carried through with the great changes he promised her and the American people as a whole. Sure, he reshaped a large chunk of the globe and looked to garner a new peace dividend.

In the end, though, what really changed? That's what Camille kept asking him. Other than his personal notoriety, what changed? During his campaign, he had promised to push a plan for recirculating wealth and jump-starting capitalism put forth by her friend Johnny Long, a renowned money manager. Beck vowed to make Camille a meaningful part of his presidency if she would only do her best to help him win the women's vote. She did her part. In return, Beck paid her back by refusing to ever discuss the plan again.

"Maybe select new White House china or redecorate," he suggested instead. "That's your prerogative as First Lady. Other than that, stay out of finance and politics, baby. You don't have what it takes."

Beck got tired of Camille's complaining pretty fast. It didn't take long for his dark side to emerge. Camille always knew it was there. She'd seen the beast come out many times in their past lives together. True to form, the more he achieved, the more he wanted.

One night after a high-profile dinner, Beck was clearly displeased with Camille. She was sitting at her marble-topped dressing table removing her makeup. She was still wearing a gorgeous emerald-green Chanel gown, although she had long tossed off her shoes. The dress accentuated her green eyes making them seem ablaze.

Beck was standing behind her removing his cuff links. She could tell from the cold, flat tone of his voice that he was angry. His loathing for her was so strong, it had a physical presence in the room that she could feel.

"Did you really have to discuss those crazy ideas of yours with the Prime Minister of Australia? Pre-Life plans and all that other crap… crystalline bodies? Really? And what did I tell you about discussing that stupid financial plan you and that guy Johnny Long cooked up? Keep your nose out of my business, Camille. Know your place. You don't belong. Sometimes I wonder why I ever–"

She noticed he cut himself short. That was quite uncharacteristic of him. "Why you married me in the first place?" she said, finishing his thought.

Beck smirked. His cuff links were off, but he remained standing over her from behind. "I didn't say that, Camille."

She smiled. "But you thought it."

Beck closed his eyes and shook his head. The woman could give him a headache like a nail to the temple. "That's right, I forgot. You can read minds, too. That's part of your psychic shtick."

She applied lotion to her fair hands and arms. "For the hundredth time, I am not a psychic. I am a medium, clairvoyant, and past-life regressionist," she said. "But even a blind man can see that you despise me. I can actually feel your disgust."

Beck stood motionless. For a moment, he felt liberated. He was about to speak his mind but thought better of it. "I didn't say that either. Don't be ridiculous."

She pointed to the back of her shoulders. "Unzip me, please. You're pretty good at that."

She bit her lip the moment the words came out. All this time, she'd been playing dumb about his affairs. Now, she slipped... badly. She had no doubt that if Beck so much as suspected she was writing a book, he would do whatever he needed to keep her from revealing to the world the kind of man he really was. Although they never discussed his military past in Army Special Forces, she knew intuitively Beck had killed more people than he could count on both hands. And now, he was the most powerful man in the world. Her book could take that all away from him. Put it all together, and she had good reason to fear for her safety if not her life.

She looked up at him in the mirror. They locked eyes. She was startled to see the way he was already staring at her. She laughed. "Gosh, that didn't come out right. I was trying to make a joke about the most powerful man in the world having to do tedious things–"

He cut her off. "I know," he said. Again, that cold, flat voice chilled Camille.

Beck let that crack slide as best he could, but not entirely. He unzipped her dress with one hand but was curious to find his other hand remaining on her neck. He felt her shoulder tense and knew she felt it, too.

With his free right hand, he stroked her thick, red hair like he used to when they first met. She found it soothing... until she felt Beck's left hand slide up from her shoulder to her neck. She could almost visualize the sinews of his fingers in his powerful grip as it tightened around her esophagus and jugular. She choked a little but remained perfectly still.

Their eyes were still locked in the mirror. "Remember how you used to like this when we first met?" he said. "You used to ask me to do this to you... from behind, only you were on all fours. Remember the good old days?"

She can't speak but blinks demurely to let him know she remembers.

The president leaned in close now. "I want to keep things good, Camille. Do you understand what I'm saying?"

She blinks again. She understands perfectly.

"Great, because I'm not about to let anybody, especially you, bring down everything that I've worked so hard to build. Remember that."

He released his grip, leaned down, and kissed the top of her head. "I'll have someone come up to take your gown to be dry-cleaned."

Camille knew one thing very well – everything for Becket Rosemore became about conquest. His ego ballooned to the dismay of the few people who actually cared about him. He had to feed the monster sexually and in every other way. That night she realized there was no going back. She had to leave him. She had to publish her book. She had to let the women of the world see her stand tall and not stand behind her man like some smiling, programmed machine as previous First Ladies had done.

Once Camille made her stand in the Rose Garden, Americans finally took notice of the deceitful, adulterous man whom they so willingly ushered into the Oval Office. When *This Soul's Journey through the Eye of the Storm* hit bookstores, American women stood up to protest the president. Becket Rosemore was not who they wanted to be the most powerful man in the world.

Instead, American women united to lift Camille to new heights. The phenomenon spread. She'd won the global stage. And the higher she rose, the lower Beck sank. For the first time in their entangled history of past lives, it was Camille who ascended while Beck paid the price. No more would Camille's power, energy, and spirit be used as stepping stones for Beck or any other man with his Johnson in one hand and a weapon of war in the other.

Not even three years into his first term, and Becket Rosemore was a lame duck, a one-termer in an ignominious club with Hoover, Ford, Carter, and the older Bush. His party abandoned him as quickly as they once embraced him as a favorite son. Beck was crushed even more than he was bitter. He knew how life was in the Beltway.

He didn't begrudge politicians for their expediency. Instead, he grew consumed with hatred. He loathed "that redheaded bitch." The venom welled up inside him, seeping into every cell. In no time at all, Beck realized he had changed, had become a different man. Even his Vice President, Harry Pierson, turned on him. Beck cast himself as a modern-day Julius Caesar, playing his role for the world, scripted to fall victim to a conspiring group of politicians ignorant about his true power and prestige.

As the knives were plunged into him from all directions, Beck knew his political career was over. He could do nothing to prevent it, nor anything to retaliate now that his power was defunct. With Beck practically castrated, the country was effectively being run by the congress and Vice President Harry Pierson, who was calling the shots for his party from behind the scenes. Everybody knew it. The American people couldn't care less, not after Camille's book. The people adored Beck back when he made America great again. And now they deplored him for tarnishing the very same brand. Their adoration was fickle. In that way, they were much like the man they despised.

He could barely contain his resentment for Camille. It was inevitable, really. Before he knew it, Beck found himself stripped of his empire, locked away in the dungeon of his own sullied, depraved mind. A man like Beck, a man who defined himself by power and ego, couldn't survive as an emperor without clothes. Naked and afraid would never suffice. Everything he had worked for his entire life evaporated. In a way, Becket Rosemore was a tragic hero of sorts, falling victim to his own desires, cut down by his own hubris. At the same time, he was a comic figure like Quixote, embarking on embellished journeys into his own grandiosity, all the while tilting at windmills. He grasped for salvation by casting blame on everyone else but himself. And for this, the media pilloried him while the American people turned their backs.

Nobody wanted to be seen with him. Reviled more than desired by women now, Beck's stable was empty. He could no longer conjure up a free lay with the snap of a finger. His copious fantasies shifted accordingly. His exotic fetishes morphed into elaborate scenarios in which Camille suffered the most heinous torture. Even Beck's neuroses had neuroses. A shrink could have spent five years unpacking the layers upon layers of repressed shame and narcissistic rage. This was his way. Whenever his shame was plucked, rage bubbled up, oozing a protective coating over his fragile ego. Toward the end, deflection and anger were his primary mode of being.

Always, he was the torturer exacting his revenge methodically, painfully, punctuated with grandiose one-liners and *double entendre.* His favorite revenge fantasy would have repulsed even the few women who still desired him when they weren't busy trying to marry cons on Death Row. By the end, he was playing it out in his head at least a dozen times a day. If Fellini had an evil twin, it could have been Becket Rosemore. The action unfolded in an odd, story-land amalgam of Druid mysticism and a splash of Dark Ages topped with carnivalesque. Camille was always scantily clad, usually dressed in something wispy and white like an ancient, sacrificial robe. He was always on horseback, armed but never armoured save for his massive pecks and gorilla arms. He usually wore something resembling a kilt. Bare-chested and in command, he barked out orders, and always seemed to be pointing some phallic weapon at somebody. Sometimes, he was pointing his actual phallus.

In most versions of his dark revenge fantasy, Beck had Camille restrained in some fashion, stripped naked, and brutally raped. Naturally, he imagined her liking it at times. He was, if nothing else, a typical man. The roster of rapists and perps read like a patient list from a sinister asylum in which Beck was judge, warden, and executioner… filthy homeless, deranged serial killers, lepers, gangs of depraved, homicidal dwarves, shit-eating lunatics, howling amputees, gigantic, puerile imbeciles, lascivious watchmen. Beck imagined them all in their full grotesqueness in order to destroy everything that Camille held sacred.

With Pierson calling the shots behind the scenes, Beck was largely useless now. He retreated with his sinister fantasies to Rockwell House, his private escape in Cooperstown, New York. Overlooking

Candalargo Lake, he would ride out the remainder of his days, alone save for his security detail. Less than a head of state, he was basically a figurehead, and not much of one at that. It was there at Rockwell House that Beck finally accepted his fate. For the first time in his life, he had lost. He'd lost to Camille, a woman whom he considered a "spaced-out moron," a "whacko," a "dingbat."

How he could have fallen to a woman, let alone a woman like Camille, was beyond his comprehension. He simply couldn't grasp how he'd lost it all. He knew it was all her fault, even his cheating. It was all her fault. She was out to subvert him from the start. Why else would she write that book?

She told him it was karmic payback for what she called his "many lifetimes of mistreatment" of her throughout their past lives together. As far as Beck was concerned, the American people were just as stupid as Camille if they bought into that New Age bullshit. Screw them all. Let them all rot in a shitty new world run by liberal nut jobs like Camille O'Keefe.

To make matters worse, Camille somehow managed to team up with Harry Pierson and pull off some sort of wild rescue mission that saved 5,000 female refugees from being killed or enslaved by *Boko Haram*. Beck couldn't believe what he was seeing unfold on the world stage. Camille was trying to be *him*. What balls they had. Harry Pierson and that redheaded bitch were actually usurping his presidency.

Thinking about it only incensed him more. How could people be taken in by such a transparent maneuver? Harry Pierson couldn't give a crap about a bunch of poor, diseased African women. That was bullshit spun out for the media. Beck knew what Pierson was really up to. He knew Pierson was taking out *Boko Haram* to overshadow what Beck had done in the Middle East when he wiped out Allah's Fortune. As for Camille, Beck knew her game, too. She could barely manage a Greenpeace fund-raiser, let alone a global crisis involving military intervention.

Nevertheless, Harry Pierson and Camille O'Keefe sat atop the world after saving those women on Koulfoua Island in Chad. In a lightening flash, Camille O'Keefe was front and center for the world to applaud. And cherish her they did. A former First Lady who was horrendously mistreated by her husband, the president, Camille O'Keefe now symbolized the birth of a new period of female empowerment. Women across the globe celebrated her newfound prowess even if Harry Pierson orchestrated the entire thing.

Her mortifying book, her courageous rescue operation, and her high-profile, iconic status... it only took a few months for shame to overcome Beck like a shadow moves across a room. He wanted to spew it all out onto the pages of his final note. He wanted to rebuke the media for being mindless puppets. He wanted to mock and ridicule the American people for being fat, closed-minded, and naïve. Most of all, he wanted to hurt Camille as deeply as possible, scar her emotionally down to her soul for betraying him. He must have run the words through his head a million times during his last days.

But when it came time to put pen to paper and script his glorious farewell, he couldn't find the words. All he could touch was his own narcissism, which he summed up in a four-word suicide note to the world: "Screw all of you."

It all ended instantly for Becket Rosemore. A bullet to the head terminated his pained existence far faster than the Black Cohash terminated Camille's baby. Ironically, his final act brought even more shame and embarrassment to the country. Despite all he'd achieved in the Middle East and with China, Becket Rosemore would always be remembered as the only U.S. president to commit suicide.

Shortly thereafter, Camille sold the movie rights to *This Soul's Journey through the Eye of the Storm,* starring Julianne Moore as Camille and Charlie "winning" Sheen as Beck. Beck's legacy would thereafter be managed by Hollywood more than the annals of history. Camille knew it would torture him even in the afterlife. She could live with that.

Chapter 10

The whole vice president thing came out of nowhere. Sometime after Beck killed himself, Harry Pierson called Camille to the White House. When she arrived, he was waiting for her in the Oval Office. She wasn't used to calling him president. Ever the gentleman for appearances sake, he rose when she was escorted in. He flashed his usual toothy grin. He was tall and round, but his gray hair betrayed his age. He considered dyeing it when he assumed the presidency but opted against it. There were far too many pictures in the papers of him with salt-and-pepper hair for people not to notice. If there was one thing Harry Pierson couldn't tolerate, it was the thought of people snickering at him behind his back. Better he look a bit older than be made fun of.

"My day has suddenly brightened," he exclaimed while stepping out from behind his desk. He dismissed his security and stood next to Camille.

"Really?" replied Camille mockingly. "Some things change, Harry. But they don't usually change that much, know what I mean?" Her long, crinkly yellow skirt billowed a bit as she strode in. Her white pull-over blouse, embroidered with fine, red trim, was accentuated by a large jade pendent that matched her green-ruffle wedge sandals.

"Seriously," said Pierson. "I have something very important to discuss with you."

Camille froze with suspicion. "What's that now? Should I be afraid?"

Pierson snorted. "Not at all," he said. "Not at all. Quite the contrary in fact."

He took her by the arm and turned her toward the large, hand-carved desk that had become iconographic. They both stood facing the three large window panes. Sunlight flowed in, providing a prescient glow to the moment.

"Just look at that," he said.

Camille smiled. "A desk?" She was toying with him.

"Not just any desk, Red. *The* desk. Billions of people around the world recognize that desk. More importantly, they associate the man sitting behind that desk with absolute power."

Camille glanced at him askew. "Always a man, huh?"

The president laughs. She took the bait. He clucked his tongue. "Funny you mention that. See, this is what I'm thinking. If you play your cards right, that seat could be yours after my second term."

This made Camille laugh out loud. "Oh my God, like I would want that. Now I really am afraid, Harry." She knocked her fist against his shoulder. "Silly boys with your silly toys."

Pierson turned to Camille and looked her square in the eye. "I'm being totally serious. With your help, I can distance myself from Beck's diseased legacy. After my second term, it'll be your turn to run for president, Camille. You need to see the big picture. This is more than just a desk. It's a symbol."

Camille scowls. "Yes, a symbol. Well.... I can only imagine what Beck did on that desk... sorry, on *the* desk."

Pierson adjusted the knot of his red tie and stretched his crisp, white collar. He was a bit uncomfortable because, well... she was right. He knew for a fact that Beck screwed more women in the Oval

Office than Big Billy, and that was saying something. He wasn't sure if Camille knew, but he sensed she had a pretty good idea.

"Yes, he certainly tainted the honor of this great room," he agreed.

Camille looked at him, but he felt like she was looking through him. "He's not the first, Harry. And he's not the last. That's the kind of legacy I'm looking to distance *myself* from," she said.

Pierson could feel her pull away. "But look where you are now, Red," he said. "And look where he is."

"Beck may have passed in this lifetime, but I'm afraid he and I have many more lives yet to live together. We have yet to work out our karmic burdens."

She tried to change the subject. She turned toward him and took his tie in her hand. "You should try something different to accent your appearance, make you stand out from all the stuffed shirts you surround yourself with. Maybe a pastel color or something? I bet people would take to that."

Pierson pursed his thin lips. "That's not very presidential. Clarification, standing around a bunch of stuffed shirts is rather presidential. Wearing a pastel tie, not so much."

Camille flipped her mane to one side. "Neither is calling me 'Red.'" She held up her hand. "Just sayin."

Pierson feigned offense. "Oh, come on. I've called you that for years."

"And for years, I've told you how much I hate it," snapped Camille. "It's almost as bad as Red Dragon Lady. Who the hell came up with than anyway?"

"Some broad over at the *Post*," replied Pierson.

Red Dragon Lady... that was the name the press gave her a while back. It stuck. The world knew her as Camille O'Keefe, the Red Dragon Lady. Given her unique blend of spiritual enlightenment and flat-out tenacity as a human-rights advocate, it seemed fitting enough. Camille appreciated the sentiment, but she hated the name. She was tall and thin, but neither frail nor glamorous. She had a natural beauty accentuated by her soft voice. She preferred loose, flowing dresses and bare feet to Chanel gowns and Prada shoes, although she'd grown uncomfortably attached to her *haute couture* world while First Lady. She found herself clinging to material things for lack of genuine love and affection in her life.

She worked diligently since then to unwind the bloated role material things played in her life while married to Beck. It wasn't going to be easy. Even she had to admit how stunning her 5'10" milky body looked in that champagne pearl-embroidered Givenchy dress she wore to Beck's inaugural dinner. Giving up all those shoes was no easy task either, especially since she was always a bit insecure about having big feet. It didn't help that Beck referred to her as Sasquatch with his staffers behind her back. Word got back to her soon enough. It really hurt because Beck meant it to be derogatory and malicious. It was just another one of the many, many ways he expressed how much she disgusted him.

Obviously, her flowing red hair made her stand out in a crowd. She often wore scarves or large-brimmed hats to obscure it. The more popular she became, the more low-key she tried to be. If anything, she saw herself as a butterfly, or something like that – beautiful, delicate, impossible to hold without killing it. The idea that she was a bright red dragon ran completely contrary to her self-image of ashy and demure. Nor did she relate well to aggression, symbolically or otherwise, and she certainly didn't consider herself a warrior type. That was Pierson's role.

Camille had yet to come into her power as a warrior. But the media seemed to have a penchant for portraying her as a fighter to the point of putting blood on her hands. Apparently, the world wanted a Red Dragon Lady who could soothe and slay one in the same. Violent and sexual… it was as if people wanted to fetishize her as a kind of earth goddess warrior princess. She learned pretty quickly that once the media takes hold of you, it's pretty damned hard to shake them off. Like attacking dogs, they only let go when they're good and ready.

She found it all rather perverse. The closest she came to a dragon was the tattoo of a Japanese dragon koi emblazed on her torso. The bright yellows, reds, and oranges appeared to glow with a sort of radiance and multidimensionality that was rare to achieve in tattoo art. The symbolism was equally important. Thought to possess the power to transform itself into a powerful dragon, the dragon koi had a special meaning in Japanese mythology. It symbolized overcoming challenges and power through a spiritual awakening. She got the tattoo on a trip to Japan with Beck before he became president. It meant a great deal to her, so much so that she made it a permanent part of herself despite the disgust it caused Beck. In a way, she knew even then that the tattoo would remain with her long after the man had come and gone.

And so it did. Unfortunately for Camille, so did the Red Dragon Lady moniker. She just wanted to be Camille O'Keefe. Harry Pierson was insightful enough to know this about her. Like Beck before him, he recognized Camille's sway over more moderate and sensitive voters. That's what underpinned his scheme to get her on board as his vice-presidential running mate. He was smarter than Beck, though. He intended to ride Camille's popularity with everyday people for purposes of winning a second term. But he also envisioned something beyond that for her and looked to also mold her into a proper vice president. Preferably, she would remain easy to control. But he recognized the need for her to be comfortable with herself if the thing was going to work. And it had to for Pierson's sake. Now that he finally had the big seat, he'd be damned if he'd give it up again so fast.

He gestured toward the desk and windows again. "When the world sees me sitting behind that desk, they see strength, they see power. That builds trust. When they trust the person sitting behind that desk, they feel secure. That's our job... make the world feel safe."

Camille laughed. "Men are so funny. It's like you really believe you can achieve peace through war. So funny...."

Pierson grimaced, but he was used to these kinds of retorts from Camille. "Go ahead," he said.

Camille looked at him quizzically. "Huh?"

"Sit... go ahead. I mean... when we win this election – and we will win – you'll be second in command. Should anything happen to me, you'll be the one sitting in that chair. So, go ahead... have a seat. Take her for a spin."

Camille stared at the brown leather chair and thought it over. She'd never been in a situation like this before. She was sure a number of Beck's women had their naked asses in that seat, but it never occurred to her that she might one day run the world. She didn't know quite how to feel about it. It was a lot of power, probably too much if she wished to remain true to her virtues.

The medium in her sparked to life. She could feel the intense energy radiating from that chair, literally the seat of world power. How easy it is to turn that power into domination. This was not the path she wished to travel. And yet, she allowed the moment to speak to her, commentary from the Masters who possessed the sagacity of the ages. They told her that power did not necessarily equate to domination, that power, in her hands, could move the world forward. But she had to take the initiative.

"Okay," she said. "I hear you."

Pierson nodded. "Good."

Camille flipped her hair again. "I wasn't talking to you, Harry." She laughed whimsically.

She walked over and touched the desk. She could literally feel the history as it flowed through her. "Boy, no wonder they call this the 'Resolute Desk.' That's the name, right?"

"Yeah," explained Pierson. "I'm impressed. It was crafted from the timbers of the *HMS Resolute* in 1875 or something like that, I think. My P.R. people know the story. Anyway, the name says it all, doesn't it? It sends a message. It says the person sitting at this desk is ambitious, never satisfied, always searching to make the world a better place."

Camille slid her hands laterally across the desk, allowing it to speak to her. "Is that really what people think when the U.S. president says something, Harry? Who was the first president to use it?"

"That's a good question. If my math is right, it was none other than Ulysses S. Grant. That man needed a desk like this... hefty, staunch...."

"Resolute," they both said at the same time and laughed.

Camille stopped, closed her eyes, and waited for it to come to her. "No... it was Hayes. And Truman added the carved eagle in front. Now *that's* fitting."

"Pretty nifty trick. Was that for real?"

"I don't do parlor tricks," she said, lifting her head.

Pierson was intrigued. What if she really was psychic? "Can you see if we are going to win the election?" he asked.

Camille lifted her hands from the desk and turned to him. "It doesn't work like that. I'm not some sort of fortune teller. God, Beck used to call me a fortune teller. It would make me so mad. Whatever, I'm used to people around here poking fun at me."

Pierson smirked. "I would never poke you, Red."

Camille remained defiant. "And laughing at me too."

Pierson held up his hands in conciliation. "No, no... that's not why I was laughing. It suddenly occurred to me that there were only three presidents since Hayes not to use this desk... Johnson, Nixon, and Ford. So, I'm saying we definitely keep it, know what I'm saying. Not exactly prestigious company if you know what I mean."

Camille smiled. "Now that's funny. No more Johnsons, Tricky Dicks."

"Wow," said Pierson. "I like my running mate to be quick-witted. But you got nothing over Gerry Ford?"

Camille cocked her head and arched a brow. "Really? His middle name is Rudolph. 'Nuff said." She winked at him like she often did when she was mocking a man. They always interpreted it as flirting. That made it particularly funny for her.

She could tell the president was eager to get back to business. She didn't think he was going to accept her refusal to be his running mate without putting up a fight. So, she just stood there, silent and calm.

The president looked at her anxiously. "So, sit already," implored Pierson. "Sit and talk with me for a minute." He gestured to the big leather chair behind the desk.

Camille walked around the imposing desk and looked at Pierson. He smiled like a used-car salesman trying to close the deal. "What can I do to put you into the White House today?"

"Go ahead," he said. "You earned it. Agree to be my running mate, and it could be yours easier than you think."

She touched the leather chair cautiously.

Pierson exhaled loudly. "Jesus Christ, woman. Sit down already. You look like you expect someone to pull the chair out from under you."

"Okay, so here goes nothing." She plopped down on the chair and wiggled into it. She liked it. She liked it a lot more than she thought she would. "I'm all ears," she said as she crossed her legs.

Pierson took a seat in one of the chairs adjacent to the desk. "It's been a while since I sat here," he said. "So? How does it feel? That's no ordinary chair, you know. It's actually a bullet-proof Lay-Z Boy Kennedy had made. I hear Marilyn loved it. Ironically enough, there's a red button and speaker under the desk that Johnson put in. The Secret Service used it to warn him when his wife was coming. I kid you not. You can't make this shit up." Camille made a guttural sound of contempt. "Men are disgusting."

Pierson nodded. "I guess that wasn't very shrewd of me. Sorry about that. Back to the matter at hand, can you see yourself in that seat as president after me? I only ask because I'm sitting in this crappy chair kissing your ass, trying to get you to be my running mate."

Camille wagged her finger. "You haven't convinced me yet, Harry. In fact, what's going to happen when you announce me as your running mate? Vice President Daly is going to go ballistic when she hears you're dumping her from the ticket."

There was a knock at the door. Both Camille and Pierson jumped up and switched seats without exchanging a word. Pierson cleared his throat. "Enter," he said in a gruff, authoritative voice.

They were still holding back smirks when one of Pierson's aides popped her head in. "Sorry to bother you. Mr. President."

"That's alright. I told my secretary to find you. Are they ready?"

"Yes, sir. The new ads are ready for review."

Pierson clapped his hands in delight. "Excellent. Have them ready for the two o'clock meeting. That's all."

The aide closed the door.

"What was that all about?" asked Camille.

"Well, it just so happens that I would like to announce you as my running mate next week. Honestly, I don't see how you're wavering on this? We've got to strike now. So, I had several new T.V. spots made out of the Koulfoua Island footage. Awesome stuff. The footage of you addressing those refugees after saving them from slaughter by *Boko Haram* is phenomenal. By the time the election comes, people are going to drop to their knees when you walk by."

Camille ran her hand through her hair. "That's not exactly why I'm in this," she said. "I helped those women because those disgusting terrorists were going to either slaughter them or sell them into slavery, forced brides."

Pierson interrupted her. "I know... I know. That's okay. I'm just saying. The world loves you. Whatever they want to call you... Camille O'Keefe, the Red Dragon Lady, Madam Vice President... they can't get enough. When these new ads run, you and I might as well start picking out the new china."

Camille threw her head back and laughed. "Oh my God, that's what Beck told me to stick to, picking out the china."

Pierson grunted as if clearing a bone from his throat. "Yeah, well, I guess I put my foot in my mouth again. I can sympathize with you. To be honest, I'm pretty sure my wife has hated me for years. I don't know. I still say all this First Lady stuff is good for her, gives her something to do. What the hell else would she be doing? Walking around Whole Foods? Going to Pilates class? Please... spare me."

Camille shrugged. "Harry, I–"

He cut her off. "But boy does she love your book. Let me tell you. It's all she talks about. She's all about her female sovereignty now. I really do have to thank you, we haven't had sex since she read it. She's convinced I was up to the same antics as Beck."

Camille cringed. "That is way too much information, Harry. But it is quite a contrast to the last man who sat in that chair."

There was a heavy pause.

"That said," she continued, "I appreciate your offer, but politics isn't really for me. Even if I was interested, it's going to be hard for me to come back here. There are so many bad memories."

This was the part Pierson feared. As much as Camille distrusted him, he distrusted her. He needed her but questioned whether she had the fortitude to follow through with their deal.

"I understand," he said. "But we can make a deal, right? There has to be something you want that you can only get through acquiring political power. I mean, you always have some big cause you're pursuing. Surely, there are obstacles you cannot currently circumnavigate."

Camille took a deep breath. "Yes, I know. It's true. But a lot has changed since Beck. I've done a lot of soul searching, a lot of thinking about my purpose for being here this time around."

The president leaned in toward Camille. He pressed harder now. "And where did that lead?" he asked.

"Everything happens for a reason," Camille responded. "We are always right where we are supposed to be. I have no doubt about that."

Camille's answer irked Pierson to no end. He felt like setting her straight right then and there. He felt like telling her to forget about all that New Age bullshit and take control of her life. He wanted to tell her that he's the most powerful man in the world offering her an incredible opportunity to do something that she would never be able to do for herself.

It took all the self-control he could muster to choke those words back down. "That's interesting. I don't usually look at things from that perspective. See, that's your value in all this. A good V.P. is a good partner, dutiful and loyal but also able to contribute a unique perspective to the relationship."

Camille considered his comments for a moment. "Maybe, Harry. I don't know. It all sounds good, but that's your job. You spin out pretty words. I made a pre-life plan before I came back to this dimension. I just haven't figured out what my purpose is yet. I will. There is one thing I do know for sure, though, Harry."

Pierson bit his lip and tried to make it look like a tight smile. "That's a start at least," he said. "What is it?"

Camille looked at Pierson sympathetically. "You're not going to like it, Harry. I'm not as willing to compromise my values to resolve problems anymore. I've got to stay true to my purpose, true to myself."

Pierson viewed this as Camille's personal weakness rather than her strength of conviction. "I thought you didn't know what your true purpose is?" There was genuine confusion in his voice but also a hint of calculation.

Camille nodded. "I did say that. I'll know it when I see it. In the meantime, like I said, I'm not going to compromise my values to resolve problems anymore."

The president smirked like a chess player whose opponent just stepped into checkmate but didn't yet see it. He exhaled methodically, trying to convey an emotional connection. It was a decent simulation. "And risk not solving the problem? That doesn't sound like the Camille O'Keefe I know. You've done some amazing things in the name of problem solving. If that required some compromise on your part, so what? What you gave to people far outweighs what you took away, right? Maybe look at it that way?"

Camille uncrossed her legs and then re-crossed them to the other side. She was struggling with it. Pierson could see that. That is good, he thought. Maybe he is penetrating her wall.

"I'm listening to you, Harry," said Camille. "I really am. I promise. I totally get what you're saying. I... I just... I've been through so much, you know? The whole time I was with Beck, I thought I was fulfilling my pre-life plan, you know? And look where that path led me? I am tempted by your offer, but I need to be sure. I can't go down the wrong path again, Harry. I can't. I just don't have the energy for it anymore." She sat back abruptly and blew the hair from her face.

Pierson had reached his threshold of tolerance. He threw his hands down on the desk. "Come on, Camille. The press releases are already written, for Christ's sake." He looked off to his left and shook his head in disbelief. "For Pete's sake, Camille, you're leaving me sitting here with my dick in my hand."

Camille looked at the president. "That's what the last guy who sat there used to say," she taunted.

Pierson had to laugh. She was hard to pin down, man. She was proving more wily than he anticipated. "Look, you can't bail on me now, Camille. The world needs you. I... need you." He had trouble getting out those last few words. "Don't you remember what you did in Nigeria? Saving all those refugees, all those women and girls from those terrorist scumbags?"

The president leaned in. His eyes were piercing now. He was done dicking around. This was the make-or-break moment for him. Not for a minute did he think she would balk on the opportunity to become the first elected female vice president. And yet, here she was, giving him some bullshit about pre-life planning and life without compromise. What the hell was wrong with her?

"I have to be honest," he said. "I am more than a little surprised. I mean... I'm offering you the chance to be the first elected female vice president. Sure, Jennifer Daly is my V.P., and she's a woman. But I selected her from Congress as a compromise to everyone when Beck decided to take the easy way out just like I bumped up to president. Screw that. That's not how I want to be remembered. The Twenty-fifth Amendment allows me to pick a qualified vice president. If I change my mind before the next election, so be it. Congress must vote their approval."

Camille lowered her head. "I thought it would be easier, Harry. I really did. I still have nightmares. It's horrible. I mean... it's horrible. Look, I know we saved all those refugees from a disgusting fate. But I feel like my hands are bloody, you know? It runs deep, Harry, I don't expect you to understand the source of my feelings. But I do expect you to respect that I feel them truly."

Harry Pierson didn't know what move to play next. A minute ago, he thought he had Camille checkmated. Now, it seemed that he was exposed and in danger of losing the whole damned thing.

"When I first started out in the CIA," explained the president, "I was as green as a cucumber. I mean I didn't know a spook from Mother Jones." He sat back and ran his hands through his hair. "I remember the first time... you know, my first time."

Camille caught his drift. "It's hard, right?" she said. It wasn't often that Camille O'Keefe and Harry Pierson could commiserate.

Pierson's demeanor neither confirmed nor denied his feelings. "So, I remember my first time. I pulled the trigger accidentally. He wasn't supposed to be there. We had intel that the target was in that hotel room. Turned out he let his brother crash there for the night or some shit like that. The guy never knew what happened. I had a suppressor on my H&K, cleaners made it all disappear, we reprioritized the target, and wrapped it up within 24 hours."

Camille looked horrified. "My God, Harry. How did you feel?"

Pierson smiled. "Yeah, well... that was the night I ripened. Don't get me wrong, that guy was part of the problem. His number was going to come up before long. Eh... you know... the timing was off, that's all. The point I'm trying to make is that things happen in the field. After that day, I wasn't green anymore."

"Why?" asked Camille.

Pierson looked at Camille. "Because, I learned how to stop feeling."

"What?" asked Camille, in shock.

Pierson stroked his chin. "I learned how to stop feeling. It's as simple as that. You can't control everything, Camille. Shit happens. No plan survives contact with the enemy. That's just how it is. It's the nature of the game. After that day, I was good to go."

Camille shook her head. "I don't like to play that game."

"I don't blame you," replied the president, thinking about what Camille had said up to that point. "But you were called to action by your fate. You can't control that, Camille. You said so yourself. Your advantage, Red, is that you *can* feel. It's like a curveball. I don't know how else to explain it really. People connect with you. You make them feel safe. That's a tremendous weapon."

"I am so sorry you see it as a weapon and not a bridge," replied Camille. "I really am. After witnessing all that killing... how many was it... fifty, sixty, seventy people?"

Pierson sat back and tried to reel her in. "Whoa... whoa... we killed about fifty *Boko Haram* terrorists, rapists, and pimp scum. That's true. I don't feel bad about that, and neither should you. My conscience is as clear as a mountain spring. They deserved to die. I understand you lost a good friend in Kofi Achebe. That's never easy. Believe me, I've lost close friends, too. It goes with the territory. But you can't lose sight of the most important thing, Red. You are the reason... you, Camille O'Keefe, are the reason why 5,000 women are alive today. It's that simple. If that's the result of a compromise, so be it. So, let's go, already. It's time to step up and accept the fate that has been waiting for you like low-hanging fruit."

Camille starred out the bullet-proof French windows behind Pierson. The Rose Garden looked resplendent. "That's exactly why I don't want to be a part of that landscape, so to speak."

Pierson noticed her looking out at the Rose Garden behind him. "Do you remember the last time you were in the Rose Garden, Camille?"

Camille smiled. She'd been waiting for him to push that button. She knew exactly what he was getting at. "You know I do, Harry. So, what's your point?"

"The last time you were in the Rose Garden, you called an urgent press conference. Not even Beck knew about it."

Still staring out the window, she shrugged and smiled. She was replaying it in her mind's eye. "Yeah, he must have been a tad bit upset."

Pierson laughed to himself. "Upset? I was the one who called him and told him to flip on the television. He shit a brick. S.H.I.T. a brick." With each letter, he pounded his finger into *ol' Resolute* for emphasis.

She directed her gaze back to Pierson now. "You never told me that, Harry. I didn't intend for that."

Pierson pressed on. "More important, Camille, was what you *did* intend. You served notice to Beck and men like him that you weren't going to take it anymore. You, the First Lady of the freaking United States of America, actually stood in the White House Rose Garden and announced to the world that you were leaving the president. Good God, you even cracked a joke about sending his stuff to the Watergate Hotel. It was a thing of beauty. Really… I was very impressed."

She didn't answer.

"You say you don't like politics," said the president. "You say you don't like compromise and you need to wait to see the way. I say bullshit, Camille. You're just making excuses. Your path is laid out before you as clear as day. From the moment you stood up to Beck, you were an activist, a role model, an icon. And I hate to tell you this, but you became a politician, also. Then came those refugees, all those women. You knew full well what you were getting into when we made our pact. Your friend Kofi took a grenade for you. The shrapnel that killed him would have killed you. He knew that. That's why he threw himself on top of you. You can't turn back on all that now. You can't turn your back on him."

She held up her hand. The memories were flooding back in a sea of red. "Enough."

Harry Pierson got up and went over to the bar. He poured Camille a tall glass of fresh-squeezed juice and handed it to her.

"Have a seat over here. Relax for a sec."

The president sat back down behind his desk. "You say you're looking for your path? Well, I've got news for you. You're on it. You've been on it. Accept it. I want you to be my vice president. Take the mantle. Accept your fate."

"You have a vice president. Her name is Jennifer Daly, remember?"

Pierson laughed. "Jesus, Camille. We're not talking about dumping my wife for a younger woman here. This is business."

"It's worse. It's politics."

"Okay," replied Pierson with hands extended in a sort of plea. "This is the top of the pyramid here. Jennifer Daly will just have to get over it. Frankly, I don't care what she thinks. The distance between us is a chasm. It's that way for a reason."

"I guess we're going to find out about Jennifer Daly soon enough, then," said Camille.

Harry Pierson was thrilled although he did his best to play it low key, "So, I've earned your trust? You're on board?"

Camille unfolded her legs, stood up and stretched her arms over her head. "Let's not get too carried away with the trust business. The last time I checked, your name was still Harry Pierson."

Pierson stood up, too. He was delighted. "So then, we're a go. That's excellent news. And Camille... thank you."

They shook hands.

"I need a little time to let this all settle in," said Camille. "I hope you don't mind if I wrap things up."

Pierson checked his watch. He had about fifteen minutes before his meeting with the Secretary of Defense. "Not at all... not at all. We'll talk tomorrow and settle things. Thanks again."

Camille left the Oval Office. Sitting back at his desk, Harry Pierson buzzed his personal secretary.

"Yes, Mr. President?" she said dutifully.

Pierson searched for the right words. "Find me someone who actually understands what the hell Camille O'Keefe is talking about."

Chapter 11

Harry Pierson kept his word. Several days later, he announced Camille O'Keefe as his running mate. And just as he'd planned, he had the spotlight instantly. They were the "suicide president's odd lineage" as one reporter put it – his former vice president, now president, and his zany, spiritualist ex-wife on a ticket to govern the world. The media couldn't get enough. Pierson viewed them as a means to an end. He considered himself a sculptor, the Michelangelo of politics. In his mind, he saw American voters as a raw, unshaped mass of people. Using the media like a sculptor uses a fettling knife, Pierson knew how to transform people into something glorious in his own image.

As Camille predicted, there was only one problem. Her name was Jennifer Daly. Pierson's current vice president wasn't going to acquiesce quite as easily as he assumed. Camille was right. But like Pierson told her, he didn't care. His success working with Camille to save all those refugees on Koulfoua Island put him in good favor with the public. Naming Camille as his running mate would throw him over the top.

Camille tried to maintain her composure. She was inundated with interview requests. Pierson's people tried to control the process, tried to keep her on a short leash on the president's order, but it proved more difficult than expected. For one thing, she'd been a media darling for some time despite Beck and Pierson. She had her honesty, resilience, and charisma to thank for that. Even if she preferred to shy away from the spotlight, she knew how to handle herself on the world stage. She could simply be herself. That's who the world wanted. That's who the American public wanted. That's why both Beck and Pierson picked her.

Camille was accustomed to the rigors of the campaign trail and presidential politics. She was learning life lessons every day and was allowed to imagine a world in which she was vice president and maybe, just maybe, president thereafter. It was overwhelming to think about, and she tried to keep her feet firmly planted on the ground while still allowing her mind to journey freely across time and space.

Only a couple of weeks had passed since she agreed to be Pierson's running mate and the number of interviews she had to endure seemed interminable. But it was an off-the-record reunion of sorts with an old college roomie that solidified her resolve in what she was undertaking. Camille and her former roommate Lula were a few Chardonnays in before long. They were safe in Camille's apartment, away from prying ears and loose lips. Camille trusted Lula. For the first time in a long time, she felt like she could speak her mind without worrying about the repercussions. She really needed to vent her misgivings about pushing out Jennifer Daly and taking her place as Harry Pierson's vice-presidential candidate. Even so, Lula's question took her completely by surprise.

"How does it feel to be the other woman?"

Refills on the wine gave Camille time to let the question settle in. Lula's comment was so much like something Pierson would say.

"What do you mean?" asked Camille to keep the conversation from running off the rails.

Lula was equally struck by Camille's apparent naiveté. "You know… the current Vice President Daly, whatever her name is… she's a woman, and you're kind of shoving her out so you can take up with the president, no?"

Camille's first instinct was to laugh. It summed her up perfectly. "What? It's so funny you say that," she said. "Do you know you're the second person to use that analogy?"

This intrigued her friend. "Really?" said Lula. "And who might that be?"

"None other than the president himself," answered Camille. "It's just what I need, people thinking that I have no problem stabbing a prominent woman in the back to help my own career."

Lula considered her wine glass. "Maybe it's her people? Maybe it's the other party floating it out there? Maybe it really bothers you that much? Does it really bother you if people say you are one thing or another? Like this glass... half empty or half full? Who cares? As long as people get their wine, that's all that matters."

Camille looked at her for a moment, completely unsure whether her friend was being serious or sarcastic. It had been many years since she last saw Lula, but she remembered her former roommate as an easy going but principled California gal.

"It most certainly does matter," said Camille. "I'm surprised you would say that, Lula. I remember when you used to protest everything from nukes to leather."

Lula shrugged and thought nothing of it. "Look, I used to be as idealistic as the next kid when I was younger. I wised up. Now, I figure the most important thing is getting people elected and in power who can actually make change happen... you know, like... make dreams come true. Otherwise, they're just dreams, you know? What good does that do? In the end, change is the only thing that matters."

Camille thought about it. "Yeah... I think I do." She shook her head. "I assume I'm one of those people?

"Like I said," reiterated Lula. "It's a results-driven world, Camille. Women have been excluded from politics and Wall Street, like, forever. Look at the 'Me Too Movement'. Times are changing, girl. Look at the Supreme Court. The stakes are totally high. Women in America are all in. We don't really give a crap that the current vice president is a woman. That's ancient history. We want a woman at the top who will actually *do* something," she urged. "A woman who can lead us all into a new future. It's not personal. It's about finding, promoting, and supporting women who can make change actually happen. I'm sorry to tell you, my friend. The time has come for the Red Dragon Lady."

Camille choked on her wine. "Oh my god, don't ever call me that again."

Both ladies laughed. Lula held the empty wine bottle upside down. "Oops," she said. "All gone."

It wasn't the second bottle of wine they drank so much as the newfound sense of power that lifted Camille's spirits that night. For the first time in a long time, she threw off the cloak of shame and accepted that there were times when making lofty ideals a reality was more important than the ideals themselves. When she agreed to help Pierson plan a military strike against *Boko Haram* to save 5,000 women from a brutal demise, Camille was faced with the very same dilemma. What is more important, the pristine, abstract ideal or the realization of that principle in such a way that actual lives are changed for the better? In the months following the raid, Camille O'Keefe forgot how to walk that tightrope.

"Thanks for helping me see it again," Camille mentioned to Lula a few days after their impromptu reunion. "I guess I was too caught up in the media circus following the attack to recognize the very same challenge staring me right in the face again."

Lula laughed. "Um, yeah. His name is Harry Pierson. What is it with you and these warrior-type men, anyway? Do you have a fetish or something? Seriously, you work with a bunch of douche bags. I hope you know that."

Yes, thought Camille, I work with a bunch of douche bags. As she headed up to her new office Pierson cleared for her in the Eisenhower Building right there on the White House grounds, she felt optimistic. She felt things might just fall into place, and humanity would be a whole lot better for it. That was the whole point, right? This new, exciting chapter in her life was all about moving people forward. Not just the wealthy or those privileged enough to be born in a developed, industrialized country.

For Camille O'Keefe, this new chapter was about the masses of other people who did not yet have the opportunity to participate in the wonders of the modern world. It was about making dreams come true for millions of people who barely had clean water and basic sustenance. It was about making real and meaningful change instead of spouting off all the time about lofty ideals with no real plan for execution. God, she was tired of all that self-righteous bullshit rolling down into the gutter from up on Capitol Hill.

It was enough to make her turn negative, and that was not her style. As a light seeker, Camille O'Keefe fed off positive energy and returned it in kind. More than anything else, this was the metric by which she measured her success as a spiritualist and as a human being in general. This was her life's work. Paying it forward was the code she lived by.

Camille said yes to Pierson although her next great cause was not yet clear to her. She was keeping her eyes open for that special someone who could provide the spark needed to propel her into her next great adventure. Humanity was always the treasure she sought. Sometimes the price of discovery weighed heavily upon her. She struggled with that when Pierson made his offer. At the same time, she knew life was risk to reward – nothing great ventured, nothing great gained.

Although they didn't yet know it, the Phoenix and the Red Dragon Lady were heading toward each other with history hanging in the balance. So, too, were Camille O'Keefe and Jennifer Daly, although that would be something entirely different.

It was awfully nice of Pierson to set her up with an office. Even though she was his running mate, she was still an outsider of sorts. In order to assign her space, Pierson had to make Camille a "special consultant on electoral affairs." The office was in the Eisenhower Building, and bore all the signs of power and prestige... huge oak desk, deep-grained panelling, inset bookshelves, dark leather chairs, paintings of dead white guys. He was trying to steep her in traditional genealogy.

The office was way too dark and full of phalluses for her taste. For the moment, Camille was thankful for a space of her own and content with redecorating her new digs. She had to admit, there was a certain allure to it. It was seductive. At times, she was tempted to give herself over to the power of his-story. Each time she felt Pierson's shadow creeping over her, she had to reaffirm her purpose, reminding herself that she was playing out the role that karma had scripted for her long, long ago. And while she had come to learn through her tumultuous relationship with Beck that her life was about fulfilling her own potential and not her man's, she also recognized she was but a piece in the universal puzzle.

She knew the right opportunity was waiting out there for her. Whatever it was, it would be important. She would change the world for the better. Exactly how that would manifest remained to be seen. Maybe this opportunity with Pierson was the moment she was waiting for? It wasn't for her to decide. She understood intuitively that there were far greater forces at work – universal forces – in which she was but an obedient soldier of light.

People like Harry Pierson could not understand how Camille O'Keefe drew tremendous power from this realization. To people like Harry Pierson, spirituality was a weakness. At best, career politicians affirmed God for sound bites they could later cast out to catch the religious right. In actuality, they believed only in their own will to power. In contrast, Camille knew on a cellular level there was a higher power behind all things that bound all people together. This, more than anything else, drove her forward in her search for a mission.

Sitting behind her huge new desk reminded her of Beck and how the trappings of power and ego could become a barrier separating a person from the people of the world. Pierson was quite proud of himself for setting her up with such regal accommodations. He called it the "Running Mate Suite." He and Camille both got the joke. She and Harry Pierson were honeymooners, wedded now "for better and far worse," as she liked to quip. Camille O'Keefe and Harry Pierson were indeed strange bedfellows for better or worse.

Camille looked at the picture Pierson had one of his aide's place on her desk. A bit tongue-in-cheek, it was a photo of the two of them standing together in the Rose Garden waving to the cameras after Pierson announced Camille as his running mate. It was so like Harry Pierson to have someone photographing or videotaping them around the clock. And damned if he didn't have a team of publicists spinning everything into gold, a veritable army of minions for the Rumpelstiltskin of the Beltway. She had to give it to him, though. They looked pretty good together. Not in a sexual way, of course. Rather, Camille found the picture full of hope and promise.

The engraving on the frame made her chuckle every time she saw it… "*To My Work Wife*," written in a sort of goofy script font. It was his way of busting her chops. She reached out and adjusted the Bodhisattva statue she brought to adorn her desk to serve as a sort of counter-balance to all the masculine energy circulating that building. It was a personal gift from the Dalai Lama himself. They met when Beck was president. It really pissed off Beck's buddies in the Chinese government with whom he scripted the Rosemore Middle-East Accord, but she answered to a higher authority.

Her interaction with the Dalai Lama was short. Nevertheless, Camille never forgot two things he said to her. "Happiness is not a packaged product. We make our own happiness." He also told her that, "Whatever the difficulties in our life, losing hope is the real tragedy."

His words were prescient at the time. That brief meeting changed her life as she re-dedicated herself to kindness and love, the only religion that ever worked for her. The statue was a gesture, her mark upon this otherwise alien world intended to offset the patriarchal energy of the president's "*Work Wife*" jibe. Even at this early stage, Camille was certain Harry Pierson needed her now as much as she once needed him with the refugees. She figured there had to be universal order somehow in that.

She exhaled loudly and blew a big, red curl from her face in great exaggeration. The stress hit her like a brick. She was beat. Pierson's people were sticking her on just about every morning talk show they could in hopes, of her grabbing the women's vote. Plus, they were gradually working her into the late-night talk-show circuit in order to grab the hipster and Millennial voters the way Hillary Clinton paraded Al Gore around talking about climate change when she was running against The Donald.

So far, it was working. Her approval numbers were through the roof, and Pierson's once-sinking ship was lifted along with the rising tide of good will toward his new running mate. Pierson played it off like he never had a doubt. "I'm a freakin' genius," he declared to his staffers every time a new poll number rolled in. "That's why I'm the Rumpelstiltskin of the Beltway. I can turn shit into gold. You give me shit, and I give you back gold. Just like that. That's it." He always snapped his fingers after "just like that."

Unfortunately, the genius overlooked one person... his Vice President Jennifer Daly. Don't ever piss her off, and don't ever call her Jen. Unfortunately for Camille, Daly was now one pissed-off woman. It wasn't that he overlooked her so much as he simply ignored her.

"I need to shut the bitch out," was how Pierson explained it to his majority whip. Pierson couldn't care less about Big J.D., as he called her. He found her useful in some instances. For the most part, though, she annoyed the shit out of him. He didn't give a crap about her background or her aspirations.

He summed her up with a single word... sourpuss. "You've got the perfect sourpuss for funerals and other somber diplomatic bullshit," he once told her. He didn't mean anything by it. He actually meant it as a compliment as if to say, "You look like you should be doing funerals."

Big J.D. was Pierson's vice president on a technicality and nothing more. That's how he saw it, and there was no way in hell he was putting a sourpuss from Iowa on his ticket when he could have the stunning, wildly popular Red Dragon Lady instead. The irony of Pierson's own ascension by technicality when Beck killed himself escaped him. More likely, he buried it deep inside with everything else that might otherwise foster empathy and humility, two emotions Harry Pierson spent years killing off. The remains were buried all over the world.

Despite the conservatism of her Iowa constituency, Jennifer Daly was not one to be passed over without speaking her mind. She did not become Speaker of the House by allowing herself to be shoved aside. Nancy Pelosi set the standard for a woman standing her ground among a gang of resentful men. Daly roamed the Hill with the same swagger. And if the president referred to her as Big J.D., it was Big J.D. he would get.

Camille was still sitting at her desk contemplating her Bodhisattva when she heard it... the distinctive stride... the unmistakable click of heels... the gale-force sense of self that preceded her. Camille looked up with a growing sense of horror, as if a dark entity was headed straight for her door... and one was. The clicking of heels grew louder as the entity drew nearer. Then, the footsteps stopped. Camille exhaled loudly. She hadn't yet hired a secretary, and there was little they could have done anyway when confronted by the vice president.

Nothing but the door stood between Camille and Jennifer Daly. There was a brusque knock. Camille watched the doorknob turn. Time seemed to stand still. A Secret Service agent popped his head in and was immediately pushed aside by the vice president.

"She's expecting me," Daly lied. She looked straight at Camille with intense, dark eyes. "Isn't that right, Camille?"

Camille just nodded. The last thing she needed was for word to get out that Daly barged right into her office unannounced like Camille was some sort of petulant child hiding out in her room about to be scolded by her mother.

"Please have them send me up some matcha tea," she said to the agent. "Nothing for the vice president. She won't be staying long."

The agent nodded and left the two women alone. Camille hoped her announcing that Daly wouldn't be staying long would stave off the vice president. It seemed to have the opposite effect.

Jennifer Daly clicked up to Camille's desk and shot a sarcastic glance at the Bodhisattva. "I'm quite sure his people didn't put that here."

Camille smiled. "It's a personal touch. Something that says 'Camille O'Keefe' is here."

Camille's nonchalance irked Daly. It was precisely the kind of attitude that threatened her because she was so much the contrary, a sourpuss, the Big J.D. "I suppose you like having your name on the ticket, too?"

Camille shrugged. She was still genuinely ambivalent about the whole thing. "I haven't decided how I feel quite yet."

That sent Big J.D. over the top. "Never in my entire political career have I seen someone like you get to a position of such importance."

Camille sat back and smiled. "Honestly, Jennifer, I don't find it all that important. I'm not invested in all this like you are. I can walk away any time. I guess that's what makes me valuable."

Daly shook her head in disbelief. "Is that right?" she said. "I think what it makes you is dangerous. I'm not sure what your game is exactly, Camille. You surely can't be this naïve, this simple. I know you're hiding something. God only knows what you have on that old son-of-a-bitch that he would choose you over me."

She ranted on about how Camille wasn't qualified to be vice president and how she actually posed a great threat to national security should she ever become president someday. "What's more," she added, "I don't see how you can possibly do the job as well as I can. I mean…." She scoffed and threw her hands up. "I mean, you are some sort of psychic or something. This is truly unbelievable. It's a complete mockery of our political system."

Camille stretched her shoulders before speaking. "Or maybe it's exactly what our democracy needs? And I'm not a psychic. I'm a medium."

Daly couldn't believe her ears. "Really? That's your response? Do you have any idea what's required to be vice president?"

Camille decided to have a little fun herself. "Yes… I suppose it can get tricky juggling all those diplomatic dinners and travelling around the world to attend formal events of state. Of course, the funerals are a bummer, but you look like—"

Jennifer Daly turned crimson. "Don't you dare say it."

"Say what?"

Daly pointed at Camille "You know what."

Camille shrugged. "Honestly—"

"That I have a face for funerals" Daly hissed. "It's bad enough the old man calls me 'Sourpuss.'"

Camille did her best to choke back a laugh.

"Oh, what? Like you didn't know he calls me that? Christ, he even says it to my face. He says I've got a face for funerals. I'm a natural, a real sourpuss. Isn't that lovely, Camille? That's your new boss. Oh, but you'll find out soon enough, my dear."

Camille thought better of pushing Daly's buttons. She really hated confrontation, and it wouldn't help things to make an enemy of her.

Jennifer Daly was not similarly inclined. She came to vent and vent she would. "Everything about you undermines what I have achieved," she said. "I lead the way for women looking to rise to the top of a man's world. Surely, you can see that? Surely, you know you are not the sort of person to lead women into the future. I'm on top of everything. I'm in control of things. That's what the women of the world need to see."

Camille closed her eyes and tried to stay cool. "They need to see you?" she said.

Daly pointed at Camille. "Exactly, O'Keefe. You can hide behind that big desk that daddy bought you, but you must know it's going to get real sooner or later. I'm what women need. You...." she laughed to herself. "You are most certainly not. You live in some far-off world in the clouds from what I hear. You're in space. Me? I'm firmly planted in this world. I'm...." She struggled for the right word. "Hell, I'm Teutonic."

Camille couldn't resist playing the dumb redhead. "You mean like the earth's shifting plates?" She threw out her best doe-eyes.

Daly's upper lip quivered. "Jesus Christ, that's tectonic. I am *Teutonic*... as in strong, deeply rooted, bound to the nature of things."

Camille nodded. "Ah... I see. Funny, your feet don't look that big. I have a sunflower tattoo on my foot. Do you wanna see it?"

Daly stared at Camille. Thoughts were racing through her head, each one more disparaging than the last. How else was she to respond to this dingbat, ex-wife of a loser president? Opting for some psychic over her, the current vice president and former Speaker of the House, was nothing short of an insult, a direct affront, another example of Harry Pierson's misogynistic, egotistical bullshit. She wore these thoughts plainly on her face, which was now fully both sour and a puss.

"Did you screw him? Is that it? Is Pierson just like his old boss? I mean, for all we know, you and your ex-husband were two peas in a pod when it came to sleeping your way around the world. We could ask him, but oh... wait... we can't because he blew his head off. All thanks to your book, by the way. Will you double-cross Pierson like that, too, Camille? Will you double-cross the American people while you're at it? Where do your loyalties lie? That's what I want to know."

Jennifer Daly was on a roll now. She started pacing and gesticulating. Camille noticed it was the same thing Beck did every time he launched into a rant against her. And Daly's personal attacks were just as hurtful.

"What do they call you? The Red Dragon Lady because of your hair and some rumor about a giant tattoo? Are we going to park a trailer on the White House lawn, too? Maybe throw in an old Buick up on blocks? Ladies and gentlemen, it is my pleasure to introduce the first female vice president to have her entire midsection tattooed."

Daly walked over to a painting of George Washington. The deep oil paint glistened a bit in the light. "What do you think he would say? Oh, this is George Washington, by the way. I'm not sure if you know that. Anyway, I'm not so sure he would approve."

Daly gestured at the six or so other paintings hanging on the walls. Together with Washington, they represented Harry Pierson's favorite presidents. It was another tongue-in-cheek message to Camille that Daly totally missed. "Look at them... a bunch of rich, dead, white men. Do you know what I don't see? I don't see any damned women.

I could have changed that, Camille. And I'm sorry, there's no Red Dragon Lady, or whatever the hell they call you, going to become president of the United States. Not now, not ever. Sorry to break it to you, Red. That's what the president calls you, you know. Red... like you were some sort of little kid."

Saddened by Daly's behavior, Camille just sat back and studied her. She was thinking what stark opposites they made. Daly's choice of attire matched her demeanor. As was the case today, the vice president usually opted for a dark-blue pants suit and white blouse. Her brown hair was cropped into a very respectable bob. She wore a wedding band and an antique-looking Cartier watch, both of which were lost against her pale skin. All in all, Jennifer Daly's appearance made her unobtrusive and inconspicuous. There was nothing frivolous, nothing loud, and by God, certainly nothing alluring in her closet. That was precisely according to plan.

In contrast, Camille looked exactly as one would expect from D.C.'s most famous medium. Before meeting Beck, she preferred loose, flowing skirts and blouses. Always opting for vibrant colors that accentuated her hair, Camille's appearance was synchronous with her spirit. She was a child of the millennia. Her accessories almost always included an array of energy stones in different settings... necklaces, anklets, pendants, that sort of thing. She hated wearing shoes and was barefoot and "earthing" as often as possible.

If anything, her look conveyed a sort of free-spirited sexiness most men couldn't resist. Becket Rosemore was just one in a long line of admirers. Once she became First Lady, Camille found herself constantly surrounded by the finest of everything... exquisite accommodations, lavish trips around the world, regal state dinners. The greatest designers fought to drape her body in their clothing. She had closets full of *haute couture* and an army of accompanying footwear from Prada to Jimmy Choo and every other sort of fabulous shoe a woman could want.

As if suddenly in Oz, Camille didn't know who or where she was anymore. In her brief tenure as First Lady, Camille transformed into a fascinating creature, an artistic pastiche that was part ingénue and part Hollywood star with hair like a red comet. As things began to fall apart for her, Camille recognized that all those "material thingies," as she called them, had grown into a grotesque monster that almost swallowed her up whole. It was hard, but she managed to dispose herself of the trappings and artifice that divided her.

Now that she was running for V.P., she agreed to let Pierson's handlers roll her out in Burberry and maybe de la Renta for more formal occasions, but that was about it. Well... Prada stayed onboard, too. But that was as far as she was willing to go to play the Red Dragon Lady. "A girl has to have her limits," she told them tongue-in-cheek. In exchange, she was allowed to wear flip-flops while at home (so long as they were wedges with a little bling) and all the flowing blouses her heart desired so long as she wore a bra at all times. It was a fair deal.

Jennifer Daly loathed the way people bent over backward for Camille O'Keefe. Daly had to work her way up, fighting sexism the entire way. But not Camille. Oh, no, she was everybody's favorite ingénue. Daly couldn't understand why everyone kissed Camille's ass. She was stylized, accessorized, promoted, supported, endorsed, philosophized, and aggrandized. All that privilege. What did she ever do to deserve that? Daly resented it deeply. Had she been afforded all that special treatment, the world would love her, too. She was sure of it. Camille O'Keefe was nothing special. She was simply the product of a marketing machine, an amalgam of Grace Kelly and Marilyn Monroe. How disgusting.

As a congresswoman from Iowa, Jennifer Daly came from another world entirely. She was far more conservative than Camille. During Camille's stint as First Lady, Daly resented and openly criticized her for putting her personal indulgences above the dignity of her office. In fact, Daly was one of Camille's most strident critics. She didn't like Camille, nor did she respect Camille's world view. Daly felt that Camille O'Keefe, with her frivolous psychic mumbo jumbo and casual appearance, should never be given the spotlight because she set back the cause of women struggling to make it in a man's world. Daly respected only total dedication to the job, an endless work day, constant availability, and the struggle against fiefdom, hierarchy, and compliance that made it so tough for women to make their way to the chief executive job whether in the corporate or the political arenas.

"Never, ever should there be a question about personal whimsy when there is a job to be done on the scale of equality and women's rights," Daly once said on a Sunday morning news talk show. And she meant it. She was a fierce woman warrior in a world dominated by men. She bore the scars to prove it. But she didn't parade them around for everyone to see. She preferred to fight from inside the system, to explode it from the inside rather than implode it from the outside.

Jennifer Daly spent her adult life working her way up from an accountant's daughter to Vassar, Speaker of the House, and now vice president. She didn't give a shit how she landed in the White House. She earned every inch of that progress. The important point was that she was there, on the inside, one small step removed from the Oval Office and becoming the most powerful person in the world. From there, the gains she could affect for women had no end. She truly believed she could push the country to gender equality, and what was so wrong with that?

In stark contrast, Camille believed deeply in personal freedom and saw women like Jennifer Daly as problematic. Camille was an empath and could tell easily that Daly wasn't a nasty woman at her core but rather conditioned herself to behave that way in order to fight the system from the inside. It made sense to Camille. After all, if Jennifer Daly was going to work from the inside, she would first have to gain access. In order to gain access, she had to pass muster and appear to be part of the system she wanted to change.

As Harry Pierson once said in confidence to one of his Secret Service detail, "I swear that woman straps on a dick every morning before going to work." It was the kind of thing that only a man could say and only a woman could do.

The ironic thing was the way in which Daly was driving a wedge between herself and the president. It wasn't Harry Pierson. He was a politician adept at the usual maneuvering. The circumstances were entirely different, given the way both he and Daly came into power. He wanted to portray Jennifer Daly as a wholesome, blessed woman who'd ascended up the ranks by respecting the system and playing nice. Daly just couldn't flip the switch. She associated Harry Pierson with everything that was wrong with American politics. She finally hit her Peter Principle. She couldn't play the role. She was done.

Camille sensed the seething cauldron inside Jennifer Daly. It seemed to be heading toward an ugly end. Nobody doubted Daly would scorch the administration in the press once she was out of office. And yet, Camille felt this wasn't set in stone. Her intuition kept telling her that there was another narrative waiting for her and Jennifer Daly waiting to play out if only someone could script it. Daly had tremendous potential as an ally. The problem was, being in the system for so long, she may have lost sight of the way out and head right off the cliff instead.

Camille understood the theme at the heart of this other narrative. Here they were, two very powerful women, who could continue advancing themselves to historic heights if only they could work together, if only they could keep moving forward. Instead, Daly chose to attack Camille with a series of low blows that only separated the two of them. That was the sad part for Camille. Everywhere she looked in politics, there was divisiveness and hierarchy. Everything seemed ego driven and power hungry to her. She felt unique in her desire to bring people together for a change. Accordingly, she felt very alone. Her confrontation with Jennifer Daly only served to drive that home.

Standing there in Camille's new office, Jennifer Daly sensed none of this. A salty veteran of political malignancy, she was waiting for Camille to fire back. Camille's restraint disgusted her. She considered Camille a weak woman completely unfit for office.

"Don't you have anything to say for yourself?" she spat like a cat revolted by a mouse that doesn't try to escape. Where's the sport in that?

Camille smiled and carefully considered her options. "I am a bit disappointed. I hoped we could work together. The world needs more of that."

Daly was floored. She dropped into a chair in front of Camille's desk and leaned in intensely. Camille could feel the heat radiating from her. "What? Really? Are you that obtuse? What world do you live in that you could think I wouldn't be completely offended by this ridiculous scheme Harry cooked up in that sinister brain of his?"

Camille tried to explain her position without inciting too much confrontation. "I have a powerful gift. I can communicate with other dimensions. I have access to the wisdom of millennia, all human experience. What happens in my mind is so far removed from your material world, it's hard for you to even imagine it. So, I never speak just for myself. I speak for all people, everywhere across time. And I know there is another path for you. It could even intersect with mine. I'm not sure yet. I can't see it clearly. But I know it's there."

Daly wasn't having any of it. "What a load of crap. Pierson isn't going to let you spout that New Age shit in public. You know that, right?"

Most people would be offended after being dressed down like this, but not Camille O'Keefe. She found Daly's perspective amusing more than anything else. She was fascinated by the extent to which Daly had assumed a masculine energy while cutting off her feminine side almost entirely. Even her self-proclaimed feminism sounded like a bar-stool pissing match.

Daly sensed Camille's amusement. It vexed her terribly. "Why do I get the feeling that you find this whole thing funny?" she asked.

Camille laughed out loud this time. She accentuated her laugh with one of her characteristic little snorts that popped out whenever she burst out with genuine laughter. "Because I do," she said.

Daly smoothed her blue pants. "At least we're being honest."

Camille replied. "Honesty doesn't have to be hurtful. I'm not going to allow your harsh words to hurt me. That's a power I have that no one can take away from me unless I let them. And anyway, I don't agree with you at all. Think about it, Jennifer. I mean... if we're being honest, as you say. Who's more popular, me or you? When I speak, masses of women react. When you speak, nobody even knows."

The calmness in Camille's voice gave her words an eerie aloofness that penetrated Daly's armor. She'd heard that Camille wasn't prone to a war of words, and she'd always considered it a weakness. Having gone at Camille so vehemently with her personal attack, Daly was trying to push every button she could in the hope that Camille would fire back with guns blazing. So, when Camille spoke with no acerbity whatsoever in her voice, it threw Daly off her game.

For once, Madam Vice President was at a loss for words. "I... look... well... say what you will, Camille. It's a tough world out there. Things can get pretty rough." She stopped suddenly. She didn't know what else to say. She felt incredibly exposed and vulnerable and hoped Camille would not press on.

Camille was not inclined to leave off. She'd been through too much shit from the moment she met Beck to this very minute not to speak her truth. "Believe me, Jennifer, I am not the sheltered, red-headed dingbat Beck's people made me out to be. As for the media, they don't have it right, either. They're like zoo animals and Harry Pierson is the zookeeper. I'm not the Red Dragon Lady or whatever nonsense Harry's press people feed them. You're right about that. But you're wrong if you think I'm stupid, as evidenced by the fact that I am quite aware of everything going on between us right now."

Camille rubbed her temples in a futile attempt to clear the landslide rumbling through her head. She stole a glance at Jennifer Daly, who was rolling her eyes.

Camille shook her head sadly. There was genuine remorse in her words. "You're rolling your eyes at me, Jennifer. I know. The two of us arrived at the White House through such different paths. And yet, here we are, two women occupying prominent positions of power that no two women have ever enjoyed simultaneously in American politics. If only we could join forces. The potential is vast. Unfortunately, so too is the space between us."

Daly said nothing. Camille welcomed her restraint. Sensing she'd made a connection, she opted to expose her vulnerability.

At the very least, she hoped it would subside the intensifying pounding inside her head.

"I'm going to tell you something I've only revealed to a handful of people," said Camille. "Honestly, there are maybe three or four people in the world who know this about me. I don't even know why I'm telling you this. I feel compelled to tell you for some reason. I don't know why. Maybe I'm just looking to connect with someone right now."

For all her experience and political savvy, for all her dexterity navigating the treacherous terrain of the Beltway, the first woman vice president in American history found herself allowing a strange feeling to escape. For the first time in a long time, Jennifer Daly felt something strangely akin to solidarity with another highly positioned political woman.

"Curiously, Camille, I feel compelled to listen in earnest." She laughed. "I'm not quite sure how to feel about that. But there it is, so go ahead and disclose away." She couldn't help looking at her watch. "Now would be the time."

Camille let out a long, deliberate, cleansing breath. She was ready to speak.

"People look at me and think I am weak, flighty, weird and stupid... the list goes on."

Daly chuckled. "So I've heard."

"So, you've said," clarified Camille.

"Touché," replied Daly, nodding slightly. "Fair enough."

Camille breathed again. "People assume I tread on the softer side of life. I get that. What they don't know is that I've squared off with some very bad people... and won."

Jennifer Daly nodded again. "You sure stuck it to Beck even though he was president."

Camille shakes her off. "No, no... well, yes. I'm pretty sure Beck tried to have me killed by doing something to my car. Sure, that's pretty bad, and I survived. But I'm talking about things... people... it's far worse... covert."

Jennifer Daly smirks. "I'm the vice president," she said. "I'm read in on all this."

"Then you know that I've stared down the barrel of a gun on more than one occasion, had the shit beat out of me in my own kitchen by some goon hunting down Beck."

Camille could see from Daly's expression that she hadn't, in fact, heard about this. The assault in her kitchen by a hired thug occurred before Beck was elected.

Camille continued. "I survived a terrible car accident. Like I said, I'm pretty sure Beck had something to do with it. I even saw a close friend have his stomach blown apart in Nigeria when he jumped on a grenade to save my life. I actually held his intestines in my hands. And you're telling me it's a tough world? Have you ever tried to stuff your friend's intestines back into his body?"

Daly was stone-faced. "Who knew?" she said with a shrug, averting her glance. Then she thought better of it and looked Camille square in her green eyes. "Honestly, Camille, I didn't know. We all have our emotional hills to climb, dear." She regretted that last bit as soon as she uttered it, for it was not her intention to patronize Camille, at least not at that particular moment.

"I'm surprised you didn't know," said Camille. "I mean, Jesus, my story has been plastered on every newspaper, magazine, and tabloid in America. I've made, what... a dozen television appearances in the last two weeks alone?"

Both women sat quietly staring at each other for a moment. It felt like a duel, like a test of wills from a bygone era.

Camille spoke first. "To be quite honest, Jennifer, if you don't know my story, it's because you don't want to know. That's your choice because you can't read a newspaper or magazine, you can't turn on the T.V. without seeing or hearing something about me."

Camille assumed this would prick Daly. She was right.

This time, Daly did intend to sound patronizing. "When you've been around politics as long as I have, Camille, you learn how to play penis politics." She leaned in closer to Camille's desk. "Fact, I don't have one. Neither do you."

Camille glanced down at her lap, looked back at Jennifer Daly, and smiled. "Sure, we do. It's just that we have innies instead of outies." She laughed robustly and mumbled something as if speaking to some unseen friend sitting next to her. Knowing Camille O'Keefe, maybe there was.

Jennifer Daly bit her lip hard. "See," she said. "That's exactly the sort of comment that sets us back decades." She sighed and shook her head.

Camille sat back in her chair. The soft leather took her in gently. She looked... bemused. "Us?"

"Women, Camille. By 'us' I mean women in politics."

Unable to decide if the redheaded beauty was brilliantly coy or a space-brained dolt, Daly opted to be frank. "There's something about you, Camille. I can't put it into words."

"I'm ineffable," said Camille with a dramatic flip of her locks. "That's my thing." She smiled and rolled her eyes.

Jennifer Daly squinted as she wondered to herself how it was that a woman like Camille O'Keefe could manage to push her buttons like a seasoned interrogator while coming off like a complete dingbat?

"I'm wondering," continued Daly. She was aware of a vitriol rising inside her that she couldn't suppress even if she wanted to. She had no idea where it was coming from, but it was going to be very nasty. She couldn't pull it back. "Consider Beck–"

"Oh, God," blurted Camille. "Here we go."

Daly focused her bitterness. "Do you think it was a coincidence that a douche canoe like Becket Rosemore latched on to a woman like you?" she taunted.

The smirk on Camille's face dissolved immediately. "A woman like me?" repeated Camille, sharply now.

Daly bobbed her head from side to side mocking Camille. "Well... you know... someone... like... you know... someone all...." She searched desperately for just the right word. "Someone... soft like you. Not that that's a bad thing, mind you. It's just not the sort of woman a man eyeing the presidency would choose to become his First Lady. No offense, mind you. It's just... you know... look at you."

Camille laughed out loud. Her response unnerved Jennifer Daly. Camille sat back in her chair and thought for a second.

"Soft is not the same thing as weak, Jennifer. It's important to make that distinction around here, that's for sure. All these powerful men running around with their egos hanging out of their pants, and what do we have to show for it? Nothing has really changed much for all their blustering."

For a moment, Daly actually cracked a smile. It was brief and both whimsical and disparaging at one and the same time. She fashioned it after Franklin's picture on the hundred-dollar bill.

"You're telling me?" said Daly. "I've been saying for years that when Congress is in session, you can smell the Ben Gay and scotch wafting through the Capitol Building. That bunch of codgers keep mistaking Viagra for prowess, if you know what I mean? Why do you think they all love you so much?"

Camille wasn't quite sure what Daly meant by that, but it didn't sound flattering. "Look, Jennifer, I don't expect you to like me. But you should at least recognize that there are masses of people around the world looking to make something of their lives. From the terribly victimized to the terribly affluent, people all over the world know my name. You may never respect me, but you should respect those people. Unfortunately, they are the same people who like to call me the Red Dragon Lady, but I guess that comes with the territory."

With that, she laughed whimsically to herself.

Her perceived nonchalance both offended and fascinated Daly. How... why? The answer eluded her. She couldn't put her finger on it. She wondered if Camille's ability to move between personae was the key to her popularity with all those people she referred to. As the lame-duck V.P., Jennifer Daly sat staring across the desk at Camille, and she felt a sense of surreal disbelief creeping across her consciousness.

Again, she had to wonder... how... why? As she looked at Camille simply sitting there smiling and looking beautiful, Daly's world began to teeter where usually she was a hermetically sealed political machine. This, though, she was having trouble keeping down. After everything that went down with Becket Rosemore, the last person she thought would take her out – the very last person – was Camille O'Keefe.

Camille O'Keefe, the beautiful redhead Harry Pierson tapped to replace her as vice president. Camille O'Keefe, this populist champion of downtrodden women he chose over her. Camille O'Keefe, some spiritualist and medium who knew jack about the world of politics.

It was enough to make Jennifer Daly scream. Inside, she was. Inside, she was loud and angry, and the hermetic seal was cracking. To Jennifer Daly, Camille O'Keefe was dangerous, a subversive threatening her way of life and everything she'd worked her ass off to achieve, including becoming Speaker of the House and the first woman vice president.

With that, she decided she'd had enough. She stood up and smoothed out her pants first and then her jacket. She did this whenever she was perturbed. She started humming. She did this whenever she was really perturbed.

She smiled dryly at Camille. "The one thing they will never call you is Madam Vice President. Of that I can assure you," said Daly. "The old man must be crazy. Either that, or you're one hell of a good lay. Either way, your days in politics are numbered. You just don't know how to play the game."

Camille shrugged. "I certainly hope you're right, Jennifer. I want to be Camille O'Keefe, not some manikin with a title. As for having a short political career? Politics is not where I want to spend my energy."

Camille's response made Daly's blood nearly boil. "Why, then? Why do this?" she asked Camille through gritted teeth.

"Well, there is a world of people who are just waiting for someone to lead them forward. From there, I trust they can continue their individual journeys alone."

Daly could only chuckle at the thought. Camille was about to stand up and escort the vice president to the door but thought better of it. She'd had just about enough of Daly's bullying for one day. Better she remained seated behind her big, official desk than give Daly the slightest accommodation. She wished her security guy would hurry back with her matcha tea so she could excuse herself and get Daly the hell out of there.

"You question if I am the right type of woman to hold such an important office," said Camille almost as an afterthought. "But my question is: What is the right type? History has been dominated by a particular type of person, usually a man – power-hungry, ego-driven, violent, and greedy. Blah, blah, blah... we all know the story. But for some reason, throughout history only a few people have ever asked where has that really gotten us? We're still fighting the same old battles for thousands of years. Even though you're a woman, you fight like that as well. Just look at yourself."

Jennifer Daly made a loud, grunting noise. "You'll go nowhere in politics with an attitude like that. Christ, O'Keefe, you're worse than Jimmy Carter. Like it or not, men are in control. Why the hell would I fight the people who hold the keys to every locked door blocking my way? That's counter-intuitive, is it not?"

Daly turned more aggressive. "Good luck trying to change the system from the outside, O'Keefe. It doesn't work. Do you hear what I'm saying? Trying to change things from the outside doesn't work. As far as I'm concerned, working within the system is the only way to move up in this world. Shit, it's the only way to change the world. But you know it all. You go, girl."

Camille refused to engage anymore. She was done fighting for the day. Daly grimaced. She surveyed Camille's Burberry business suit. It made her sick. It was all a show. If only the world could see the real Camille O'Keefe, the freak with the giant tattoo. That would be the end of the Red Dragon Lady for sure. As far as Daly was concerned, that idiot Harry Pierson was casting away a good, savvy woman like herself in exchange for some fly-by-night temptress like Camille.

How like a man... how very like a man, she thought to herself.

Daly could barely look at her. "My constituency is middle-of-the-bell-curve," she said. "We know the difference between a man and a woman, and we have a solid sense of decency."

"That's not my battle, Jennifer," replied Camille, hoping her security guy would get back with her tea. "What I want the world to understand is that we are bound together by a great force. I know what people are going to say. I heard it all the time when I was in the

White House. People like you say things like, 'Camille O'Keefe is a weirdo,' or 'Camille O'Keefe talks to ghosts'.

"Nothing could be further from the truth. I don't care about gender. Gender is very Third Dimension. It doesn't really matter. In this day and age, what is gender anymore? Millions of people are changing their physical gender. So, for me, gender is not the issue. For me, *energy* is the source of everything, every one of us. There is masculine energy and feminine energy. People think that's weird. And yet, Harry Pierson chose me because the world has chosen me. And by the way, the last time I checked, they never voted for you. You have what you have because my slimy ex-husband put a bullet through his head rather than atone for his sins. How's that for a solid sense of decency?"

Daly turned and made for the door. She opened it just as Camille's man arrived with her tea. He stumbled trying to avoid running into the vice president. He spilled scalding hot tea on his hand. He said nothing except, "Excuse me, Madam Vice President. I apologize for my clumsiness."

Daly shook her head. "No wonder you got this assignment," she said to the agent. She turned back to Camille to lob one last mortar. "Remember this talk, Red. If there's one thing you'll learn about politics, it's that payback is the real bitch around here, not me. But then, you did write a book burying your ex-husband while he was still the president. No wonder he killed himself. So, I guess you already know about payback... and about being a real bitch."

In an uncharacteristic display of confrontation, Camille decided to draw some boundaries. "Jennifer, one last thing."

Daly turned back.

"I know people talk behind my back and call me names. But if you ever call me Red again, you will, indeed, learn first-hand how big of a bitch I can be. And that's about all the time I'm going to spend today with a lame duck."

Camille dismissed Jennifer Daly with a wave of her hand. "That will be all."

She began jotting down some thoughts for later entry into her journal. The Secret Service agent brought over the tea and laid it on her desk. "Here you go, ma'am."

Camille noticed the bright red mark on his hand where the hot tea spilled. She put down her pen and looked into his blue eyes. "Do you see how easy it is for people to turn on each other and hurt each other? I just fell into the same trap… woman against woman. That's the first thing that has to change."

The agent kept his distance as he was trained to do. He was an up-and-comer hoping for a spot on Camille's personal detail should she become vice president. He looked as if he was born in that blue suit and white shirt.

"Yes, ma'am. Can I get you anything else, ma'am?"

"Yes. Go to the infirmary and have them take a look at that hand."

The agent chuckled. "No worries, ma'am. I have thick skin."

Camille returned a vacant smile. "Yeah," she said. "That seems to be a requirement around here."

The agent smiled. "Let me know if you need anything, ma'am. I'll be covering you tonight."

He turned to leave Camille to her thoughts.

"Oh, wait," said Camille. "I heard your daughter will be two in December?"

The agent turned back. "Yes, ma'am."

"Well, make sure to put in for Christmas Day off this year."

"But I'm scheduled for your detail this Christmas."

Camille smiled. "I'll stay in the White House. In-house staff will cover me. Make sure you take the day off."

Camille sipped her tea and prepared to refocus on her writing. "One last thing, Paul."

The agent turned back.

"What do you guys call me? You know, my call sign. Be honest."

"Ghost Whisperer," he replied.

Camille nodded. She was clearly pleased. "Excellent. That's much better than Red Dragon Lady."

Meanwhile, as Jennifer Daly walked back to her office, the clicking of her heels reverberating down the polished marble hallway, she could only laugh to herself in dismay. Camille O'Keefe stood her ground. Who knew what the future held? She stopped short and looked at a rich, thickly brushed oil painting hanging on the wall.

Her mind raced back to her teen days when she was winning awards for her pastel landscapes. Concerned for her future, her parents pulled her from public school and sent her to the Windsor School where, they were assured, their daughter would be firmly entrenched in the classic canon. As she abruptly turned away, she finally admitted to herself that she was jealous of Camille O'Keefe.

Chapter 12

Jennifer Daly didn't understand the curious relationship between Camille and Pierson. It had been that way since before Beck took office. The bond they shared was forged as much by struggle as by triumph. That seemed to sum up Beck's legacy as a whole. Where Camille might have been offended by many of the things Pierson said to her had they come from Beck, she took it light-heartedly from the older man. Beck was a callous, hurtful, and vindictive adulterer. Harry Pierson wasn't cheating on her. More importantly, he didn't loathe her like Beck did. Becket Rosemore was a dark man with a darker past who preferred to live in the shadows, emerging only to feed his voracious ego with sexual conquests.

When Pierson lost his temper or patronized his little "Red," it wasn't mean spirited. Pierson didn't come at her from a place of hate. Like a Great Horned Owl sitting high atop the mess of bones that piled high and higher with each fresh kill, Beck took no care to hide the carnage. In contrast, Pierson's affairs were buried, clandestine, and political. He made sure there were no bones lying around when he was done. His handling of the rescue mission was a perfect example. The world saw only what he wanted them to see. None of it was aimed at hurting Camille. So, she tolerated it, maybe even appreciated it more than she was comfortable with. The only thing she knew for sure was that she wasn't crying at the end of each day like she did when she was with Beck. She wasn't thinking about dying or wishing she could simply vanish into another dimension.

Bottom line, point blank − with Beck, Camille felt harried, accosted, and humiliated. She hated herself, her sex, and her sexuality. Most of all, she felt threatened. With Harry Pierson, Camille O'Keefe felt safe for the first time in a long time. For her, this trumped everything else. She needed stability in her life, a return to normalcy to the extent it was even possible, given her celebrity. Add to that a vice presidential nomination and God knew what was to come should she and Pierson actually win.

Camille was the woman Harry Pierson wanted as his running mate. Early on, he recognized in Camille a certain genuine beauty that people couldn't resist. She even held sway over his cranky ass from time to time, something his wife hadn't managed to pull off since their crystal anniversary. The old man was banking on Camille finding her power once more despite the number Beck and his cronies did on her. If Camille could tap her spiritual wellspring and regain her emotional balance, she and Harry Pierson would walk right back into the White House.

But if Camille failed to find her former self and harness the spiritual power she once wielded, if she failed to realign with the universal forces she knew flowed through everything and everyone, Pierson's candidacy was sunk along with his career. Camille could always move on to some project or cause that interested her. Her baseline popularity seemed stable enough. In that regard, her life was moving forward. Harry Pierson did not enjoy Camille's freedom of choice, her affability, or her popularity. He was often aggressive and dour, a cantankerous hawk who clung to the past like a life preserver after he jumped from Beck's sinking ship.

Pierson was very different from Beck in another significant way − he respected Camille and expected his people to toe the line. He knew Camille could be flighty, but he demanded she be treated with every courtesy his running mate deserved. A veteran leader, Harry Pierson knew he couldn't control how people felt about Camille. But he damned sure could demand that those who didn't like her keep it to themselves. He also expected each of his staffers to treat Camille as if she were the most important woman in the world because to him, she most certainly was.

As much as he hated to admit it, Camille O'Keefe was the center of his universe. Everything revolved around her. This made Camille uncomfortable. It was a process; enjoy the ride. That's what she kept telling herself. At least things were headed in the right direction. She appreciated this, especially since she enjoyed far more status with Harry Pierson than she did with Beck when he was alive. She was, after all, Pierson's running mate. And despite the death stares Jennifer Daly shot at her every day, Camille had to integrate into the power structure as best she could.

Process or not, the next month moved at a furious pace. Camille felt like she was in a hurricane. Pierson's people had her out in front of the public at every opportunity. Meet and greets, talk shows, magazine interviews, current-events spotlights… one puff piece after another. Pierson kept a low profile himself. His plan was to fix the American gaze on the Red Dragon Lady. Better they lavish their affection on Camille than find reason to take issue with him.

Finally, Camille got a morning off. Since accepting the nomination, most of her time was spun into a whirlwind of preplanned, prescripted events. She needed a breather. She used the opportunity to have a much-needed sit down with the president. She felt too much like his puppet. She needed to create some space for herself. She reckoned that was why he tapped her in the first place. Of course, concept doesn't always translate into proactive, she realized, especially with politicians.

Pierson was waiting for her in the Oval Office. Sitting there in his tailored white shirt and clean, solid tie, he looked crisp, rested, ready to take on the world, which was, for the president of the United States, a daily occurrence. Camille looked frazzled, fatigued, and generally out of sorts. With no appointments scheduled until dinner, she donned a casual pants suit that made her look far too much like Jennifer Daly, only without the spunk.

"Jesus, Camille," said the president, as soon as Camille walked in. "You need to get to a spa and make extra time for the makeup team before your fund raiser tonight. And where'd you get that suit? If I wanted Jennifer Daly, I would have chosen her. I like you in flowy stuff when you're off camera, so to speak. Although, there's really no such thing as off camera. That's a good lesson for you to learn early. Someone with a camera is always watching."

Camille plopped down on one of the two couches in the middle of the office. "Thanks, Harry. You really know how to flatter a girl."

Pierson sat back in his big leather chair. "You're missing my point," he said. "I want as many people as possible to see you, as often as possible. Let's face it, Camille. The less attention they pay to me, the better off I am."

"I can't argue with that, Harry. I'm sure Jennifer Daly would prefer the media shine a huge spotlight on you, huh?"

Pierson paid it no mind. "Who, her? Big J.D.? Who gives a crap what she thinks? She's small potatoes compared to you, Red. Whatever it is about you, people can't get enough. You're exactly what the world wants."

Camille looked at him sceptically.

"I'm serious," said Pierson with an impish smile, really pouring it on now. "In fact, you're what the world needs, Camille."

Camille arched her brow. "I think so, too, Harry. But I don't think for a second that you do."

The president threw his hands up, feigning innocence.

Camille smiled. "Yeah, yeah," she said. "But I'll tell you this, Harry Pierson. I don't care if you are the president of the United States. I don't care how many years you were with the CIA. I don't even care that you're my boss. There's only one thing that should concern you about me."

Pierson absolutely loved this side of Camille... coy, playful, sexy, a few barbs on her tip. "And that is?"

"I'm exactly what *you* need," she said.

Pierson smiled. "Exactly, Red. Am I a genius or what?"

Pierson was squirmy like that. Camille knew it. Debating with him could be like trying to stab a walnut with a fork. He went about his business like Camille's conviction in his candidacy was a foregone conclusion. It wasn't. She may have accepted the nomination, but she wasn't yet on board emotionally. For a woman like Camille O'Keefe, this meant a great deal. Her lack of emotional connection was for her a sign that something was amiss. That was going to be a problem for Harry Pierson.

Camille still wasn't comfortable stepping back into the Oval Office. Too many bad memories hung there like fruit waiting to be picked so they could poison her again. Despite Pierson's frequent assertion that he knew nothing at all about Beck's philandering, Camille found it almost impossible to believe. Now that she'd accepted the nomination, she had to make peace with the fact that she'd be partnering up with yet another man in the White House who would lie to her face... often.

She told herself it would all balance out in the end. There were greater universal forces at work. If she maintained the right intentions, everything would fall into place. That's what she told herself, and she believed it most of the time. Now that she was back in, she had her doubts, coming to realize that perhaps she, too, lies to herself in an attempt to assuage her misgivings about the sudden change in direction her life had just taken yet again.

She felt mounting pressure to maintain leverage over Harry Pierson. She was beginning to realize how difficult that might prove. He was a handful, especially for Camille, who avoided conflict as a rule. Pierson was many things... former CIA director, master of manipulation, seasoned politico, vice president, and now president. The man had done so much and seen even more, much of it the sort that could never be discussed. The ease with which he orchestrated the rescue operation underscored his power. The globe was his chessboard, and he took great delight in playing either color.

Like Beck, Harry Pierson had lived many lives as a warrior. Camille had no illusions about his power or the possibility that he would someday shove her aside like he'd done to Jennifer Daly. And yet, she sensed vulnerability in him. She knew one thing for certain – he needed her more than she needed him. Intending never to give up that power, she vowed to remain indispensable to Pierson. The most effective way for her to do that was to stay connected to the American people first and "world humanity" thereafter.

Pierson poured himself some coffee and took a seat on the couch opposite Camille. He swirled the coffee with a spoon and listened to the metal tinkle against the fine china cup.

"I find that sound soothing," he said. "I guess you prefer fairy bells, huh?" He laughed to himself and took a sip.

Camille rolled her eyes. She knew he was just trying to get a rise out of her. "Do you know there's one hovering right over your shoulder?"

Pierson looked right and then left. "Are you sure? I don't hear any bells."

"Keep listening," she said. "You'll hear them soon enough."

The president sipped his coffee carefully so as not to spill any on his shirt. "You know, we're sitting in the same spot as we did when I asked you to be my running mate." He put his drink down and thumbed through his schedule for the remainder of the day.

Camille sighed. "We have a lot of work to do, Harry. You're like a mass of unshaped clay. You need me to help shape you into a work of art the entire world can admire."

He didn't look up from his papers immediately. He tugged on his French cuffs while he finished reading through his schedule. "Have you looked in the mirror this morning?" he shot back.

He sipped his coffee again, tossed the papers on the table, and looked up at Camille. "Troglodyte… that's what you usually call me. So, I guess a mass of unshaped clay is better. See, things are looking up already."

Camille just smiled.

"You know, I redecorated the Oval Office myself." He sat back and crossed his legs. "I don't recall you complimenting me on my fine taste."

Needing something weighty, Pierson chose a burgundy fabric with gold stripes for the couches. He opted for a light rug, regal enough, with a neoclassical pattern around the perimeter. Gold curtains framed the large, iconic window behind the *Resolute* desk. Beige walls brought it all together. He found anything resembling "eggshell" too feminine for a U.S. president. Most importantly of all, the space was purged of everything brought in.

Camille looked around to appear interested. "It's a bit too King and Court for my taste, but it suits you well." She smirked. "Your Highness."

Pierson rolled his hand in a regal gesture of approval. "Would you like to kiss my ring?"

Camille shot him one of her looks. "Um, no. But you can kiss something of mine."

Pierson just loved this gal. She had so many facets, it would be impossible for his opponents to pigeonhole her as this or that.

There was a knock at the door.

"Enter," said the president.

A kitchen butler came in and placed a cup of steaming matcha tea on the table in front of Camille. He turned and left.

Pierson looked at his watch. "Eleven… right on schedule," said Pierson.

Camille winced. "You know that I have tea every morning at eleven?"

Pierson smiled broadly. "Not just any tea. You prefer matcha green tea." He urged her on like an excited boy on Christmas morning waiting for his sibling to open their best present. "Go on… taste it. It's a very limited batch grown outside Kyoto. The Japanese Prime Minister sent it to you personally."

Camille sipped reverently. For her, drinking tea was akin to meditation. As with the Japanese of old, respect for the tea was a form of reverence. The Japanese also valued gift-giving. She made a mental note to send the Japanese Prime Minister something special. Pierson was right. The tea was extraordinary. For a split second, she even smiled. And then she gritted her teeth.

"If the Prime Minister sent it to me, why do you have it?" she wondered aloud.

Pierson smiled. "Well... let's just say I prefer to handle some of your foreign affairs... not like Beck's affairs, mind you. You know what I mean. It's better this way."

Camille put her tea cup down. "The tea is lovely. Thank you. But, how do you even know I like matcha? For that matter, how the heck do you know I have tea every day at this time?"

Pierson shrugged. "Information is my business, Camille. You of all people should know that by now. How does a man make sound decisions or, for that matter, stay in power without a constant flow of accurate information?"

"He doesn't," answered Camille.

"Exactly," said Pierson. "I see it as job security for the both of us. Not knowing is dangerous. That's something else you'll learn on the job."

"Once the CIA Director always the CIA Director, huh?" said Camille.

Pierson nodded. "What can I say? It's in my blood."

Camille looked pissed. "Harry, I thought we agreed you would stop spying on me?"

The president leaned back and stretched. "I can't help it. As you would say, Camille, it's in me on a cellular level."

Camille was not assuaged. "Seriously, Harry... it's creepy. You need to stop."

"Sorry, sorry. I totally understand."

Camille put her tea down and sat back. "You don't sound the least bit concerned. You couldn't care less about personal privacy, do you?"

"Does Google?" replied Pierson. Seeing she was still ticked off, he tried to explain. "Look, it's important that I keep an eye on you. I assure you, there's nothing malicious about it. It's for your good as well as mine. It's just how I operate, Camille. You still love me, don't you, Red?"

"No," said Camille. "I think it's gross to invade my privacy like that. God only knows if you have cameras in my house, too. I'm gonna feel totally weird taking a bath."

Pierson's silence screamed, "no comment."

Camille's jaw dropped. "Oh... my... God, Harry. You have cameras in my place?"

"Come on, don't be like this. It's silly. Drink your tea while it's hot."

She stared at him with a blank face. "Lovely," she said. "And I'll drink my tea when I am ready."

Pierson laughed and stood up. "Yes! That's the spunky Red Dragon Lady the people love. Gentle but firm, calm but strangely passionate. You're a damned paradox, and they can't get enough."

Camille looked around the room. She felt controlled. She felt the weight of history pressing on her chest. Things like that happened to her all the time. She was acutely aware of her surroundings on a multi-dimensional level that transcended everyone else around her at any given time. Maybe it was the striped fabric on the couches? The place needed some floral patterns... maybe some exotic birds flying freely? If Harry Pierson was connected to the world of shadows, Camille O'Keefe was connected to the plane of light energy. In a weird way, this connected them like yin and yang.

"Anyway," she said, trying to get it out of her mind that some NSA newbie was sitting around watching her bathe. "Am I still doing *Saturday Night Live* this weekend?"

"Of course, you are. If Bill Clinton could play the sax on Letterman, you can do the monologue on *SNL*. We've almost got it finished."

Camille pursed her lips. "Um… you wrote my monologue?"

"I didn't write it, for God's sake. One of your publicists did. That was part of the deal for letting them book you. Do you think I'm letting that socialist Lorne Michaels write it? Negative on that. He'll try to turn you into the next Tina Fey. Don't worry, you're gonna be great."

Camille breathed deeply and counted to ten... fifteen... no, twenty. "I need to read it first."

The president walked around a bit as he was apt to do when he was excited. "Nonsense. Your publicists are the best in the business. They can make Jeffrey Dahmer look like a gourmand. Things are going great for us, Camille. You're holding up your end of the bargain like a real champ. Thank you for that."

"We've got a long way to go, Harry. And you made promises I expect you to keep, as well. The universe will hold you accountable."

"Stop over-thinking things. Christ, you turn everything into an existential crisis. You sound like that depressing guy Kierkenbaum."

She corrected him. "Kierkegaard. He was a philosopher."

The president nodded. "Yeah, yeah... all that angst and God stuff. Who needs it? Not the American people, that's for sure. They want to eat cake, so give them cake. Just stick with me. You're going places you never dreamed of."

Camille sighed loudly and folded her hands in her lap.

"I hate when you do that," Pierson complained.

"Do what?" She reached for her tea. It was exquisite. There was no sense letting it go cold. She made her point.

"When you sigh like that," Pierson answered. "It takes the wind right out of my sails. There's no time for that. Like I said, we can make a great team under the right circumstances. What we need... yeah, what we need is a crisis. It needs to be something big, something terrible. Terrible always gets people's attention. Nothing cataclysmic, mind you. Something large enough to capture the world's attention, yet manageable enough to allow us to swoop in again like the dynamic duo and save the day. That will put us on the front pages for quite some time."

Camille nodded. "I know. But I still think there is something better waiting for us out there, Harry, something completely different from politics as usual."

The president hung his head and chuckled. "I certainly hope so. You're supposed to be helping me win re-election not putting me out of a job."

Camille cocked her head. "Listen, Harry. I really, really believe we are coming together to unite the world, bring people closer together, spread prosperity to more people than ever before."

The president sat down again, this time back at his desk, and began perusing papers, signalling the meeting was coming to a close. "Do you really believe that, Camille?"

Camille stood and smoothed out her outfit. She said, "Of course, I do. I wouldn't be here if I didn't. I'm not made for politics. It's too third dimension and low vibrating for me to function. My interests lie elsewhere, Harry. You know that."

Pierson mocked her playfully. "Of course, I do. I wouldn't be here if I didn't."

"Oh, Harry," said Camille, closing her eyes. "Harry, Harry, Harry... what am I going to do with you. Trust me. The universe is magical. Something wonderful will reveal itself. You wait and see. And it won't be anything negative like the terrible crisis you are waiting for so you can manipulate things."

Pierson snapped his fingers and pointed at Camille. "Then go find it for us. Be the Red Dragon Lady. Bring me something I can sink my teeth into and make a splash for our campaign, and I promise I'll consider it seriously even if it's...." He coughed sardonically. "Even if it's something... dare I say it? Something positive? Oh, God, not positive."

She walked over and put her hand on his shoulder. "Watch out what you ask for, Harry Pierson. You may actually like it."

"Yeah," said the president. "Sounds like a trip to the dentist in a world without novocaine."

Chapter 13

It didn't take long for Pierson's wish to come true. About a week later, the crisis he was looking for – something terrible but not catastrophic, something captivating but manageable – landed right in his lap during the morning briefing. It was tailor-made, a global crisis that fit him like a handmade suit.

Every morning, the president and his team of advisors assembled in the Situation Room to address the critical issues of the day to come. Located in the basement of the West Wing, the Sit Room provided the president and his advisors with a state-of-the-art facility for important meetings. Recognizable for its long, rectangular wooden boardroom table and sleek, black, high-back leather chairs, the Sit Room has been the site for countless high-level meetings when the stakes were very high. Large, inset flat screens provided instant visuals anywhere in the world from a drone fifty-thousand-feet above all the way down to a foot soldier crawling through shrub brush. State-of-the-art, real-time coms shrunk the globe to a tiny ball. More leather chairs lined the perimeter walls in case a slew of participants was required.

The Sit Room was also where the president took his morning briefing when in residence. That's when Pierson first got the news. He opened the "morning book" that lay in front of him just as he did every morning. This was the State Department morning summary, a collection of reports and summaries detailing the important diplomatic issues and world crises requiring Pierson's attention organized in tabs ranging from "Hot" down to "Further Consideration."

Today there were two reports in the "Hot" tab. The first was financial, revealing a serious economic crisis looming. The report was a well-prepared, deep-dive into the Italian banking system and concluded that Italy was insolvent. This, in itself, was not particularly earth-shattering. Economists had been predicting such an event could and probably would occur. What jumped out to Harry Pierson was the second conclusion in the report: The German central bank, the *Bundesbanc*, had been orchestrating an ongoing, systematic cover-up of the Italian insolvency in order to stabilize the Euro and the entire EU economy in the wake of Brexit. According to the report, the cover up went as high as the German Chancellor.

The second hot issue of the morning involved a company called Liquid Sky and its CEO Rickey Ormand. The issue was summarized in a one-pager rather than an in-depth report as with the Italian crisis. Apparently, Liquid Sky made claim to some sort of radical new energy source. At a recent socio-tech festival called Burning Man, Rickey Ormand claimed to have discovered gravity power. Numerous YouTube videos depicted Ormand flying some kind of remote-control aircraft capable of incredible acceleration.

Highlighted in the summary was Ormand's claim that the machine was "powered by gravity and would change the world forever." Also noted was Rickey Ormand's propensity for boasting and theatrical self-promotion. The matter was deemed indeterminate and marked for further consideration. Subsequent surveillance – "spying" to Camille, "verifying" to Pierson – by both the NSA and FBI, including communications surveillance via wiretaps and email scans as well as cell phone and database hacks revealed a program called Liquid-Drive, did, in fact, exist. The purpose of the program was the development of a gravity-powered engine.

During the investigation, NSA discovered the existence of a computer in Ormand's office that was a stand-alone and completely off line. Deemed suspicious, this computer was classified a high-priority informational target. Further "probing" was deemed necessary. By hacking into a smart, Bluetooth refrigerator in the CEO's massive, man cave of an office, NSA personnel were then able to hack into Ormand's Alexa and convert the wireless accessory into a bugging device in much the same way as they did with Ormand's cell phone.

The final comment in the summary was italicized, highlighted in yellow, and important enough to warrant inclusion in the hot tab. "NSA surveillance has determined that Rickey Ormand is developing a top-secret, military platform called Liquid-Drive utilizing gravitational energy in various forms and applications including but not limited to armored transports, tanks, strike aircraft, surface-to-air missiles, and assorted small firearms. At this point, it appears that Mr. Ormand is developing the Liquid-Drive program off the grid and without the knowledge of the Liquid Sky board of directors or the required approval and license of the Department of Defense."

Even so, Pierson preferred to run with the Italian banking crisis. "This Italian thing's got legs," he noted. "If we stroke it right, it'll run a marathon for us. Not to mention, the Italians think the way they do things makes them loftier than everyone else. A good, capitalist bitch slap will do them some good." He grinned at the thought.

Nate Barnes, Pierson's chief security advisor, tried to direct the president's attention back to Liquid Sky despite the relative brevity of the report.

"Mr. President," said Barnes. "The details about Liquid Sky developing some kind of gravity engine have significant economic implications. Moreover, the idea that their CEO, Rickey Ormand, may be engineering a rogue military program is deeply concerning. Taken together, Liquid Sky poses an immediate threat to national security."

Pierson was quickly thumbing through the Italian report. "I'm looking for a springboard, something that's melting down globally that we can swoop in and fix, so we look like heroes. If this German cover up hits the press, the Italians will be screwed. The Germans, too. If we flex some muscle with the Germans, let them know that we know and sincerely hope it doesn't leak to the press, what choice do they have but to bend over? Italy's an easy fix. They don't know how to manage a piggy bank, let alone a national economy. We'll fix it and look great in the EU for a change."

He looked up at his chief security advisor, nodded, and returned to the report.

Nate Barnes understood where the president was going, but he also felt something disturbing was going on at Liquid Sky.

"At the very least, we should expand the investigation, maybe get an asset inside Liquid Sky," he suggested. "See what's really going on."

The president finished reviewing the report. His eyes lit up as he scanned the final paragraphs. "People, I don't have to read past the summary of conclusions on page one to see that this Italian thing is the opportunity we've been waiting for."

As he went on to explain, it was exactly what he was hoping for... a crisis they could leverage. He tried very little to mask his enthusiasm. "It is always a great day when we catch someone with their hand in the cookie jar. It's even better when they try to lie about it even while they're standing there with their hand in the damned jar. At times like this, they have little choice but to hand over their cookies and also take the blame for eating them even though we took them for ourselves."

He rested both hands on the table and leaned in with a competitive fire aglow in his eyes. "Complete victory is so very hard to come by. But every now and then, it falls in your lap. This is such a time."

The room was silent. Everyone sitting around the large, rectangular oak table had their eyes on the president. Pierson loved it. He lived for these moments... times when he had complete command of a room. All eyes were upon him. He was the star. He was the most powerful man in the world. What he decided to do sitting there at that table would reverberate throughout the world as soon as his press secretary uttered the words. And boy did Pierson have himself one weaselly bastard for a press secretary.

The guy could lie to his wife with another woman's panties around his neck and even get an apology from her for ever doubting him in the first place.

Nate Barnes tried again to redirect Pierson back to Liquid Sky, and again Pierson blocked him.

"Hear me out first, Nate," said the president. "This is exactly what we need to put me on the front pages for weeks to come. If we play this thing just right, we could solidify me as foreign-policy guru at home and a savvy diplomat abroad. Heads could roll in the EU if this gets out. That means only one thing, folks - opportunity. This is good. This is 'fortuitous,' as Camille would say. And what about Camille? We'll figure out some way to position her in this and make her look like some great envoy or something. That will give her clout in the election. Does everyone see what I'm getting at? It's a no brainer."

He shot a glance over to Jennifer Daly. She was staring at him with this sort of frozen smirk... a total bitchy resting face. Yes, he thought... that's it. It wasn't a sourpuss face at all. No, it was a bitchy resting face.

All this and more was running through the president's head as he cleared his throat. "Your thoughts, Lonny?"

Pierson's top economic advisor, Lonny Harris, backed him up. "Mr. President, we do have a very serious situation brewing in Europe. It's manageable, but we can work it to our advantage if that's what you seek to do. There are many inherent risks should it spiral out on us, however."

Pierson didn't seem bothered in the least by Harris's last cautionary words. Everyone was hanging on the president's next words. Camille could feel it. She was more than a little uncomfortable having a seat at this table. She never stepped foot in the Sit Room when she was with Beck. He would never allow her such privilege or power. Were he alive to see it, Beck would surely have burst out in a tirade of invectives. During the previous regime, Beck regularly patronized, belittled, and humiliated her in front of his staffers. In turn, like children emulating their father's boorish behavior, they treated her the same way. Day after day, their hurtful barbs tore away at her sense of self and stripped away her ability to love freely and without self-doubt.

This was what Camille regretted most about her pervious time spent in the White House. The steady tide of acerbity eroded her greatest gifts… love and compassion. All she had left was an empty space inside her soul that she had to refill somehow with the sweetness of life as she once knew it. Only then could she reunite with her true self, a child of the universe both innocent and full of grace. Jennifer Daly knew this and vowed to exploit it as much as possible in hope of someday watching Pierson and Camille crash and burn.

The rest of Pierson's people pretty much followed Lonny Harris's cue – highlight the trouble in Italy, note the cover up, go on record with a few cautionary comments about the risk, defer to the president and his plan. True to form, Camille did not follow suit. The president's plan was not a sound option. She bit her lip and prayed nobody would solicit her opinion even though she knew Jennifer Daly would do just that.

Lonny Harris looked around the table as he adjusted his silver tie. He liked consensus to the point of it being a need. "Mr. President, the Italy situation poses significant instability."

He looked around the table for nods. There were nods. Consensus....

Harris cleared his throat, one of several nervous habits, and continued. "At the same time, it's manageable. Should the United States intervene, there are political gains to be garnered."

He looked around again. More nods. Nods, that was good. Consensus....

Harris felt emboldened and ventured to stray into the dangerous, dark forest of personal opinion from which many like him in D.C. have failed to re-emerge. "The situation really is quite serious, and the German cover-up makes it much worse. Europeans take to the streets over stuff like this… cover-ups, disclosure, corruption."

More nods. He was scoring points with the big man.

He stepped deeper into the forest. "It's much like our mortgage crisis of 2008, only this time it's hitting Europe. I don't have to tell you that the EU has too much on their plate already."

Pierson looked around the table, eyeing each one of his advisors. A bunch of gawking empty suits... that's what he saw. That, and a lot of nodding. Sitting there, he felt something akin to disgust for the entire lot of them. Did any of them have a dissenting opinion, he wondered. Who knew? More importantly, he thought, who would be so bold as to voice their dissent? That was the question. Most likely not a single one of them would speak up.

When, at last, he came to Camille, he saw right away that she was not with him on this. He knew this because she gave him one of her patented "don't you dare" looks. In a way, he was pleased. He smiled at her and volleyed back with his own favorite look... his cherished "just watch me" face.

Camille grimaced and bit her lip again. Pierson loved it. He patted the cover of the morning book. "Just so we're all on the same page here. What we're talking about here is a real kick in the balls, right?"

Lonny Harris took a deep breath. "Yes, Italy's on the verge of a total economic meltdown, and Germany's covering it up."

Pierson grew eager. "That makes me think there is tremendous leverage for us. The Italians probably don't give a crap if they're found out. They always do what they want. But the last thing the Germans want is a big scandal like this."

Lonny Harris began to shift visibly, not just in his seat but in his thinking as well. He slowly held his hands in front of his face as if praying. He approached economics as an objective science. The more Pierson fleshed out his plan to manipulate a foreign economic crisis, the more uncomfortable Harris became. He now felt like he did that time he discovered his ex-wife's lover had been leaving spare clothes right there in his own closet for months. There were things going on right in front of his eyes that he was too blind to see. What looked to him at first like a valuable report on a fiscal crisis brewing in the EU's third largest economy now seemed like a plan for sneaking around behind people's back to rob the honeypot.

He looked around the table. He felt like everyone was staring at him disapprovingly. No more nods... no consensus. He suddenly found himself lost in the forest. He felt like whichever way he turned would only lead him deeper into trouble. The president never really liked Lonny Harris. He relied on him for critical data and trusted him to provide accurate information in that regard. But Harry Pierson viewed bookish intellectuals like kickers on an NFL team. You needed them in their limited role, but they sure as hell weren't football players. More to the point, they were completely expendable. One was like any other. The president felt the same way about economic advisors.

Lonny Harris slid two pale, bony fingers into his collar and tried in vain to stretch it out. He suddenly realized that the president of the United States was using him to justify a back-channel political maneuver that, if it went wrong, could trigger a total meltdown of the world's banking system. Facts, he reminded himself, stick to facts.

Pierson sniffed out Harris's fear immediately like a vulture on carrion. "You're turning green, Lon. That's your waffling complexion. I'd recognize it anywhere. Why are you suddenly ill, Lonny?"

Lonny Harris cleared his throat. He was desperately thirsty. Facts. He must stick to facts. That might get him away from personal opinion. Facts might lead him out of the forest.

"The quantitative numbers don't lie, Mr. President," he said. "The more I look at the facts, the more I think –I mean, the more it becomes evident – that the risks might outweigh the rewards."

Harry Pierson glared at him. A moment ago, he was lamenting his team's lack of gumption and the resolve to express it. Now, that seemed to him a waste of time. He knew what he wanted to do, so why the hell did he need to sit there listening to some bookish academic type opining on policy? It was like letting a kicker play quarterback. Kickers and quarterbacks were two different breeds.

Pierson considered himself a QB and Harris a kicker. They should stick to their respective roles.

"You're waffling on me, Lon. You know how I feel about that?"

Lonny Harris nodded. "Yes, sir."

"Good," replied Pierson sitting back in his chair nonchalantly. "Then you know how much I hate it. So why are you doing it?"

Lonny Harris had reached a crossroads in the forest. The path he followed now broke off in two different directions. He'd been around long enough to know he was screwed either way. There was no good choice.

He decided to go with the facts and try to pass it off on his research staff. "If what my quants tell me is correct," he explained as calmly as possible, as if he was just a messenger and not one of Pierson's chief economic advisors, "Italy has been insolvent for some time now, and the major European players, at the behest of Brussels, have seen fit to keep it a complete secret. They have been going about their business as if nothing is wrong."

Pierson held up his hand. "Wait. You're saying this is bigger than a German cover up? You're saying this goes all the way up to Brussels? It goes all the way up to the top of the EU?"

Lonny Harris turned a darker shade of green as a bolt of fear shot up his ass. Had the president just raised the stakes? That was the exact opposite response to what Harris sought. Yes, he concluded, the president just raised the stakes. Lonny Harris was now so far into the dark forest of personal opinion, he could feel the predators eyeing him and salivating. He could think of at least five people who were angling for his job. When they got wind of this, they would be all over the president.

A second bolt of fear shot up his ass. The shock must have jarred something on his motherboard because his next words bore no sign of either prudence or temperance.

"It's a cluster mess. I mean... I mean... straight up to the top. They're completely screwed. If you call their bluff, what can they do? They'll have to kiss your ass for as long... good God, for as long as you're alive."

Stunned silence muzzled the room. Jennifer Daly closed her eyes and shook her head. It was a wonder he was even born, she thought. The guy couldn't find his way out of the womb.

Pierson broke the silence with his euphoric praise. "That's fantastic," exclaimed Pierson. "I mean totally fantastic. Christmas is coming early, people. And Lonny," he added almost as an afterthought. "Whatever happens with this Italy thing, I'll make sure it connects back to you." He looked round the table. "I think we can all agree that this should roll up to Lon, right?"

Nods... lots of nods. Consensus....

Lonny Harris thought he would surely vomit. Where did unemployed economic advisors go to die, he wondered? He had no idea. Was there a support group? He had two degrees from Yale, and yet he felt at that moment like becoming a barista might be a welcome change.

If there was any doubt a minute ago, it was now clear that Lonny Harris was horrified at where this was now headed. As a reputable economist, he was worried that his research was being used as a weapon.

"Yes, Mr. President," was all he could muster.

As for Harry Pierson, he was giddy inside. It was all sweet music to his ears. "It sounds like a damned Ponzi scheme," he deduced with vigor.

Everyone around the table cast glances at each other.

Lonny Harris really didn't want to speak. He preferred to simply die right there at the table. That would be infinitely easier. The president just sat there staring at him. He tried desperately again to stretch his collar.

"We're waiting, Lonny," beckoned the president.

Harris swallowed hard. His throat was so dry. He sipped some water. "That's not a bad analogy Mr. President. Factually, it's not correct, of course. But essentially, you are correct. The EU has been propagating a huge lie and falsifying just about every financial record there is regarding Italy. Like a Ponzi scheme, they are transacting business based on assets and solvency that just aren't there."

Harry Pierson steepled his fingers and raised them to his pursed lips. He loved the pensive affect. "This is very... interesting." He unclasped his fingers and laid his hand on the table. He was smiling broadly. "Very, very interesting, indeed."

Camille decided she couldn't sit and hide in silence any longer. "I don't like this, Harry," said Camille.

All eyes suddenly turned to her... and then back to Pierson. Was she calling out the president?

"*Au contraire*, my dear running mate," said Pierson, pleasantly so as to diffuse the situation. "This is good. This is opportunity. We can have anything we want. It's like a hungry bear discovering a buffet table."

Camille knew she had a bit of latitude with Pierson. She knew he didn't want to blow her up in front of the others. That was something Beck would have done. "It seems to me," said Camille, "there could be a waterfall of negative repercussions that could rock the world if it gets away from us. Is it worth the risk?"

Camille was correct. Pierson didn't want to show her up in front of the others. He turned to Harris. "Lon?"

Lonny Harris blinked hard. His tone was cautious on the verge of being afraid. Thus far, everything he'd said only led deeper into the forest. "My people ran some macro models using some quant algorithms to estimate the derivatives and so on. It's complex. Anyway, yes, if my quant team is correct, we're talking about a worldwide fiscal meltdown should we have a loss of confidence even remotely like we had here with the mortgage crisis. Take the U.S. in 2008 and extend it to the EU. That's what could happen if this thing gets away from us."

Pierson smirked. He really disliked people with extremely large brains. They were so one dimensional. God forbid they had to calculate and kill somebody at the same time.

"Really?" said Pierson scratching his face to convey his displeasure. "You do understand what we're talking about here, right? I understand your concern, I really do. But this thing is not going to get out of hand. I assure you. We can control it. And, like I said, Lon. I'll make sure everything ties back to you. This could be the most important moment of your entire life."

Camille tried to make eye contact with Lonny Harris, but he kept his eyes down. "But what if it does go wrong?" she said. "Is it worth all the pain and suffering that would ensue just to bolster our campaign?"

Pierson breathed methodically and nodded. "I understand your trepidation, Camille. You're like Lonny, here. You're not politicians. But you need to learn how to be one. That means understanding the game. No one understands it better than yours truly. Power politics is a redundancy. They're synonymous with one another. Everyone in this room except you and Professor Economics over here understands the immense power this could give the administration. The EU? I can squeeze their balls until they burst in my hand just like this." He demonstrated with his hand. "I'll get the EU leaders to campaign for me. We'll be untouchable, Camille. It will set the stage for the next eight years at least because I fully expect you to become president after me."

Camille closed her eyes. She knew he was right about that. She had seen it in a dream. She was only just beginning to understand what it really meant.

He addressed his next comments to the group as a whole. "As for the rest of you, I don't need to remind you that we all have our jobs because the former president blew his brains out. We still have to distance ourselves from Becket Rosemore. We're not free of that shit storm just yet. Unless you all want to be unemployed soon, get on the bandwagon."

Cynthia Roberts chimed in. A former Stanford professor, she now worked for Lonny Harris, specifically keeping an eye on the Federal Reserve. She was one of the people gunning for Harris's job. She smelled blood, Lonny Harris's blood. It made her salivate.

"What we're talking about here, Mr. President, is the economic meltdown of the entire EU and, by extension, the rest of the economic world," she said with an air of pride. "The German exposure here is quite significant. But if this thing goes all the way up to Brussels, I cannot imagine a weapon more powerful for you. It's... it's brilliant actually. I can see why you're sitting in that chair, Mr. President."

"Oh, good Lord," heckled Jennifer Daly from the cheap seats.

"This is much, much bigger than Italy," added Lonny Harris in a cracked voiced, once again unable to control himself.

Camille was never one for treacle and tea cakes. She had to add a healthy dollop of reality to the mix, something of an irony, she thought. "If this ever gets out, it will hit the U.S. stock market hard. I'm not a professional politician like most of you, but that seems like the last thing we need going into an election. If something goes wrong – and I'm not saying it will – but if something leaks or somehow spins out of control, it will make us even more vulnerable, won't it?"

Pierson had an amused look on his face. "No, no, no, Camille. You have it backward. This is exactly what we need. The way things stand now, each and every one of us – myself included – will be looking for a job next year, right?" He perused the table. "As for me, I plan to do something about that."

Camille looked at the president disparagingly. "Just so we're all on the same page here, are you saying you actually want a global financial crisis so you can play the hero or something like that?"

Pierson pressed his eyes. He was tired. "Look, the EU has it coming to them. It's fraud. Apparently, everybody in Brussels knows the bonds they're buying aren't worth much more than Italian toilet paper. But they're buying them anyway," he said slowly as if drawing the final conclusion in an intricate mystery.

"Why?" asked Camille, wondering how politics became such a mess.

"I'll tell you why," replied Harry Pierson. "It's a means of artificially propping up the Italian government, the Italian economy, one great, big fraudulent meatball. It's wonderful. I mean, I couldn't write this scenario any better if I was Earnest Hemingway. I can see the story develop in my head. I agree with Cynthia. It's a brilliant plot, if I do say so myself. And, let's face it. We've done nothing positive to make this administration really stand out to the voting public."

Camille clucked her tongue and shot Pierson another one of her looks. "We need a crisis to do that?" she asked.

"I stick to what I know," said Harry Pierson. "There is a dynamic, a back story to everything that occurs whether you're included in those decisions or not. Most of the time, it's above your clearance. So, why would any of you concern yourself? Let it be."

Cynthia Roberts shook her head. "Well, that's that then," she said in dismay. "I just hope it doesn't come back to haunt you, Mr. President."

"I'm not worried. I never allowed myself to be tied directly to anything that could blow up in my face." He looked at Lonny Harris as if to say, "That's what you're for, Lonny my man."

"Things blow up in other people's faces," quipped Jennifer Daly.

"Exactly," replied Pierson. "Things go south all the time. Ops go awry, people get hung out to dry. I've never been one of them, and I don't intend to start now. That's how you survive decades in the CIA. I thrived because I have a knack for attaching myself to great American achievements and distancing myself from the embarrassing screwups."

Pierson sat back and allowed the silence to settle in. His people were thinking. They were damned smart, he had to give them that. What they lacked, in his opinion, was political savvy. That was his job. He was certain he could turn this thing into his advantage.

After a moment, he turned back to Cynthia Roberts. "Your previous comments did not go unnoticed, Cynthia. I appreciate it. You're on top of things at the Fed, right?"

She nodded. "I like to think so." She smiled.

Pierson smiled. "Well... the question is. Can we get the Federal Reserve on board if we need them?"

Cynthia Roberts looked at Lonny Harris. How on earth did he get the job, she wondered. His analysts did all the work. She eyeballed him while he sat there. He was virtually cowering. She sat back, still staring at her boss but with a broad, self-satisfied smile spanning ear to ear.

"What are you looking at him for?" blurted Harry Pierson. "I asked you the question. I already know what Lonny thinks. He's been saying the same shit for the last six months already."

Cynthia Roberts turned a similar shade of green as her boss, which was saying something considering she was African-American. She made eye contact with the president immediately. The way he looked at her said it all. She had no doubt Pierson knew exactly what she was thinking and was putting her in her place.

She stuttered a few times and looked up at the ceiling as she released a herd of "ums," "wells," and "'that is to say" from their corral as she inevitably did when nervous.

Pierson grew irritated. At first, it looked like he could groom her into an excellent protégée. Now... maybe not so much. "Look at me," he commanded. "I'm over here."

Cynthia Roberts stopped staring at the fly on the ceiling and returned her gaze to the president.

"I'll make this as simple as possible for you because, apparently, all you brilliant economists understand esoteric algorithms but lack any shred of political savvy. Okay, so this is what I want to know. Is Fed Chairman Gretsch going to play ball, or do I have to replace him after we win this damned election? If you're not sure, then say so. Don't give me made-up bullshit because you think you need to sound smart. Better you figure out the lay of the land first."

Cynthia Roberts looked scared. The president of the United States was asking for her opinion on something that might have vast global economic implications.

"I believe the Fed will facilitate, Mr. President."

Pierson nodded as he digested her answer. "This is Lonny's gambit, you know. This is his idea. He has everything riding on it."

Lonny Harris tried to protest. He looked around the table. Surely everyone knew it was the president's idea to manipulate a global banking crisis.

"Lonny's the mastermind behind this thing, not me," reiterated Pierson, laying one more whack on the nail he'd just driven into Lonny Harris's heart.

Lonny Harris looked around the table. He saw nodding... so much nodding... consensus but the wrong kind... my God, such the wrong kind.

Cynthia Roberts looked at Lonny Harris. She saw a little bead of sweat run down his face from his temple to the middle of his jaw.

"Absolutely," she said, with newfound confidence. "The Fed will be on board. In the end, Chairman Gretsch works for you, sir. He knows that. Maybe you have to remind him you're the boss. But he gets it."

Harry Pierson rubbed his thumb over his lower lip. He liked the sound of that. She may yet have a future. He slapped his hands down on the table. "Excellent. Camille... thoughts? You'll need to formulate an opinion on this once the *schiesse* hits the fan, as the Germans say."

Camille figured she had to give it another shot. Maybe she could come at it from a humanistic angle on the outside chance she struck the miniscule portion of Pierson's heart that still felt compassion. "Is the German government going to bear the full brunt of the Italian failure? If so, how will it affect the German people?"

Pierson acknowledged what his running mate was up to. "See that? She goes right to the emotional heart of the matter. That's why people love her. She actually cares about them. It's fascinating."

He could feel Jennifer Daly shooting hate-tipped daggers at him from her seat at the far end of the table. He loved it. The animosity made him feel like he was governing with an iron will and a strong sense of purpose.

Camille felt she needed to keep asserting her own perspective. "I agree with the president. What we need is something weighty to ride into the election. But I don't want to lose sight of people along the way. In the end, that's why we're here... to help everyone prosper."

Pierson again offered praise tempered with condescension. "God, I love this woman. She really believes in all that stuff. It's truly fascinating."

He'd said his piece. He was done explaining his motivations. He addressed Lonny Harris again. "So then, Lonny, do you have anything else to add?"

Lonny Harris thought it through a bit before answering. He honestly didn't know what to say or do. He opted for the truth. "My people have run several different scenarios."

Pierson held up his hand. His mind was pretty much made up. Polling his staffers was merely for appearance, to make them feel involved. He really didn't care what Lonny Harris had to say. As far as the president was concerned, his next visit to Brussels was going to be an abrupt wake-up call for the world not unlike prison sex. Brussels was gonna be his bitch. That's what he was thinking, and it worked pretty well for him.

So why not bust Lonny's balls for the hell of it? Pierson was planning on dumping him when he and Camille won another term anyway. Why not have a bit of fun at Harris's expense? That's how Pierson was feeling.

"Did you say your 'people'?" Pierson questioned.

Harris looked confused. "Yes, that's right."

Pierson smiled wryly. "Who the hell are your people? Your people are my people, aren't they? Or do you have a secret stash of brains I don't know about?"

Lonny Harris couldn't tell if the president was kidding.

Lonny Harris tried to explain. "Well, my quants," he said in a voice much softer than he intended. It made it seem like he was hiding something. He closed his eyes and cursed himself as soon as the words passed his lips. He could feel Cynthia Roberts's ridicule.

"Whoa, whoa, whoa," boomed Pierson. "Your quants. What the hell does that mean?"

Lonny Harris emitted a meek whinny. "My quantitative analysts, sir. They run macroeconomic models based on complex quantitative algorithms to help you make informed and timely decisions that are data driven and actionable."

"Excellent," said Pierson. "You can put that nice little blurb on your resume when you're looking for a job next year." He looked at Cynthia Roberts. Why not bust her chops, too? "You, too, Roberts. Maybe the both of you can find a package deal."

Nobody dared speak lest they become the target of the president's ire. Pierson had complete control of a room full of over-paid stiffs who were praying the president would not ask them for their opinion.

Pierson returned to Lonny Harris. "So, Lon, you have a bunch of Indians stuffed away in a room doing your work for you when they're not too busy betting to see who can calculate pi to a million places?"

Harris didn't know what to say. He still wasn't sure if Pierson was serious or not. He looked to Cynthia Roberts for help.

"Don't look at her," said Pierson crisply. "Why are you looking at her? Does she have quants, too?"

He turned to Cynthia Roberts. "Ms. Roberts, do you have a closet full of quants? Now's the time to come clean." He threw up his hands and feigned disgust. "How come everybody has quants but me? I'm the president. Why don't I have a team of quants? Where are my Indians?"

Cynthia Roberts sat up erect. "Actually, Mr. President, they're Chinese."

Wrong answer. Pierson sharpened his gaze, but inside he was hysterical. She took the bait. He might get a laugh or two out of this gag yet. "Who's Chinese?"

"The quants, sir. They are Chinese," she explained.

The president leaned in and pointed at one of his advisors across to his right. "Bob, you're my immigration Tsar. I want a bunch of Chinese guys… these quants… I want them hanging around me like Christmas ornaments on a tree. And I want them calculating stuff whenever I'm on camera. Get me Chinese people who can calculate stuff… you know, stuff nobody understands. Get some shots of that out to the media outlets."

Bob Jonas pursed his lips and glanced from side to side trying to gauge everyone's response. "Um… I'll make some calls, Mr. President. Is there anything in particular you would like them to calculate, Mr. President?"

"How should I know?" replied Pierson. "Whatever looks good. Tell the press they're curing cancer. What the hell do I care?"

Bob Jonas was scribbling notes furiously.

Pierson sat back. "Excellent. And throw in some Indians, Bob. Those people are good at math, right? Eh, it doesn't matter. People think they are. That's the only thing that matters. Couldn't hurt. Indians and Asians... it's all good."

Bob Jonas stopped writing and looked up. "Which Indians are Asians, Mr. President?"

Harry Pierson was surprised. "What now?"

Bob Jonas's feet began to sweat something awful. That was his nervous habit. His wife made him wash his feet first thing every night when he came home. "I was just saying, sir, that Indians and Pakistanis are actually Asians." He pursed his lips, waiting for the fatal blow.

It came. "Bob, did I mention Pakistanis? Pay attention, man."

He surveyed the room, somehow managing to keep a straight face. He knew if he looked at Camille, he would burst out laughing from the look of horror no doubt frozen on her face. He loved that look of hers.

"People... people," said the president, chuckling a bit now. "I'm joking. Relax. You're such an uptight bunch of popsicles. You know... popsicles... with a stick up your—"

He began mocking Bob Jonas. "Err... um... Indians are Asians?"

Camille thought it wise to interject again. "Mr. President...." She thought about the best way to present her thoughts to a room full of people she considered slightly left of war mongers. Add to that her precarious position of having no formal position at all.

"Mr. President," said Camille, "it's just that... well, I feel we're all a bit concerned about what we're hearing. The Italian banking system may be inconsequential to you unto itself–"

Here, the president stopped her abruptly. He felt it was his job to train his running mate. "Unto itself? What does that mean?"

Camille smiled and nodded. "Sorry, sorry.... I mean as a theoretical concept, the Italian banking system is just an organization, a construct, a thing. We may pour money in it, but it's not really something we would put our hearts in, know what I'm saying?"

The president looked at her crooked. "The only thing I'm sure of is that I have no idea what you're saying."

Camille continued explaining. "I don't think we're too concerned with a banking system. I think what worries us is the people who are impacted by that system, or, in this case the collapse of that system. Millions of lives could be ruined. If the ripple effect is going to be as bad as Lonny and Cynthia say, we may have quite a problem on our hands."

Harry Pierson rubbed his chin and thought about it for a moment. "You mean a humanitarian problem?"

"Precisely," replied Camille. "If the EU is like a house of cards, a mistake on our end could lead to a humanitarian crisis. Do you really want that on your hands?"

This got the president's attention. "Did you say, 'humanitarian crisis'?"

The way he was grinning concerned Camille. "I can't tell from the look on your face if you find that frightful or delightful."

Harry Pierson sat back in his executive chair. "The jury is still out on that. I need more details. This humanitarian crisis... it could be a good pivot. You could actually be a genius, Camille."

Camille reminded him that, "These aren't cards. We're talking about real people here."

Pierson stopped drumming his fingers. "I know that, Camille. We're talking about a lot of social pressure that can be applied."

"What about Rickey Ormand," said Camille desperately grasping for something. "I have to say, I'm a bit surprised the news about some guy inventing gravity-power would not steal the day, especially if he's developing a secret weapons program."

Camille had been following the Liquid Sky breakthrough ever since she saw footage of Parker Fitzgerald at Burning Man on YouTube. Camille was blown away by the brilliant robo-woman, by Rickey Ormand, gravity power, the whole spectacle fascinated her.

Pierson looked unmoved.

Camille tried again. "I saw their presentation on YouTube. They're doing amazing things. Did you know the lead scientist is a woman who is half a robot?"

The conversation came to a sudden stop.

Camille looked around the table.

The president suddenly seemed interested. He had a big grin on his face. "Half robot, you say? A half woman, half robot? For real?"

"Yeah," replied Camille. "Her name is Dr. Parker Fitzgerald. I was looking up her story. It's amazing."

The president held up his index finger. "Hold that thought, Camille."

Camille wondered whether she could turn Pierson's attention away from the humanitarian firestorm he was looking to ignite and somehow get him to focus on something she considered much more productive.

"But, maybe this gravity engine–" She tried in vain, but Pierson cut her off a second time. "Hold that thought, please. I'm thinking. You've piqued my interest with this robo- woman thing."

After an uncomfortable silence, the president instructed Camille to continue what she was saying a moment earlier.

"You and I approach the world very differently," she said. "Positive influence always plays better. We saw that with the female refugees, right? I'm sorry, I just don't think we should intentionally start a catastrophe just so we can look good riding in to save the day, you know?"

On a whim, Jennifer Daly decided to enter the fray. She was getting bored and figured stirring things up might provide the pick-me-up she was looking for. "I can't believe the German government owns billions in worthless bonds," she said.

Everybody in the room knew she was trolling Camille except Camille herself.

"And they are lying about it, Camille," added Jennifer Daly with a robust and pernicious gleam in her eyes. "What do you think about that?"

"To be honest, this all sounds horrific," answered Camille. She looked around the table. To a person, nobody else really seemed to care.

"Oh my God," gasped Camille. "It's like you're playing some sort of board game. But there are millions and millions of lives at stake."

Pierson looked at her sympathetically. He could fake anything. "It'll never get that far, Camille. Trust me."

Camille wasn't buying it. "How many times have I heard that before? Isn't anybody concerned?"

Hank Andrews, a three-star general and one of Pierson's top military advisors from the DOD, threw his two cents in. "Mr. President, I don't feel good about a destabilized Eurozone right now. Major economic instability always gives rise to terrorist insurgency. And then there's the refugees. You saw what happened with all those Syrians. Literally millions of them spreading across Europe."

"Well, then," Daly said to the president. "It looks like you have a decision to make."

Pierson looked at her sharply. "What are you talking about? I've already made up my mind."

Chapter 14

"So that's it?" asked Camille, again looking around the table for support. Her power was, it seemed, momentary at best. "You've made your decision regarding Italy?"

The president smiled. "I said no such thing, Camille. And even if I have made up my mind, I'm not about to disclose that at this table."

Camille looked confused. "So, you can't say 'yes.' And 'no' could mean 'no' but just as easily mean 'yes'?"

Harry Pierson smiled wryly. "Yes. You're learning."

Surprisingly, it was Jennifer Daly who chimed in. She wasn't quite sure why, and she wasn't quite comfortable with it. It was Camille's charm, her appeal. Daly had to admit it. The redhead had a certain strength and power. She wasn't quite comfortable with that, either.

"If I may offer a suggestion?" said Daly.

The president turned his head sharply. His tone was almost whimsical. "Really?" In a way, he was proud of his two girls.

Daly cracked her knuckles. Was she really going to do this? She had no reason to get involved, no reason in the slightest. In a couple of months, she'd be free of all this bullshit. She relished the thought. And yet, something inside – she referred to it as her "goody-two-shoes morality" – was commandeering her tongue. She thrust her jaw out, attempting in vain to resist the force. She knew from experience that it was no use. That goody two shoes, she thought.

"Well," said Daly pausing, her tongue now under the sway of the goody two shoes. The sound of her voice cut through the room like a needle sliding across a vinyl record. She had everyone's attention if for no other reason than the perversity of her putting herself out there for no apparent reason whatsoever. "Well," she repeated, "it seems to me that both you and Camille make good, albeit opposite, points." She swallowed hard. "In this regard, you make a good team."

She swallowed hard again. Keep pressing forward. There are much bigger stakes than her ego, she reminded herself.

She continued on deliberately. "Although I will be stepping aside…."

Deep breath followed by three firm blinks.

"Even so, I agree with the president that this administration very badly needs something big to catapult us – I mean you, of course…."

God, that was a hard bit to get out. She fought back every word, but there it was.

To her horror, her tongue kept moving and words kept coming out. "You need something big, huge to get you past Rosemore's distasteful legacy and into the spotlight. Like the president said, every great administration needs conflict or crisis to forge itself."

"Crisis and conflict," reiterated Harry Pierson. "You got that right, J.D."

Jennifer Daly looked up at the ceiling as if asking for God's strength now that she was sure the goody two shoes would issue forth a compliment of Camille.

"That said, I see… yes, I see the wisdom in Camille's approach, as well. She is special. People connect with her positivity. She gives them hope, the most powerful of emotions. And with hope comes enthusiasm. So, give people hope, receive their enthusiasm in return. It's the greatest social contract there is."

She couldn't believe what her tongue just put forth. If there was a sharp knife handy, Jennifer Daly may well have sliced off her tongue rather than utter those words. Now that the words were out for everyone to hear, she had a brief moment of empathy for the ancient Samurai. Had she been one herself, she would surely have committed ritualistic suicide. Lame-duck V.P. commits *hara-kiri*.

Harry Pierson and Camille O'Keefe looked at each other. Their mutual gaze spoke volumes.

"People connect with positivity," repeated the president, not so much as a question as an out loud verbalization of the concept to see how it felt, like trying on a suit to see how it fit. "Interesting. I... I don't really know much about that."

Jennifer Daly nodded. "Except for New Yorkers."

Nods circulated around the table like the wave at a ball game.

"Perhaps taken together, the both of you are onto something big," granted Daly. "Maybe you're both right. Find something really big, but it should be overwhelmingly positive."

Daly paused. Her brain wanted to explode like the gray matter was C-4. She wanted her brain to explode. That her final gesture in office after being shoved aside was to kiss up to the very two people who shoved her aside was beyond humiliating. And yet, there it was. It came from some unknown part of her where her goody two shoes lived.

"That's all I have to say about that," she said.

Pierson and Camille were looking at each other again. When he saw the fire in Camille's emerald eyes, he was genuinely inquisitive.

"What are you thinking?" he asked.

"Liquid Sky," replied Camille. "Rickey Ormand, Parker Fitzgerald... this amazing gravity engine or gravity car, or whatever it is. It's going to change the world, right?"

"I can put some of my people on it," offered Lonny Harris, seeing a way out for himself.

"There's really no need," said Pierson. "There's no question about it. If this thing actually works, the world as we know it is about to change overnight."

He scratched his chin. It was clear he was out of his comfort zone. "I'm not sure I see that as a positive," he said. He stood up and started pacing. He looked down at his black wing tips. They were so well polished, he could almost see his own reflection.

Camille closed her eyes and searched for the right way to convey to Harry Pierson exactly what she was thinking. If only he were clairvoyant like she was, communicating would be so much easier.

"The implications associated with a new energy source are significant," Camille said. "And if someone has truly figured out how to harness gravity power and actually make things powered by gravity, I don't even know where to begin forecasting the effects of... how would you put it, Lonny?"

"Forecast the effect of immediate, worldwide adoption of the technology," fired off Harris.

The president stopped pacing and turned sharply. "That's precisely what worries me."

Camille pushed back her chair and cranked up her charm. She knew Harry Pierson. There had to be a thousand negative thoughts each with a thousand counterproductive scenarios running through his head. She had to redirect his negative thinking.

"This could be really huge," she said enthusiastically.

Pierson started pacing again.

"Really, really huge," she stressed. "Think about it... Mr. President."

That last bit didn't sound right coming from Camille, and she knew it. She smiled coyly and tried to shrug it off. The rest of the folks around the table smiled, too. Only a handful of staffers were on a first-name basis with the president. In staff meetings such as this, that number was limited to two: Jennifer Daly and Camille O'Keefe.

He stopped, turned to Camille, and pointed at her. "So, now it's Mr. President, is it?"

He walked over to the table in the corner of the room, grabbed his blue coffee mug with THE BOSS stencilled on it, and poured himself a steaming cup. The mug was a gag gift from one of his staffers last Christmas, but Pierson rather liked it anyway.

With his free hand, he snatched a handful of chocolate-chip cookies. Cookies in hand, he turned back toward Camille. "And for your information, Ms. O'Keefe, I am thinking about it. Believe me, I'm thinking about it. It's just that you and I come at things from very different perspectives."

He returned to his seat at the head of the table and carefully placed both his beloved Boss mug and the cookies in front of him to his left. He then proceeded to line up the chocolate-chip cookies in a horizontal row from right to left. The team was clearly perplexed.

"Lest any of you think about tipping off my doctor about my eating habits, these are for demonstration purposes only," he said, referring to the cookies.

"I can explore this gravity-power thing before you make a final decision on Italy," pleaded Camille. "What harm could that do? Let's see what is really going on at Liquid Sky."

Pierson wagged his finger. "Not so fast, Red. Okay, so what's the thing people love about chocolate-chip cookies?"

The groups shot confused looks at one another. Pierson looked around the table waiting for other input. None was forthcoming.

"Thanks for your input," Pierson quipped. He held up one of the cookies. "What people like about chocolate-chip cookies is that each one is different. No two cookies are the same."

"That would not have been in my top million answers, Harry," said Camille.

"Still, my point remains. How does that commercial go?" He broke the cookie in half. "Any way you break it, it comes up chocolate chips. Every cookie is different but not to the point of being unpredictable or inconsistent."

He tossed the two pieces of cookie into a nearby trash bin. It echoed inside the empty metal canister.

"Interesting," said Lonny Harris, still desperate to save his political career.

Pierson lowered his chin and sighed. He slid a cookie over. "Have a cookie, Lon, and leave the jokes to me." He lifted his mug making sure THE BOSS was facing out and took a pronounced sip. "It's all about subtlety, Lon."

"You have an idea?" asked Camille, trying to keep the president on point.

"Ah," said Harry Pierson. "My point about the cookie is simple. There's nothing wrong with variety so long as there are hard and fast limits. For example, no two cookies have the exact same...." He looked to Lonny Harris for a prompt.

"Distribution," said Lonny.

"Yes," said the president, smiling broadly. "No two cookies have the exact same distribution of chips. But you can be damned sure they all have the same amount of chocolate. It's controlled. What's more, we sure as hell know that each cookie will be exactly the same size. Variety, yes, but limited, controlled, consistent, predictable. That's what maintains stability."

Pierson slid a cookie into his hand and sat back. He dipped the cookie into his coffee and nibbled off the soft part. "Coffee and a good chocolate-chip cookie. So simple, and yet it embodies the principles that make this country great."

He finished the rest of his cookie in silence while his point sunk in. Three cookies later, the president wrapped the meeting. "Okay, folks. I think we've covered quite a lot of ground for our morning briefing. One of my aides will run through the rest of the binder."

He slapped both hands down on the table as if about to stand up ceremonially.

Camille was unnerved. "But what about Liquid Sky? I thought we were going to at least explore what's there for us?"

Pierson sighed and cocked his head. "Did you understand my cookie analogy, Camille?"

Camille scratched her head. She had absolutely no idea what the president was getting at with those cookies, and assumed he really just wanted an excuse to eat a few.

Camille looked at Pierson. "All I am asking for is a few days to look into this Liquid Sky thing. That's all. You can still make the necessary preparations to bring the Europeans to their knees." She blew a curl out of her face. "Lord knows we can't take that pleasure away from you."

Pierson held up his hands. "Hey, I said nothing about that. That was Lonny Harris's idea."

Camille pursed her lips and sucked through her teeth. "Uh-huh."

The president shrugged. "Did anyone hear me say that?" he asked, looking around the table.

Shaking heads.

"It was Lon's idea."

Nods all around... except for Lonny Harris.

"See," he said, returning his attention to Camille. "That's not my plan at all. Forcing the EU to their knees like a cheap hooker? Not my style. Talk to Lonny. Apparently, he has a penchant for that sort of thing."

Camille was frustrated by Pierson's glib evasiveness. "But–"

This time, Pierson cut her off much more sharply than before. "Camille, I understand your personal agenda leans toward spiritual ideas–"

Camille cut him off in return. She surprised herself almost as much as she surprised Jennifer Daly. "Harry, that's exactly why you brought me on board. I know what people want. Even Vice President Daly said it."

Jennifer Daly nodded demurely. "I did say that, didn't I?"

The steely glint in Harry Pierson's eye signalled to Camille that he was done pulling punches for the sake of appearances. Her assessment was correct. The president adjusted his tie and straightened his cuffs before speaking. Was he going to blow his stack? Is the Red Dragon Lady's bid for the White House over already? That's what the staffers were all thinking.

"Camille," said Pierson, the strain showing in small vocal quivers. "Let's assume that you're correct. Let's assume that this gravity engine is for real, and Liquid Sky rolls out a gravity-powered car or something like that."

"Okay," said Camille, thankful, at least, they were still discussing it.

"Good," said Pierson. "Let's assume that happens tomorrow. What comes next?"

Camille squinted and brought her hands together. "I imagine the energy crisis will be over, and people all over the world will have access to cheap energy because gravity is abundant. More importantly, nobody owns gravity. It's part of our planet, part of our universe. Therefore, it belongs to everyone."

Pierson rubbed his face, mostly in dismay. Can she possibly be this naïve, he thought? He stole a look over toward Jennifer Daly. She returned a faint smile.

"Is that your full take on it, Camille?" he asked. "Because, that would be nice. That would be such a lovely world, maybe with some Smurfs, and talking donkeys, cats and dogs and kumbaya. Lovely, right?"

"It's something to aspire toward," returned Camille. "It would be a really nice change."

Pierson managed to control himself. A few times that morning he wondered to himself what possessed him to opt for Camille O'Keefe over Jennifer Daly. He looked at Camille. Her bright green eyes, flowing red hair, and that damned look of hopeful optimism cooled his ire. He laughed to himself. He'd just seen why.

"Okay," he said, trying his hardest not to go off on her. "Let me ask you something, Camille."

Camille swept her hair aside, leaned in and beamed at the president. "Fire away... Mr. President."

"So, you really think this new energy source will be good for the country?" asked Pierson.

Camille took the bait. "Not just the country. If gravity power is for real, this could be a great moment for the entire world. We've got to think big here. A few minutes ago, you were saying how we need to land something big in our corner. You being you, Harry, you gravitate toward some complex, clandestine operation that ferments insurrection and instability."

The president frowned. "I wouldn't put it quite that way, Camille."

"It makes perfect sense," she said. "That's what you know. That's who you are. It's served you well all these years. But I see something different, a different way. We can truly lead the world into a wonderful new future."

Pierson steepled his fingers and brought his hands to his lips. "How's that?"

"If this gravity power thing is for real," said Camille, "it could lift up the entire world, A totally new paradigm... just imagine what would happen."

Camille's enthusiasm was palpable. She meant every word she said. She believed in the idea. She believed real change could happen, would happen, was about to happen.

The president ran it through his head. If it was anybody other than Camille O'Keefe, he would be demanding their resignation. But there was something about Camille that soothed his senses and made him actually enjoy stepping outside his box.

"Lonny," he snapped.

Surprised, Lonny Harris sat bolt upright. "Yes, Mr. President."

Pierson slowly walked to the table for another cup of coffee. Over his shoulder he said, "Lon, what do you think about this totally new paradigm?"

Jennifer Daly closed her eyes and squeezed them. She saw Pierson's endgame and knew he was playing it out masterfully. She tried to interrupt, but the president motioned her to remain silent. "I'm talking to Lonny."

He prompted Harris to continue. "You were saying, Lon?"

Lonny Harris scratched his neck nervously. He needed to find a middle ground, but there was none at the moment because Pierson was using him as a foil against Camille.

Lonny Harris stuttered a bit. "Well... uh... paradigm shifts... paradigm shifts are neutral in and of themselves. The impact of the shift is determined by the net results it yields." Pierson poured a fresh cup of coffee into THE BOSS and nodded without turning around. "And what if it's true? What if Liquid Sky has actually invented a way to use gravity as an unlimited, zero-footprint energy source displacing every other energy source we have today?"

Pierson turned around and returned to his seat, but not before snaking two more cookies.

Lonny Harris nodded. "Yeah, well... that's the big question. I mean... assuming gravity power is a reality and that a single company owns the exclusive rights to it. I... I can't begin to posit the size of the global impact. Everything, I mean everything, will change overnight. Not only that–"

He stifled himself.

"No, no," said Pierson gesturing for more. "Please continue. This is your plan."

Lonny Harris did a double take. Did the president just tag him for a second crazy scheme? Over the next five seconds, Lonny Harris's brain contemplated no less than seven scenarios all of which ended in his being homeless and living in a refrigerator box under some bypass.

"Well," Harris explained, rubbing his face, "I agree with Ms. O'Keefe that the possibilities are endless."

Camille beamed a radiant smile his way. "Thank you, Lonny."

Lonny Harris scratched his neck. "At the same time, that's precisely what concerns me."

Camille's smile faded quickly. "Go figure," said Daly, sardonically.

"Yes, Lon," beckoned Harry Pierson. "Please expound on that?"

Jennifer Daly exhaled loudly, sat back in her chair, and crossed her leg in annoyance. Was she now siding with her goody two shoes?

Lonny Harris drained his water glass and ran his tongue around the inside of his dry mouth. "What concerns me, Mr. President, is too much change, too fast."

"Ah," said the president. He knew exactly where his man was going. "Lonny remembers the cookie," he said, wagging his finger at them all.

"What does that even mean?" asked Jennifer Daly.

"It means," replied Lonny Harris nervously, "that an invention like this could change the world as we know it overnight. I mean...

literally… overnight. I can't even imagine the immediate impact on the global economy. I mean…."

He stopped. He waved his right hand in the air as if trying to conjure up the answer to an inestimable question.

"Don't stop now, Lon. You're on a roll," said Pierson.

"Frankly," continued Harris, "I think the impact of gravity power would send shockwaves throughout the world. I think entire industries would be obsolete in the blink of an eye."

"The blink of an eye," said Pierson, wagging his finger again.

Lonny Harris wasn't anywhere near done. "Oil, heck anything remotely connected with the fossil-fuel industry like drilling, exploration, natural gas, transportation, good Jesus how about the automotive industry? And the airlines? And anything remotely connected to *them* as well?"

He pounded his forefinger onto the table to underscore his point. He couldn't control himself. He was desperate to derail the president's gambit in the EU and yet here he was spinning the alternative like it was the end of the world.

He couldn't stop talking. He pressed on like there were two entirely different people living inside him, each set on an opposite agenda.

"The energy sector as a whole would explode, Mr. President. There would be widespread turmoil throughout the Middle East, Nigeria, and the Northern European Countries. If you think Venezuela is in bad shape now, imagine what would happen if oil was suddenly deemed obsolete? A loaf of bread will cost a thousand dollars in the oil-producing world."

Pierson raised his hand. "Thank you, Lonny. That will suffice."

He folded his hands and nodded solemnly. "So, you see, Camille, we can't allow an upheaval like this to occur."

Camille laughed at the absurdity she heard coming from Pierson. "That's exactly why we should find out what's really going on at Liquid Sky."

Camille pressed her temples in a vain attempt to quell the row taking place between her ears. "Lonny, if it's true about gravity power, is it all so negative?"

"The thing is," replied Lonny Harris, "all the benefits you desire would be there, Ms. O'Keefe. But at what cost? How far do you let it go? Do you let the global order of things completely collapse so that people can have clean energy and the poor get it for free? Something like this could make the Italy thing seem like a flea bite on a whale. Can you imagine the mass unemployment across the globe? I mean… I can't even imagine the predictive modelling for an event like this. The paper would fill a room. We would need a freaking supercomputer."

Camille was not content to leave it at that. "You're focusing on the negative, Lonny. You are focusing on extremes. There's no guarantee all that chaos will ensue. And again, this is why I say we need to investigate. What if Liquid Sky rolls this thing out next week? What then?"

Camille's inexperience in the political arena was beginning to show. She was unwilling to compromise, and that was making things difficult for Harry Pierson. When Camille agreed to be Pierson's running mate, she did so only because she felt becoming the nation's first elected female vice president would provide her with a powerful platform from which she could promote her agenda of universal respect, human interconnectedness, and, above all, kindness and love. Now, she felt Harry Pierson using Lonny Harris to wall her off, and she began to feel like she was back with Beck all over again. That was a pattern she swore never to repeat.

She addressed everyone now. "I get where Lonny is coming from. I really do. But we can't hide from progress. We can't keep replaying the same, tired game of politics based on deceit, economic subjugation, and war. All the back-channel, clandestine deals, the covert military operations, flat-out wars… none if it moves the world forward. I worry that we won't really stand out like we want to if we do the same old thing as other administrations have done. If we want to stand out, we should do things differently. The Italy crisis won't make us stand out."

Harry Pierson was forged from the raw materials of the Cold War. That's what he knew. Those were his ways. To him, anyone

who thought the Cold War ended was ill-informed and a danger to
national security. The Cold War was still very much alive for Harry
Pierson. Only now, Russia hid behind an oil curtain rather than an
iron curtain. Pierson believed to his core that Vladimir Putin was
pulling the strings behind every struggle the United States had in the
Middle East. For Harry Pierson, "Islamic terrorism" was merely the
Russians engaged in clandestine guerrilla warfare against America.

Pierson admonished his running mate. "I wish the world was like
that, Camille. You might think I'm an anachronism. It depends. As
long as there is a Putin, there needs to be a Pierson."

General Hank Andrews went way back with Pierson and saw
eye-to-eye on most issues, especially where national security was
involved. He'd been brooding about something for the last fifteen
minutes.

"With all due respect," he said. "We can't forget the comment
in the report about Rickey Ormand running his own, secret military
program using gravity power."

"Assuming such a technology even exists," said Pierson.

"We should find out," said Camille. "That's all I'm saying. Let's
not dismiss this out of hand."

"Actually," said General Andrews, "I have to agree with Ms.
O'Keefe. The weaponization of gravity power really concerns me. In
fact, the more I think about it… yes, I'm scared as hell. We mentioned
all the socioeconomic implications. Yes, they will be very, very
impactful. Too much change too fast can be a real problem. There's
no way the world can swallow and digest it. I may not have a bunch
of Punjabi brainiacs locked in some broom closet cranking out fancy
models, but I have a lifetime of experience dealing with shit storms."

"Thanks for the lovely image, General," quipped Jennifer Daly.

"Let the man speak, please," said the president.

General Andrews hardly heard her anyway. "My point is that
I know a dangerous thing when I see it. And this gravity engine,
gravity power, whatever the hell it is… it's a damned dangerous
thing any way you slice it. Like your cookie."

Pierson was beaming. "See, he gets my cookie analogy."

Harry Pierson trusted Hank Andrews. They both cut their teeth hunting and killing communists. They were fashioned from the same stuff. So, when General Andrews spoke with such conviction, it got the president's attention and fast.

For the majority of his professional life, from his days with the CIA right up to the presidency, Harry Pierson understood the world was one giant sea of gray. Mission success meant everything. He was paranoid as only a life-long CIA man could be, about everything he knew and everything he did not know at one and the same time. Sitting there listening to General Andrews lay out his concerns only underscored the extent to which Pierson had to weigh his options very, very carefully regardless of Camille's agenda or anyone else's for that matter.

"I'm listening," Pierson said to General Andrews.

Andrews sat up a little taller. His voice had a deep, guttural quality to it that made him seem perpetually angry.

"Like I said, Mr. President, I don't deal with economic paradigms or fancy algorithms. That's like a fantasy world to me. I deal in life and death, real lives and real deaths. The biggest threat I see with the introduction of some radical new power source is its military applications."

Camille nodded. "I'm not sure what you're imagining, but it sounds like we need to investigate."

Harry Pierson was interested in what Andrews had to say. They spoke the same language, whereas he and Camille had completely different worlds of understanding.

"I know this is a bit impromptu, Hank, but can you elaborate a bit more?"

General Andrews squeezed his bottom lip between his thumb and forefinger a few times while staring off into the corner of the room. He was running scenarios through his head in much the same as Lonny Harris did. But the similarities stopped there. Where Harris dealt in dollars, Andrews dealt in death.

Andrews elaborated as requested. "I agree with Mr. Harris, sir, that large-scale economic upheaval would ferment uprising around the world. I also acknowledge that any sort of power-play using an Italian banking collapse for leverage could very well bring about an upheaval of its own. Naturally, my concerns revolve around armed conflicts that might ensue. But I see that as mostly helping out here and there as required."

"This gravity-power thing is very different, though. If it's true, it's a complete unknown. We have no models incorporating this type of technology. Accordingly, I can't begin to assess the risk potential. It could be astronomical."

Pierson scratched is head. "This is very different from what Camille is advocating. Camille, you seem to be interested in gravity power to unite the world. Hank is worried about it being used to destroy it."

Camille saw his point. "I'll have to think about that a bit more. But certainly, we can all agree that we need to learn more about what's going on at Liquid Sky."

General Andrews added the support Camille needed. "I agree," he said. "We need to know what Liquid Sky knows. If this technology exists, and there is already a secret weapons program under way as the NSA report suggests, will Liquid Sky sell it on the open market? Will they operate a clandestine marketplace? Are there weapons? What makes them different? Can we protect ourselves? The questions are endless, but the answers we have at this time could fit on a matchbook."

Pierson thanked him for his opinion.

I'll say this in conclusion, sir," added Andrews. "We do not have control of this situation."

Harry Pierson nodded. "Good point."

Hank Andrews stood up and stepped back to the white board hanging on the wall behind him opposite the president. He grabbed a marker and drew a big circle. Inside the circle he wrote "Liquid Sky."

"Assuming it actually exists, Liquid Sky owns the technology,'" he said poking the tip of the marker inside the circle he'd drawn. The marker dotted the board as he continued speaking. "Which means Liquid Sky has all the power."

He indicated the circle. "This is the circle of power." He labelled it as such.

He then drew a wavy line at the top of the white board well above the circle of power. "This is us, Mr. President. We're far removed from the circle of power."

Camille didn't like the direction this was heading. At the same time, she needed anything to persuade the president to look further into gravity power and drop his crazy idea about taking on the EU.

"Why does that worry you so much, General?" she asked.

Andrews' steely eyes narrowed. "Where do I begin?" he said matter-of-factly. "For starters, I'm assuming that gravity power functions as long as there is gravity present. Accordingly, Liquid Sky could develop an entirely new generation of fighter aircraft, missile technology, and ground-combat vehicles that are not limited by conventional miles-per-gallon. As such, it would redefine strike capabilities. With new propulsion systems, the physical requirements of our aircraft could potentially be lessened. Is it possible to design a new generation of combat aircraft that is even more undetectable than our stealth technology? We just don't know."

He drew arrows radiating out from the Liquid Sky circle of power. He labelled each line by weapon type.

"The list goes on and on, Mr. President. For example, consider our friends in North Korea. Current intercontinental-ballistic-missile technology limits them from striking the United States with a nuclear payload. They haven't figured it out yet. Well, if by using gravity power, they have access to new technology that allows them to strike anywhere in the world, what then?

"Can you imagine the instability when the world wakes up one day and discovers some guy named Rickey Ormand owns the key to a technological Pandora's Box that could level the world?"

"Global panic," shouted Harry Pierson. "It would be mass hysteria." He tossed his pen onto the table. "Liquid Sky could become a monolithic supplier of military technology that could overturn the world's military power structure overnight."

General Andrews snapped his fingers. "Bingo."

He turned back to the white board and wrote: Liquid Sky = Threat #1 and underlined several times for emphasis. "Threat number one, Mr. President. Threat number one."

Everyone was silent. Pierson stared at Camille. "Camille, I don't know whether to hug you for bringing this to our attention or lock you away for ruining my day."

"I'll hold out for a third choice," replied Camille. She looked casual enough. In truth, her head was spinning. None of this ever occurred to her. Why would it? She wasn't wired for this kind of stuff. Her brain filtered out negativity, she thought to herself; these people actually seek it out. Is it any surprise they find what they're so determined to find?

General Andrews picked up a red marker and drew a second wavy circle around the circle of power. "The degree of instability is unimaginable. We all heard Lonny Harris explain the depth of the economic fallout that would ensue from a new technology that radically displaced oil and gas. Now add to that new military threats that were the stuff of science fiction yesterday. Maybe even space travel is impacted? Who knows what this Rickey Ormand guy has in his Pandora's Box? Plain and simple, Mr. President, we must figure out if this gravity power really exists."

"And if it does?" asked Pierson.

General Andrews drew a deep breath. "If it does, I strongly advise you to control the technology by any means necessary." He drew a thick black line around Liquid Sky. "Wall off Liquid Sky, Mr. President. Box in Rickey Ormand."

Harry Pierson sat back and took in the board. "Thank you, Hank."

The general returned to his seat and sat quietly with the rest of them like a churchgoer does while waiting for the rest of the parish to take communion.

It was Camille who broke the silence. "We should be doing exactly the opposite. We should be breaking down walls, not erecting them," she said. "This is amazing technology that could better the world."

The president wagged his finger at her, indicating for her to stop talking. He looked at his watch. He opened the brown portfolio containing his schedule for the rest of the day.

"Okay, listen up," he announced. "Here's what we're going to do."

Everyone sat upright, leaned in, and prepared to take notes except for Camille.

"Put your pens down," said Pierson. "No written notes."

They did as instructed. He turned to Jennifer Daly. He instructed her to, "Collect everyone's phone and leave them outside."

The vice president did as she was told and promptly returned to her seat.

"No recordings," he said. "No notes, no recordings, no minutes, no leaks. If I so much as hear one single word of this anywhere outside this room, I'll know it came from one of you. I'll get rid of all of you, and so help me God I'll see to it that every agency at my disposal makes your lives living hell for as long as I hold this office. Do I make myself absolutely clear? I mean crystal clear?"

Everyone nodded and voiced their consent.

"Good. Now that we've established my expectations, let me tell you what we're going to do about Mr. Ormand and his little black box of magic tricks."

He turned to Jennifer Daly. "How generous was Ormand during Beck's campaign?"

She returned a disapproving look. "Not very. Like everyone else in Silicon Valley, he depends on India, Pakistan, and China for engineers. He was... how should I put this? He was stridently opposed to President Rosemore's push to restrict immigration. If I'm not mistaken, he chairs the *Freedom of Movement, Freedom of Ideas Foundation*."

The president looked angry. "Well la-dee-da. Mr. Ormand is one of those. He considers himself special. So then, we'll treat him that way. At this point, it seems Liquid Sky might pose an imminent threat to national security. That determination is really all we need to bring the hammer down hard enough to crack this guy's coconut in half."

Pierson looked at General Andrews and smirked. The general returned a nod and a wink. Camille caught it. So good ol' boy, she thought, shaking her head. Somehow, she figured, this was all going to end very badly, and that would be a shame.

Harry Pierson stood up and collected his things. "I think it's safe to say we no longer require the Italians in order to make our mark in history. I strongly disagree with Lonny Harris's suggestion that the United States would use critical economic data in a pernicious way against its allies."

He smiled at Camille. "You have your wish, Camille. For the immediate future, Liquid Sky needs to be brought under this administration's control by any means necessary. I don't care what it takes. If my attorney general has to devise a way to take over that damned company, so be it. We are going to wall off Liquid Sky no matter what it takes. As for Rickey Ormand, we are going to box him in, at least until I understand exactly what he has and what he intends to do with it."

Pierson put his papers back on the table, rested his hands on the table top as well, and spoke plainly. "Look, people. I don't know what this guy is hiding. But he's sure as hell is hiding something. I want to know what it is. If it's something I want, some sort of technology that will reinvent the energy world and maybe power up a new era of American military might, then we'll take it. I don't care how. I don't care what it takes… in the name of national security, whatever the AG decides. Whatever label we have to pin on it, Ormand will have no choice. There's no way this thing can be allowed to run loose in the marketplace, do you understand me? No way. The world as we know it will disappear overnight. And with it, all the privilege each and every one of our supporters enjoys. I can't let that happen, not on my watch."

Something occurred to Jennifer Daly. "Harry, are you suggesting that this administration step in and take over a private company in order to take control of their proprietary technology?"

Pierson was caught off guard. It was such a pointed question, so carefully worded. He looked Big J.D. over for a moment. "To clarify,

Jennifer, it was Camille O'Keefe who posited the idea that we investigate Liquid Sky more thoroughly. Like she said, we need to know if there is an energy technology. We need to know if any military applications exist. I completely agree with Camille. If such technology exists, it's in the best interests of the United States to take them under control in the name of national security."

He smiled at Jennifer Daly. "Is there any question that something like this is best placed safely within the confines of government control?"

Nobody answered. Camille looked over to Lonny Harris. The two commiserated through a silent stare.

Camille was the last to leave the Sit Room. She sat quietly running it through in her head a few times over, trying to comprehend what just went down. At least the whole Italian plot was shelved, she thought. That was a triumph for sure. But now, she and the president were in direct opposition regarding Liquid Sky. She wanted to share this amazing new technology with the world; Harry Pierson wanted to grab it for himself and stash it in a vault.

She didn't trust him. She never did. She only turned to him when she had no choice. She went back to her office and dialed Pierson's cell.

"I would like to ask a favor," she said when he answered.

"And what might that be?" asked the president.

"Let me see what I can find out about this gravity power before you go after Ormand with guns blazing."

Pierson was intrigued. "Really? What do you have in mind?"

"Earlier, when I brought up the topic in the first place, I mentioned that I watched a video of Parker Fitzgerald on YouTube. She works for Liquid Sky."

Pierson snapped his fingers. "The she-bot."

Camille bobbed her head. "Yes, yes, the she-bot. She heard about me from the whole *Boko Haram* thing and wants to meet me. I researched her and there's some sort of big Liquid Sky gala coming up. Get me into the gala. I can work my way around and find out what I can. You know how people like to tell me things, Harry. It's what I do, after all."

"Great idea," said Pierson. "Get someone inside the circle of power, right? I like it. It looks like the Red Dragon Lady is going undercover. Oh, and by the way, I don't remember any of this conversation."

"Of course not," she replied.

"You're coming along quite nicely, O'Keefe."

"Thanks," she answered. "It's a good thing I'm not trying to make it in this town."

Camille hung up and smiled. "We'll see who has the power," she whispered to herself.

Chapter 15

When Camille first heard the particulars of Harry Pierson's scheme to "get my hands on that arrogant prick's gravity machine or whatever the hell it is Rickey Ormand's got," she was less than thrilled. His plan was certainly less sinister than his designs for the EU. She had to applaud herself for sticking it out through that roller-coaster of a decision-making process in the Sit Room. On the face of it, investigating Liquid Sky made common sense and represented an unusual departure for Harry Pierson.

Camille relished the moment in retrospect. Had Beck been sitting at the head of the table, he wouldn't have permitted her to be in the same wing of the White House, let alone actually participate in making a major decision. More likely, Beck would have found some other moment to ridicule her mercilessly in front of as many staffers as possible, humiliating her to teach her a lesson about having opinions regarding matters that were clearly over her frazzled little head. He wouldn't have slugged her in the privacy of their bedroom, but she hurt just the same.

Reservations aside, she acknowledged that Harry Pierson asked her to join his ticket and also included her in major decisions. That, in itself, moved her light years ahead of where she was mired with

Beck. Camille had no illusions about what went down in the Sit Room. It meant a lot to her that the president included her in the meeting. For the most part, though, he paid her some lip service to help build her clout. She knew that. It was General Andrews that really tipped the scale in favor of pursuing Liquid Sky rather than the Italian bond scheme.

Camille couldn't help smiling. What an odd alliance. It wasn't even an alliance at all but rather some sort of strange alignment of totally disparate agendas. Perhaps, she thought, politics held more surprises than she originally thought. She was optimistic about the universe of possibilities open to her. Still, that good-ol'-boy thing between Pierson and Andrews worried her. It worried her a lot. Her intuition told her there was a heavy conflict building on the horizon and that she would find herself sitting smack-dab in the eye of the storm.

She didn't have much time to think about it. Pierson's approval for her to attend the Liquid Sky gala on a fact-finding mission meant she had to reorient herself and do it quickly. Pierson's people built a cover story for her. It was simple enough. The best covers are. San Francisco – that's where they were sending her the weekend of the Liquid Sky gala. They couldn't just call Liquid Sky and request a spot on the guest list for Camille, nor could she simply show up at Ormand's door. That would raise too many red flags if he was, in fact, hiding some sort of secret weapons program or anything clandestine involving gravity power.

"Less than innocuous," was how Pierson phrased it. For a man like him, that was never a good thing to be. "We can't have Camille O'Keefe fishing for an invite like Charlie Sheen trying to work his way into a party at the Playboy mansion."

But if Camille happened to be in the area at the time, if she happened to be, say, in San Francisco as part of her campaign for the vice presidency, it would seem like a tremendous boon for Rickey Ormand to land a guest as distinguished as Camille O'Keefe. Little did he know. The plan was to dangle her out there right in Ormand's back yard. Pierson knew the Liquid Messiah could never resist reeling in such a prized catch for his trophy wall. It was planned out exquisitely. Camille had little more to do than fly cross-coast and be herself. "The rest," explained Harry Pierson "will take care of itself." She would do a book signing at City Lights Booksellers, the fabled, beat-era bookstore started by Lawrence Ferlinghetti and frequented by all the famous beatniks, including Ginsberg, Keenan, and Kesey. Pierson's people arranged the event, which included her signing copies of her heart-wrenching exposé *This Soul's Journey through the Eye of the Storm*. In addition, Camille would share her thoughts on the role of global conflict in shaping modern U.S. foreign policy. The president had no qualms given the "bunch of leftists and Sixties throwbacks" that would make up the majority of the audience.

The event was more than a cover. Much like Camille herself, it doubled as a campaign stump speech. Nothing could be less Camille and more Harry Pierson. The president's people scripted the words to put in Camille's mouth. In deference to her, they kept it mercifully short. It was more of an indoctrination than anything else. Everyone including Camille knew a topic like that would be a tough sell in a city like San Francisco, not to mention a vanguard poetry shop like City Lights. That was the point. That's why Pierson picked her as his running mate. These were the voters he hoped to pull over.

In her pre-event briefing, one of the White House publicists advised that she "consider it a sort of hazing. It's part of the process."

To which Camille replied, "That will certainly come in handy the next time I decide to rush a sorority and do some keg stands."

At Camille's insistence, however, her short stint in San Francisco included her doing a tarot reading for three random people in the audience. Harry Pierson didn't know what the hell that was, but he didn't really have a choice if he wanted Camille to run this op.

"Out of curiosity, what are you reading?" he inquired.

"Their cards," she said.

"Like, their business cards?" asked the president. "You can vibe them or something that way?"

"Yes... exactly," said Camille. Harry Pierson liked the idea that his running mate was out on the campaign trail beaming her pearly whites and flipping her waves of ginger locks. Camille liked the idea that her running mate had no clue she was talking about reading tarot cards not business cards, and she would woo her way right through his otherwise stolid defenses.

That's how they got along, each of them turning a blind eye to what the other favored most. It's what most marriages lacked.

After receiving her orders, Camille had just one point to make. "How do you know Ormand will take the bait? I mean, that's what I am, right? Bait. You want him to reel me in so you can get your hands on his goodies while he's thinking he's going to get his hands on mine. You obviously have your own designs for the technology. I don't believe for a second that your goal is simply to prevent global instability. After all, you were just detailing a scheme for creating massive problems in the EU. So, I am more than a little bit suspicious, Harry Pierson."

The president grinned. "Kudos to you, Camille O'Keefe. I might make a politician out of you yet. Listen, I like you in this role. I like you in public developing opportunities for me. More to the point, I like you in this op. I think you're exactly the kind of–"

"Bait," she interjected.

"Person," said Pierson.

"Bait," she said again.

He paused, choosing his words carefully. "How about this? I like you out there like my falcon tacking down prey and bringing it home. Does that image work for you?"

"Just as long as I don't have to perch on your hand," replied Camille. "And, you didn't answer my question. How do you know Ormand will invite me to this grand *soiree* of his? You may be able to control a lot of things, Harry, but these tech billionaires aren't exactly puppets on a string. They can be an unruly bunch."

"Ah, yes," said Pierson. "Those pesky Silicon Valley liberals and their sweatshirts."

Camille corrected him. "They're called hoodies now, Harry. I think the sweatshirts went out with *FlashDance*."

The president stood up to see Camille off. He had a large grin on his face. "It's time to go to work, Camille. You're going to earn your field badge."

Camille cocked her head and smiled. "At least I still amuse you, Harry."

"Let me teach you something about power, Camille. It takes something intangible to get to the level we're at. I say 'we' because I'm including you in this. I am the most powerful man in the world. If all goes according to plan, you will be the most powerful woman in the world."

He waved his hand in the air as if swatting away some gnats. In actuality, he was clearing away a few counterpoints that popped into his head. "Yeah, yeah," he said. "The Chancellor of Germany is a woman. But that's Germany. Nobody cares. The reality of the situation is this, Camille. It takes a certain intangible quality, something totally unique that separates you from all the rest. You have your powers of intuition. People gravitate to you. Run with it. Lead the pack."

"I knew you were going to say that," she joked. "My intuition told me so."

"Indeed," said Harry Pierson. "That idiot Beck never understood your power. I do."

Camille lowered her eyes. The mention of her ex-husband and dead president still stabbed her soul. "So, what's your superpower, Harry?"

Pierson stroked his chin. "Knowing what makes a person tick. I mean really knowing what buttons to push."

Camille laughed. "So, you're a super button pusher? My God, do you have any idea how funny you really are?"

The president laughed a bit, too. "Yeah, you and I see people differently. How do you put it? I see people as a panel with a bunch of buttons, and you see them as... how do you put it?"

Camille swept her red hair to one side. "Spirits having a human experience not humans having a spiritual experience." she said.

Pierson snapped his fingers. "That's it. Yes, I've got to remember that one. Anyway, you come at it from a different angle. We complement each other."

"Well, it's the truth," Camille interjected.

Amused once more, Pierson smiled again. "For you. But for me, people are nothing more than robots, machines that all share the same circuitry on the most basic level."

"Just a bunch of buttons," said Camille flatly. "That's what makes it so easy for men like you to annihilate masses of people."

Pierson returned a cynical smirk. "Nice try, Red. Of course, on a certain level, you're absolutely correct. Every soldier knows it's easier to kill something that's been dehumanized."

"Someone," said Camille. She was feeling a bit empowered herself.

"Something," reiterated the president. "That's the whole point. Removing the humanity from people is a gift of mine."

The president waved away more of those imaginary gnats. "Sure. You talk about this mother goddess inside all of us. What do you call her?"

"Gaea," clarified Camille.

"Right," said Pierson. "You talk about Gaea the mother goddess inside each of us, and I talk about the motherboard inside each of us. That's what controls all of our basic instincts and stuff like that. We're still just biological robots... like that robo-chick who works for Rickey Ormand."

"Dr. Parker Fitzgerald," said Camille.

"Right. Sounds like she is exactly what I'm talking about. After the mother board and whatever makes a person unique, it's just artificial intelligence."

Camille just stared at him now. The ease with which her running mate and most powerful man in the world transitioned from humanity to circuitry was a clear reminder that she was teaming up with a man who didn't feel very much at all.

"I'm serious," said Pierson. "I'm teaching you something invaluable about power. You have to understand how to make all these robots do what you want. I am an expert at knowing exactly what makes each person – each robot – tick. Once I know what motivates a person, I know exactly what buttons to push. After that, I own them."

Camille looked at her watch. "You must own quite a collection," she said.

Pierson caught the bit of sadness in her tone. He nodded, to himself more than anything. She was going to take some work, this running mate of his. But once he reprogrammed her, once she finally capitulated and allowed herself to fully become the Red Dragon Lady, she would prove an invaluable ally for him and a formidable adversary for anyone standing in his way.

"You really need to get to your next briefing for the op. But as for this Rickey Ormand guy, you wonder how I am so certain he will jump at the chance to land you at his gala?"

"Yes," said Camille. "That was my initial question... so long ago."

"I know these tech types. I know what they can't resist. Rickey Ormand can't resist Camille O'Keefe."

Camille looked disgusted. "It feels good to be pimped out?"

Pierson looked equally repulsed. "Don't be stupid," he retorted. "I'm not talking about sex. Well, not in this instance. Ormand can bang anyone he wants. That's not why he wants you."

"Gee, thanks," said Camille, checking her watch three more times in involuntary succession. "I can't win either way."

"Ricky Ormand wants you because he wants me. He thinks if he can get you on his home turf, he can wow you enough to get a sit down with–"

Camille finished his sentence. "With the most powerful man in the world."

The president nodded. "Exactly. See what I'm saying. The man calls himself the Liquid Messiah, for Christ's sake. The bigger the douche bag, the easier it is to set the hook. It's almost too easy with this guy, although you never know."

"Yes," she said. "Big douche bags are easy prey. Their ego is their Achilles heel."

Pierson wagged his finger. "You are making a left-handed reference to me, of course. But you know from personal experience, Camille, I can be a very dangerous man. That's why you asked me for help in Nigeria. My point is, I know this Ormand guy like a book. Like all those Silicon Valley assholes, he pretends to be above everybody else. But guess what? He's a robot like everyone else. I've read the owner's manual a thousand times. He's looking to take this gravity-drive thing to the next level. People think Rickey Ormand wants to improve the world, but he knows he needs me in his corner. That's why he needs you."

Camille was interested by something Pierson glossed over. "So Ormand doesn't want to improve the world?"

Pierson shook his head. "Not really. That's the story he spins out there for the masses of people who don't know any better. All those arrogant pricks in Silicon Valley like to paint themselves as great saviors and altruists. Let me tell you something, Camille. It's a bunch of bullshit. Rickey Ormand doesn't want to improve the world. He wants to control it. Rickey Ormand wants to be the most powerful man in the world, a world that—"

Camille finished his sentence yet again. "A world that he creates and controls. I see where you're going with this."

"You're starting to see the big picture now, Camille. That's a good thing, believe me. Rickey Ormand isn't the kind of man to settle for what a thousand other men have. No… no, not this guy," he said suddenly pensive. "This guy wants it all."

"And he thinks he has it with this gravity thing," confirmed Camille. "I get it."

The president smiled and nodded. "Indeed. This is a big deal, Camille, a really big deal. It's a matter of national security."

"National security," repeated Camille through tightly-pursed lips.

Pierson nodded again and walked Camille to the door. "Sending you in is like a rope-a-dope. The prick is scheming to gain an audience with me." He snickered. "But really, I want an audience with him. That's why you're going to deliver a message for me, in person, right there at Liquid Sky, right there at Rickey Ormand's magnificent celebration of his own grandiosity. And the way things are going now, if he doesn't watch his step, his ass and his invention will belong to me."

Camille looked at him. "You mean it will belong to the American people."

The president gestured his acknowledgement. "*Touché*. But of course, my dear. That's what I meant to say. National security is always about the American people. I am in office solely to serve the people... as you so often like to remind me."

"I can't be anything other than be myself," she replied, a twinkle in her eyes.

Pierson touched his index finger to the side of his nose. "Exactly."

Chapter 16

Not long thereafter and exactly as Pierson predicted, Rickey Ormand snapped at the bait. Pierson couldn't have scripted it better had he been sitting next to Ormand when the tech mogul read in the *Mercury News* that Camille O'Keefe was coming to San Francisco for a book signing. As luck would have it, it was the same weekend as his gala. As the Liquid Messiah sat having breakfast in the massive formal dining room of his residence, Liquid Palace, his mind was frenzied about the countless ways he could garner even more notoriety for his grand event. And of course, making friends with Camille O'Keefe would open a direct channel with President Harry Pierson. Ormand's grin grew bigger and bigger as he played it out in his head. Suddenly, the grand dining room of Liquid Palace seemed to him the center of the universe.

Calling Liquid Palace a personal residence was like calling the Palace of Versailles a country estate. Liquid Palace was Rickey Ormand's homage to himself and to the greatness of his imagination. The rectangular dining room where Ormand ate breakfast every morning was massive and decorated in ornate rococo style. The inlaid wood flooring was intricate in design, a series of interconnected three-dimensional cubes accented with four different shades of contrasting parquet. Gold leaf adorned the elaborate moldings and framed the many frescos running around the perimeter of the walls just below the ceiling. The ceiling itself was a marvellous display of plaster Archangels, trumpets raised to lips, and enough gold leaf to cast a warm golden glow over the entire space below. The massive chandelier was crafted from the finest Murano crystal and gleamed like the North Star above the long dining table that seemed to stretch on forever.

Designed as a reformulation of the Oval Salon in the *Hôtel de Soubise* in Paris, the dining room was but one of the many lavish excesses Ormand dreamed up for his palace, which was, more than anything else, a message to the world that he was a new type of monarch. It was important to him to be seen as sitting atop the growing pile of wealthy tech entrepreneurs. Indeed, the growing number of wealthy tech gurus represented for Ormand a burgeoning new class that would inevitably rule the world behind the great, amorphous cloak known as "the cloud." Ormand believed whole-heartedly that this new ruling class would overthrow the old-guard *illuminati* and drive the world forward into modernity. It was all good so long as Ormand felt like he was controlling that revolution.

The table where Ormand sat was long enough to accommodate thirty guests, on par with a regal state dinner. Every morning the Liquid Messiah made an odd figure sitting at one end of the giant table, hoodie-clad, eating alone save for the staff as he worked his way through the stack of newspapers that sat neatly piled next to him like a stack of pancakes.

The whole thing seemed a bit lonely to the household staff at large. Not so for Rickey Ormand. He cherished those few moments of solace and solitude, the quiet before the storm that beset him each work day. He enjoyed the escape of consuming the morning news, searching for mention of himself. He was the center of his universe.

He pushed back the baggy sleeve of his $1,200 maroon Plain hoodie and glanced at his original-issue, 1934 Ingersoll Mickey

Mouse watch. 6:15 in the morning. He knew Parker Fitzgerald was up. He assumed robots didn't sleep.

The more he thought about it, the more he liked it. Camille O'Keefe would be a delicious prize, a rare delicacy in a buffet for guests who had every conceivable amenity at their disposal. That settled it. Rickey Ormand was determined to land Camille O'Keefe at his gala. Who in Silicon Valley could top that? He smiled lasciviously just thinking about it. Camille O'Keefe... First Lady, vice presidential running mate, best-selling author, transcendental medium, spiritual warrior, and inspiration to women the world over... the list went on and on.

Ormand figured it was a can't lose situation. He was totally stoked. As with Burning Man, he was looking for something big, really big, to keep him on the front pages for another few months until his first Liquid-Drive product was ready for release. Parker Fitzgerald was the perfect card to play. Woman to woman, thought Ormand, Fitzgerald, the Phoenix, and the Red Dragon Lady together under his roof. Their meeting would elevate Liquid Sky to another level of credibility. He had to have it. His P.R. people could spin out some crap about emotional IQ and all that.

Once he had Camille O'Keefe under his thumb, he could get to the president. He could get to Harry Pierson. Parker Fitzgerald would slip inside and leave the lock open. After that, he would slip right in Camille's back door.

He tossed the newspaper aside and swallowed his mouthful of poached egg. "Someone find Parker Fitzgerald," he barked. "Bring her to me right now."

One of the domestic staff squaring away the room put down the bouquet of flowers she was arranging on the marble-topped buffet behind Ormand. Like all the other women on the domestic staff, she was Latina, fully documented, no older than thirty-five, pretty without being conspicuously "hot," and dressed in classic French black-and-white with skirt at or below the knee, never above it.

"I will arrange it, Mr. Ormand," she said.

Ormand half-turned and responded over his shoulder. "Send a car to her place. Use that new guy. That buffed-up guy? Looks like Rickey Martin. What's his name?"

"Humberto Salvador?" said the woman.

Ormand picked up another paper and began scanning the first few pages. "Humberto, sure, if you say so. Whatever. Fitzgerald loves the guy. Use him."

The maid requested clarification. "What shall the driver tell Dr. Fitzgerald?"

"Just tell the driver I said not to return without her, or he can look for another job."

"Tell Humberto?" clarified the woman.

Ormand huffed aloud but did not turn from his paper. "Jesus Christ, stop asking me asinine questions and bring me Parker Fitzgerald," he yelled.

The maid quivered a bit when he yelled. Then she beat it out of there to find Humberto.

Ricky Ormand peered out from his paper and looked at the plate sitting in front of him… mocking him… taunting him. The offender in question was a green goddess, sausage, and mozzarella "V-egg" vegan omelette.

His mood turned instantly. He got like that sometimes in the morning, especially when his stomach was grumbling. "And can someone please get this crap out of here," he growled. This was definitely not how he wanted to start this day.

Immediately, a buff and bronzed young man sporting a tight cut that framed his dark, penetrating eyes and cleft chin stepped forward. It was Dirk, a butler of sorts in charge of the four domestic staff working breakfast service.

Dirk wasn't quite sure what crap Ormand was referring to. "Are you referring to the newspapers, Mr. Ormand?"

Ormand looked up and scrunched his face. "Really, dude? Um, no. I am referring to whatever it is you allowed the chef to place upon my plate. I thought you liked me, Dirk?"

The butler wore a look halfway between hurt and distress.

Ormand kept his gaze locked on him like he was targeting through a scope. "You look confused, Dirk."

Dirk did his best to clear all expression from his face lest he antagonize the tech mogul. He tried to explain his confusion. "It's just that… well… there's sausage and green goddess in your omelette. And those are V-eggs, Mr. Ormand. It's a fabulously healthful combination, and, I should add, quite the rage in San Francisco."

Ormand laughed to himself. Not only did Dirk like balls, he evidently had a brass pair on him, as well. "Healthful, huh? San Francisco? I bet it's real popular in West Hollywood, too, huh?"

Ormand tossed the newspaper he was holding on top of the offending meal. "Dirk, is there some sort of conspiracy to turn me into a vegan?" he asked.

Dirk wasn't at all surprised by Ormand's acerbity. He returned a vaguely vacuous smirk. "Not that I'm aware of, Mr. Ormand. It's more of a personal choice."

Ormand chuckled. "Yes, we must be very picky about what we put in our mouths, Dirk." He pushed his chair back abruptly. "Let me explain something to you, Dirk. The word 'omelette' refers to eggs. The word 'egg' refers to the white, oval thingies squatted out of a hen. That's what I want. Does that make sense to you?"

Dirk steepled his fingers and bowed slightly. "Understood, Mr. Ormand."

Ormand returned a sardonic, tight-lipped fake smile. "So, please remind the chef he works for me. If I find anymore sausage or green whatever on my plate, I'm going to replace him with a teenager from McDonald's and save a ton of money in the process."

The chef in question, Bernard LeGrange, happened to be Dirk's lover. And although Dirk had no clue that Bernard's real name was Barry Lefkowitz, he knew enough to understand what happened to people who found themselves under the scrutiny of Rickey Ormand.

"I will tell Bernard to make you a real-egg omelette right away, Mr. Ormand." He tried not to show the disgust he was feeling just thinking about eating chicken fetuses.

Ormand pinched the bridge of his nose. "You know what?" he said. "Never mind. Just send somebody to get me a couple of sausage McMuffins with egg before I get hungry. You won't like me when I'm hungry."

Dirk nodded. "Yes, Mr. Ormand." He turned to leave.

Ormand cleared his throat conspicuously. Dirk stopped and turned back. Ormand waved his hands at the plate still sitting in front of him. "You can take this with you... please."

Dirk quickly removed the plate and fled to the kitchen where he knew Bernard would hurl it clear across the room. It wouldn't be the first time. It happened at home, too. Occasionally, things escalated to physical violence when Bernard got upset, but only at home, only when nobody else was around to witness him hit Dirk. But Dirk figured he had it coming and would do his best not to upset his sensitive, artistic lover.

The emotional turmoil in the kitchen never reached Rickey Ormand. Even if he knew how upset his chef would be or how violent he could get at home, Ormand had but one person on his mind – Camille O'Keefe, the Red Dragon Lady. If he could get her on board with his grand vision, he could work his way right to the president. From there, the possibilities for power and influence were boundless. What he could offer Harry Pierson in terms of gravity power no president could resist. Ormand knew that. He also knew that the real power of gravitational energy had nothing to do with replacing fossil fuels or designing new cars. No, the crux of his radical new technology boiled down to one thing and one thing only for Rickey Ormand – the power to completely reshape the world.

What president could turn that down? What man could turn that down? If Liquid Sky were the preeminent technology company in the world now, what would it become after gravity power became a reality and Ormand joined forces with the president of the United States? If Rickey Ormand was one of the richest and most brilliant men in the world, what would he become after joining forces with a man like Harry Pierson? The world was what it was, as it had been for the last century. What would it become after he and Pierson crafted a brave new future led by Liquid Sky and Liquid-Drive?

This was the question Ormand replayed in his mind over and over again. Any way he cut it, it turned up chocolate chips. He loved it. He got giddy just thinking about it despite his disappointing breakfast. Let people think what they want, he thought to himself. A new ruling class was about to be forged, and all anybody would see is the façade of a new energy source. What he was building behind the scenes was something much more powerful... a new ruling class.

By the time Parker Fitzgerald finally arrived, Ormand had finished with his papers along with six cups of coffee. When she walked into the dining room, he was scribbling copious notes outlining everything he wanted to cover when he met Camille at the gala and, more importantly, with Harry Pierson thereafter. The list was growing by the minute.

He turned and scanned his creation up and down. She was wearing dark-blue skinny jeans, off-white ostrich-skin cowboy boots with teal tooling that matched her black-and-teal leather belt accented with a blingy rhinestone buckle. Her white, designer button-down fit just snugly enough for Ormand to discern the shapeliness of her breasts while still remaining clean-cut and professional by Silicon Valley standards.

Her blonde hair, now cut pixie style, gave her a spritely air as she seemed to glide over without the slightest hitch in her stride. Those robotic legs of hers were truly a work of art, thought Ormand as he admired the Phoenix like Michelangelo admired his David. Her pins were absolutely perfect, no way to tell they were artificial even in skinny jeans. His eyes lit up and grew to the size of biscuits when he spied the McDonald's bag in her hand.

"My God," he said. "Only the Phoenix would wiggle a pair of skinny jeans over a set of robotic legs. You look amazing. Nobody would ever know. I can't wait to see what they look like at the company Beach Blast in July. You know your synthetic skin actually tans."

Parker Fitzgerald gave him a disgusted look. "That's almost as creepy as the Frankenfood you're about to eat."

Ormand threw his hands up. "Speaking of which, you are truly a welcome sight in more ways than one. I'm starving. Not to mention that I have some big news for you."

Fitzgerald grabbed a seat at the table and slid the coveted food bag over to her boss. "I hate to see a starving billionaire. We can't have you malnourished, can we? Who would rule the world if you were gone?"

"You read my mind, Fitzy. How do you do that? Hey, you should be thanking me. I sent that stud driver Hugo to pick you up."

"You mean, Humberto?" she said.

"Yeah," he replied. "What you said. I think you have the hots for him, robo-gal." Ormand smiled widely, revealing a mouthful of McMuffin.

Fitzgerald made a sour face. "Please swallow before you talk. I don't know how you eat that crap first thing in the morning. I mean, there's not even any tequila to denature all the carcinogens."

Ormand laughed. "That's right. I forgot about your love affair with tequila." He took another ravenous bite. "As for me, I would love some Mickey D's."

Fitzgerald leaned in, filled an empty coffee mug from the carafe sitting between them, and breathed in the aroma emanating from the steaming coffee. "Clears the senses."

"Tell me about it," he said. "That's the third carafe this morning."

Dirk walked in briskly carrying a service tray.

"And here's my breakfast," said Fitzgerald, sitting up straight. "I asked my 'stud' driver to have the kitchen whip me up something considering you had him drag me out of bed."

Ormand polished off the first breakfast sandwich, balled up the familiar yellow wrapper, and tossed it in the bag. "I figured you would have dragged him into your bed."

Fitzgerald looked queasy. "Creepy again, Rickey. Very creepy."

Ormand smiled like a misbehaving boy as he wiped his mouth with the sleeve of his Plain hoodie, making it a $1,200 cloth napkin.

Dirk arched his brow sharply and shot Parker a glance while he laid the service tray in front of her. He lifted the cover off the plate revealing a perfectly-folded V-egg omelette exactly like the one Ormand rejected earlier. It was accompanied by a tall glass of something viscous and green.

Rickey Ormand looked at his prized scientist in disbelief. "Tell me that's not the same mess you tried to serve me this morning, Dirk."

Dirk looked at the Liquid Messiah with the flattest affect as he could muster. "It is, Mr. Ormand. I mean... uh, sorry, not the same omelette that was on your plate but the same type of omelette." He omitted the fact that, as predicted, chef Bernard launched Ormand's spurned plate across the kitchen.

Parker Fitzgerald was delighted. "Wow, Rickey. I didn't peg you as a sausage and mozzarella kind of guy. I'm impressed."

"Don't be," said Ormand in disgust.

"He sent it back," whispered Dirk as he leaned to refill Fitzgerald's coffee. "Look what he's putting in his mouth," he whispered again.

Ormand pointed the remains of his second McMuffin. "Watch your step there, Dirky. Let's not get into what we put in our mouths."

"Oh, stop, Rickey," said Fitzgerald. "We're just busting your chops. This isn't the East Coast, it's Palo Alto. We're happy to be different. Look at us. I'm half a robot and you're a billionaire CEO who thinks a hoodie is a suit coat."

Dirk took that as his cue to go stand attentively back by the buffet.

Fitzgerald raised her glass. "Here's to my green goddess." She plunged her upper lip in deep enough to leave a green moustache.

In return, Ormand tore a savage bite from the remains of his second McMuffin, chewed it into a brown, pasty mash, and then opened his mouth to taunt Fitzgerald.

"Okay, John Belushi," she said. "You win."

Ormand washed down the mouthful of muck with a loud slurp of coffee. "Don't fret, Fitzy. The java is organic, fair trade, rain-forest certified, and no slave-labor brewed."

Fitzgerald laughed and began eating. "So, what's this big news you have that prompted you to drag me from my lovely slumber. I didn't even have a chance to oil my hips."

Ormand balled up the second sandwich wrapper and stuffed it in the bag. "Well," he said, "you're right."

Fitzgerald put her utensils down delicately as if she were the Queen of England. "Wow, that was a rare occurrence. I may bring you Frankenfood every day. What, pray tell, was I right about?"

He pushed up the sleeves of his hoodie and rested his arms on the table. His vintage Mickey Mouse watch seemed both perfectly at home and conspicuously juxtaposed at one and the same time. "I always win. That's what you said, and you're right. But everything I've achieved–"

She cut him off. "You mean everything *we've* achieved. I don't see you missing the lower half of your body."

Rickey smiled. "Point taken, Fitzy. But then again, you owe me your life." He paused for effect. "I have something else to tell you. It's pretty big actually." He breathed deeply and took a pronounced sip of his coffee.

"Give me one second," he continued. He stood up and summoned Dirk over.

Dirk hustled over. "Yes, Mr. Ormand."

Ormand pulled his baggy sleeves down like they were French cuffs. "Clear the room," he ordered. "Everyone... out now."

Dirk bowed slightly, turned away, and motioned his hands ceremoniously. "*Vamanos, todos.*"

The four women working the room responded immediately. If their alacrity wasn't impressive enough, their attention to detail under pressure was. They buttoned everything up and exited the formal dining room without the least hesitation thereafter.

Parker Fitzgerald sensed the gravity of the moment. She and Rickey always had that sort of brother-sister bond, supportive at times, oppositional at others, platonic always. She polished off her glass of green goddess and slid her plate and the uneaten half of her omelette to the side. She folded her hands on the table.

"So much secrecy, Rickey. You've got my attention. You usually don't order people to vacate your presence until after lunch at the earliest."

Ormand rubbed his hands together like a hungry fat boy contemplating a defenseless dinner buffet. "Guess who's coming to dinner?" he said.

Fitzgerald tongued her top lip. "I assume it's not Sidney Poitier? He's still alive, you know."

Completely off script, Ormand just stared back blankly.

Fitzgerald grimaced. "Really? *Guess Who's Coming to Dinner?* Sidney Poitier... Katharine Hepburn? The famous movie?"

"You're, like, completely derailing my train of thought," said Ormand, a bit flustered.

"I know," replied Parker sitting back and folding her arms across her chest. "It's fun."

Ormand made a series of gesticulations. "Anyway, I was alluding to one Camille O'Keefe, the Red Dragon Lady herself. I do expect to get her here for the gala."

Fitzgerald did a double take. "Wait a minute," she said, barely able to contain her excitement. "Are you telling me that Camille O'Keefe is coming to the gala? For real?"

Ormand held his hands in the air like a boxer after he's announced the winner. "Does Rickey Ormand rock, or what?"

"How did you manage that? She's running for vice president, not to mention the fact that she's, like, one of the most famous women in the world. She kicks ass. I'm a huge fan."

Ormand smiled. "She's doing a book signing at someplace in San Francisco the day before. I bet she's a big fan of yours, too. Think about it. You're the Phoenix and she's the Red Dragon Lady. It's a celebrity friendship made in heaven. And the Liquid Messiah will be right there in the middle."

Fitzgerald watched Ormand stroke his chin gently and dared not speculate on what exactly he was envisioning.

"So, she's coming to Liquid Sky after the signing?"

"Sure," said Ormand. "Great idea. You can tell her when you speak to her."

Fitzgerald was ecstatic. "Speak to her? That's just so amazing." Her thoughts immediately turned to her gown and a million other necessities for the event that suddenly became much more important.

"Yes," said Ormand. "Someone has to invite her to the event."

Fitzgerald's enthusiasm hit a wall. "Wait, what now? So, she hasn't agreed to come to the gala?" She propped her elbows on the table and folded her hands under her chin.

"Well," said Ormand, "the way I figure it, if anyone can get Camille O'Keefe to show up, it's you. Get her publicist's number. It can't be difficult to find. Tell them who you are. Her people will eat it up. Give them the whole spiel about the gala, the announcement, changing the world, all that glitzy sizzle shit. I'll leave that to you."

Fitzgerald sat back and threw her hands up. "Don't you have, like, an army of P.R. people to do this?"

Ormand shook his head. "You and Camille are cut from the same cloth. The Red Dragon Lady and the Phoenix leading people forward into a brave new world. It's so perfect, somebody should write a book, or make a movie, or series, or something like that. I'm telling you, Fitzy, it's perfect."

Parker Fitzgerald knew Rickey Ormand was onto something here. "Not bad," she said, nodding. "I'm not sure exactly what you're up to, but you're definitely up to something."

Ormand cocked his head quizzically. "Really? What on earth do you mean?"

"Oh please, Rickey. I know you too damned well."

"Not buying any of it?" he said.

"Not a word," she said. "What you want is for me to schmooze the next vice president. Knock wood." She rapped her knuckles on the table. "I create a little friendship with Camille O'Keefe, giving you a clear pathway to President Pierson. It has nothing to do with Camille O'Keefe or me. It's all about you. How am I doing?"

Rickey Ormand slapped his palm down on the table. "You are every bit the genius I say you are. Speaking of geniuses, isn't this plan brilliant? I mean… like I said… the Red Dragon Lady side-by-side with the Phoenix. Who can resist that? The two of you might even overshadow my announcement about Liquid-Drive. The media will eat it up."

"Yup," said Fitzgerald. "And I'm sure President Pierson will love it, too. That's why he picked Camille O'Keefe in the first place." She shook her head slowly. "I gotta hand it to you, Rickey. You're a crafty son-of-a-bitch."

Ormand sat back and gloated. "You got that right, sister. And let me tell you something else there, Fitz-O. President Pierson may look like some hip champion of women, but don't kid yourself."

Fitzgerald shrugged. "Never," she said flatly. "Apparently, you've got it all figured out."

"Damned right I do. Let me tell you something, Fitzy. A salty tiger like Harry Pierson doesn't change his spots... ever. You can take that to the bank. It's an immutable fact of human nature. People don't change. The times around them change, and most people die off. And then, of course, there's the few like us. We are the enigma behind the semblance of democracy and normalcy that everybody else calls everyday 'life.'"

He paused and took a long, deep breath. Bacon, Downey, and armpit... the smell of brilliance.

"Trust me," he repeated. "Harry Pierson? He's a cagey son-of-a-bitch. That tiger ain't changing his spots."

Fitzgerald smirked and sniffed a couple of times. "Um, leopard."

Ormand scrunched his wiry brows. "Huh?"

"Tigers don't have spots," she noted. "Leopards do."

Ormand closed his eyes and shook his head slowly. "What is this, *National Geographic*? You know what I mean. That guy is old school. Wasn't he, like, running the CIA at some point? He's one of those scary guys Americans like to put in power."

Fitzgerald laughed. "Which is exactly what you want for yourself. You're funny, Rickey. One of you two men running the world."

"Exactly," said Ormand, completely missing the irony. "That's what I'm saying. Once I get an audience with Harry Pierson, I can explain the real potential of gravity energy. Pierson won't be able to resist. Power... control... influence... the economic and military applications alone are mind boggling. Once the president knows what I have, we'll be in tighter than Haliburton was with Bush and Cheney."

Fitzgerald sighed out loud. "So, you want me to do some P.R., lay the ground work, that sort of thing?"

Ormand nodded. "No, I want you to get Camille O'Keefe to come to the gala. Then I want you to schmooze her shamelessly. Do that voodoo that you do. Reach out and lock it down with Camille O'Keefe. That's all I ask. Get her to my gala by hook or by crook. The two of you can promenade around and work the room. The media will trip over themselves to cover it. Tell her Liquid Sky will provide all the P.R. and media support she wants."

"Whatever she wants, huh?" asked Fitzgerald.

"Read my lips," replied Ormand, slowly accentuating the movement of his mouth. "Whatever Camille O'Keefe wants, Camille O'Keefe gets. Understood? Shit, if this goes according to plan, this empire I've built will look like a sandcastle in comparison to what Liquid Sky will be ten years from now. And rest assured, your role on the business development side will continue to grow."

Fitzgerald bristled when she heard that last bit. "Business development?"

Rickey Ormand stood up abruptly, his chair making a sharp noise as it slid over the parquet. "Yes," he said. "I don't really need more scientists. I've got plenty of the temperamental, socially awkward geniuses working for me. I don't need you in the lab. I need you out there in the world clearing the way for me. It's a much bigger role."

Hearing that she was being shoved out of the lab and onto the rubber chicken circuit offended her. She was about to fire back but thought better of it. For the moment, the chance of meeting Camille O'Keefe eclipsed everything else.

"Okay, Rickey," she said. "Whatever you say. You're the boss."

"I never get tired of hearing that," replied Ormand. "It's a perfect plan, an absolutely perfect plan. It can't fail." He pointed a finger gun at her, dropped the hammer, winked, and was gone.

Chapter 17

Rickey Ormand saw only what he wanted to. He was fixated on Camille O'Keefe and saw her merely as a means to an end. Like so many other men, he underestimated the demure redhead, reducing her to some sort of vapid minion of unremarkable intelligence and thus easily manipulated. As such, his plan to curry the president's favor amounted to little more than wowing his ditzy running mate. He assumed the bedazzling excesses of Liquid Palace ought to do the trick. It usually did. He would also assail her amiable femininity by foisting Parker Fitzgerald on her.

His plan reflected Ormand's philosophy on women as a species. It pretty much boiled down to a single, primitive impulse – security.

"Women only care about one thing," he told a friend whose fiancée insisted on regular shopping trips to Paris and Geneva. "Just one thing. It's simple really. They need to feel safe. What makes them feel safe? Three things – money, money, and more money. Unfortunately for you, your fiancée is a woman."

That was as warm and fuzzy as Rickey Ormand could get. He lacked the genetic makeup for any deeper level of empathy. He carefully crafted the opulence of Liquid Palace to lull women into a deep sense of security, thus rendering them harmless to his ego.

As he explained to his friend whose fiancée had a penchant for Hermès, Chanel, and Dior, "there are some things a man can get from women simply by having a hefty pair of brass balls he can swing around like Thor's hammer. Truly special women, though, require something special. Their senses need to be reeled in by a level of opulence so massive that it suspends reality and makes them feel like they can transcend the total mundaneness of their lives... as women, of course."

Ormand saw only the bait Pierson hung out for him. He did not see Camille O'Keefe the human being. He never saw that big, nasty hook upon which Camille was so delicately bobbing before his eyes. He saw only the glint of his own rising star, not the glint of sharpened, barbed steel. Pierson was counting on Rickey Ormand clinging to his arrogant myopia and delighted in the irony that was actually manipulating Rickey Ormand in exactly the same way Ormand thought he was manipulating Camille. There was just one difference – Pierson, and by extension Camille, saw right through Ormand's thin façade whereas the Liquid Messiah had absolutely no idea he was about to get reamed big time.

A few days later, Parker Fitzgerald reported back that Camille's people jumped at the opportunity. It would take some juggling – Ms. O'Keefe was quite busy – but they would figure out some way to add the Liquid Sky gala to her schedule. Count on her being there.

Both Ormand and Fitzgerald were brimming over with exuberance. Fitzgerald could hardly believe she was going to meet Camille O'Keefe. She'd been obsessed with the idea since Ormand mentioned it. And now, she was actually playing hostess of sorts.

Rickey Ormand saw matters a bit differently. "The hook is set. It's an absolutely perfect plan," he explained. Soon, he thought, he'd have the president as an ally. Damn, it was a perfect plan.

"It's a freaking perfect plan," exclaimed Harry Pierson, gesticulating all over the place, when Camille confirmed that she would wear Christian Lacroix to the Liquid Sky gala.

"Beautiful," he said. "Both you and my plan. It feels good to have that squirmy little bastard right where I want him."

Camille's response was classic. "You know what's funny, Harry? You and Rickey Ormand think you're so different from each other, but it's not so."

Camille occupied a precarious place between two very powerful men. There was no escaping it. The middle ground was the battleground. Camille recognized this; the men did not. Harry Pierson and Rickey Ormand were both so intent on out-maneuvering each other that neither saw the hook Camille cast out. While the men were focused on snagging each other, Camille decided to once again use herself as bait and hook them both. Neither of the men saw it coming.

Camille knew playing games like this could exact a hefty toll, especially if the president felt she was duplicitous or otherwise untrustworthy. But she felt she had to. If there was one single belief, one holy mantra, Camille clung to it: "I answer to a higher power called the Universal Divine."

She said it often, a declaration of her will and intent to stand her ground. It made Harry Pierson chuckle every time without fail, but she was serious. It was the code she lived by, the bedrock of her ethical being. Sometimes it sounded to her more like an apprehensive question than a definitive statement. As she prepared for the gala, she was worried. She had to cast her line carefully lest she wind up hooking herself accidentally like a child.

Chapter 18

Camille looked out the window of Rickey Ormand's personal helicopter, a sharp, black-and-gold Bell 429 GobalRanger with smoked windows and tan leather interior. Ormand had the bird, a favorite among billionaire businessmen, waiting to take Camille from her book signing in San Francisco right to his doorstep in the epitome of style. Camille was a special woman. As such, Ormand dangled as much opulence in front of her as possible. This would give her that sense of security he believed all women craved like an addict and their next fix. A sense of security, he reasoned, would win her trust. Her trust would gain him a new ally in the White House named Harry Pierson.

Ordinarily, Camille wasn't easily swayed by rich boys and their toys. It was all too much fuss. What did it really amount to? But now, as she looked out upon the endless acres of green grass and forest that framed the Liquid Palace grounds in their full majesty, she had to admit that maybe the helicopter ride wasn't such a bad idea after all. She reminded herself that there was such a thing as simply enjoying oneself.

There was much to enjoy about Liquid Palace. It was nothing less than a living monument to spectacular craftsmanship and human

ingenuity. Rickey Ormand built Liquid Palace intending to make
it his full-time residence. The project was like a blank canvas for
Picasso. The $500 million estate was the most expensive in the world,
for the time being at least, although developer and film producer Nile
Niami was said to be designing a Bel Air residence he hoped to list
for over $600 million. For the time being, Ormand's hunger for more
was satiated.

Liquid Palace afforded him and his guests every luxury
imaginable and was maintained by a housekeeping and grounds
crew that was 75 percent A.I. Originally, Ormand's pad was slated to
cost a meager $100 million, give or take. But when he heard Markus
Persson, creator of the ultra-low-tech *Minecraft* video game, built a
house for about the same money, the race was on. There was no way
Rickey Ormand, founder of Liquid Sky and capitalist extraordinaire,
was going to be outdone by a 16-bit Swede.

Rickey Ormand hated *Minecraft* with its low-tech, lo-fi
arrogance. That was the real reason he squished Persson's mansion
under his foot like a bug. Ormand set his sights higher, though.
He sought to create a living space that eclipsed even the famous
Cedars mansion perched high atop *Saint Jean Cap Ferrat*. Once
the home of Belgium's King Leopold II, The Cedars was now the
£860 million retreat belonging to one of his biggest competitors. It
irked him to no end that he could not erect for himself something
grander. When asked bluntly whether he felt overshadowed by
the European opulence of his competitor's *Cote d'Azure* palace,
Ormand bristled in that ornery way of his that his Millennial
followers so loved.

"What America lacks in antiquity, I will make up for with
ingenuity. A Belgian King may not have resided in Liquid Palace, but
what need of a king do Americans have? Quite the contrary, Liquid
Palace reflects America's ability to achieve a great deal in a very
short period of time. No other country in the world is capable of
achieving so much so fast, and there should be a sort of multiplier
added to everything we create. And, I feel obliged to add that my
esteemed competitor now residing where kings once slept did little

more than select the china. I, on the other hand, have built Liquid Palace from the torrent of my imagination, sounding the depth of my creativity in a way I can only compare to Walt Disney."

In a way, he was right. The only thing limiting Liquid Palace was Ormand's imagination because his pockets were certainly deep enough. Despite it's being a completely over-the-top retreat, Liquid Palace impressed visitors for what it offered the average citizen. Anyone visiting Liquid Palace came away with either a newfound or deepened appreciation for Ormand's generosity. He really spared no expense and sought to include average folks. If nothing else, it softened his image and afforded him a bit of good will during one of his "awkward" moments.

This was the other side to Rickey Ormand, the side few saw up close. Despite his arrogance and blind ambition, Ormand sincerely believed he was moving the world forward into a better future for all people. Within his bristly persona, the shell that most often eclipsed his kindness and humanitarianism, there was a core of humanitarianism that shined like an incandescent yolk inside a cracked egg. On a certain level, Rickey Ormand sought to improve life for people. It just wasn't his primary goal. Still, few other men in history had both the grand ideas and the pragmatic wherewithal to turn dreams into reality like Rickey Ormand. And for this, he expected his ring to be kissed.

A walking, breathing paradox to be sure, Rickey Ormand did give back to the public. Tipping the scales in his favor in the court of public opinion was very important to him. Camille O'Keefe may have been a cherished champion of women, but Rickey Ormand was revered by more than only those measuring progress and success by dollars and downloads. He cut across and defied every preconceived stereotype, demographic, or pigeonhole one could come up with.

In Ormand's opinion, few people really wanted to pull back the curtain and discover the wizard was a hoax. "That kind of crap is for bores and revolutionaries. And what have they done for the world?" he was famously quoted as saying in *Rolling Stone*. "The world doesn't need people like that. We need people who can imagine something marvelous and then make it seem real. That's what inspires people. Stripping magic of its sleight of hand is a beastly thing to do. It is the way of the bitter and cynical."

What kind of fun was that? Nobody really cared about what Rickey Ormand was up to so long as he threw money at enough causes and kept pumping out the best, coolest, hippest, mind-blowing tech and toys imaginable. The people wanted cake, so why not give it to them? Let them eat cake. All he had to do was keep the public entertained. His philanthropic giving enabled everyone, including himself, to assuage their guilt.

With this in mind, he designed Liquid Palace to be more like a resort than a house, boasting every amenity, including a casino and a salon and day spa staffed and fully operational before and during special events. The hotel-quality kitchen, overseen by a former executive chef from the Atlantis resort in the Bahamas, could run around the clock if necessary. Ormand even built a little-league stadium to host local tournaments. Escalators, elevators, self-driving golf carts, A.I. people movers of all sorts, even a scaled-down locomotive pulling three wonderful reproductions of Victorian lounge cars running throughout the entire Liquid Palace and Liquid Sky properties teased the imagination of every visitor.

For guests looking to get closer to nature, the Palace stables offered an array of well-bred horses to accommodate riders from children through the most accomplished equestrians. Miles of trails circled the property, and an Olympic-quality jumping course delighted riders looking for something a bit more challenging. Aside from squash, which he played every day, Ormand was an avid polo player. With a scar just below his right eye that made him think he was ruggedly handsome, he was the sort of man who populated the pages of a Kozinski novel in which the churning froth of the equine beast mingles with the odors of aged leather and Ralph Lauren in such a way as to suggest money old and plentiful. The fact that his favorite outfits always seemed to include some sort of $100 T-shirt only served to underscore the casual air about him that only self-made billionaires could sport so well.

A devout bachelor in everyone's best interests, Ormand had no children and only three paternity suits lodged against him, all of which he beat with a simple cheek swab. He may not have been much of an athlete growing up, but he still embraced an idealized notion of Americana with its baseball, hot dogs, and apple pie. He made his Little League stadium accessible to thousands of families participating in youth baseball. Every Memorial Day, Liquid Sky hosted a baseball tournament for kids with serious disabilities in which participating families had free use of the palace grounds. A lifelong Cubs fan and avid statistician, Rickey Ormand made sure Liquid Sky sponsored its own youth baseball team, as well, the Liquid Launch. Their home field sat proudly a few thousand yards from the palace. Built as a mini-replica of Wrigley Field, it was one of his most precious crown jewels.

This miniature Friendly Confines could seat 1,000 spectators in the most comfortable bleachers a suburbanite ass had ever enjoyed, something between a gentle caress and loving squeeze. As if the stadium wasn't enough, Ormand personally designed a quaint Main Street USA that looked like it was time warped from 1955. Built by a company that constructed a number of Hollywood back-lot sets, the elaborate stretch of Americana included everything from a 5$^{\mathbb{C}}$&10$^{\mathbb{C}}$ store to a soda shop, bakery, ice cream parlor, even a drive-up burger joint with roller-skate-and-skirt service. Needless to say, home games were very well attended.

The boat house – as charming as any sitting on the banks of the Schuylkill or Charles Rivers – rested on the thirty-acre lake separating the palace from the Liquid Sky campus. Here, guests utilized recreational watercraft such as paddle boats and sailboats, as well as motorized bass boats should someone wish to grab a rod and test the waters. The lake was so well-stocked with bass, trout, and perch, it was as if Ormand had men under the water putting fish on your hook. If their rod didn't bend, they forgot to tie a hook on.

The whole setup was classic Rickey Ormand. He gave back to the people in exchange for his success. Liquid Palace was his way of paying it forward for the successes of Liquid Sky. This was

Ormand's kinder, gentler side. Make no mistake about it. As much
as Rickey Ormand built Liquid Sky "so that all the good people of
the world could experience first-hand all that America has to offer in
the way of opportunity," he also built it as a monument to himself.
In one interview, he claimed that Frank Lloyd Wright "would look
enviously upon Liquid Palace and rightfully so. I aspire to be the
closest thing to aristocracy we can have in America, which, sadly,
has no royal lineage to speak of. Instead, we depend on the great
entrepreneurs such as myself to hoist this country up to the level of
royalty in the world."

Yes, Rickey Ormand was a paradox. He wanted to touch people
and find within himself some metaphysical meaning in that. But
it was Angry Rickey who broke ground on the Palace like he was
storming Normandy. The project was yet another challenge for him
to prove himself the greatest at everything. Is he really doing that?
How on earth is it so big? That sort of thing. That's what he heard
in his head. He never believed in keeping himself in check. In this
way did the Liquid Messiah fertilize himself. He walked both sides
of Main Street. He wanted to carve out a genuine slice of American
greatness and serve it up to the average family. At the same time, he
was putting on a grandiose show rivaling any Hollywood production
as an *homage* to his own brilliance.

It was a matter of opinion. People who had been to Liquid Sky
came back spreading the praises of the Liquid Messiah, while many
who had never made the trip could easily find all too much. True
to form, Ormand remained focused on his own vision. For him,
Liquid Palace was the city upon the hill, ancient Greece, Atlantis,
and Lemuria rolled into one. More than a residence, more than a
monument, Liquid Palace was as unique an experience as meeting
Rickey Ormand himself.

Good, clean family fun, always congenial and often a bit
whimsical... such was the part of Liquid Palace that was open to the
general public.... The private grounds, on the other hand, housed an
opulent adult playground accessible by invitation only. Within those
confines were unique pleasures and delights that "special" guests

never forgot. The Palace beach, for example, consisted of genuine pink Bermuda sand. The upper pool area, referred to as "The Gables," was modelled after the Biltmore Hotel in Coral Gables, Florida. The pool house was an actual scaled-down, 6,000 square-foot model of the historic hotel itself. The pool was shaped like an immense palm tree to suggest the resort island of Palm Jumeirah in Dubai where Ormand owned several properties personally and Liquid Sky owned a seventeen-story building housing its EMEA headquarters.

Peacocks roamed the private grounds freely. But not all the free-range animals on the property lived as carefree. The exclusive, five-hundred-acre hunting forest was home to almost two-hundred different species of wildlife selected primarily for their wall-mounting appeal and overall tastiness. Although he'd logged hundreds of hours playing *Call of Duty*, Rickey Ormand had never fired a real gun. Inherently distrustful of any animal more feral than a kitten, Ormand delegated complete oversight of the forest to his animal-husbandry team.

The hunting grounds afforded Ormand ample opportunities to rub elbows with many politicians and other rich, influential hunters who visited Liquid Palace for sport. Rarely did Ormand ever join an excursion. That "delicate consistency" thing again. If anything, permitting hunting on his property drew negative attention from activist organizations like PETA who threatened to pillory him publicly unless he agreed to donate an undisclosed number of turkeys to food banks across the state every Thanksgiving. It didn't matter to him. He determined long ago that giving people what they want is the best way to get ahead so long as he convinced them of what they wanted in the first place.

By far, the favorite among private guests was the lower pool area. Referred to as "Eden," it was a lush, adults only, clothing optional paradise. Eden was the site Ormand chose for his yearly Back to Nature *fête,* during which his most privileged guests were permitted to camp overnight in the hunting forest provided they adhered to a strict carry in/carry out policy. Only once did some PETA activists manage to sneak onto the property during the festival. Other than their assemblage of martyrdoms, they did not carry anything in, but they did attempt to carry out as many animals as possible. One activist was severely injured by a particularly nasty beaver.

Hairy, unshaven animal-rights activists notwithstanding, the world's beautiful people fought to make the Liquid Palace guest list for Ormand's premier party of the year, a veritable rite of Spring, an unbridled bacchanalia called Ride the Valkyrie, held every May in honor of Richard Wagner's birthday. Ormand kept his R-rated lagoon fully stocked with a glorious array of California beauties, visionary artists, disaffected writers, trippy musicians, and globe-trotting correspondents as if they were works of art themselves. The lagoon complex even came equipped with a concert-quality stage for impromptu jam sessions and a full-size movie theater complete with snack bar and imitation butter.

It was all part of the creative process for Rickey Ormand. There was no separation between work life and home life for him. In a way, this was his genius. "Liquid Sky... the convergence of mind, body, and spirit. Liquid Sky... propelling humanity into the future." That was one of his corporate tag lines. It described his philosophy for living, and loving, and moving forward into the future.

By design, Ormand was a sworn bachelor with a lyrical sensibility. He let few people in close enough to see that he was at war with himself in his head. Ormand intended the distance between himself and everyone else to be a tangible measure of his prowess. He made similar use of his appearance. He wanted to embody juxtaposition. So, he would often wear a $600 hoodie with, say, tapered Versace slacks and a pair of cheap-ass sneakers to show people he could flaunt convention. Similarly, Ormand had no qualms about stroking his ego in front of his fans. They took it in the face willingly every time. Even so, the rich and powerful hovered around Rickey Ormand because he always made them look both rich and *avant-garde* without expecting them to do much of anything to prove it.

Chapter 19

Ormand instructed his publicists to leak Camille's attendance. On the night of the gala, the grand ballroom in Liquid Palace, modeled after the magnificent ballroom in Blackpool's Tower, was abuzz with anticipation. Everyone wanted to catch a glimpse of the famous redhead in person. Ormand's custom Armani tux fit him to perfection. His yellow-and-red Hermès tie and pocket square danced against his flat-black jacket and crisp white shirt. He looked suave, even debonair. At his side was Dr. Parker Fitzgerald, stunning in an ultra-hip Matija Cop that was part *haute couture* and part industrial Steam Punk with patterns suggesting mechanical design prints. The dress accentuated Fitzgerald's robotics, and it celebrated her marvellous uniqueness.

Camille took it all in. She looked at Parker Fitzgerald in admiration and winked. She then turned her attention to her host, Rickey Ormand. She extended her hand gracefully. Ormand seized it a bit too eagerly with two hands as if greeting a good buddy were he actually to have one. It startled Camille.

"Welcome," said Ormand. "Welcome to Liquid Palace, the most amazing, fantastic place on earth."

A bit put off by her boss's naive exuberance, Fitzgerald interrupted. "She used to live in the White House, Rickey."

245

Ormand leered at Fitzgerald sideways but quickly smiled again for fear of appearing too conniving. "Indeed," he said, bowing slightly to Camille. "It's just that I am so very excited to have you as my distinguished guest."

He bowed again. "Madam First Lady."

There was a brief, uncomfortable silence during which he realized he was still clutching Camille.

He dropped her hand like it was hot toast. "And soon to be vice president, we hope," he added, trying his best to recover.

Camille folded her hands gently at her chest. The gesture was soft but just guarded enough to communicate to him that she was not wide open and unwitting.

"The tux suits you," she said decorously. "It's a nice change."

Parker Fitzgerald snorted. "Ha," she chortled and poked Ormand in the arm. "I do believe she's referring to your collection of fine hoodie wear." She couldn't help chuckling.

"Well," said Camille through an impish smile. "You look so smooth." She applauded herself in her head. Good choice of words, she thought. Smooth... she knew Ormand would eat it up. And he did. He perked right up.

"Oh," he said. "If you put it that way, maybe I can have my guy at Armani design a tux-hoodie for me."

Fitzgerald rolled her eyes and waved to one of the waiters offering flutes of champagne. She then turned her attention to Camille. "Ms. O'Keefe." The two women looked at each other. For the first time in a long time, Dr. Parker Fitzgerald was at a loss for words.

Now it was Rickey Ormand's turn to laugh. "I do believe the good doctor is a bit starstruck." He poked Fitzgerald in the arm.

Camille held out her hand. "Camille," she said to Fitzgerald, who was quite embarrassed. "Call me Camille. We can't very well be friends standing on formalities, now can we?" She twirled her index finger in the air. "What's in a name, anyway?" she said. "It's all so dull and 3-D."

Parker Fitzgerald was delighted. "I love when you say stuff like that. I have read your book twice. And…." She paused. She wondered if she was coming off as too doting. What if Camille really meant that bit about being good friends? Even Taylor Swift had a bestie.

Camille sensed Fitzgerald's discomfort but also her genuine honesty and openness. "Go on," she said. "You were saying?" she asked, touching Fitzgerald on the arm.

The gesture pleased Fitzgerald. She smiled and bobbed her head. "I was just going to say that I think you're an amazing woman. The things you've been through. Everything you've achieved. I'm sure I don't have to tell you, Camille. That is to say, you are a hero to women. I mean... wow, the really amazing thing is how you've touched women all over the world… so many different women from so many different countries."

Ormand was virtually beside himself with delight. Things were going splendidly between his Phoenix and the Red Dragon Lady. He couldn't have scripted it any better himself.

"It's true," he mused aloud as if his opinion held some sort of sway over Camille O'Keefe. "You're the Red Dragon Lady."

It was horrid. It was disruptive, it was as if he'd suddenly dragged the ladies' faces along a rough-hewn stone wall.

"Ech," grunted Camille, flipping her hair. "Good Gaia. Enough with that name already."

"Please," said Parker Fitzgerald. "You're talking to the guy who has dubbed me the Phoenix." She moved her bent arms up and down to simulate dragon wings.

Trying valiantly to erase the sour look on Camille's face, Parker Fitzgerald refocused the conversation. "Anyway, you're an inspiration to women and… and, to girls, young women… all of us, all over the world. What you've been through, what you've done."

Not one to enjoy effusive praise heaped upon her, Camille was immeasurably relieved when a neatly tuxedoed waiter offered forth a gleaming tray of the finest silver embossed with multiple *fleurs-de-lei* around the edges and the Liquid Sky logo in the center. On the tray stood a copse of paper-thin flute glasses filled with champagne. Thin trails of bubbles were flowing from bottom to top.

Parker Fitzgerald led the charge as all three helped themselves to a glass.

"I've no doubt this is one heck of a wine," said Camille.

Rickey Ormand smiled. He lived for moments like this. "Krug *Clos du Mesnil*, 2000. Nothing but the very best for our Camille."

Ormand's use of "our Camille" irked Fitzgerald yet again. She leaned in toward Camille. "That particular waiter only serves Rickey's A-list guests. The other guests aren't sipping Krug, believe me. The A-list wait staff actually memorizes the head shots of the A-list guests. Isn't that a little creepy?"

Camille returned a sympathetic look. "Actually," she said, "I'm used to that. The White House has a bull pen full of aides with photographic memories whispering in the president's ear at social events. You'd be surprised how much the president depends on his support staff to get through an event."

Parker Fitzgerald nodded. Lesson learned. Rickey Ormand held his glass of champagne. Camille and Fitzgerald raised theirs as well.

"Camille," said Ormand. "Would you do the honors?"

"I would be honored," Camille said. "Let me start by saying how happy I am to be here." She looked at Ormand. "Thank you for your incredible hospitality, Mr. Ormand."

The three of them enjoyed a few sips.

"Damn, this is good champagne," said Ormand.

Camille smiled and waited a moment before continuing. "And, I feel obliged to note, Dr. Fitzgerald that you can say what you like about my personal challenges. But we all know it's your story that deserves attention. You're the hero, not me."

She noticed Fitzgerald avert her eyes. Camille felt the intense physical and emotional pain of her ordeal at Lake Titicaca that still remained despite Fitzgerald's miraculous rescue and revolutionary robotics.

They sipped their champagne and allowed for a moment of quiet reflection.

Camille touched Fitzgerald's arm again. "I know your story, Parker," she said. "Doesn't everyone?"

Fitzgerald scoffed and polished off her glass. She beckoned for the waiter to return. "Ah, some more of the good stuff," she said, swapping her empty flute for a fresh, effervescent replacement.

Rickey Ormand tipped his glass and swapped it for a fresh flute as well.

Fitzgerald took a healthy sip before speaking again. "I'm a bit surprised. That's all." She looked at Ormand and then to Camille.

Camille frowned. "How so?"

"Well, you know, I'm surprised you know my back story. I'm a nobody."

"Back story?" said Camille. "From what I understand, it was nothing short of a miracle." She thought better of her phrasing. "What I mean to say is that you stood on the precipice—"

Ormand imposed himself once more. "Quite literally. The compound stood on a cliff, like, on a mountain plateau."

"As I was saying," continued Camille, asserting herself a bit more. "You actually died up there on that mountain, died for a magnificent discovery that will help millions and millions of impoverished people around the world. You died for something you believed in, Parker. And now, you're standing here part woman, part machine, but so much more than either piece alone. You get that, right?"

"Of course, she does," said Ormand, holding up his glass.

Neither woman clinked it. Instead, Camille and Fitzgerald looked at each other. Their gazes locked, creating an ethereal bridge across which they exchanged their deepest emotions in a moment that was at once fleeting and outside linear time. It was uniquely feminine.

"You get that, right?" Camille repeated, more emphatic this time.

"Yeah… no, not really. I've been way too busy to do much in the way of self-reflection." She scratched her chest and finished her champagne.

Camille smiled. "You've been through a lot. I can feel your pain."

Fitzgerald smiled. "Of course, you can. You're Camille O'Keefe. That's what you do. That's why people love you."

With a smile on his face reflecting a bit of delight and a bit of fear, Rickey Ormand was following the two women like he was watching a tennis game.

Camille shrugged. "You have absolutely nothing to feel uncomfortable about."

Fitzgerald smirked. It seemed to Camille to be more self-deprecating than sardonic.

"Come now," said Camille, thinking about the NSA profile on Fitzgerald she read earlier that week. "I know the whole story."

Camille noticed Fitzgerald's mood change precipitously. Perhaps it was the two glasses of champagne in rapid succession? She watched as Fitzgerald held up a fist, made her best blank bitch face and cocked her head, first right then left.

She rapped her knuckles against her right leg as she waved her empty flute... blasé, la-de-da. "Metal," she said. "Not flesh. Hydraulic fluid. Not blood."

It was Camille's turn to be a bit surprised. She was not expecting Fitzgerald to go negative like that. She made a mental note to add that to Fitzgerald's NSA profiles when she got back to D.C.

Camille shook her head sympathetically. "Oh, you're so much more than that, Parker." She pinched Fitzgerald's thin forearm. "This stuff is nothing more than clay. It doesn't matter. That's like saying Leonardo's David is just a big block of marble. It's much more than that. There's a life force, an essential energy from the universe that connects us all to the Source, right? It's quite palpable. I can feel it flowing through you. I mean that, Parker. It doesn't matter what your legs are made of. I know you can feel it, too, right?"

Fitzgerald's mood lightened instantly. Camille had the ability to send her positive energy to others even if they were a continent away. As a medium, Camille could tap non-linearity and, thus, travel between dimensions in her mind's eye. She punningly termed it her "present of presence" in her numerous books on past-life regression therapy.

"Yeah," said Fitzgerald with a newfound smile brightening her face. "I totally feel it right now. Thanks for the energy boost. It's better than a vitamin B shot." She shook her head as if clearing out cobwebs and winked.

Ormand was now completely lost. "Whoa, I can smell the estrogen burning," he said. "I have no idea what you two are talking about, and I consider myself a pretty smart guy."

"Oh, that's as clear as this crystal," said Camille, flicking her champagne flute with her finger nail.

The women laughed; Ormand just stood there as the joke sailed over his head.

"You know," he said at last. "That so-called 'battery' the Phoenix is referring to is not exactly a Duracell." He finished his second glass of champagne. "In point of fact," he said, pointing the empty flute at one woman and then the other like a stern teacher from a bygone era, "the Phoenix is powered by a self-charging gravity power pack. It's the only one of its kind… completely revolutionary."

Camille turned to Ormand and suddenly grew serious. "Believe me, we know all about it." She held him in her gaze for a long moment, silently communicating to him that there was infinitely more – more to her, more to her visit, more to gravity power – than the great Liquid Messiah knew.

"So, you see," said Fitzgerald. "You and I are both kinda connected to the universe but in different ways. Isn't that so cool?"

Ormand looked at Camille. He wasn't sure what the hell Camille was getting at, but he damned sure caught a whiff of something cooking. "We?" he said suspiciously. "Who's we? Wait…."

Camille ignored him. She was simply testing the waters, determining how easy it was going to be to set the hook. Too easy, she determined. Not even a good challenge in the catch. She sighed. He really was little more than a walking, talking penis who somehow had more money than God herself. She found the combination completely unappealing and totally boring. In fact, looking at him now in his tuxedo, she noticed how slight he was, and, if she wasn't mistaken, his smart-looking glasses were not prescription at all but purely cosmetic, obviously to make him appear more intellectual, bookish even.

"Tell you what would be amazing" said Fitzgerald. "Can you imagine if there was some way…." She couldn't quite put her finger on it.

Camille scrunched her face and nodded. She intuited what Fitzgerald was trying to verbalize. "Yeah, something on the next level, something truly world changing." She gestured to Fitzgerald's legs. "Something with the body, you know?"

Fitzgerald rapped her knuckles on her leg again, only this time she spoke with pride instead of self-pity. "Something like me, only universal for all people to benefit as people or something to that extent."

Bang, crack, stop the tape. It was as if a lightning bolt struck both women simultaneously. Both ladies felt it and smiled delicately. Universe… power… energy… human energy? There was an idea lurking there somewhere for sure.

Ormand wasn't impressed. He was starting to get a weird feeling about Camille, like she knew things and was checking him out. He couldn't care less about whatever the ladies were yammering on about. He had other things on his mind. He thought about his secret weapons program. She couldn't possibly know. That was impossible.

Camille looked right at him. Ormand did a double take. He got the chills. He could almost feel her inside his head reading his mind.

"We've taken an interest in Liquid Sky," Camille said flatly.

Ormand stiffened. His stomach leapt. "We?" he repeated tentatively. "We who? Who is we?" The fake smile melted away. His lower lip trembled even as he bit it.

Camille noticed Ormand was rocking back and forth from foot to foot. Yes, she thought, he's skittish. She let him see the threat in her eyes. She couldn't help it. He just rubbed her the wrong way. Look at him tugging at his shirt collar. He was like a kid with a gazillion bucks who had to get his way, or he would throw a wicked tantrum.

Camille twitched her head. The few thick, ginger curls that artfully hung down from her meticulous hair snapped back in place like a crisp salute. Yeah, she thought… gotta play with this guy. "I'm sorry?' she said. She shot a coy look over to Parker Fitzgerald.

Ormand was getting edgy now. "Two minutes ago," he said more sharply than he intended. "I was talking about the battery system in her." He raised his chin in Fitzgerald's direction.

"Were you?" said Camille with honey on her tongue. She pursed her lips as if trying to recollect.

Ormand scratched his chin rapidly and shifted to his other foot. Pretending not to notice his puerile impatience, Camille turned to Fitzgerald. "We will have to follow up on this grand idea of ours, Parker. We put it out to the universe, so we need to follow it up before someone else plucks it."

Fitzgerald nodded. "Yes, yes. I would love that. I can't believe I'm becoming friends with Camille O'Keefe. This grand idea of ours which isn't really an idea yet, but we'll come up with something."

Camille threw her hand in the air and pointed up toward the gilded dome ceiling that seemed to hover majestically over their heads and finished Fitzgerald's sentence.

"Idea of having an idea," she proclaimed.

The two ladies laughed heartily. They high-fived with a vigorous clap that irked Rickey Ormand from head to toe. Too much women's bullshit.

"So, yeah," he said. "I hate to interrupt your girl-power moment, but I am still wondering about your comment. Ms. O'Keefe." He was really getting pissed now.

Camille winked at Fitzgerald and turned back to Ormand. "Which comment was that?" she said. She could see the ire rising like putting a lid on a pot of boiling pasta. She rather liked it.

"That bit when you said you and unnamed others know all about the Liquid-Drive technology," replied Ormand through the tiniest slit between his clenched teeth. It was more of a hiss than anything else.

Having seen the signs of Rickey Ormand about to blow like a volcanologist can read a volcano, Parker Fitzgerald grew tense. The clenched teeth gave it away. Ormand clenched like a pit bull locked on a ham bone when he reached the end of his fuse. She'd seen it enough to know you didn't want to see it. That's when the "other" Rickey Ormand came out. That Rickey Ormand would fire an employee on a whim and then pull every string he could to blacklist the poor bastard so he never worked in Silicon Valley again. This was Rickey Ormand the "Liquid Annihilator," as many ex-employees called him.

Parker Fitzgerald glanced at Camille. She wasn't so much concerned for her new friend. After all, standing before her was a former First Lady and presidential running mate. No, she was concerned for her boss, Rickey Ormand. Fitzgerald knew that, for the most part, Rickey Ormand preferred the company of weaker women who, if not charging him by the hour, would be equally submissive in the face of his power. Most people simply kissed his ass. Fitzgerald never once considered Camille among their ilk. Quite the contrary, Fitzgerald was seriously worried that Rickey Ormand might lose his cool and let the Liquid Annihilator loose. And that would be the end of Liquid Sky.

"Um," said Fitzgerald uncomfortably. "Rickey, I'm sure Camille was just making polite conversation."

Ormand made a mock gesture of sympathetic understanding. "I see, I see. No doubt."

But Camille decided to bust his balls a bit more. "Oh, no," she said. "He's quite right. We know all about it."

She turned to Rickey and smiled.

Fitzgerald's heart must have skipped three beats. All she could think was, "Oh…My…God!"

Ormand somehow managed to keep his cool. He wanted a tie to the president so badly, he was willing to let a woman mock him at his own event. He made a mental note that he owed Camille a good kick in the ass. For the time being, though, Rickey Ormand acquiesced. "Yes, of course, of course."

Pause… uncomfortable silence.

Remembering her marching orders like a good soldier, Camille sidled up to Ormand and put her arm through his. "All of it, Mr. Ormand. We know all of it."

Ormand scanned the room desperately for any wait staff. He saw some Latino guy heading across the room serving something. Ormand put two fingers in his mouth and let fly with a shrill whistle.

"Jesus, Rickey," complained Fitzgerald. "You're not calling the beer guy at a baseball game."

The waiter hustled his ass over to the boss and held forth the shiny, silver tray. "Sir," he said, bowing his head lest he risk rousing the Liquid Annihilator.

Ormand downed some sort of puff pastry and washed it down with some of his champagne.

Camille allowed him to finish his *hors d'oeuvre* before leaning in toward his shoulder. "All of it, Mr. Ormand. As in everything. We know everything there is to know about you. And in your case," she eyed him from head to toe and then back up to his midriff. "We rather think the imagination is quite a bit larger than… then the actual thing itself, shall we say?" She turned her head suddenly. "Of this, I can assure you, my friend."

She flicked her hair as if waving a straight razor in Ormand's face. Parker Fitzgerald wasn't sure what the hell was going on, but she sure as hell figured it would result in an ugly end.

Ormand unlocked arms with Camille, a contemptuous look on his face. He maneuvered around her exquisite teal Zanotti suede sandals. Camille smiled to herself. He was gonna lose it.

"So," he said, smirking at her.

His charisma was plain to see. But Camille found it more like artificial jelly. "So?" she said. "A needle pulling thread."

Ormand was about to fire back with some witty barb but stopped dead in his tracks. He was so not expecting that comment.

He tried to force his way in a second time. "Um… yeah. So, you and your Washington D.C. buddies know all about me, huh?"

Parker Fitzgerald may have feared her boss would lose his cool and blow himself up, but she had to admit she was kind of enjoying it. She thought back to her days at MIT. There was this guy, a chess master, who used to hang outside the Au Bon Pain in Harvard Square during the spring and summer. He used to wear a weathered, khaki safari hat, short-sleeve plaid button down, jeans, and grungy Converse Chuck Taylors. People would come from all over the area to plop down their $5 and promptly get their asses kicked.

Nobody could beat the guy. Camille reminded her of this chess guy. Rickey Ormand was all too willing to pony up his money and get his ass kicked. Only with Ormand, there were a lot more zeros tacked onto that $5. And this time, the grand master was not some abstracted Cambridge savant sacrificing make-believe pawns in a game of war but Camille O'Keefe, the famous redhead whose record of achievement impacted very real people in very real ways. Her bid for the White House was real, so real, in fact, that Rickey Ormand was willing to shell out astronomical sums to curry her favor.

But now, he seemed to have forgotten all that. Now, Rickey Ormand was peeved as hell and teetering on the verge of going ballistic.

"You know," Ormand said, "I'm used to people saying things like that. You'd be amazed how many times a reporter has said to me, 'Oh, we know all about you, Mr. Ormand.' I mean, think about it… I'm a great story."

"Bottoms up," urged Fitzgerald.

Ormand obeyed by downing his second glass in the short time they'd been chatting.

Camille took a deep breath and smiled. She ran through Harry Pierson's instructions in her head before speaking. "Only I'm not some reporter looking to write a puff piece. I'm not here to revel in your great story… Mr. Ormand."

Rickey Ormand got the confirmation he was looking for. There was another agenda in play, one that was not his own. He found it quite unsettling.

"Why are you here?" he said cooly.

"First," replied Camille, "I wanted to meet Dr. Fitzgerald in person. As I said – and I really meant it – *she's* the one with the great story. Not you. Not me. I've made a new friend."

Ormand somehow managed not to roll his eyes. "And the second reason?"

Camille switched modes on cue as she set the hook like an expert angler. "I guess you can say that I came to deliver a message."

Ormand's jaw dropped as the orchestra struck up a lively rendition of Duke Ellington's "Take the A Train." He began to fidget. "A message? You have a message for me?"

God, he was so patronizing. "In a matter of speaking," replied Camille.

"What the hell does that mean?" snapped Ormand before seeing Fitzgerald gesture for him to tone it down. He held up his hand accompanied by a conciliatory look... lots of pathos, totally fugazi.

Camille turned to Fitzgerald. "Would you please excuse us for a moment?" she said. "I need to talk to Mr. Ormand in private. You understand."

Fitzgerald returned a concerned look but tried to keep it positive. "It was a dream come true meeting you in person, Camille O'Keefe. When you come as close to death as I have, moments like this mean a lot."

Camille smiled. "Oh, death exists only in this 3-D world. We all just come and go, one life into the next throughout the millennia. Remember, we're spirits having a human experience, not humans having a spiritual experience."

"You know I love that," exclaimed Fitzgerald.

Ormand sighed heavily. "Yeah, yeah... we are spirits in the material world. Didn't Sting beat you to that one?"

"Don't mind him," said Fitzgerald waving him off. "He doesn't even like the Police. As for sarcasm, Rickey's too rich to be genuinely sarcastic."

"Anyway," added Camille almost as an afterthought because, for her, it was a done deal. "We'll find each other later. I know intuitively we are going to be good friends. I'll find you."

With that, Parker Fitzgerald pivoted on her robotic heels as smoothly as if she had ball bearings in the soles of her shoes and was off to mingle and drink some more of Rickey's best bubbly. Her dress rippled in time with her magnificent body.

Camille admired her. She was so very sporty and so very chic at the same time. She turned back to Ormand. "Now, where were we?" she taunted.

"Look, Ms. O'Keefe," said Ormand impatiently. "In a few minutes, I have to get up in front of all these people – broadcasting live to the world, by the way – and announce the greatest discovery of all time. I was hoping that you could say a few words, too. You know… like an endorsement."

Camille laughed. Did he really just say that?

"Oh, dear," she said. "Is that why you invited me to your grand gala? To get my endorsement of your gravity-power program? I wonder, does that include your secret weapons program, as well?"

Ormand froze instantly. His stomach dropped a thousand feet and his throat clenched tighter than his sphincter which, given the size of the stick the Liquid Messiah kept up his ass, was saying something. All he could do was stare back at her.

"Oh, dear, indeed," repeated Camille. "You're standing there like a statue wondering how we know about your gravity power, and your gravity weapons, and all that, aren't you?"

Still unable to utter a word, Ormand could only nod. A shrill sound akin to a banshee's scream was bouncing around inside his head.

Camille bit her lower lip. "I told you, Rickey. We know everything."

His tongue finally loosened. "Everything?" asked Ormand.

"Yeah, everything as in everything… everything as in there is nothing you have done, are doing, or will do that we don't or won't know."

Ormand finally managed to pry his dry lips apart enough to speak a full sentence. "You certainly have a way with words."

"Believe me," said Camille, "I'm not entirely comfortable delivering this message. But a girl's gotta do what a girl's gotta do, right? That's something you would say, isn't it?"

Ormand tried to defend himself but only stuttered.

"Of course, it is," said Camille, patronizing the Messiah just a bit. "And like I said, this kind of stuff makes me uneasy. But I am going to occupy the White House someday. I know this.

I have seen it. So, I might as well get used to all this man talk if I'm going to offer something different with my newfound power, right?"

Ormand shrugged, his jaw low, wondering what the hell was happening.

"Anyway," said Camille with a laugh, "we've been paying close attention to Liquid Sky. We've been paying close attention to you, too, Rickey Ormand. Think of it as the most in-depth proctological exam in the world. And what we've discovered–"

"We?" muttered Ormand.

"Right up to the top," said Camille.

She held up her forefinger and turned an ear toward the stage. The orchestra had Ellington's tune in full swing. "I love this part." She wagged her finger in time with the music.

Ormand looked at the orchestra, looked around the huge room, and then returned his attention to Camille. "The top?" he said softly.

Camille regained her focus and nodded. "Oh, yes. The top. Of course, I would never bring his name into it, but you know who I'm talking about."

"President Pierson?" muttered Ormand.

"Like I said, I would never bring his name into it. Suffice it to say, you have attracted significant attention. You're on the radar. That's not a good thing, my friend. I use the term loosely."

She reached over and plucked a blonde hair from Ormand's shoulder. "Right, right," said Camille. "Just a few more things from my mental list."

Ormand swallowed hard and closed his eyes as if standing in front of a firing squad.

"I'm not sure what you're planning to say in your little speech. But I am sure that we will be paying very close attention. In fact, we're here now… watching, listening, studying your every move. We have access to every nook and cranny of Liquid Sky, not to mention your personal life. I mean… I'm not necessarily endorsing that sort of thing, but that's beside the point, right? The decision came from way, way up the ladder. Use your imagination."

Ormand tried to mount a defense, but it amounted to nothing. "I don't know what you mean," he said weakly.

"Case in point," she continued, "what's up with this whole secret military program you have tucked away somewhere. Why on earth would you want to attempt something like that? Only a crazy egomaniac would think he could launch a weapons program using unprecedented technology without the government finding out eventually. What were you thinking? I know what you're thinking now though. How did we find out? That's what you're wondering."

Ormand nodded. Camille shrugged.

"I don't really know. If I did, I certainly wouldn't disclose that. I get all my information from out there." She waved her hands in the air, indicating her psychic connection with the universe.

"As for the men I work with, who knows? Correction, they know. They know everything about you. As such, you must be very, very careful what you say to the world right now. And then you must be very careful what you do going forward. There are people watching your every move, Rickey Ormand. I'm not sure they like you very much. You probably don't hear this often, but I wouldn't want to be you."

"I don't understand," said Ormand.

"Oh, you do. For some reason, Rickey, you think you can redesign the world with your new technology, corner people into depending on your new energy source for virtually everything in their lives, build new weapons of mass destruction to use against those who dare to resist, and make yourself not only the richest but the most powerful man in the world. How did I do?"

Ormand held up his hand. "No, no, Ms. O'Keefe. With all due respect, you have the wrong idea."

Camille tapped her right temple. "Remember, you're talking to a medium. I can intuit certain things as concretely as reading them in a book."

Ormand protested yet again. "No, that's not me at all. I want to help the world."

Camille smiled. "Of course, you do. That's great news. So then, I can go back to Washington and tell my people that you don't mind sharing everything you're working on with the government."

"Wh... what?" stammered Ormand.

"Well, sure," said Camille. "Gravity power is certainly going to change the world. You are right about that. But once you started thinking you were going to centralize everything under your providence, you began to pose a threat. In case you've been living under a rock for the last two years, threats don't exist long around this president."

Ormand's stomach was in his mouth now. "A threat? Me? How?"

Camille wagged her finger. "You see, Rickey, you are lying. I can sense it. The problem is that introducing a radical new energy source like gravity power is going to cause immediate upheaval. The system as we know it will suddenly collapse. There will be mass hysteria. In fact, you're counting on it, aren't you? That's terrible. You call Dr. Fitzgerald the Phoenix, but it is you who plans to rise up from the ashes. We cannot allow that to happen. We cannot allow one man to bring down the entire economic system. And we certainly cannot allow one man to develop a new type of weapon for which there is no defense. I have to ask again, what on earth were you thinking?"

Ormand caught site of Robert Jarvis over Camille's shoulder. Jarvis was the founder and CEO of the largest software company in the world. The man was famous for many innovations. But for Rickey Ormand, Robert Jarvis was a hero for another reason. The United States Department of Justice brought two anti-trust suits against Jarvis, and he beat the rap both times.

Seeing Robert Jarvis must have lit a fire deep inside Rickey Ormand. He cleared his throat. He'd heard enough. In a moment of near insanity, he decided to talk. "Take a good look around, Ms. O'Keefe." He held up his hand and gestured wide to the right and then wide to the left. "Does is look like I am afraid to take risks? Does it look like I am easily intimidated? This is my company. This is my house. I don't have to take your Big Brother bullshit. This is America. Things don't work that way here."

Ormand was on a roll now. He cracked his neck left, then right. Camille could only smile as she watched him slide the noose over his own neck.

Ormand raved on. "Let me tell you something, I put half of those assholes in office, and I can sure as hell take them out. Why do you think they're pressing me? It was the same when those fascists from the Justice Department went after Robert Jarvis, who's here, by the way. Remember that? Like I said, I put those guys in office, and I can take them out, as well. It's about the money, Ms. O'Keefe. It's always about the money."

Camille just shook her head in disbelief. Things were going perfectly.

"Yeah, look at Robert Jarvis. I'm even bigger than he is. He beat the feds not once but twice. The bastards haven't bothered him since. The man's a hero. I'll introduce you. Anyway, my point is that this is America. Free enterprise is what makes us great. The Chinese haven't figured that shit out for themselves, so they come to guys like me for answers. Gravity power will do away with oil. China is the world's largest manufacturer, but they're also the world's largest consumer of oil. They'll love me so much over there, they'll probably make me an honorary Chinaman. Do you know what that means, Ms. O'Keefe?"

Camille shook her head. "Nope."

Ormand rolled his eyes. "I didn't think so. China wants a big boss to provide them with an alternative energy source. Sure, no problem. I'll charge them half of what oil costs, maybe less. The Chinese save themselves billions, which, as I'm sure you know, goes right into the pockets of a few high-placed Party officials, if you know what I mean. What do I care about corruption? I don't give a shit what they do so long as they buy my gravity power. Actually, what choice will they have? And it's totally clean energy, so people are happy about that. I make more money than I can hope to count in a lifetime. Liquid Sky shareholders... we can't forget about them. They'll make a killing as the stock skyrockets. I hire more and more people. The U.S. government collects more and more taxes. I contribute to the right campaigns, it's all good. That's the business cycle. Your people should know this. So I really don't know why they would send you."

"You make everybody happy," said Camille.

Ormand took her comment at face value. "Bingo! Now you're getting it," he exclaimed proudly. "I'm in control of the future. It's just how it's going to be. What do you want me to say? Deal with it. The only people who are not happy are the Saudis and the Russians. But you know what? Who gives a shit about them? Screw them. Let them come up with their own idea or else get in line to buy mine. You say a few politicians are pissy, too? Whatever... it's just about the money. I'll figure out how to ingratiate myself through the almighty dollar. Don't you worry your pretty red head about it."

"What about all the people you will put out of work when just about everything we have becomes obsolete?" asked Camille.

Ormand waved his hand in disgust. "Who cares? They will retrain, get new jobs. Remember, once the world moves from oil to gravity power, we will need to remake everything. So really, I am creating more new jobs than the last twenty presidents combined. And if I want to sell weapons, too bad. What's wrong with that? All those stuffed shirts you work with are just pissed because their precious military industrial complex won't be spoon fed by Lockheed Martin, Boeing, Raytheon, and General Dynamics... all of 'em. They're literally dinosaurs. They're extinct after I speak tonight. You are right, Camille. There is a new order of things coming, a new power structure. And you're looking at the man who's gonna be sitting on top. I'm sorry if that bothers you."

Camille gave him one last chance. "Is this the response you want me to bring back to Washington?"

"This is a done deal, Camille. Checkmate. Rickey wins. That's why those pricks up on Capitol Hill sent you here. They'll come around sooner or later. Trust me, they always do. They want to line their pockets like everyone else, so they get a little cranky when their allowance is taken away. But they'll get it back... provided they play nice with Rickey. Those who don't will get my gravity-powered foot up their ass."

Camille nodded and shrugged. "Look, I am just the messenger. I'm sure you're right. This is probably some kind of misunderstanding."

Ormand smirked and straightened his bow tie. "Now that's more like it, Ms. O'Keefe. A beautiful woman like you shouldn't be used as a cheap messenger by some guy who backed into his job. You're too beautiful to be making threats."

Oh boy, thought Camille. What a guy... what a guy.

"Just so I get it right when I'm back in Washington... I can be a little ditzy as I'm sure you've heard."

"So it is said," replied Ormand.

"The message you want me to bring back is that you aren't particularly worried that gravity power will topple everything we have now, right?" she said in the most naïve voice she could muster.

Bite the lower lip just so. Bat the lashes. Flip the hair.

"That's right," replied Ormand. "And if anyone has a problem with that, tell them to grow a pair and come see me in person instead of letting a beautiful woman do their dirty work. It's beneath you, Camille, although that sounds like a wonderful place to be."

He winked. He might as well have farted on her. She found the thought of both equally disgusting.

Having spent himself, Ormand craned his neck trying to find Robert Jarvis. "Robert... Robert," he called out.

Jarvis saw Ormand and strode over to greet his host. The two men gripped hands. "Hell, Rickey. You do put on the best parties in Silicon Valley."

Ormand laughed. "That's nothing, old boy. Just wait until you hear about my new toy. You're gonna want in really bad. Trust me."

He introduced Camille.

"I was just telling Ms. O'Keefe that there are many, many dinosaurs still roaming this planet."

Jarvis laughed. "Yes, I believe the *senatorus rex* is flourishing still."

"Indeed, indeed," said Ormand as he clapped the older Jarvis on the shoulder. "You know, I was also telling Ms. O'Keefe – Camille – about how you beat the Justice Department twice. Amazing…."

Jarvis rolled his eyes. "A bunch of uptight assholes," he said in a low voice. "But I never said that."

Ormand laughed. "I say bring on all challengers. After you hear what I'm rolling out, you'll see there's nobody who can derail Liquid Sky. I don't care if it's the president himself, whom I am hoping to meet actually."

He turned to Camille. "In fact, I am hoping you can arrange that."

Robert Jarvis patted Ormand on the shoulder. "Look at you with all that vinegar in your blood. Just so long as the government doesn't play the old National Security card. If they go National Security on you, you might as well hand over the keys to your entire operation. You're toast. Did you know the government has the right to come right in and take everything you have? Believe me, if they play that card, there's not a damned thing you can do about it. But hey, they didn't go 'national security' on me, and I make their encryption software."

Camille was all light inside. This was going to be a real good finish.

Jarvis put his hand on Ormand's shoulder. "Okay, Mr. Messiah. I've got to hit the head. I don't want to miss your speech. And by the way, fantastic champagne. I feel bad pissing it out."

The orchestra brought the A train to a climactic end. Some woman from the Liquid Sky public-relations office stepped up to the mic and began introducing Rickey Ormand.

Ormand gestured toward the stage. "It's time," he said. "You're going to love this, Camille. Really, we got off on the wrong foot, but I think we can become very close friends."

He turned to walk away, then suddenly turned back. "That stuff about how the government can just take what they want in the interests of national security and stuff. That can't be true, right? Not in the United States of America."

Camille took a long, deep, cleansing breath. She exhaled through a radiant smile. "Actually, he's right. If President Pierson deems something to be critical and in the best interests of national security, there are very few limits to what the government cannot do to you."

Ormand was shocked. "How is that even possible in the United States?"

"It is possible *because* this is the United States."

Ormand just stared at her.

"Think about it," she said. "You'll figure it out."

"Anyway," said Ormand light-heartedly. "Like Richard Jarvis said, they didn't even do that to him, so I'm not worried."

Camille tapped her lower lip as she thought. "And yet... I wonder if Richard Jarvis threatened to shove his gravity-powered foot up the president's ass? I think that's how you put it, right?"

This got Ormand's attention. "I was only kidding about that. Please, my God... that stays between you and me."

They were now calling him up to the stage. His big moment was here.

"I really have to go now," he said. "But I would love to spend some more time with you... later tonight."

"You say that now," replied Camille.

Ormand looked confused. Then he turned and started toward the stage.

"Oh, Rickey," called Camille, behind him.

Ormand turned. "Yes, my lovely. Miss me already? I'm hard to forget, I know."

Camille tapped her forehead. Bat the lashes. Bite the lower lip... just a bit of tooth showing. "Jeez, I forgot what I was going to say. I forget more than I thought I knew," she quipped and threw her head back.

Rickey Ormand half turned. "I've really got to go. But I'm sure we can jar it lose later tonight." He winked.

Camille snapped. "Oh, I remember now." She thumped her forehead with the heel of her hand. "I can be such a ditz, sorry. There was one other thing I was supposed to tell you. I forgot all about it. I really do apologize. I'm not good at this sort of thing. My head is literally in another world."

Ormand rolled his hand to hurry her. "Come on then. What is it?"

"I'm supposed to tell you that, based on the intelligence we have at this time, your Liquid-Drive program as well as any other Liquid Sky program, concept, initiative, invention, idea, or patent involving gravitational energy that exists now or may exist at any point in the future in perpetuity – that's a fancy way of saying until the end of time – is hereby deemed a matter of national security and, therefore, may become the sole property of the United States government at any time and without notice."

Rickey Ormand stood dumbfounded, jaw agape, eyes suddenly glazed.

"Sorry," said Camille again. "You know me. I forget stuff sometimes."

Camille swivelled her head until she spotted Parker Fitzgerald, which wasn't too difficult because Ricky Ormand decided to make her 6'3" when he selected her robotic specs. He always liked his women tall and leggy.

Camille left Ormand standing agape and glided up to Fitzgerald's side. "We need to talk," she said.

"I had a feeling," said Fitzgerald. "What the hell did you just say to Rickey? He looks like he just died a hundred times over."

Camille smiled and looked at Fitzgerald sideways. "Never mind Rickey Ormand. He's got far bigger things to worry about. What I'm interested in is us… the future… us in the future… our future."

"I had a feeling," Fitzgerald repeated.

The two locked eyes. The power was palpable. A beer and Solo cup frat boy might get lightheaded or giddy at the possibility that the gorgeous redhead and the hot robo-chic might make out. In reality, there was nothing sexual about it. The energy moving between Camille and Parker was deeper than that… much deeper. Acutely aware that there was something extraordinary connecting them, both women smiled. The moment was gentle and warm. The moment was unity.

"What?" said Parker Fitzgerald coyly.

Camille enjoyed the connection immensely. She tugged on her right earlobe like she often did when receiving a message from some source outside normal perception. "You're holding something back," she said. "Why?"

Fitzgerald averted her eyes for a split second, but it was enough to break the bridge between them. Camille nodded. It was confirmed.

"I don't know what you're talking about," said Fitzgerald, smoothing out her dress. She gestured with her chin toward the podium. "Rickey's getting ready to speak," she said.

The magnificent chandeliers dimmed about halfway as did the real gold-leaf sconces gently illuminating the entire perimeter of the lavish, two-story ballroom. Rickey Ormand was getting ready to take the podium.

"Eh," commented Camille. "Whatever he's going to say, I bet we've heard it a million times before from a million different people."

Fitzgerald held up her index finger. "A million different men," she clarified.

"Indeed," said Camille. She then promptly returned to her previous line of inquiry. "I bet whatever it is you're not telling me is much more interesting."

Fitzgerald pretended not to hear her.

Camille smiled, stepped next to Fitzgerald, and turned to face the podium as well. "You know," she said, "I am absolutely certain there is something you and I are supposed to accomplish together."

Fitzgerald looked down at Camille standing next to her. "I wish I could be so certain about important things like you are."

Camille sensed her new friend's fear. "Is that why you're hesitant to tell me?"

Parker Fitzgerald shook her head. "Tell you what?"

"Whatever it is you're hiding," replied Camille.

"What makes you say that?" she asked, trying to laugh it off. But the nervous edge to her chuckle betrayed her efforts at nonchalance.

Camille reached her arm around Fitzgerald's waist. She squeezed just a bit. She felt no give in Fitzgerald's space-age alloy hips. "Because I know," she said.

"You know I'm hiding something, or you know what it is I am hiding?" asked Fitzgerald.

Camille slid her arm up from around Fitzgerald's waist and patted her on the shoulder. It was a bit of a reach up. All the same, she could tell Fitzgerald found it comforting.

"Maybe both. I'm content to leave you wondering… for now."

There was a far-off look in Fitzgerald's eyes, somewhat clouded, a poignant mixture of regret and yearning. Overall, it reminded Camille of the very same look in her own eyes. Camille glanced to her right and noticed that Fitzgerald was biting her lip. There was something weighing on Parker's conscience. Camille was certain of it. And yet, she could also feel tremendous anticipation, even positive energy, radiating like crazy from her new, semi-robotic compatriot.

Camille rapped her knuckles on Fitzgerald's alloy thigh. "Anybody in there?"

"Would you go knocking on the Tin Man like that?" asked Fitzgerald.

"Oh, Parker, you are nothing like the Tin Man. You, my dear, have a gigantic heart. You are full of love and ambition. Combining those two life forces can create something very powerful. But I think you know that."

Fitzgerald liked the thought of it. "Yeah, for as long as I can remember, I wanted to do something really great, you know? Something, like, off the charts, you know? I have the brain for it. I know that."

"It requires emotional intelligence as well. We've entered a new phase. It's time for feminine energy to rise up—"

"Like a Phoenix," joked Fitzgerald.

Camille laughed. "Yeah, exactly. I'm not talking about gender though. Let me make that clear. I'm talking about energy. I can feel it everywhere. Centuries of masculine energy." She gestured to the grandiosity of the magnificently gilded ballroom in which they stood.

Fitzgerald grunted. "Men... their structures are too big and their penises too small. You think feminine energy can displace the centuries of masculine energy that brought us all this? God, I hope you're right. Right now, all we get is nothing but fancy constructs and cocktail weenies."

She gestured toward the podium with her chin. "Speaking of which."

Rickey Ormand was still standing out in front of the podium lingering in conversation with a beautiful, leggy blonde in a stunning blue gown. She was with a V.C. firm and there to court Ormand's business or Ormand himself if necessary. Seeing that Ormand was on his own schedule, one of the P.R. women working the event rolled her hand at the orchestra director. He turned to his guys, counted off, and they dove into a Count Basie tune again.

"Cocktail weenie," quipped Fitzgerald. "That blonde will be very disappointed."

"Oh my God," said Camille, giggling. "I can't believe how... right you are. Seriously, though, it's not about gender. It's about energy, masculine and feminine."

"Like yin and yang," said Fitzgerald.

Camille nodded. "Actually, yeah."

"Like I always say," joked Fitzgerald, "a billion Chinese can't be wrong."

"Hmph," muttered Camille. "Yes, they can. Believe me. Do you know that the last era of the feminine culminated in the Renaissance? The Renaissance. Can you believe that?"

Parker Fitzgerald was delighted. "See, that's what I'm talking about. A new era of wisdom and creation."

"Feminine creation," added Camille.

Fitzgerald smiled at the thought. "Yeah, exactly. A new Renaissance, Camille. Just think about it."

"I do. All the time."

"Damn," exclaimed Fitzgerald. "There are so many ideas running through my head right now, I can barely organize them."

"Don't," said Camille. "Let your ideas run free like wild horses. They will organize themselves as they will according to their own laws, just like horses. It's not for us humans to control the universe of ideas."

"We're just along for the ride, huh?" said Fitzgerald. She exhaled loudly. "There's a damned stampede in my head."

Camille O'Keefe turned to face Parker Fitzgerald. "Know what the best part is?" she asked coyly.

Fitzgerald shrugged. "I wish I knew."

"Oh, you know," said Camille.

"How's that?" said Fitzgerald.

Camille rapped her knuckles on Fitzgerald's alloy thigh again. "You don't have to look any farther than that mirror over there."

The two women turned to face a mirror on the wall near where they were standing. It must have been twelve feet high.

"How's that?" repeated Fitzgerald.

Camille chuckled. "You are brilliant, Parker Fitzgerald. But you're naïve, too. It's cute. Just take a look at yourself. You are the idea. You are the Renaissance, my dear. You are the living, breathing embodiment of art and technology. You represent the feminine future that is now unfolding."

Parker Fitzgerald turned away from the mirror. "Or a freakazoid," she said flatly.

Camille shook her head and flipped a curl from her face. "You are so funny," she said. "I used to turn away from the mirror after my accident. I was in a car crash that almost killed me just like you and the earthquake. Rest assured, Parker, there are no freakazoids in the feminine realm. There's only crystalline energy, a true force of change. You are the new."

Fitzgerald thought on that for a moment. She reached out and took Camille's hand in hers. "So then, if I represent the technological future, you know, the future of the material world, you must represent the spiritual future."

Camille smiled. "Now you're starting to get it. Let those horses run."

Fitzgerald thought some more. "So... no more cocktail weenies?"

"No more cocktail weenies. In this new feminine era, people will sustain themselves on the energy that unites us all."

Parker Fitzgerald tensed up a bit. "Camille, you have no idea how right you are," she said.

"Oh, yes I do, Parker. I most surely know already. You'll reveal it when you're ready. Let those horses run."

Parker Fitzgerald almost let her secret slip but caught herself. Camille knew it.

"Like I don't already know," said Camille. "I'm a medium. It's who I am."

Chapter 20

Ormand coughs into the microphone. He is clearly still reeling from the heady mix of Camille's threats, which he finds outrageous, and the blonde investment banker's promises, which he finds invigorating. He would love to have both women, preferably at the same time, but with Harry Pierson's words staining Camille's lips like she is a vampire, the great Liquid Messiah is beginning to regret inviting her in the first place.

He's disappointed. Worse yet, he feels a bit foolish. He loathes both. His intentions were innocuous enough. All he wanted was to charm the panties off the famous redhead and land himself an introduction to the president. Was that so much to ask? Instead, he got a swift kick in the bullocks and not even a glimpse of what lay locked up and buried inside her treasure chest. As for meeting the president? Well, it seems now that the president is summoning him, not the other way around.

As if getting his body punted across the ballroom floor at his own party wasn't humiliating enough, he'd actually asked Camille O'Keefe to speak after him. Panic creeps in. He cannot trust her with the microphone after what she's said to him. It occurs to Ormand that he hasn't been this stupid since... since... since he doesn't know when. He sees now that Camille O'Keefe is a big pain in the ass. She actually thinks she can strong arm him. Ormand finds the entire concept preposterous.

Ormand figures Camille's got issues with successful men like himself. Everybody knows how weird she is. He figures she probably needs to feel powerful or something, so she goes after successful men and kicks them in the balls. She probably needs that to feel good about herself. She's a total bitch and a total pain in the ass. Yeah, he figures, Camille definitely has issues, but they're definitely not the kind of issues he likes.

Rickey Ormand likes chicks with daddy issues. That's it. That's the only baggage he allows onboard his private jet. Daddy issues mean fun. As for Camille O'Keefe, Ormand knows what she needs to straighten her out – a ball gag, a good spanking and a new wardrobe when all is said and done. If he said it once, he said it a million times: The problem with modern women is their demand to be equal with men. He never understood that. Why on earth would a woman want to be measured like a man? Screw that. As far as he's concerned, women wield power of their own and should stop worrying about being treated like men. He would never admit this in public, but everybody at Liquid Sky understood... Rickey Ormand does not hire women for positions of authority, Parker Fitzgerald being the one notable exception. Women are way too much trouble. He wants no part of it. All this bullshit about "Me Too," and "corporate governance," and finding women to sit on boards as directors only underscores how much trouble women can cause.

Camille O'Keefe is a huge disappointment for Ormand. When he first had his idea to invite her in, he really thought she was different. Now, he's lamenting the whole stupid thing. It's too bad, really. He's never had a real redhead. Alluring as that is, though, he doesn't like Camille one little bit. She's a bitch. She's trouble. He enjoys dealing with women like the investment banker babe. He finds them so much more accommodating. Chicks like that are all about closing the deal. They'll do all the work where it matters most, the three B's… the bedroom, the boardroom, and the bank. What the hell could be better than that?

All this is running through his head when the orchestra comes to a crisp and complete stop for a second time. Ormand realizes that he's missed his second cue. Suddenly, he can feel one thousand eyeballs fixed on him. They came to hear the Great One's announcement, and now it's time.

He turns and the spotlight hits his eyes. He isn't prepared for that and squints. It makes him look sheepish. "Um… hello and, um…."

Okay, he has to admit, not the best start. He stares back at the camera that is taking in his visage and recasting it onto a gigantic, wall-size screen that was lowered from the ceiling dramatically several minutes earlier. His bowtie is choking him to death. Camille's words have taken his mind hostage. He can feel himself start to sweat. Gravity power is the most amazing discovery of the millennium. Gravity power is going to change the entire world overnight, and he, Rickey Ormand, the Liquid Messiah, will finally take his rightful place atop the pyramid. He will be the all-seeing eye whose powerful gaze sees all… knows all… controls all. Does the president have the power to simply confiscate everything he spent his life creating?

Yeah, the more he thinks about, the more pissed off he becomes. This is America. True power rest with the technology innovators, not the politicians. True power stems from Silicon Valley not Washington, D.C., despite whatever self-deluded narrative the president and his blowhard congress choose to believe. All you have to do is watch footage of his buddy Mark Zuckerberg run circles around those pompous, know-nothing senators when they try to hold him accountable for business decisions, they knew nothing about.

For Christ's sake, his boy Zuck was worth more than all those clowns combined, and they were lecturing him on running a business? Just wait until the next election. Money. That's what elections always come down to, and he was about to have more than God Himself. And the more he thinks about it, the more he's sure that Zuck and JB are gonna lay some wood to every incumbent right on up to the freaking White House if they think the president thinks he can simply swoop in and steal their technology.

He smiles to himself. He's not alone. The other CEOs will come to his rescue. His sudden pivot from taciturn to amiable soothes the anxious crowd. Suddenly, Ormand's tie seems a whole lot looser. His composure returns as Camille's lilting, almost sing-song voice evaporates like dew on a summer's morning. Yeah, come to think of it, he's the king of both realms – D.C. and Silicon Valley – which pretty much makes him king of the world.

He sees Robert Jarvis standing in one of the balconies to his left. The two men make eye contact. Jarvis tips his glass. Ormand nods. Then, the Liquid Messiah clears his mind and refocuses on his dreams, which are about to become reality.

"Ladies and gentlemen, my distinguished guests, welcome to Liquid Palace. Tonight, you will hear about a new technology that will make everything in the world obsolete before dawn. Everything in the world, that is, except Liquid Sky. Liquid Sky is the future, and I am Liquid Sky."

He quickly finds Camille and locks in on her before continuing. He shoots her a nasty, defiant glare that's caught for all to see on the giant screen.

"Nothing will stand in my way. Nobody will derail this company's momentum. The entire world is going to change right now, and there's nothing anyone can do to stop it from happening. I have seen the future, and I adore it like my child. I have created the future, and I love it. I am the Liquid Messiah... and I love that, too."

The applause is tremendous. The screen behind him erupts with color. Wagner's "*Ride of the Valkyries*" descends upon the magnificent ballroom like thunder rolling across the sky. On screen, a speeding concept car is shown from high above hurtling down a pin-straight desert highway. From the right-hand side of the screen, a bullet train catches up to the car and then passes it. Out of nowhere, again from the right, a jet appears, overtakes both the car and the train before climbing high into the sky... vertically. There is a loud boom as the jet blows past the sound barrier. It's simply amazing.

The scene dissolves into an aerial shot. This time, it's a bunch of oil-well pump jacks, the rocking-horse kind, standing defunct, looking more like relics from the Old West than contemporary technology. Helpless birds covered in oil from a tanker spill fill the screen next. They fade into images of industrial factories belching dark clouds from their stacks, and references to global warming populate the screen. The camera locates a floating chunk of ice set adrift in crystal-blue water. Diving down, the camera reveals a lone polar bear stranded on the ice raft, awaiting his agonizing demise.

The message is clear. Ormand speaks again. As usual, he's completely unconcerned with the gross contradiction between what he's about to say and the facts of his life.

"The world has changed. More specifically, it has stumbled under the tremendous burden human beings have become. We have caused irreparable harm to the planet that wants only to nurture all living things. How do we repay that? We pollute it, we overpopulate it, we strip it bare of its precious resources in order to feed a bottomless well, the greed of a few powerful men. All the while, the majority of human beings have been abandoned, left to battle starvation, disease, and staggering poverty, alone with no hope of survival."

Ormand pauses for effect. His heart is racing. He has them eating out of the palm of his hand. He feels omnipotent, and it drives him on.

"I will change all that," he continues. "We have an obligation to make good on our debts to Mother Earth. And I am going to pay the tab for all humanity. It's time to change the world. Pay close attention to what I'm about to say. After tonight, we are no longer enslaved by the oil industry. And the laws of physics as we know them will crumble, as well."

There is a palpable buzz of excitement connecting everyone in the audience. Ormand lets it seep in like he is dipping an old-fashioned donut into a cup of coffee.

"I stand here before each and every one of you prepared to give the world a gift that will instantly change the game."

Large gold letters spell out Liquid-Drive on the screen and then dissolve into a picture of our galaxy.

"Imagine an endless power supply surrounding us at all times no matter where we are or what we are doing," continues Ormand. "Imagine instant energy independence with a zero-carbon footprint, clean, efficient, unlimited power. We owe that to our Mother. We owe that to ourselves and our children."

Ormand smiles. He knows the real "clean, efficient, unlimited power" refers not to gravity but to the power he, the Liquid Messiah, is about to wield over the rest of the world. He likes the hidden meaning of it. It makes him feel good. He doubts anyone is really going to get it anyway.

"Power," he continues. "Imagine that kind of power, the kind of power that can totally redefine human existence. Do you understand what I am talking about?"

The audience cheers riotously. Yes, yes! We know! We know!

Sure, you do, he thinks to himself. If his smile gets any wider, his skin will tear.

"And so," he says, "without further delay, I give you Liquid-Drive, a propulsion technology using nothing but gravitational energy for fuel."

The room goes silent. All eyes are fixed on the screen. Jaws hang agape.

"Sure," said Ormand, "there are those among you who were at Burning Man or who have otherwise heard tell of this miraculous technology capable of converting gravitational energy into an endless, clean, zero-footprint source of power."

Ormand steps out toward the audience. A silver disk, no more than two inches thick and about three feet in diameter cruises out silently from somewhere off to his left. It is lit with blue neon around its perimeter and its top surface is fully illuminated in cool white LED. The disk stops in front of Ormand's feet, hovering a few inches off the ground. He can hear his guests gasp.

"Jesus may have walked on water," he says. "But did he walk on air?"

Rickey Ormand steps onto his Liquid-Disk. The surface immediately changes from cool white to deep purple. "They don't call me the Liquid Messiah for nothing," he exclaims.

This is the big reveal everyone's been waiting for. The disk rises up to about five feet and begins to circulate around the ballroom with Ormand standing atop like Poseidon rising from the ocean depths. Applause fills the room as the disk moves the Messiah about... high, low, left, right, front, back. Ormand appears to be floating. He even ascends as high as the balcony level. The audience is awestruck. Love him or hate him, there are two things about Rickey Ormand everybody knows. First, he's a natural-born showman with a gift for the dramatic. Second, he loves to drop a bomb on convention. This is why they came.

Ormand keeps talking as he flies around the room. "Yes, it's self-driving. And yes, it's powered entirely by gravity. Inside this thin disk is a unit no bigger than a nine-volt battery. You don't need to know how it works. All you need to know is that it does work. It works perfectly, silently, cleanly efficient."

The audience, once demure, well heeled, and affluent, gives in to the moment. Countless cell phones are raised in the air, live streaming the momentous event... just as Ormand planned. When the Liquid-Disk brings him to the rear of the room directly across from the podium, it climbs high, elevating Ormand high enough so that his feet are even with the balcony railing. He steps off the Liquid-Disk onto the railing and uses a large pillar to his right to brace himself.

"I was never one for gymnastics, let alone standing on a railing the size of a balance beam thirty feet in the air," he says. "But these are new times. I feel emboldened. They don't call it a 'brave new world' for nothing. I am unafraid of the future."

There is a spontaneous gasp as Ormand steps off the railing. Time freezes during that fraction of a second before gravity plummets him to his death. But this is all part of the show. For no sooner does Ormand step off the railing than the Liquid-Disk flies in – silently and in the wink of an eye – and provides... a step.

"Amazing," he proclaims over the cheers. "Gravity would have caused my death. Instead, when harnessed to my advantage, gravity actually saved my life. It's a metaphor, people. Gravity power is going to save the planet. Gravity power is going to save civilization."

The synchronization is flawless. No sooner has Ormand stepped onto the disk that saved him from falling to his death then a second disk, and a third, fourth, fifth appear creating a flight of steps for Ormand to descend.

The audience goes berserk, frenzied like a mass of satyrs and nymphs before Dionysus descending from Olympus. Ormand strides off the last Liquid-Disk and is back at the podium.

"A moment ago, I said Jesus may have walked on water, but I can walk on air. Let me now put it to you another way."

He pauses to take in the cheers and whistles.

"Tonight," he says when things die down a bit. "Tonight, I am serving notice to the world."

Applause... enthusiasm... admiration are all thrown at the Messiah. Rickey Ormand drinks it in.

"That's right," he declares, staring straight at Camille again. "Liquid Sky is about to crush the antiquated, disjointed, and disconnected paradigms that govern our world. Just imagine a new future where completely new principles govern the world. Isn't this the purpose of change? Isn't this the meaning of progress?"

The support is so raucous even Camille is surprised. She is worried, as well. She sees Ormand's gift for connecting to people by making promises to deliver grand ideas he has no intention of keeping. She senses his disdain for those very same people and cynicism for those very same ideas. At the same time, his hunger for power is palpable. She can taste it, acrid on her lips. There is a fight coming. She knows this now.

Ormand shifts to his nerdy, techie, *sympathetic* persona. "Wanna know something?" He says in his affected, dork voice.

The mass of enthralled guests beckons him to continue. Yes, they want to know. They want to know something.

"People are going to be very threatened by my discovery," he says. "In fact, I'm already getting threats from very high places."

A series of boos rises up from the audience.

Ormand nods. "That's right, that's right. And I bet you can all guess who's threatened the most. The people at the very top... Big Oil, who want us to stay hooked on their filthy fossil fuels for the next hundred years... the transportation industry, the manufacturing sector. Oh, let's not forget the industrial military complex, right?"

Boos emanate from the collective.

"Yeah, I know," he says, egging them on. "The powers that be, right? Well, tomorrow, they're going to be the powers that *were*."

There is tremendous applause.

Ormand is on a roll now, man. "How about all those terrorists in the Middle East? They depend on oil money secretly funnelled to them to fund their heinous attacks on innocent civilians. I bet they're feeling pretty threatened right about now, too, right? Everyone who ponies up to the White House is about to feel the pain of change by the people for the people."

Ormand laughs robustly. The audience laughs with him. This is all honey to their ears. He turns to Camille yet again. "I say burn the entire shit house to the ground. And you can quote me on that," he declares. "Put it on bumper stickers. Put it on T-shirts. Put it on banners. Embrace the future. The houses of the holy are really just shit houses in disguise. Burn them down, baby."

The applause is deafening. Affluent as these guests are, they are happy to hand over monopolistic control of the entire world. Camille looks down, closes her eyes, and shakes her head. This is all wrong, she thinks. It's all so wrong.

Ormand puts on a little duck face as he hops back onto one of the Liquid-Disks. It circulates him gently through the audience about five feet in the air.

"Bring it down and rebuild it," says Ormand. "That's what I say. The Russians, the Chinese, the Saudis, Big Oil, Big Government, Big Military... you name it. The rule of the global oligarchy has come to an end. The era of the people is upon us."

Camille looks at Parker Fitzgerald. They both roll their eyes.

"Let me translate," says Fitzgerald dryly. "He's ridding the world of an oligarchy in order to install himself as a monarchy. It's so Rickey Ormand. He has no filter. You know that, right?"

Camille closes her eyes. "It's a good thing actually. At least he goes on record with all this. His playbook is wide open for everyone to see. He's like the exact opposite of the president."

Camille pauses for a moment before continuing. "So, he actually thinks like this?"

"Oh God, yes," replies Fitzgerald. "Whatever's in his head comes out of his mouth."

Camille chuckles. "Well, it comes out. As for what orifice... that's up for debate."

Fitzgerald shakes her head and laughs.

Camille sighs. "Sadly, it's probably what makes him so successful... thinking like this, I mean."

Fitzgerald pats Camille on the shoulder. "But like you said, a new era is dawning. And it's most certainly not the one Rickey's talking about, right?"

Camille turns back to face Ormand. She nods and bites her lip. "Should we tell him?"

"Nah," said Fitzgerald. "Let's see how long it takes him to figure it out."

They realize that Ormand is drifting toward them.

"Oh, God," says Camille. "He's heading this way. What's he up to now?"

"Isn't that always the question?" asks Parker.

As Ormand methodically wends his way over to Camille and Parker atop his luminescent disk, he keeps on firing up his group of distinguished guests. "All current modes of transportation... obsolete tomorrow. Every sort of engine or motor powered by electricity... obsolete tomorrow. Global warming, pollution, and energy scarcity... gone. In their place will be Liquid-Drive powering the world. Of course, I know it will take some time to build a new infrastructure, but I'm sure you all share my vision and get my point.

Everything you can imagine will be obsolete come tomorrow. Thank God for that."

He hovers about five feet in front of Camille and Fitzgerald, blows them both a kiss, and then rotates to face the center of the ballroom. He holds up his hand to silence the crowd.

"And do you know who is most afraid of this wonderful new technology? None other than Harry Pierson, the president of the United States, the most powerful man in the old world... until tomorrow. You all know what happens tomorrow, right?"

As if on cue, the sea of guests yells out, "Obsolete!"

"Yes," says Ormand. "Obsolete!"

He floats his way back to the front of the ballroom. The crowd of guests is elated. This is exactly what they came to see. This is exactly why they love the Liquid Messiah.

Ormand holds up his hand again, beckoning for quiet. "Thank you, thank you. Now, lest anyone think that Rickey Ormand is crass or somehow afraid to face his critics, I have a special surprise for you. I mentioned the president a moment ago – the same president who feels I am a threat to national security, by the way –"

The crowd cuts him off with a barrage of boos and whistles.

Ormand extends his arms to the side and flaps them like a quarterback at the line of scrimmage trying to silence a boisterous home crowd before a big play.

"The only thing a politician hears is the click of the ballot lever and the whoosh of bills through a money counter. But you will have your chance to be heard come election day in a couple of months. For now, however, I want to introduce you to a very special woman whom you all know. Even though she works for the president, I asked her to say a few words today... because Rickey Ormand is that kind of guy... fair and balanced."

He has piqued their interest.

"And so, without further ado, I give you the Red Dragon Lady herself, the one, the only Ms. Camille O'Keefe, candidate for vice president of the old United States and special guest of Rickey Ormand because, again... I'm that kind of guy."

Camille tenses when she hears her name. Ordinarily she is casual, if not a bit awkward, speaking in public. After all, she communes with souls and masters across multiple dimensions and across millennia. But Ormand has unnerved her with his aggression. She really doesn't like conflict, and Ormand's self-aggrandisement strikes her as flat-out throwing down the gauntlet.

Either way, she knows that Harry Pierson is going to take the gloves off. Once again, she'll be right where she doesn't want to be… standing in the stream of a pissing match between two powerful men fighting over the power of their magic. What is it about her decision making, she wonders, that she keeps ending up in this position?

Most of all, she's troubled by Ormand's nasty rhetoric. It's indicative of a raging narcissist. He's ignoring the facts in lieu of his ego's alluring charm. Camille knows that Harry Pierson is dead serious about invoking national security and seizing the entire gravity program. She has no doubt that Ormand will fire back with all his vindictiveness. They were headed for a massive confrontation, each man with his cocktail weenie in his hand, as Parker might have said. Unless a deal could be struck, only one would emerge victorious.

Camille felt a bit guilty just then. Rickey Ormand had no clue what he was up against. Harry Pierson could crush him like a bug and would gladly do so just for sport. Ormand was engulfed by his ego and unable to see past the fog of his self-aggrandizement. She knew this. In fact, she was playing off this. Perhaps her plan to bait and hook these two men was ill-conceived. In the end, Rickey Ormand would be in tatters, and Harry Pierson would somehow manage to hold her indebted to him for it.

Camille feels Fitzgerald poking her ribs and returns to the present moment. The audience is applauding robustly once again.

"Camille," says Fitzgerald. "You're on, sister. Come on. How much longer do you want them to clap for you?"

Camille shakes the thoughts from her head and looks at Fitzgerald. "What?"

She is suddenly aware that the orchestra is playing a lively rendition of "In the Mood" to set up her approach to the podium.

Fitzgerald points to Rickey Ormand. "You're on, sister. The Messiah awaits. It's show time."

Camille turns toward Rickey Ormand as her focus returns. Ormand is facing her with his arms outstretched as if he's her husband welcoming her home after a long trip abroad.

"I suppose it is," says Camille.

Parker looks at her quizzically, but Camille is already striding toward the podium. Ormand is waiting for her, arms still extended. Camille stops short of an embrace.

"Photo op," Rickey mumbles through his plastic smile.

Camille glances toward the audience that fills the room to her left. She can feel their excitement. She feels honored and even a bit humble. Their intentions are genuine. But she's certainly not going to let Rickey Ormand wrap her up in his arms so the pic can go viral, making it seem as if he has both her and the president of the United States in his pocket.

No, she decides, that will definitely not do. She's been around enough to know better.

She takes one more step toward Ormand. He leans in to engulf her in a smothering hug and, she has no doubt, a slimy kiss on the check. Instead, she stands erect, stares off the Liquid Messiah, and extends her right hand.

The large wall-screen depicts it all... Camille's warm smile... her right hand extended, bent at the wrist for Ormand to kiss... the Messiah's stunned look.

Camille raises her hand up and down slightly as if flicking a lure, her bright, pale skin radiant under all the lights. "Photo-op," she says.

Suddenly, Ormand feels like his bow tie is strangling him again. On screen, he looks flushed and aloof. Realizing that everyone is awaiting his next move, he takes Camille's hand in his, bows slightly, and kisses it without once looking at her.

Camille can only wonder if he is this clumsy in the boudoir, as well. She thinks of Parker Fitzgerald. She half-wishes she could have Fitzgerald's snarky wit. And Fitzgerald's amazing physical prowess doesn't escape Camille's notice, either. As she watches Rickey

Ormand finish his clumsy kiss, she notices the slug trail of saliva
he leaves on her hand and imagines Fitzgerald squishing the little
man between her immensely powerful, robotic legs. It makes her
feel better.

She casually wipes the top of her hand against her beautiful
gown and smiles. Show time, indeed. She nods to the band leader
who instantly brings his musicians into a thrilling crescendo full of
vibrato and excitement. She turns to face the throng of guests and
waves energetically. She is rewarded with a prolonged round of
enthusiastic applause. She blushes a bit, holds her hands at her chest
palm to palm in a Buddhist prayer position, and bows slightly.

It takes several minutes for the cheers to subside. She is Camille
O'Keefe. She is the Red Dragon Lady. And they love her here as they
do everywhere. Camille stands still while one of the tech crew clips
a mic to the nape of her gown. Rickey Ormand is still standing there,
not next to Camille but not too far away either. He is close enough
to look like he's trying to glom onto her while, at the same time,
appearing too weak to do so even in his own palace. In the end, he just
stands there frozen in a state of limbo, snared on the redhead's hook.

This is the thing about Camille O'Keefe that Harry Pierson values
enough to make her his running mate. The woman has presence and
magnetic charm that's hard to resist. Camille senses that Ormand has
just learned that for himself. She also senses that he doesn't much
like it. She relishes the thought. It bolsters her confidence and helps
dissipate the reluctance she was feeling a few moments earlier.

When the tech motions to the clip-on mic and gives the thumbs
up, Camille really turns it on. She looks at Parker Fitzgerald. Even at
this distance, the half-bot dominates everything around her.

"Ladies and gentlemen, friends of Mr. Ormand, fans of Liquid
Sky, kindred spirits… it is my great honor to stand here before you
tonight."

She begins walking around the front of the ballroom without
straying too far from the podium.

"Judging from your warm welcome, most of you know who I
am. I thank you for that." She holds her right arm out to the side and

points with her full open hand palm up to Ormand. "I also want to thank Mr. Ormand for this opportunity to speak to you tonight as well as his great generosity. It's not every day that I get to step into a fantasy world."

She pivots back the way she came and sees Parker Fitzgerald laughing. She gets the *double entendre*. The audience applauds, but Camille doubts many of them get the joke.

"You know," continues Camille, "I cannot travel through the air on little silver gravity saucers, but I can certainly travel through dimensions and back centuries with the same ease. To some, that makes me weird. But seeing you all here tonight reminds me that the world will always have a contingency of people looking for something different, looking for another way. Who knows? Maybe come election time, that new way is me?"

The applause is far more than Camille expected. She looks at the Liquid Messiah and winks. It pierces him like an arrow through a paper tiger.

"Yes," says Camille, "I am different. But you know what? That's what makes me powerful. Difference is power. Difference is the future. Difference is the way to genuine progress. Take my new friend, for example."

She heads toward Parker Fitzgerald who has suddenly turned a shade of red that can best be called mortified crimson.

"I'm sure you all know Dr. Parker Fitzgerald. I mean... is she incredible or what? I won't go into too much detail about her personal struggle. Suffice it to say, Dr. Fitzgerald is the heart of Liquid-Drive. I hope you all know that. This woman right here is the real essence of this company. I hope you tell everyone you know. Tweet it."

She waits for the laughter to subside.

"Anyway, Parker Fitzgerald represents the future of the physical world, a world that will transcend simple flesh and bone and introduce us to brand new manifestations of exciting ideas recast in totally new forms."

She returns to the center near the podium while allowing her analogy to seep in.

"As for me," she says. "I represent the future of the spirit. The spirit inside each and every one of us is like our own personal chariot to the heavens. It's wonderful."

Pause... draw it out... wait... draw it out....

She takes a deep breath making sure that the mic picks it up. "Unfortunately, our chariots have been stuck on the ground for many, many years... for centuries, in fact."

She lowers her eyes and nods several times. She is contemplating her next words and thinks she might as well jump into her theory about male and female energy. She then reconsiders it. Better that she translate the concept into something more palpable so everyone can easily understand. That is, after all, her role as a running mate.

"Yes, yes," she says, "we are about to enter a new era, one in which energy means everything."

There is loud applause. Even Rickey Ormand thinks he's won the day now. "You got that right," he says into his mic."

He grabs a glass of the good stuff from a passing waiter, places it atop one of his Liquid-Discs, and sends it out to Camille. He gets rousing laughter and applause from his guests.

Camille raises the glass to her host, takes a small sip, and then sets it back atop the disk. She's comfortable now. She feels she can say what she must in a way that will be well received.

"Well, those of you who have read anything I've written know that I am all about progress, right? Just think about it, gravity power is here, and the world is going to change in the blink of an eye."

Rickey Ormand sees an opportunity to insert himself again. "Like I said, people. I will lead us into a brave new world."

Camille can only close her eyes and droop her head. She wonders how many in attendance have actually read Huxley's novel about bleak totalitarianism and a society in which individuality is stamped out like a burning ember underfoot in the name of progress and modernity.

Ormand looks around wondering what he can interject next. Parker Fitzgerald crooks her index finger at the tech standing closest to her. "If his mic isn't turned off in the next six seconds, you're going to see me get all nasty ass. And listen… nobody wants to see a nasty-ass robot. I mean it."

The tech scurries away and switches Ormand's mic off. Fitzgerald smiles and nods to Camille as if to say, "Please proceed."

Camille returns a smile and a nod of her own. "Gravity power is something totally new," she says. "But I wonder… is that the same thing as progress?"

She pauses to let her question sink in.

"I mean," she continues, "what exactly is progress? The discovery of gravity power has infinite possibilities and can create unprecedented opportunities for even the most impoverished and downtrodden in the world."

She snickers.

"I mean, gravity power – in the form of this proprietary product called Liquid-Drive –has got to mean more than a flying serving tray with a glass of champagne, no matter how good that champagne may be, right?"

She is pleased to get a bit of laughter as she segways into a harsh criticism of Rickey Ormand in his own house. The lines have been drawn. On one side is the Liquid Messiah ready to pounce. On the other is the president, Harry Pierson, also ready to pounce. Camille feels a lot like a piece of raw meat thrown in between. So be it if this is her calling. So be it if this is her fate.

Camille clears her throat. "I want each of you to close your eyes and follow me on a short journey."

She smiles at Fitzgerald and then turns to the band leader. "Perhaps something light and airy?"

The conductor raises his arm. On the downbeat, the piano and stand-up bass ease into a lazy rendition of "Summertime," sliding in and out of the space the drummer creates chipping on his high-hat.

Camille smiles a perfect smile for the perfect tune. Her voice is gentle and rides along atop the sultry, sweet notes. It is almost hypnotic. She begins walking the floor.

"Okay, so imagine a source of energy that is everywhere around us and readily available. This energy is constantly flowing and comes from the universe and not from some oil refinery or utility company. No one company can monopolize this energy because its source is the universe. It belongs to all of us. No one man can claim it as his own because its source is the vital essence that flows through each of us, and no one man may own another."

A sort of rapt attention spreads over the crowd of distinguished guests like the sun rising on an August morning. Camille interprets this as a general awareness that she and the Liquid Messiah may be on different paths. She looks up at the folks in the balconies. She wonders how many billions in net worth are standing around her. For that matter, how many of these guests run companies that govern the world? Here at the Liquid Palace, in the heart of Silicon Valley, it could be any number of them, she realizes. And yet, all these billionaires, all these power brokers, have lined up to hear what Rickey Ormand defines as the future of the world that he plans to carve out for himself.

It's fascinating. She can't help wondering, is it really that easy? Is it really so simple to control people, even the handful of über elite who run the world? She nods. She assumes so.

"Yeah, I know," she says, "intellectual property rules the day here in Silicon Valley. All this talk about universal rights sounds a bit too strange, even in California."

She gets a good laugh with that one. She is relieved. She needs a delicate transition. She looks up and addresses the people on the balcony level.

"Did Camille O'Keefe just say 'universal rights?' That's what you're asking yourself. I know. I'm a medium, remember?"

Laughter... not as much as before but still welcome.

She knows where this is headed. Rickey Ormand will be furious. Harry Pierson will be furious. The two most powerful men in the world... both will want her head. She has no doubt about this. But she cannot betray herself. Speaking her truth might piss off these two men and countless others. But that wasn't betrayal, not for Camille. Speaking her truth can never be a form of deceit, disloyalty, or treachery.

If anything, the contrary is true for Camille. Were she to gag herself or somehow hold her tongue, she would be betraying herself. Standing there in front of all these powerful people, she still knows this much.

She looks over at Parker Fitzgerald. The eagerness in Fitzgerald's eyes encourages her. Fitzgerald makes a fist and pumps it at her waist. "Go for it," she mouths.

Camille nods. "Yeah," she mouths back and winks.

She spins around and faces Rickey Ormand, who looks like he does not know where this is heading, and having his mic turned off at the same time is kicking his ass.

"Rickey Ormand," shouts Camille, holding her right hand out toward him. Her sudden burst of high energy surprises people, especially given the soothing music the orchestra is still dishing out. Ormand nearly jumps out of his tux which, by now, he would gladly trade for a hoodie and some khakis.

"Great house, great champagne, great guy," says Camille, although not particularly enthralled with any of the three. "And yet, is this all there is?"

Ormand looks around as if trying to find out who just tapped him on the shoulder. The orchestra fizzles out. So much for "Summertime."

Camille looks around the ballroom. Stunned silence. She grits her teeth and sucks air through her pursed lips. Yeah, she thinks, I'm about to lose some friends right here.

"I mean," she continues, "his discovery of gravity power is something with collective potential, is it not? Collective potential, right? The implications are definitely staggering. First of all, I am sure there were many people involved, not the least of whom is Dr. Parker Fitzgerald."

Camille points her out with her left hand. Fitzgerald raises her hand and waves tentatively. There is acknowledgement from the guests.

"As you probably know, Dr. Fitzgerald was really the first person – and a woman at that – to discover that gravity could be harnessed to amass a whole lot of energy. Yeah, and it almost killed her."

Camille is pacing side to side at the front of the ballroom now. She is building momentum.

"Wait," she says, stopping dead in her tracks. She turns her head to the right, toward the mass of people. "You didn't know that?" She chuckles sardonically. "You all don't think Rickey Ormand discovered gravity power... do you?"

Dead silence. Somewhere outside the gilded ballroom a tray full of empty glasses crashes. It happens all the time, but now it seems almost slapstick.

"I guess that fella didn't know either."

Yes, there is laughter. But it's nervous laughter. There's no doubt about that.

Camille remains undaunted. Her truth is truth to herself and to the great collective of humanity. "Now, it's true," she continues. "Without Rickey Ormand, this great discovery would never become a *thing*. We need things. The *world* needs things. But most of all, more than anything else, we in the world need each other to share things. Otherwise, what do we really have? Isolation, not interconnectedness."

At this point, Ormand is feeling his pockets for some sort of magic mute button... or a gun. He would definitely take a gun if no mute button is available. He turns to the technical staff dragging his forefinger along his throat. "Kill her mic," he mouths... to nobody. But to his dismay, there's nobody manning the audio controls. They walked out a minute or two earlier at Fitzgerald's urging.

As Ormand so often says, he gets everything he deserves. That's as true right now as it ever was. Camille O'Keefe doesn't know about this little *coup*. She just keeps giving it to the Liquid Messiah. She is there, after all, to nail his ass up. So why not nail his ass up?

"There's no question about it," says Camille, her arms outstretched to her side at shoulder height. "The discovery of gravity power will change the world in the blink of an eye. I get all the lip service about making the world a better place. But let's face it. When has that ever driven stock prices, right? And I'm sorry to burst bubbles, but the true potential of gravity power does not lie in some balance sheet or stock price. If you are living in dire poverty somewhere in Africa or South America, how concerned are you with your 401(k)? More likely, you are thinking about what you can possibly scrounge up that passes as protein to feed your starving children whose bellies are distended like basketballs from kwashiorkor. Of course, you have no electricity or heat or fuel of any sort for cooking, lighting, or transportation because you cannot come close to affording electricity, propane, or gasoline. The oil industry must have its revenues. And so, only those who can pony up the dough deserve the luxury of light and a cooked meal… provided, of course, they are able to find some grubs or bugs under a rock or fallen tree."

Silence… uncomfortable coughs as Camille's excruciating ironies penetrate the well-lotioned soft skin like thorns.

Ormand mutters his protest to Camille through a tight fake smile. "Come on, O'Keefe. At my party? Really?"

Camille just shrugs.

"People," beckons Ormand, "I'm the greatest innovator this world has ever known.

It's my job to make as much money as possible for my shareholders. Driving profits and creating shareholder value… at the end of the day, that's my only job, and Rickey Ormand is damned good at it. I mean… think about it… cars, planes, farming equipment, drilling devices, water, oil, gas services, medicine, heating and cooling, the military, pollution. Who knows? Maybe even interstellar travel, unlimited speeds, and levitation become a reality. With Liquid-Drive gravity power, there are no limits anymore. That's right… Rickey Ormand has erased all those boundaries."

Fitzgerald looks around the room. Everyone is eyeballing Camille and Ormand like they were two school kids about to brawl on the playground. She sees people leaning in toward one another whispering what she can only assume are crass criticisms of both.

Camille is less concerned. She also sees people whispering, or primping their hair, or adjusting their ties and collars. "Mr. Ormand is correct," she says. "It's marvellous. It really is. And I know, I know. I see a lot of you fidgeting and wondering to yourselves, 'Is this redhead completely nuts?' It's okay. It's all good. I've made you uncomfortable. Never be afraid to feel uncomfortable. Look at me. I lived in the White House for God's sake. What could be more uncomfortable?"

She's got to work her way back slowly.

"But I'll tell you one thing. I sure learned a heck of a lot about politics, about men, Democracy or whatever it is we actually have, and about myself. That's the point. We humans are strange. It's a peculiarity of this Third Dimension. The Fourth is full, by the way. And the Fifth... that's where the fun is. Anyway, we humans are here to learn, grow, and fulfill our spiritual potential. It's really that simple. When we reach our apex, we reach enlightenment and no longer need to come back incarnate. Once we resolve our individual karmic baggage, we transcend. We become Masters, spirits advising those who are still struggling to overcome their karmic debt.

"Here on earth, things are so slow and dense, we have life lessons crammed into everything. This Third Dimension is slogged, and bogged, and grossly uncomfortable. But for that reason, it's where the fastest learning happens. So, remember this – learning happens when we are uncomfortable. Soft and comfortably unconscious people neither learn nor grow. Of this I can assure you. Discomfort is the soil for personal growth."

Crickets. A few coughs. That's about it.

The awkward, uncomfortable silence is shattered by hearty laughter. It's Rickey Ormand, and he's laughing his ass off.

"Oh, my," he says. "That was certainly entertaining. Thank you so much for being yourself."

People can't hear him without his mic on. She feels she's losing the crowd. She already knows Parker Fitzgerald is striding toward her. Seconds later, the Red Dragon Lady and the Phoenix are standing side-by-side in front of a ballroom full of posh guests.

"One last thing," says Camille. "This is Dr. Parker Fitzgerald. I mentioned her earlier. This is the woman who first discovered the potential power of gravity. She represents a new breed of woman, part human and part machine. This is the potential of technology.

My role is to remind the world that the potential is far bigger than any one individual. Gravity power should be shared with the entire world, with everyone everywhere every time regardless of profit or loss.

"Access to the most important discovery of our age should not and cannot be restricted, rationed, sold, or otherwise controlled. Liquid-Drive can catapult the entire world forward for the better. That's progress. We heard a lot of nice, fanciful promises tonight. But I promise you this. I keep my promises. Most of you already know that about me. In fact, this is so important to me, that I have asked the president to make this a matter of national security. What more than elevating the lives of the world's most vulnerable would make our country more secure? This, I ask you to ponder."

Camille removes her clip-on mic and hands it to Fitzgerald who tosses it aside. It makes a little crackle when it lands.

"Not much of a mic drop," says Fitzgerald under her breath.

Camille chuckles. "Yeah, not much of a speech, either. I left out the most important parts."

The two women stop.

"So, go back up there and say what you came to say."

"That's the thing," says Camille. "I came to Liquid Palace to deliver a specific message from the president, which I did."

"And?" prompts Fitzgerald.

"And," says Camille sighing, "Ormand threw it right back in my face. He basically flipped the bird to the president of the United States."

Fitzgerald shrugs. It's nothing she hadn't seen a million times before during her tenure at Liquid Sky. "That's Rickey Ormand for you. He's like a petulant child. He doesn't like being told no, and he throws a tantrum whenever he doesn't get what he wants. Liquid-Drive he wants more than anything else in the world."

Camille bites her lip. "Yeah, well... after hearing him speak, I changed my comments and said what I felt had to be said."

Fitzgerald puts her hand on Camille's shoulder. "Sort of," she says.

"Sort of," says Camille. "Maybe next time."

Fitzgerald laughs heartily. "My friend, I can guarantee you are never stepping foot in Liquid Palace again. Believe me, when you cross Rickey Ormand, you're dead to him. And you, I'd venture to guess, are as dead as roadkill as far as the Liquid Messiah is concerned."

Camille snorts in disgust. "Eh, Liquid Messiah," she says. "What balls."

Camille O'Keefe and Parker Fitzgerald continue toward the door when they hear Ormand clearing his throat. It sounds like thunder because Ormand is holding Camille's discarded mic up to his mouth.

"Well, thank you for that, Ms. O'Keefe," he says. "Don't we all just love to be preached to by a politician? I mean… people in Washington find it so easy to tell us what to do with our money and our businesses."

His barb earns laughter from his guests.

"Isn't that right, Ms. O'Keefe?" he says.

"He's taunting you," whispers Fitzgerald. "That's what he does."

"And you, Dr. Fitzgerald, would do well to remember that all of this…." He gestures to the opulent surroundings. "Comes at a price that very few people can pay. So, pick your allies wisely."

He turns his attention back to the guests. "That's what I always say. And I venture to guess that you've all enjoyed what I have laid out for you tonight."

There is a solid round of applause for the Rickey Ormand, the Liquid Messiah.

Camille looks up at Fitzgerald.

"It's now or never," says Fitzgerald. "You'll not step foot on this campus ever again. Now's the time to let it fly."

Camille musters her resolve and walks over to Ormand.

Ormand feigns delight. "Look, folks. The Red Dragon Lady returned."

Camille walks right up to Ormand and takes the little mic from his hand. His mocking, sardonic smile vanishes instantly. The last thing he expects is for Camille O'Keefe to stare him down like she is doing right now.

"Don't mind if I do," says Camille, holding the mic in front of her like a reporter on location. "Radical mutuality," she says. "Look it up in one of my books. Radical mutuality, that's what I'm about. It's a deep interconnectedness among all people of this planet. It binds us all to each other like a giant needle and thread. We, all people, are the fabric from which life is woven."

A waiter starts clearing a table next to Fitzgerald. She reaches out and seizes his arm. He looks up at her, shocked. She shakes her head. "Show some respect," she says.

"I'm sure most of you are wondering what the heck I'm talking about, but really it's quite a simple concept. You see, it's all a matter of intentions. Results concern me much less than the original intentions. The time of Enlightenment science, the time of Cartesian causality and this stuff about mind-body separation, has come and gone. That duality doesn't exist any place other than in our own imaginations.

"If you've ever read one of my books, you know I am always saying that ideas are things… ideas are things. Until very recently, what I meant was that each of us has the power to manifest an idea, turn it from idea to reality. Take Mr. Ormand, for example. He is perhaps one of the greatest men in history when it comes to manifesting an idea, that is, taking something abstract and turning it into something real.

"Recently, however, I learned about something called noetics. I see a lot of confused looks out there. Rest assured, noetics is a real science. There are actually three major institutes in the United States, including one in Princeton and one right here in California called Ions. Noetics is the study of internal intelligence, intuition, from an empirical, scientific perspective. It is science and enlightenment beyond anything we have ever known. It's not just a science about science, not just a meta-science. It's science so far beyond anything we have today, it's almost wrong to call it just science. Noetics has proven that ideas are things and actually have mass. So, forget what I said about manifesting ideas into things."

She throws her hands up and blows a curl from her eyes.

"Because guess what? Ideas already exist as things in our mind. It's amazing, isn't it? What's more," she continues, "our ideas have the ability to link up and form something far greater than ourselves, something huge, and something that can be trans-global. The possibilities are endless. So, it is with gravitational energy as well."

Camille stops and looks over at Parker Fitzgerald. Fitzgerald cocks her head and scrunches her face. Two thoughts race through her head.

First: How did Camille get inside my head?

Second: I'm not saying a word. No freaking way.

Camille smiles and turns away. "The science of noetics tells us that we can build individual ideas into something like bridges that connect everyone everywhere so that we don't have to exist on an island of self. That was the old Descartes stuff. That's obsolete in the wake of noetics. But geez, I've known that for centuries. Anyway, follow me...."

She turns her back to the room and walks behind the podium. She stands tall behind it and rubs her hands together. This is the moment she has been waiting for her entire life. This is the moment when she casts off the shackles of politics and inside-the-box expectations in exchange for the bonds of human transcendental experience.

She clips the mic to her dress. "Now, I'm no theoretical physicist, but I am a theoretical transcendentalist. That's enough to know if ideas are things - which noetic science has proven - then ideas have *mass*. And if ideas have mass, they have what else?"

She lets the question hang out there for a few seconds. Nothing. She waits a few seconds more.

It is Parker Fitzgerald who calls out. "Gravity!"

Camille throws her other hand up. "Yes! Ideas have gravity. Radical mutuality. Remember that. Radical mutuality means we exist in a meta-system. All you Silicon Valley techies know what I mean. A meta-system is an overarching system that monitors individual micro-systems but also combines them into something far greater than the sum of the parts. Radical mutuality. Each human being is a subsystem, and we are all part of a universal meta-system that, when tapped, can generate a power far greater than anything this world has ever known.

"Radical mutuality... ideas have mass. Therefore, ideas have gravity. Thus, gravitation energy is flowing through us at all times, connecting us to both the universe at large and the universe of human intuition."

Parker Fitzgerald is blown away. She never would have guessed that someone like Camille O'Keefe would ever figure out things together like this. "*Quod erat demonstradum*," she says. The situation demonstrates the truth, abbreviated *QED* at the end of a formal proof.

Camille turns to Fitzgerald again. "What was that, Dr. Fitzgerald?"

"That's absolutely correct," says Fitzgerald. "Gravitation energy affects us on a sub-atomic level. I have proved it in the lab."

"None of this is what I came here to say today," continues Camille. "What I came here to say is that Liquid-Drive will never, ever be the sole property of Liquid Sky, its shareholders, Rickey Ormand, or any other select group of people. I promise you this. Before that happens, President Harry Pierson will transfer the technology to the government in the name of national security."

The mass of guests is floored. So much for lending Camille a sympathetic ear. It's one thing for Camille to be all peace, love, and New Age. It is quite another for her and the president to start collectivizing private companies. Most of these people have never heard anything remotely like this before. Conversations erupt throughout the ballroom as people try to figure out the extent to which their personal power and privilege will be affected. After all, these are the very people who pump the lifeblood of capital and intellect into Silicon Valley. To hear the president's running mate sounding like a communist is mind boggling. What else can you call it? That's what they're wondering.

By this point, Camille has to speak her truth. "Listen to me. Gravitational energy can unlock an entirely new existence. This is so much more than an engine, or a patent, or earnings per share. It is so, so much more than that. Free your minds. Let your ideas run like wild horses. Remember, we are all God, and noetics is the science of our Godly power."

She turns to face Fitzgerald. "Free yourself," she says. "Taken to its extreme, gravitational energy can sustain life all by itself."

Parker Fitzgerald hangs her head. I'm not saying a word. No freaking way.

Not long after, the gala quickly descends into a maelstrom of debate. One of the distinguished gentlemen in attendance stops recording video on his cell phone and makes for a service door. In fact, he is neither distinguished nor a gentleman. Rather, he was sent by the NSA to assess the event. He's been live streaming Camille's speech back to the White House where Harry Pierson and a select group of his advisors sit watching.

Pierson's jaw is agape. His face is red but turning purple fast. He has been feeling numbness in his fingers lately, and he's had a bout or two of dizziness. But right now, he would gladly suffer a massive coronary if only he could reach through the screen and choke the life out of Camille O'Keefe.

The three men with him are all staring at him for a cue.

Pierson rubs his face before speaking. "How many of those people would you say have cell phones?" he asks.

The men look at each other, afraid to answer. Finally, one of them finds the courage to speak up.

"All of them, Mr. President," he says.

Pierson clears his sinuses a few times. "And… just roughly… how many do you think were recording all that?" He clears his sinuses a few more times.

"Maybe all of them," the man said again.

Harry Pierson nods. "I want O'Keefe, Ormand, and that freak robot woman in the Oval Office," he says in an eerie, calm voice.

"Yes, Mr. President," all three advisors say at once.

Pierson stands up. His face is almost purple. "Get out of my office," he orders in the same eerily calm voice.

The three men bolt up and make for the door.

"And find me a noeticist or whatever they call themselves. What the hell was she talking about? Does it even exist?"

His voice is raised now. "And get the damned doctor. My heart feels like it's about to explode. That damned woman is going to be the death of me... and we're not even married."

Harry Pierson lays his face in his hands. It is an uncommon visage for the president sitting behind his desk in the Oval Office. "We are all God," he mutters. "What does that even mean?"

Chapter 21

Dr. Venk, the official White House doctor, put it bluntly. "Too much stress is starting to show, Mr. President. You're too distracted. You need to focus more on your health, or the results of the election won't much matter."

The doctor slid the blood-pressure cuff off Pierson's arm, wrapped the pump around it, and placed it back into his black bag. "I'm serious, Mr. President," he reiterated. "Your numbers are getting worse, and you're starting to feel it. This is the third time you've summoned me in the last two weeks. I imagine you want to be alive for your next term?"

Harry Pierson just grunted. He had neither the time to waste on doctors nor the time to waste on changing his behavior. In his opinion, both endeavors were signs of weakness. And going into an election, appearing weak was the one thing Harry Pierson feared most.

"Don't worry about me, doc," Pierson snapped back without delay. "You're looking at one tough son-of-a-bitch. How do you think Putin would respond if I suddenly started taking yoga? Please... the American people want a leader, not a pansy. And for those who do prefer a softie, I have Camille O'Keefe as my running mate."

That was the last he spoke of it. He did, however, think twice about taking on Rickey Ormand just before the election. Ormand's immense popularity, immense wealth, and immense discovery all added up to immense political influence. And the last thing Pierson needed was Ormand getting behind the candidate looking to take the White House away from him.

With this in mind, Pierson figured it best to put off any face-to-face with Ormand until after the election, no matter how big a prick the guy was. As Camille was quick to point out, she'd already delivered a pointed message to Ormand at the gala. "He is fully aware you're looking to take him down," said Camille. "You probably should have played your cards closer to the vest."

Pierson knew she was right, but what could he do about it now? "That's old news, Camille. Offer me solutions, not history lessons, for Christ's sake."

"Wait," she told him flatly. "Don't bring Rickey Ormand to the White House just yet. Wait until after the election."

Pierson liked the sound of that. "Ah... so the clairvoyant sees a victory for us next month?"

Camille said nothing. She had what could be called a non-disclosure agreement with the universe that clearly delineated between foreseeing and foretelling. Camille considered it her moral obligation to never reveal things she foresaw if it would result in significant events changing in ways that would not otherwise have unfolded. For Camille O'Keefe, communing with the universe meant knowing certain truths and events before they occurred. It meant living outside the parameters of free will and free choice. Even if she knew these to be largely illusions, fiction humans tell themselves so they can pretend to have control of their lives, it was a necessary narrative, as necessary as the art of fiction is to our understanding of ourselves and the world around us.

And so, Camille said nothing about the upcoming election even though she knew in one month's time she would be vice president and Beck would be rolling over in his grave were he not cremated out of national embarrassment. Pierson felt confident going into the election. No matter how much of a pain in the ass she was, Camille O'Keefe was Pierson's secret weapon. As far as he was concerned, having Camille by his side was like having a trained falcon on his arm. He could release her into the sky and wait for her to return with something valuable. He liked this.

"I'll take that as a yes," blurted the president. "Your silence on the matter tells me everything I need to know."

This was the first time she'd stepped foot inside the president's Private Study since Beck was president. Pierson had the room completely redecorated, but Beck's energy still hung heavy for Camille. She could almost smell him and the other women he liked to bring there when he needed some oral attention. He said he admired Bill Clinton.

Camille walked over to the two big windows that were adorned with light-blue drapes trimmed with gold. She rubbed the silk fabric between her fingers. She was obviously deep in thought.

"Okay, okay," said the president. "I will defer Rickey Ormand's beat down until after we win... which, again, I assume is predestined, or preordained, or whatever the term is that you use. But he's definitely got one coming, and I intend to oblige him. I just want to make that clear."

Camille released the fabric from her hand and turned to face Pierson, who was sitting behind an intricately carved, ball-and-claw-foot desk. The Presidential Study was nice. Pierson's energy matched the new decor quite well. He looked so comfortable sitting there, more so than in the Oval Office. She looked at him and felt a pang of sadness.

It had been a very long time since Camille O'Keefe found herself in an ethical dilemma. She was in a double-bind and had no idea how to handle the quandary. She knew she couldn't tell him. Revealing what she knew – foretelling what she foresaw – would violate her pact with the universe. It would clearly change the course of events in ways that would reshape the world. And yet, not telling the president of the United States about what she knew was going to happen shortly after the election would also change the course of history in ways that have never occurred before.

The president misread her apprehension. "There's obviously something on your mind, Camille. Like I said, I won't stick it to Ormand until after the election."

"It's not that," she said, stopping well short of a full confession. She still had no intention of telling him what she knew would happen in a few weeks. For now, let him think it was the result of the election she was withholding. In fact, it was not. The Pierson/O'Keefe ticket was going to win. What she was keeping to herself was something far bigger.

"But this whole gravity thing needs to be controlled," he said, again thinking his running mate was concerned about a fight with Rickey Ormand. "Well, it needs to be controlled by me specifically."

There was that grin again.

The time had come for Camille to make a move. Either way she played it, she was going to violate her sacred pact with the universe. Her moral code was bumping up against situational ethics. She closed her eyes and prayed for direction. From Pierson's point of view, it looked like Camille suddenly decided to take a nap. But that's not what was going on.

Camille needed to tap a source. She quickly stepped out of linear time into a space somewhere between the physical dimension of the President's Study and the realm of infinite source. There, she moved impossibly fast through a wide range of ideas and possibilities. In what amounted to a little more than ten seconds, Camille O'Keefe was seeing things, learning things, addressing things both past and yet to come.

She suddenly sat bolt upright. She was back. She saw it. She was there, there in the very source of gravitational energy. As if in a dream state, she saw all the possibilities, and saw Parker Fitzgerald. That's when she knew. That's when she was sure. Parker Fitzgerald was the answer. And she saw Harry Pierson. She saw the thing that she knew would happen to him if she refused to tell him what she knew about his fate. Her moral paradigm had exploded. She saw her ethical self instead, her ethical self as but one string in an ever-expanding cat's cradle spanning the universe and everything in it.

She knew then what had to be done. For the first time in her life, Camille O'Keefe became a politician and a philosopher Queen at one and the same time.

"What?" asked Pierson.

Camille looked at the president. "Rickey Ormand is a big threat," she said. "You're right about that. You said it was ancient history, but I don't agree. He needs to be reigned in right now. I have seen it."

The president grabbed his chest like he was having a heart attack. "Wait, what? Who are you, and what did you do with Camille?"

Camille looked at Pierson clutching his chest and lowered her eyes. Sometimes, the universe played perverse jokes called irony. It was playing one on her now, and she didn't appreciate it at all.

"I'll tell you what you need to do," she continued.

They were both a bit startled by her assertiveness.

"Go on," said the president.

Camille strode across the room and took a seat in one of the two Queen Anne chairs next to a rectangular coffee table adorned with a Ming-style vase and an Ansel Adams pictorial book.

She continued in an authoritative voice that seemingly came from nowhere. "It's like this, Harry. You lit the fuse. More correctly, you sent me to light the fuse. I lit it. As instructed."

Pierson laughed. "Is that what you call it, that performance of yours?"

Camille nodded gracefully. She was unaware that Pierson knew about her comments at the gala. "I stand by everything I said." She thought again about what lay in store for the president. "But there will come a day when what I said about gravity power will find its place in the world."

Pierson looked at her askew. "Really? I think you said all those things just to piss me off because nobody in their right mind would voluntarily give away something so valuable and powerful."

Camille glossed over it. "Back to Ormand," she said, "he's extremely agitated. He vowed to unseat you. You wanted his fuse lit. Now that it is, you've got a bomb about to detonate."

"Who cares?" replied the president. "You already know we're going to win. So, screw the bastard."

"Wrong approach," said Camille crossing her legs, her anklet dangling against the side of her platform sandal. "Neutralize him."

Pierson sat back and raised his chin. Her words were making a deep impression. "I've never heard you speak like this," he said. "You're actually advocating for a more aggressive plan of action then I am. What's up with that? I have to admit... I kinda like all the hostility."

Camille paid him no mind. What she had to say was far too important. "Listen, Harry, you still need to reach out to Rickey Ormand immediately. Just don't call him in for a face-to-face just yet."

The president found this amusing. "What shall I say to the illustrious Mr. Ormand, then?"

Camille thought it over before answering. It was clear to her that a conflict of interest was looming over her head. It was too late to worry about it now, though. She had to trust her intuition and make a decision in the here and now. If she was to benefit, so be it. Her intuition was screaming out to her on this one... the world needed Camille O'Keefe.

"Tell him he needs to stay in check. Tell him he needs to support our ticket. Tell him he's not to throw millions and millions of dollars into some PAC or anything like that trying to derail us over the next month."

Harry Pierson laughed as he stood up from his desk chair. He walked over to the small refrigerator inconspicuously obscured behind inset panelling. He pulled out a can of seltzer and placed it on his desk.

He pointed to the can.

Camille declined. "No thank you," she said.

He opened the can and poured it into the glass he emptied earlier. The effervescent beverage fizzed to the lip of the glass, raising with it the rind of the lime Pierson squeezed into it earlier.

"Look at that, Red," he said. "Right to the top without as much as a drop spilling." He looked up and winked. "That's how I roll... exacting."

Camille nodded impatiently. "Great, so imagine Rickey Ormand is like that glass and the seltzer is your political influence. If you leave too much in the can, you leave too much room at the top."

"Okay," said Pierson.

She paused and looked at the president. Surely, he gets the analogy, she thought. His blank look conveyed just the opposite. She blew a curl from her face. "If you pour it on too heavily, you spill all over. If you don't pour out enough, you leave too much room at the top of the glass. And if you leave too much room at the top, you allow somebody else to add some of their can of political influence, somebody like, say...." She paused and motioned for the president to finish her thought.

"Like the blockhead running against me," he said. "Oh, he would just love to get his hands on a mountain of Ormand's money going into the last month. That sneaky son-of-a-bitch."

Knowing what the future held in store, Camille felt bad for Pierson. She felt a bit duplicitous, too. But she'd decided on a course of action, and now she had to stick with it. "I'm just saying you don't want to give them the opportunity to hurt us. At the same time, if you go at it too heavy-handed, you'll have a mess on your hands."

Pierson smiled. "A perfect pour... got it, no problem. Since you're on a roll, what should I say to our friend Mr. Ormand?"

Camille tapped her head hoping from some divine intervention. None came. She had to go it alone. "Why not make Ormand think you have a big partnership plan for him. Tell him you want to make him the richest government contractor in history, but only if he keeps a low profile until the election is over. Tell him, you are planning a face-to-face just as soon as the election is over."

Pierson sat in silent contemplation for a moment or two. Then, a big smile grew steadily across his face. "Camille, you're a genius. He won't be able to resist. The bastard won't see it coming when we sweep that gravity thing right out from under his ass."

He thought it over some more and then slammed his palms down on the desk. "You're a damned genius. Correction, I'm a damned genius for choosing you as my running mate."

Camille stood to leave. "I need to get going. Just please make sure you get this thing done."

After closing the door behind her, Camille turned around and went back into the study.

The president looked up from a memo he was reading. "Miss me already, Red?"

Camille took a deep breath. The double meaning of his words was poignant almost to the point of tears. "Yeah," said Camille. "I do."

Her words hung heavy in the air with enough weight that the president put down the memo in his hand. "Surely you didn't do an about-face to tell me that."

Camille closed her eyes and nodded gently. "I just wanted to thank you for everything. It's been one hell of a campaign."

Pierson put the memo down. "Oh, yeah? Just wait and see what happens when I seize control of the greatest invention in the history of mankind. There are amazing things about to come true, Camille. And the two of us will be in the driver's seat." He quickly corrected himself. "Well, I'll be in the driver's seat, you'll be in the passenger's."

"I get your point, Harry." She looked at him for a few seconds. "The universe is always throwing us new wrinkles, even as it irons others out. It all has a way of fitting together."

This time, Camille closed the door and kept walking. The deed was done. Camille O'Keefe bet on herself.

Still seated at his desk, President Harry Pierson laced his fingers behind his head, sat back, and admired himself. Sometimes, he thought, it's just too damned easy. His reverie was brutally interrupted when a frightful thought exploded inside his head. He sat up and checked his calendar... the seventeenth... the First Lady was due back from her trip to Spain and was in residence at the White House.

"God help me," he muttered.

He leaned into his phone and punched an extension. "Get me Dr. Venk."

Seconds later, the White House physician picked up. "Long time no speak, Mr. President?"

"Venk, do you have any idea what day it is?"

The doctor shot a glance at his Apple watch. "It's Friday the 17th, Mr. President."

Pierson emitted a pronounced sigh that sounded quite a bit like a large balloon springing a leak. "Exactly," he hissed bitterly. "Friday, the 17th. More precisely, it's the third Friday of the month. Do you have any idea what this means, Venk?"

The doctor thought for a second and then threw his head back. How could he be so stupid? It was monthly "relations" night with the First Lady.

Pierson got even more serious now. He was pounding his finger on the desk for emphasis. "Listen here, Venk. You'd better bring me the big boy, the 100-milligram horse Viagra this time, not that low-dosage crap you foisted on me last month. It wouldn't get a mouse hard, Venk."

The doctor rubbed his temples. "Mr. President, you shouldn't be taking that high a dosage, drinking like you do. You're going to blow something out one of these days. I don't exactly want to get rung up like Michael Jackson's doctor, you know what I mean?"

"Just make sure that big blue pill is in my nightstand per usual," said Pierson.

"Yes, Mr. President. Your pill will be there."

"Better make it two, Venk. Last week, I caught her watching *Fifty Shades of Grey*. Do you understand the urgency of the situation, Venk? *Fifty Shades of Grey*... just one shade makes my udder shudder if you know what I mean."

Dr. Venk hung his head. He figured he could make it three or four days in prison before he was raped like Bill Cosby working through a pudding cup. "Sir, I cannot give you 200 milligrams of Viagra, especially when you plan to have a drink."

Pierson sounded more serious now. "I hope you're not suggesting that I have relations sober. Just make sure there are two big boys in my dresser. The presidential Intercontinental Ballistic Missile must launch under the most adverse of circumstances, Venk. It's your patriotic duty, man."

Pierson hung up the phone ceremoniously and let his tongue hang limp on his lower lip. The third Friday, he thought. The apocalypse is upon us.

"God help me," he muttered out loud again.

The doctor tossed his cell phone on his desk. "God help her," he muttered.

Chapter 22

Going into the election, Harry Pierson made it very clear to Rickey Ormand via unofficial back channels that any resistance would be seen as treachery and would be dealt with vigorously once Pierson won re-election. The Liquid Messiah toed the line. In the end, he was no fool. As much as he resented Harry Pierson for strong-arming him and even threatening to steal his discovery, Rickey Ormand backed down. Or so it seemed.

As instructed by the White House, Ormand said little if anything about the variety of gravity-powered products and devices that Liquid Sky had in design. Similarly, he uttered nary a word about politics in public. However, the White House began to get wind that Rickey Ormand was the source of a huge influx of dollars into a PAC run by George Soros in a last-ditch effort to unseat the president. Harry Pierson considered this a slap in the face.

"No more tea and crumpets," he told Camille, barely able to restrain his ire when he found out that Ormand was defying him. "You saw where that got us," he said, and proceeded to explain how people like Rickey Ormand only understood power. As such, it was now time to remind the man who wielded the power and who kneeled down before it.

Camille hadn't counted on Ormand's rebellion. It confused her. Why hadn't she foreseen it? Something must have changed. Ormand must have made a last-minute decision to challenge Pierson. Free will, she reminded herself... free will is God's greatest gift, and there was just no accounting for it fully. She was still confident about the outcome of the election. But now, she feared Pierson's response would be violent, and it would be her fault.

As she feared, Harry Pierson decided to take a more "direct approach" as he termed it. He decided the Liquid Messiah needed a little scare. He promised Camille that nothing too serious would happen to Rickey Ormand, at least nothing he didn't deserve. Camille felt little comfort. She couldn't foresee what was going to happen, and it unnerved her. But what choice did she have?

Pierson tapped NSA for the job, and the plan unfolded with optimal execution. Feeling rejuvenated by his large donation to Soros's PAC, Rickey Ormand figured he'd made an ally even stronger than the president himself. He believed Soros was the ideal partner to help him remake the world through gravity power. Nobody he could imagine would be able to stand in his way now.

Emboldened by his newfound power, Ormand accelerated the Liquid-Drive roll out. On the day Pierson chose for the op, Ormand had put in some hefty hours, working until about ten that night. Ready finally to call it a day, he threw some papers into his leather courier bag and made for a secret path ensconced in a long, dense stretch of trees designed specifically to conceal his coming and going between Liquid Sky and Liquid Palace. The path itself ran between two thick, tall hedgerows about four feet apart and was completely unnoticeable from outside the hedges. It was beautiful in its simplicity. Ormand had it constructed in order to keep his exact whereabouts secret and because he thought it was just plain cool.

The secret hedge path was accessed from Liquid Sky via a secret tunnel. The entrance to the tunnel was hidden in Ormand's office behind a rectangular mirror measuring five feet wide and seven feet tall. A flight of stairs took him down into the well-lit tunnel. Two hundred feet away was another staircase that brought him up between the hedgerows. From there, a paved path led to Ormand's private study at Liquid Palace. He could come and go as he pleased without detection.

Feeling fatigued but empowered that night, Ormand opened the hinged mirror and made his way through the tunnel. He grabbed one of the Liquid-Disks hanging at the end of the tunnel, ascended the staircase onto the path, hopped on the disk, and headed for Liquid Palace, where a dip in the indoor pool awaited. He felt in command, totally chilling with his hood up over his Bose headphones, enjoying the night air as he hovered his way home. As he made his way between the two massive buildings, a single thought kept dancing in his head – with Soros backing him, there wouldn't be enough days in the year to cut all the deals that would pile up on his desk.

Although the two hedgerows provided complete visual cover, it was easy enough to see Ormand's heat signature from the NSA drone circling high overhead. Ormand lit up like a Christmas tree, making it easy to pinpoint his exact position. Interestingly, the gravity board gave off no heat signal, a significant military application that greatly concerned the president. As the Liquid Messiah banked into a right-hand bend, he had no idea that a team of three NSA operators was lying in wait. Each man was wearing a black jump suit, black lace-up boots, a black balaclava, and carried a Sig Sauer P226 holstered at his side.

One moment, Ormand was singing Lady Gaga, and the next he was ass up in the air, his Liquid-Disk zooming into the wall of thick *arbor vitae* to his right. He landed with a loud squeal. His headphones went flying, and his cell phone scraped along the pavement. Before he could get to his knees, two of the three NSA operators were on him, one pinning his arms and one pinning his legs while the third watched.

Ormand emitted another girlish scream before the third man stepped over to him, kneeled down, and stuffed a rag deep into his mouth. He nodded to the other two men who deftly reached into a cargo pocket, emerged with zip ties, and secured Ormand's hands and feet. The gag was soaking up his saliva like a dry sponge. The more he tried to move his hands and feet, the more the thin, white plastic cut into his delicate, calf-like skin. And his knee... he must have scraped it when he tumbled to the ground. It stung like heck. Resistance was futile. Ormand stopped struggling.

The leader of the NSA team stepped back and nodded to his two men again. This time, they raised Ormand up by the zip ties and held him a few feet in the air parallel to the pavement like they were carrying a six-foot duffel bag. Ormand strained to raise his head. His neck and shoulders burned from the effort, and the zip ties were digging in deeper every time he moved.

The team leader kneeled down in front of Ormand. "Well, it looks like the Messiah has risen," he said.

His two men grunted at the joke. Ormand tried in vain to say something. The team leader pulled the gag from his mouth like he was a magician pulling a seemingly endless multi-colored scarf from a top hat.

"Listen up, Mr. Rickey, you little prick," the leader said.

Ormand spit some blood onto the pavement below. "Who the hell are you? How did you find me?"

The two men holding Ormand suspended in the air grunted again. This was going to be fun.

"You can call me Toast. I know, I know... who has a nickname like that, right?" He snapped his fingers as if trying to remember.

"Kandahar," said his men.

"Right, right," said Toast. "Shit Hole. What a dark place."

Ormand could sense that Toast was slipping off into some unpleasant memories. That couldn't bode well for him. "What are you talking about?" Ormand whined.

"That's where I got my nickname. Kandahar.... Shit, they were some memories though."

The panic in Ormand's eyes glowed like embers.

"Toast," said the man in a menacing monotone. "Literally... car battery, wet sponges... toast."

All three grunted this time. "Love," said one of them. "I can smell this guy burning already."

Never having removed his eyes from Ormand's, Toast said, "So what do you think, Mr. Rickey?"

Ormand's head was spinning. He had no idea what was going on. "How did you find me?" he asked.

"How did we find you?" mocked Toast. "Look up. We see everything. We know everything. Really? You're funny, man. We know all about you, Mr. Rickey."

Ormand strained hard to lift his head.

"Eyes in the sky, Mr. Rickey," continued Toast. "In our line of work, there's nothing like a good drone. We can shove a Hellfire rocket straight up your ass from 25,000 feet in the air like we are slipping a suppository into your rectum. Shit, Mr. Rickey, we can even jam your security cameras from that very same Reaper up there. Just imagine what we can do when we get ahold of your little invention."

Ormand made a paltry attempt at a verbal parry. "You have no idea who you're dealing with, you—"

Toast cut him off abruptly. "Shh... shh.... Please, Mr. Rickey. Stop talking before you piss me off. Right now, it's just business. But if you piss me off, it becomes personal."

"Toast, man," laughed one of the guys. "I love that."

His gaze still locked on Ormand's, Toast said, "You have no idea who you're dealing with, little man. You must have really screwed up big time, my friend. I've gotta hand it to you. You have enemies in some pretty high places." He stuffed the gag back into Ormand's mouth. "Enough of you."

Ormand began squirming, violently trying to shake loose from his captors. Toast looked at his men and shrugged. They hoisted Ormand higher and then exaggeratedly let go, holding their hands up as if it wasn't their doing at all.

Ormand thudded to the ground smashing his head against the hard blacktop. As he lay there, one of the men kicked him in the balls. The Liquid Messiah passed out momentarily. When he came to, he could barely make out the dark outline of Toast who was now towering before him. Ormand could smell his own vomit that had pooled in front of his face near where Toast had removed and dropped the gag so Ormand wouldn't asphyxiate. His stomach was twisted like a garlic knot and his testicles felt like cracked walnuts. He could do little more than moan.

"Right, then," said Toast. He nodded to his men again, and they hoisted Ormand up.

"Look, the Messiah has risen again," mocked Toast. "It's a miracle, boys." He kneeled down close to Ormand's face. The sight of two, dark, empty eyes staring at him from behind the balaclava was more than Ormand could handle. When the men saw Ormand pissing himself, they tossed him aside like a rolled-up carpet. Ormand landed hard, again popping his head against the pavement.

Toast was miffed. He stood up abruptly. "Really, dude?" he said. "That's disgusting, and that's coming from a guy who has drunk his own urine. You pansy-ass rich guys." His voice turned sharp as a blade. "Pick him back up... now."

Just like that, Ormand found himself suspended a third time.

Toast kneeled down next to him. "We're a little pissed at you now, Mr. Rickey. That makes this kind of personal, which is definitely not good for you, know what I mean?"

Ormand saw Toast's eye narrow in the cut outs of his balaclava. He did everything he could not to release his bowels, for he was sure shitting himself would cost him his life. He was right.

Toast reached down with his right hand and drew his Sig P226 from the nylon holster strapped to his leg. The weapon was chambered with a standard 9 mm parabellum round.

"I don't suppose you know anything about firearms. Right, Mr. Rickey?"

Ormand shook his head vigorously.

Toast laughed. "Yeah, well you probably don't handle anything more powerful than your mouse. What I like about this Sig is how naked it is. I know... you're thinking what the hell am I talking about, a naked gun."

"Naked gun? Wasn't that a movie? Asked one of the men."

The other guy laughed. "Yeah, man. O.J. was in it."

"Well, movies aside," said Toast, "the Sig has no external safety. Yeah, baby... naked... there's nothing but a firing-pin block standing between the round in the chamber and your brain, Mr. Rickey. I just hope I don't sneeze or something. That would be unfortunate."

The other men laughed.

Without warning, Toast pinched Ormand's lower lip firmly between his left thumb and forefinger and pulled down. Rickey's mouth opened right up like it was on a hinge.

"See that," said Toast. "As easy as pulling down a window shade." He slid the short, black barrel into Ormand's open mouth up to the trigger guard.

His two men grunted. Sweat was now pouring down Ormand's face. That kick to the balls drained everything from him. His ankles and wrists seared with pain from the zip ties. At the moment, it was as if time stood still for Rickey Ormand. In what seemed like a split second, decades of his life blew through his consciousness, and he knew he was about to die.

He started gagging on the barrel of the Sig. Toast looked at him in disgust. "So much for your career in gay porn," he joked. The others found that hilarious.

"Two minutes, man" said one of the guys suddenly. "Wrap it."

Toast nodded and spoke to Ormand. "Here's what you're gonna do, you little prick."

Ormand opened his eyes wide and raised his eyebrows. He was all ears.

Toast breathed deeply as if he was carefully contemplating his next words. "This little gravity toy of yours can cause problems. It can disrupt every part of our society. All you need to do is play nice and continue to let the powers-that-be run the show. This way, we have a nice, smooth transition into the future. I'm told you know this. Is this true?"

Ormand nodded slightly several times and emitted a high-pitched, porcine squeal.

"Really," said Toast, growing more agitated albeit mostly for affect. As far as he was concerned, Toast was going to—

Toast interrupted his thoughts most unceremoniously. "I should slit your scrotum and let your teeny balleenies roll before I pull the trigger. You want to ruin my country? Is that what you're saying? Good Americans all out of jobs so you and your army of zitty plebes can run my country into the ground? Is that it? Because... well... shit, that's kinda what I'm hearing, Mr. Rickey. And that just makes me mad as a snake up an elephant's ass, you know what I mean?"

Ormand didn't know how to answer. Snake up an elephant's ass... was it a trick question?

"One minute, boss," said one of the men.

"You just can't play nice, can you, Mr. Rickey. Were you one of those kids that had to have the blocks all to himself? Shit, man, you just gotta whip it out and wave it all over the place to feel good about yourself, don't you? Well, you done screwed with the wrong guy this time. The big man isn't happy. And when he isn't happy, he calls us to express his... displeasure."

Ormand's eyes shifted back and forth several times in rapid succession. By his calculations, he had about forty-five seconds left to live.

"See, that's what I don't understand about all you so-called geniuses. You have no common sense. I mean... did you really think you could level threats like that at the most powerful man in the world and not have a telephone pole shoved up your ass?" He turned to his men. "No common sense at all, right?"

The men agreed.

"Thirty seconds, then we got to boogie."

"So, here's how it's gonna go down, Mr. Rickey," said Toast hastily. "You're not going to issue any stupid press releases. You've been a good boy with that. But if you donate one more nickel to any political organization, I am going to come back, and I'm gonna hurt you real, real bad before I cap you because I just don't like you. You remind me of my brother-in-law. I should kill you just for that.

"And, you are most definitely not going to release any gravity-drive products. In fact," said Toast, "until further notice, you will act as if the gravity drive doesn't exist. *Comprende, amigo?* You understand what I am saying?"

Ormand nodded vigorously.

"Excellent. Let's hope we never meet again, you slimy little puke," concluded Toast as he slid the barrel from Ormand's mouth and stood up. He looked down at his gun, which was wet with Ormand's saliva. "Jesus Christ. What are you, a baby on a tit?"

He wiped the gun off on his pant leg before holstering it. Then he took a small canister from one of the copious pockets in his jump suit and sprayed it in Ormand's face. Ormand lost consciousness almost immediately.

"We're done here," Toast told his men. "Let's get sleeping beauty home."

He pulled Ormand's Liquid-Disk from the thick shrub where it was lodged. "All this fuss over this toy?" he said.

His men shrugged and hurried down the remainder of the path with the Liquid Messiah in tow.

When Mr. Rickey awoke late the next morning, he felt like he had a terrible hangover. His first impulse was to call security. He sat upright and grabbed his cell phone from the night table next to him. Then he saw it facing him, slid over the bedpost near his feet... a single black balaclava.

Pinned to it was a draft of a news article about his death in a tragic helicopter accident.

Rickey Ormand placed his phone back on the night table, curled up in the fetal position, and cried himself back to sleep.

Not long thereafter, Election Day arrived with all its pomp and circumstance. It came as no surprise to Camille when the results came in. President re-elect Harry Pierson chalked it up to his brilliant decision to name Camille O'Keefe as his running mate. Camille, to the contrary, knew the source of their victory lay in the realm of universal law. Even so, her misgivings about knowing both the outcome of the election and what was to happen to Pierson shortly thereafter intensified. Her advice to Pierson about shutting down Rickey Ormand still troubled her. But there was little if anything she could do about that now.

For all his braggadocio, Harry Pierson was right about adding Camille to the ticket. Thanks to Camille, they pulled more women voters than any recent candidate, including Hillary Clinton. What distinguished Camille was her ability to garner an unprecedented number of Latina women voters. That's what threw Pierson over the top in toss-up states like Ohio, Florida, and Nevada. Most shocking of all, Camille was single-handedly responsible for winning California, something not even Harry Pierson thought she could do, although he quickly took credit for the historical feat.

A few days after the election, Camille and Pierson finally had a chance to sit down and discuss the plan for Rickey Ormand and Liquid Sky.

"Whatever I said seems to have made an impression on you," said Camille. "It was like Rickey went into a cave for the last month."

Pierson smiled broadly. "You like that, huh? All I'll say is this – you made an impression on me, and I made an impression on our friend. What can I say? Great minds think alike. Anyway, it's all taken care of. Our friend decided to take an extended holiday in the tropics... where they don't wear ski masks." He laughed heartily at his sly balaclava reference.

Camille grimaced. "What exactly does that mean?"

Pierson sat back and gloated. "You'll see. He's coming here next week."

Camille's surprise was evident.

"What can I say," said Pierson, noting Camille's look. "It's time Rickey Ormand and I came to a mutual understanding. And I told him to bring that robot woman with him. I've never seen one of them."

Pierson mistook her reticence as an apprentice eager to learn from her master. "There's a lesson in this for you, Camille. That is, if you want to groom yourself to become our next president. I mean it. This may be my second term, but there's no reason you can't follow me to become the first female president of the United States."

Camille shrugged apathetically. "You never know," she said. But she already did.

"Knock 'em down like pins," declared the president. "That's the secret to success. That, and make sure you've got big balls to bowl with."

Camille shrugged again. "I will be sure to find myself some big balls."

Chapter 23

Camille and Parker spoke only once following the gala, and that was shortly after the election. Camille was sitting in the White House Solarium taking in the brilliant winter view of the Mall and the Washington Memorial through massive floor-to-ceiling windows that ran the perimeter of the room. The third-floor Solarium was the invention of First Lady Grace Coolidge and served as a favorite sanctum for a number of presidents, including Ronald Reagan and Bill Clinton.

Camille relished the thought. Now, the history books could add a woman's name to the list, although she was "only" vice president. In fact, she was only vice president-elect. The Electoral College votes were all in confirming her victory. But the inauguration was still a month or so away.

When Fitzgerald rang, Camille answered excitedly. "Well, hello, you. It's been a while."

Fitzgerald was sitting in her immense office at Liquid Sky. She had it remodelled to resemble the mountaintop office high above Lake Titicaca from where gravity power first took flight. Three walls of her office were actually sophisticated virtual-reality screens simulating the exact panoramic view from the mountaintop den where she liked to look down onto Lake Titicaca.

Camille O'Keefe had her solarium, and Parker Fitzgerald had her mountaintop den. Both rooms were equally therapeutic. Both rooms were the birthplace of great ideas that would affect the world. Like each of the ladies respectively, Camille's space was grounded in the duality between history and the spirit, while Parker's space embodied the union between human and machine. Together, they encompassed a totality of potential that did not go unnoticed by the two.

"I meant to call you several times, but I figured you'd be totally tied up with the election," said Fitzgerald.

Camille was blasé about the whole idea. "Eh, it wasn't like I didn't know the outcome about... oh, I don't know... two months ago."

Fitzgerald laughed. "Really? You can do that?"

Blasé again. "I don't really do anything. The universe sends me information... ready to eat, you know? I just spread the word."

"Any of those messages mention the stock market?" joked Fitzgerald.

Camille smiled. "Actually, I get that question every day. The answer is no. But something tells me that Liquid Sky stock is going to move big time."

Fitzgerald reached into her right leg compartment and took out an emery board. Pinning her cell phone against her shoulder and ear, she started filing her left-hand nails. Her voice was noticeably more serious now. "I guess the question is in which direction?"

Pause. Was Camille on to her?

"We'll just have to wait and see," lied Camille. "Why, is there something you're not telling me?"

Pause. Fitzgerald was holding out.

"Who, me?" said Fitzgerald. "I know better than to lie to a famous psychic. Anyway, you're the vice president now. You can't be involved in any inside information, now can you?"

Quiet. Pause.

Fitzgerald decided to start pushing a bit. "You remember at the gala how we talked about all the things that could come from this new technology, all the things that will never be developed if people like Harry Pierson and Rickey Ormand control it?"

Camille corrected her friend. "You mean men… if men control it."

"Exactly," said Fitzgerald. "How strongly do you feel about that?"

"About the wonderful world of possibilities or about men crimping them to make their manhood appear to be bigger?"

Fitzgerald was relieved. It was going better than she had feared. "Both," she said.

Camille walked over to one of the large panes and looked out at the Mall. It was crowded with activists braving the winter cold to participate in a rally supporting none other than Camille O'Keefe. Her handlers thought it best she not attend out of respect for the current Vice President, Jennifer Daly. It would appear an awkward contradiction.

"Oh," said Camille, "I'm pretty sure there are lots of women waiting for my answer to that one. Let's just say there are very big changes coming. And they're coming faster than anyone knows."

Fitzgerald swallowed hard and took a leap of faith. "I have to tell you something, Camille. Actually… I have two things to tell you."

"Just dive in," prompted Camille.

"I'm not what you think I am," Fitzgerald answered.

"I know that," said Camille. "What's the other thing?"

Fitzgerald was nervous. "Well, I'm about to do something—"

Camille cut her off abruptly. Given her new position, there were clear limits to what she could hear. "Keep it to yourself," she said. "Or, at least, don't verbalize it. I'll get the message some other way."

Fitzgerald tossed the emery board on the desk. She hoped filing her nails would make her feel more aloof, but it didn't. "I… it's just… I want you to support me on this—"

Camille cut her off again. "I will always support you. Our meeting was no coincidence. There's a reason we met at the gala.

There's a reason it seems like we've known each other for a thousand years. We have. It's a fact. There are greater forces at work. I think we'd best leave it at that for now, Parker. Be safe... whatever it is you're going to do. Please be safe in every aspect of the word."

"I wish you could tell me how this will all turn out," said Fitzgerald with a touch of despair.

"I can," said Camille. "But then, you wouldn't really be making your own choices, now would you? Remember, free will matters. It's real. It's God's greatest gift. It always boils down to intentions. If yours are just, then the outcome can never be wrong."

Fitzgerald was looking for something more concrete. "I wish I knew what any of that meant. For that matter, I wish I had your optimism."

"I just tell it like I foresee it, Parker."

Chapter 24

Her steely reserve refortified, Parker Fitzgerald hung up and immediately redialed.

"Hey there, you deviant. It's Parker," she said. "I need you and that numbskull partner of yours to meet me ASAP."

She listened to the response.

"Are you crazy? It can't be anywhere near Liquid Sky."

She listened again.

"San Francisco. Tonight," she said.

She grew visibly upset at the response.

"What the hell are you two doing in Chicago? Never mind," she said sternly. "I don't want to know what you two degenerates are up to. I'll get there. I'll text you the place from another phone... a burner or something."

She listened.

"Okay, I don't know what a burner is," she lied. But, of course she did. She'd been planning this since the gala. Anyway, it was always easier to play dumb with hackers. It played right into their narcissistic egomania.

"I hear people say 'burner' on *The Wire*," she continued. "Whatever, I will text you. Just make sure the two of you are there and prepared to discuss the biggest job of your lives."

"Yes," she said annoyed now. "Of course, I will reimburse you for your time. Please stop talking now."

She hung up. She dialed another number. Her voice was so sweet, it made molasses seem like wormwood. "Hello, Rickey. It's your favorite fembot."

She listened to him flirt back and got a little queasy.

"Um," she said, "I just found out about a seminar on alternative energy that I really want to hear. It's tonight in Chicago. Can I please, please take one of the company jets?"

She smiled as she listened.

"Thanks, Rick. You're the best. I hope you know that."

She hung up and made one last call, this time from her desk phone.

"This is Dr. Parker Fitzgerald. I need one of the jets to Chicago Pal-Waukee or Chicago Executive Airport, whatever they call it now, asap on Mr. Ormand's authorization. I'll be at the hangar in ten minutes."

She seemed annoyed by the response. "Fine, if the runway is too small to land then route me into O'Hare, whatever. Just get me to Chi-Town. Let's rock and roll."

Fitzgerald was much bitchier than usual. The stress of what she was about to do was getting to her. She was sweating, which didn't make sense considering her metabolism, but there they were, pit stains on her faded-blue Allman Brothers *Eat a Peach* T-shirt. There were still things she was learning about her new self.

Fitzgerald's anxiety did not go unnoticed. Camille picked it up right away when they were talking on the phone. After Camille hung up with Fitzgerald, she stood in the Solarium, staring out over the Mall deep in contemplation. She knew Fitzgerald had been keeping a secret from the time they first met. Her intuition told her it had something to do with Fitzgerald's technology, something more than her robotics, some other technology inside her that made her a magnificent eighth wonder of the world.

Now, Camille felt Parker Fitzgerald was up to something, and she had a pretty good idea it would undermine Rickey Ormand in a serious way. She was equally sure Ormand's response would be extreme and violent. Camille feared for Fitzgerald's safety. It seemed the universe dealt another free-will wild card, one that threatened to change the entire game. While she knew Parker Fitzgerald was brilliant, determined, and wily, she also knew Rickey Ormand possessed an ego that could explode into violent rage, taking down everything and everyone around him. This was the side of Rickey Ormand that the public didn't see, but those few who really knew him knew all too well. And they were too afraid to cross him by ever uttering a word of truth about it.

It only took one brief encounter with Rickey Ormand for Camille to sense there was good reason to be concerned. There was a lot of change, confrontation, and controversy headed her way in a very short period of time. Whether Fitzgerald knew it or not, she could easily be the spark that set off a powder keg. There was another prickly aspect bothering Camille about the dynamic. It had to do with Harry Pierson, not Rickey Ormand. In the few times they'd worked together, she found herself compromising quite a bit. It made her uncomfortable largely because people died. Many innocent lives were saved in the balance, but not all of those who perished were "bad guys," as Pierson called them. Too many men, women, and children died in the name of some abstract greater good.

Too much violence and too much death, too much male ego and too much compromise seemed to rule the day when she was paired up with Harry Pierson. Only this time, she was Pierson's partner in the White House. They were joined at the hip, and she feared his world view would overtake her own. Harry Pierson may have chosen her for his vice president because her voice of alterity made him stronger, but she could not overlook the fluidity of his powerful male ego and the possibility that it could assimilate her own sense and sensibility regardless of what she or the president intended.

Parker Fitzgerald sighed as she looked out the window of the Liquid Sky Bombardier Global 6000. Through her large, custom cabin window, she saw the lights of Chicago as the jet made its final approach into O'Hare. Deep in thought, she was fully aware of the stakes, fully aware that she was about to go apostate. Jesus Christ, Rickey was going to kill her, maybe quite literally. She stared at her reflection in the window and returned her tan, leather captain's chair to its full upright position.

Trying to relax, she took a look around the gorgeous cabin of the Bombardier. The smell of supple leather... the exquisite burled-wood trim and pocket tables... the decorative carpeting and mood lighting.... soon enough, stuff like this would be hers. And she deserved it, too. After all, what was Liquid-Drive without her? In fact, she was Liquid-Drive, and Liquid-Drive was her. Hadn't she gone to the brink of death, hadn't she actually died birthing the discovery? And wasn't she something completely new, something completely unprecedented? These were the questions she asked herself. This was the litmus test she turned to many times prior to making her decision.

Yes, she reminded herself, buckling her seatbelt. Yes, she was Liquid-Drive in more ways than anybody knew, anybody except her and Rickey Ormand. But that was about to change, and now there was nothing Ormand could do about it. She sat back and smiled. She was a living marvel the likes of which has never existed. Rickey Ormand didn't own her. No, she intended to own herself, sovereign in her transitional body.

As soon as the plane started taxiing, Fitzgerald was on her phone texting the location of the meeting. She really did use a burner, a disposable, pre-paid phone she picked up at the Circle K on El Camino Real in Mountain View the day before. She smiled as her fingers deftly flew across the keyboard of the disposable flip phone. A real keyboard... so old school. It was great.

London House. Upper Wacker. Rooftop bar. 1 hr.

She waited several seconds for a response. *You paying right?*

"Dumb shit," she muttered to herself. *Don't be late*, she texted.

As soon as the steps of the jet lowered, and they were cleared by airport authorities, Parker Fitzgerald was gone. She busted it over to ground transportation. She wanted an untraceable ride to the London House Hotel. Using a car service would leave a paper trail. The same for Uber or Lyft. That was the one thing she didn't want. It would have to be a generic taxi smelling of cumin or armpit... it was the same anyway.

And with that, Parker Fitzgerald was off to the Loop to take back her body and claim what was rightfully hers.

The London House sat on the corner of Upper Wacker and Michigan Ave., where it turns into the fabled Michigan Ave. DuSable Bridge at the Chicago River. A stone's throw from both Lake Michigan and the Magnificent Mile shopping district, the London House sat directly opposite the Trump Towers on the other side of the river. The two buildings couldn't be more different.

The Towers, with its huge Trump presi-brand name and floor after floor of gleaming mirrored windows, brought to mind something alien, something from another planet suggestive of fabulous hair and an itchy Twitter finger. Think landing pod full of aliens disguised as super-affluent Whitakers and Whitleys deposited by spacecraft while the city was lulled into an extra-terrestrial sonambulance. And, of course, don't forget the ubiquitous wealthy Chinese businessmen who own many of the units, convenient investment vehicles for parking their copious profits reaped in from mainland contracts and Nigerian resource ventures reserved for the privileged few who knew how to exploit the economy of systematic "State favoritism," ("corruption" being such an out-of-date term).

Built in 1923 during Al Capone's reign during the height of Prohibition, the London House, on the opposite bank, conjured images of a bygone era like something out of a curio cabinet. Indeed, the red carpeting set against the art deco and marble interior was reminiscent of something ghostly, as if the eerie visages of H.H. Holmes's victims still roamed about these halls. And yet, perched high atop the roof is a chic roof-top bar affording stunning, panoramic views of the Windy City. The beautiful people flock there like exotic birds to the nest.

This was where Fitzgerald intended to meet her contacts. She figured it would be aptly metaphoric, the old juxtaposed against the new, the London House and the Trump Towers, a microcosm of the macrocosm to be sure. Fanciful thoughts such as these aside, Parker Fitzgerald was just as adamant as ever regarding control of her body when she stepped into the elevator at the London House. Initially content to hand everything over to Ormand, Fitzgerald found that inconsequential now. Such decisions were easy to make now that she would have massive wealth and power herself.

As far as Fitzgerald was concerned, this was no longer about gravitational energy. The stakes were about to change. She held a wild card that made her hand unbeatable. The Liquid-Drive project was one thing. But it was nothing compared to the other technology she had inside her, code name *Liquid-Life*. With Liquid-Life, Ormand was seeking to control the very essence of life. Parker Fitzgerald herself was the intellectual property. She was the goose that would lay the golden patent. As such, intellectual-property law was a century behind, as fossilized and outdated as the Supreme Court will be when an advanced Artificial Intelligence (AI) brings a case arguing for its sovereign and inalienable Constitutional rights as a sentient being.

For Parker Fitzgerald, both events were inevitable. It was only a matter of time. Her time was now. Through Liquid-Life, Parker Fitzgerald would alter the course of human history by radically redefining the definition of life, death, and human existence. Through Liquid-Life, Parker Fitzgerald would become something so extraordinary, that nothing in the world would really accommodate her fully. So, why should she allow Rickey Ormand to patent Liquid-Life when, in fact, she was Liquid-Life?

The more she thought about it on the plane ride to O'Hare, the more she figured she really didn't need anything below the head. Sure, Ormand's robotic marvels enabled her to live from the waist down. But that's not what made her unique. That technology could be replicated a million times over. What made Parker Fitzgerald radically unique was the source of her life. With Liquid-Life, Fitzgerald existed as a totally new life form capable of surviving mostly on gravitational energy and nothing more. Her life essence, not her robotics, was the real breakthrough. As such, she felt like she was the technology. She should be free to decide for herself the matters that most concerned who – and, more importantly what – she was.

She stepped out of the cab more determined than ever. Walking through the door of the London House and then down to the left into the lobby was a symbolic passage now. This was her moment, and it was palpable. The real transformation of the world was about to blow, and she was about to light the fuse. As she stepped off the elevator out and into the rooftop bar, she felt as if she'd been transported from a century before to a century ahead.

Unfortunately, it was far too cold to sit out on the large patio overlooking both the Chicago River and Lake Michigan. In the summer, the experience outside was breathtaking.

For the time being, she would have to settle for inside seating. At least the long glass wall running the length of the room where it met the patio afforded a similarly thrilling view as outside. Inside, the cool, pastel lighting scheme played well against the black lacquer bar and multiple table tops. The way the lights danced off the high shelves full of liquor bottles and glassware made the room vibrate with a sort of transcendental energy. Funky, Asian-themed artwork adorned the walls, bringing a strange sense of juxtaposition to the entire penthouse space.

Fitzgerald strode up to a high-top off in the corner where two men were already sitting. They were conspicuous, maybe too much so for the covert nature of the meet. Anonymity was important not because Fitzgerald told Rickey Ormand she was attending a seminar. The greater risk was the two men, two of the most revered hacktivists in the cyber underground. Their impressive resume of high-profile hacks not only landed them on the short list for greatest black hats of all time, it also landed them on the short list of the FBI's most infamous cyber criminals. From the viral underworld of the darknet to the antiseptic offices of Quantico, they were known as Goatse and Malfesio.

Fitzgerald took one look at these guys and remembered just how bizarre they were. Goatse was at least 40 pounds overweight and cultivated a "menace to sobriety" aesthetic that parents pray will never show up at the door asking for their daughter. Through some time-space perversion of his full-length mirror, Goatse thought he looked good wearing black skinny jeans and a muffin-top T-shirt bearing a variety of food stains and some ironic slogan. Fancying himself a man of dichotomies, Goatse was a white guy with dreads punctuated by a nose ring of significant gauge. He also sported half-sleeve tattoos covering each forearm from wrist to elbow.

As for Malfesio, he was straight out of the Morang Avenue hood in Detroit. But unlike the usual suspects back home, Malfesio was a self-stylized "Afro ragamuffin" as well as a dyed-in-the-wool Euro-Anarchist in the classic *Baader-Meinhof* vein. He toggled between both identities depending on which better served him at any given moment. They were an odd mix to say the least, and Malfesio embodied every aspect of his quixotic, Afropunk sensibility. His hair was what Fitzgerald remembered most. He wore it intricately twisted into four huge, colorful braids… yellow, red, blue, and green. The braids were tied up in a mound on top that looked like a bird's nest crafted from a rainbow. The rest of his head was shaved clean, which made the hefty-gauge bone piercings in both ears really stand out.

Fitzgerald met these two miscreants a little over a year before when Ormand secretly hired them to tighten up cyber security following an attack that very nearly cost him everything. Had it been successful, Liquid-Drive technology would have been stolen and disseminated across the globe in seconds, making gravity-power technology a free and open source. The attack failed, but there was something about the incursion that deeply offended Ormand. For the first time he could remember, he felt violated and completely vulnerable. So, he undertook a costly and exhaustive search through the darknet in search of two black hats he could buy to tighten things up. He found Goatse and Malfesio, two former Anonymous hacktivists who got a kick out of foiling their compatriots finding it quite entertaining.

It didn't take them long to detect a systematic, complex assault on the company's data network. Still, it was a Catch-22 for Ormand, who was savvy enough to find these two reprobates but not too naive to realize that foxes in the hen house would eventually act like foxes in a hen house. At the time, he was too desperate to care and too arrogant to believe that a couple of scraggly looking kids would ever decide to screw him just for fun. He considered himself as untouchable as infallible. Foxes in the hen house may inevitably feast like foxes in the hen house, but Rickey Ormand would always act like Rickey Ormand.

Ormand never discovered who was behind the cyber-attack. However, Goatse and Malfesio did report to Ormand that the technology used in the attack was, hands down, the most elegant and sinister they'd ever seen, more so even than anything they'd seen in their days with Anonymous. Ormand paid them each a cool million for their efforts. They had no problem taking Ormand's money. But they were more interested in trying to foil this ingenious attack.

If they could crack it, they would be out in front of whoever wrote the code, and whoever wrote the code was the very best they'd seen. It was all about the street credo for these guys. The rivalry among super hackers was the bigger payoff for Goatse and Malfesio. They both played a disturbingly large role in Gameover Zeus, the 2014 phishing attack that assailed over one million computers and generated over 100 million in losses. They were also involved in designing the Rocra smart-phone bug back in 2007, perhaps the most sinister malware of the new millennia in that their Red October attack targeted nuclear research from diplomatic and government agencies in Eastern Europe. In the wrong hands, the information they stole could prove devastating to a terrorist state like Syria.

Typical hacktivists, Goatse and Malfesio were more concerned with the game and the money rather than the greater good. If it all coincided, so much the better, but that was the extent of their political activism. Either way, they chose the name Red October because they believed they were revealing "the secrets of the ex-Soviet world" just as Tom Clancy's fictional Russian Captain Ramius believed he was doing when he hijacked the Red October and handed it over to the Americans. Nobody knew who contracted Goatse and Malfesio for that job. Not even they knew where their fee came from. The $2 million was paid in crypto currency. All they knew was that some organization wanted to level the playing field in order to protect humanity.

Goatse and Malfesio knew their way around the darknet like few others. More importantly, they knew their way around the Liquid Sky network. That was precisely why Fitzgerald sought them out. Despite their outlandish appearance and the illicit nature of their work, they were the perfect team for the job. The stakes were way too high for her to trust an outsider. She knew Goatse and Malfesio couldn't be trusted either, but at least they were predictably corrupt, a known entity, manageable.

Goatse and Malfesio both saw Fitzgerald approach their table but paid her little mind. They were too engaged in debate to acknowledge her with much more than a nod. Fitzgerald plopped her volleyball of a robotic ass on a high-top chair and marvelled at how enrapt these two were in proclaiming their own prowess. They were actually debating about the work they'd done for Liquid Sky. She could tell immediately she'd walked into a pissing match.

Even though he was seated, Fitzgerald could see Goatse's pale flab squishing out between the sag-ass waist of his black skinny jeans and his red *Thievery Corporation* T-shirt depicting a black-domed surveillance cam. The multi-colored dread nest atop Malfesio's head did look pretty cool in the funky lighting, but she thought the whole Afropunk thing made him look more like the demon offspring of George Clinton and Lenny Kravitz than an IT professional whom she was enlisting for the project of her life. She sighed as she wondered whether there was even a minute possibility of either of these guys having sex with a real person before realizing herself that "real" had no particular significance for either of them. Nor did the concept of "woman."

Malfesio slugged his Makers Mark and declared he was the first to figure it out at Liquid Sky. "Whoever this bastard was," he said to Fitzgerald as if she'd been present for the entire debate, "he used a variation of the Ouroboros attacks. Brilliant pivot. But really, I would have come up with the idea eventually. These things grow organically."

Fitzgerald welcomed the waiter when he mercifully appeared in his tight, white V-neck tee and torn stretch jeans... the same as she was sporting. She fired off her ample request in light of the present company. "Triple Patron.... no, I don't want ice... good God, no lime."

"And another round here, fly boy," said Malfesio, realizing his Makers was gone. He shooed the waiter away with two limp fingers and rolled his eyes.

Realizing the problem with these two cretins was the lack of a mute button, Fitzgerald resigned herself to the dirty task of reacquainting herself after over a year. She figured she might as well start things off with a bang.

"Find the waiter cute?" she prodded.

Malfesio looked at her like she was a Republican. "What are you talking about?" he sneered. "Your homosexual barbs are too passé to be funny. Actual sex with actual people has, like, been gone for, like, years. Um... no, thank you. People are disgusting. Virtual reality is where the real action is sweetheart."

"Don't let him boggle you with sleight-of-hand," said Goatse. "He's trying to distract us from his last comment. He's an ass saying he could have savagely morphed Ouroboros like that. He also knows that he can't even get a virtual 'friend' to go down on him let alone actually love him, so...." He trailed off.

And just like that, Parker Fitzgerald hit her limit of tolerance. "I have no idea what the hell you're talking about," said Fitzgerald. "Ouroboros means nothing to me. That's why I hired you Frick and Fracks."

Malfesio grunted in disgust. "All I was saying, sweets, is that whoever did that to your Liquid Sky planted, like, a surveillance bug deep in your system. Through it, they could watch everything you were doing."

Goatse nodded his consent. "Okay, okay. But it was still slick as hell. Talk about having a bug up your ass. For all we know, this guy's launching a million other types of attacks all over the world."

Goatse laughed a greezy, slovenly laugh reminiscent of moisturizing one's lips with a piece of raw bacon before continuing on in a patronizing voice as if addressing a toddler rather than a brilliant theoretical physicist.

"And so, I really have to say for, like, the fifth time in this debate, that there's no way Malfesio would have thought to script together a surveillance program to gather information *and* a sort of beachhead from which to launch the attack. No way, man."

He played with his nose ring while his dramatic pause set in.

"It felt like Sabu," continued Goatse, referring to the legendary leader of a worldwide army of hackers. "And you ain't no Sabu."

Malfesio rejected the idea immediately. "That yak? He doesn't have the finesse to write code this elegant. You're really pushing my buttons, man. What, are you still pissed off about me and your sister? Or was it your mother? Aw, shit, it was both, wasn't it? Sabu my ass, man."

Goatse was pissy. "Whatever," he hissed. "I meant the feel of it. It felt like Sabu was all I was saying. Or maybe Lulzsec. I mean, it's obvious Sabu couldn't write code like this. I mean, that's obvious. I'm not saying that. What I'm saying is that it felt political. I always felt that whoever tried to clep the Liquid Sky files wasn't looking to make money. He was going to blast it to the world for free. That's what I'm saying."

Malfesio nodded. "Definitely. I definitely agree. Definitely political. I mean, that's obvious. It's not like you're saying anything that's not obvious." He snorted in disgust. "It's obvious. I know that."

Fitzgerald silently thanked the Lord when the fresh round of drinks arrived. The constant one-upmanship between the two was symptomatic of the collective hacktivist neuroses about appearing not to know even the most esoteric factoid or not coming off as the most cynically clever anarchist in the room, a fate worse than death in those circles. She was getting frustrated already and didn't feel like listening to all their crap. Given the billions of dollars at stake, the hack could constitute the single greatest loss of its kind. First, though, she had to get these two guys to take the enterprise seriously.

Fortifying her will with a robust quaff of tequila, Parker Fitzgerald donned her proverbial cowboy hat and became a nerd herder. Keep it simple; herd the nerds.

"I don't understand exactly what goes on inside your heads. I'm inclined to think it's far less than you imagine. That said, you know... I'm going to ask you questions," she explained in a voice edged with intensity. "And you are going to give me very precise answers in language a six-year-old can understand. Do I make myself clear?"

Even though both men could probably bring Liquid Sky to its knees with their devious skills, not to mention drain Fitzgerald's checking account before anyone knew what was happening, they just nodded and awaited further instruction.

"Good," said Fitzgerald, sitting back in her chair, snifter of tequila in hand. "Let me preface this by saying there is a highly secret program at Liquid Sky. I doubt Rickey even mentioned it to you guys."

Goatse arched an unruly black brow in dire need of waxing. He flipped his white-guy dreads. "Oh, that doesn't matter, sweetie." His was a pronounced hiss and clearly laden with some sort of innuendo that Fitzgerald dared not decipher without a body condom.

"Know about it... don't know about it... it doesn't matter a lick."

He slowly and lasciviously licked the air like there was an ice cream cone there.

"I assure you. We can find anything. It's just a matter of having a way in is all. Especially when we're dealing with new technology that's hard to crack open."

Again, Goatse's intonation was suggestive, and Fitzgerald had little doubt she was the "new technology" he was referring too and her mechanized groin was what this overgrown child wanted to "crack open."

The thought of Goatse's jiggly rolls and stank-ass dreads all up on her made Fitzgerald yearn for the solace of a convent. She slid down half of what remained of her triple tequila shot.

"Stick to virtual reality, my friend," she said. "The real thing would be too much for you to handle without shrivelling up."

Goatse looked crestfallen. He played with his nose ring and started to stutter causing a little string of spittle to stretch between his blue lips like a single thread of spider web. "Oh, I... oh, don't... don't worry about me... my handling—"

Fitzgerald smiled and cut him off. "Let's just assume speaking is not your thing. But you feel confident that you can crack it open, as you say, and get these top-secret files."

Malfesio nodded and took over for his stuttering partner. "Sure. Sure. At Liquid Sky? Sure. We left a beautiful backdoor."

"And you're sure it's still there?" she asked, hoping against hope. Could it really be that easy?

Both men laughed at the absurdity of her question.

"Uh... yeah. Of course," sneered Goatse, sensing an opportunity to reattach his balls after she just lopped them off, tossed them on the floor, and crushed them underfoot.

Fitzgerald decided to move forward with the plan. "Great," she said flatly. "Then you can get me those files?"

"Get you those files?" asked Malfesio, stroking the wispy hairs on his chin he called his "flava sava."

Fitzgerald nodded slowly. "Get them... steal them... bring them to me and delete them from the Liquid Sky servers."

Both hackers smiled broadly.

"Now we're having us some fun," said Goatse.

"Yeah, fun is good," added Malfesio philosophically.

"You know what's really fun?" said Goatse, sensing an opportunity to pay back Fitzgerald for emasculating him. "Money. Money is really fun. So, how much you got for us? This don't sound like some beef you got with your fascist pig of a boss. Nah, this sounds like something big, isn't that right?"

Fitzgerald closed her eyes in pain. "We'll get to that... provided I decide to hire you. But you're right, this is no joke. It's a very serious task with very serious consequences if you get caught. And if you get caught, I get caught. That's unacceptable."

She sensed the two hackers weren't showing much concern for her warning. In fact, Goatse was staring off at the Trump building and fondling one of his dreads while Malfesio was admiring one of the famous London House gargoyles atop the patio wall.

Fitzgerald's anxiety was beginning to show now. Were they stoned? She felt droplets of sweat running down her stomach from where they had pooled under her breasts. She also felt the tension rising in her head. Their nonchalance, their condescension, their entire anti-establishment, jackass hacktivist demeaner... it was moments like this that she was apt to lash out, and these two guys were fixing to get an earful if things progressed.

Goatse and Malfesio were beginning to get to her. Until recently, Parker Fitzgerald gave everything she had to Rickey Ormand and Liquid Sky, even very nearly her life. And the more she thought about it, the more she realized the stark implications should this technology be completely controlled by Rickey Ormand or, even worse, the U.S. government. Ormand cared only about his own power and fame. She knew he would reduce this amazing technology to a facile instrument for promoting his own rise to unrivalled power. As for the douche canoe of politicians right on up to the president, Fitzgerald had even less esteem. God only knew the myriad ways in which a politician would corrupt the greatest technology in the history of human civilization.

And where all but two people thought gravity power was the revolutionary technology Fitzgerald feared losing, only she and Rickey Ormand knew the truth. Liquid-Drive was merely a smoke screen, an elaborate red herring to keep his secret hidden until he was ready to reveal it to the world. Liquid-Life was the real revolution.

Parker Fitzgerald was Liquid-Life, and Liquid-Life was Parker Fitzgerald. As far as she was concerned, the two were indistinguishable from one another. Somehow, she'd become the invention, the greatest human achievement in history. She laughed to herself every time she thought about it. People actually thought the gravity-powered battery that ran her robotic lower half was the pinnacle of modern technology. Compared to Liquid-Life, it was little more than the six-volt lantern battery kids use to make a volcano foam like a rabid dog at a middle-school science fair.

Rickey Ormand was more of a magician than anything else. Misdirection was his greatest skill. While people were looking in one direction at something all sparkly and grandiose, it was just sleight-of-hand in the end. The real machinations were taking place where nobody was looking. Nobody was looking at Parker Fitzgerald. Or, at least, the people who were looking at her saw only what Rickey Ormand wanted them to see – a miracle half-robot scientist sporting a lower body powered by gravity. Just imagine all the other ways gravity power could be harnessed. That's what Ormand wanted them to see. What they didn't see was the way in which Parker Fitzgerald was life itself.

Liquid-Life.

Where do I draw the line? She kept struggling with that question. Her decision to steal the Liquid-Life technology and make it public to keep it from the monolithic control of a handful of men was based on moving the world forward into a better future for all people without regard for who, what, where, when, or why. Why was this so important to her? Because only Parker Fitzgerald and Rickey Ormand knew the truth. Liquid-Life was an implanted device that collected and converted gravitational energy into a life force that sustained all cellular activity.

The theory was simple enough. The human body ran on tiny electric impulses that powered and signalled the organized, metabolic process called life. At its most basic level, life stems from the constant energy running through our bodies on the cellular level. People ate, drank, and performed countless other daily activities in order to power the body. Liquid-Life replaced the need for all this by harnessing gravity as a constant energy source. Parker Fitzgerald lived on gravitational energy. It powered her on a cellular level. She had no need of external resources such as food. Her life pool was the omnipresent field of gravity that surrounded her everywhere on earth. In fact, it was this very same energy that connected all living beings in a greater spiritual sense.

With Liquid-Life, everything was part of this dynamic web. Since all people with the Liquid-Life implant could conceivably live on gravitational energy, all people could unite inside a total, encompassing energy source and consciously experience a very real collective consciousness binding us all together at the very wellspring of life itself.

Once again, Rickey Ormand made this dream a reality. But Parker Fitzgerald knew this was different. This was about something encompassing all of humanity and, therefore, deserving of much more than the profit-driven world of Silicon Valley. That model would not do for a technological breakthrough of this magnitude. The person called Parker Fitzgerald was indistinguishable from the technology called Liquid-Life. In this new paradigm, person, place, and things were melded indistinguishably.

How could Rickey Ormand slap a patent on her life? She felt no person should control another's access to a better life or, for that matter, life in general. That's why she decided to steal Liquid-Life and disseminate the technology free of charge to the world.

Goatse and Malfesio hardly noticed Fitzgerald was off somewhere deep in thought. As usual, they were too busy arguing with each other. Malfesio asserted vehemently that human civilization will inevitably implode when it no longer has enough food to feed its wretchedly overpopulated masses. Goatse saw the entire premise as moot because Artificial Intelligence will most certainly have replaced human beings by then. At one point, it looked as if Goatse was going to fall down when he stood up abruptly. As it turned out, he was just hiking up his slouching skinny jeans enough to cover his crack, no doubt a welcome adjustment for the folks sitting at the table behind him.

Fitzgerald shook her head. She was one of only two people in the entire world who knew for certain that they were both wrong...

and she was the proof. Yes, everybody seemed so preoccupied with the mundane, with the banality of everyday life. Just wait until she gave Liquid-Life to the world, a world which would never be the same again.

She leaned in toward Goatse and Malfesio and rapped her knuckles on the table symbolically. "Hey, knuckleheads. Listen to me."

Thinking she was trying to get his attention, the waiter hurried over. Fitzgerald handed over her empty. "Another triple for me. Nothing for them. Not even water."

The waiter scurried off, leaving them with some privacy once more.

"I hope you're listening, boys, because if you screw this up, we're all toast. There'll be no one to save your asses. Speaking of asses, the both of you better get used to the idea of yours becoming a playground for a long line of inmates who don't appreciate the value of lube. I'm pretty sure they have a different understanding of mouse finger in the big house, but hey... I could be wrong. What do I know, right?"

She sat back when the waiter returned with her glass, laid it in front of her, and left. "Know what I'm saying?" she said.

Whatever it was she said, it caught their attention this time. Goatse nodded his head and grinned. "Oh yeah," he said with more than a hint of menace in his voice. He ran some dreads through his fingers and then smelled them. "We get it... believe me. You couldn't find better people for this gig. We know the Liquid Sky system like we built it."

"We did," added Malfesio with delight.

"Yeah," continued Goatse, "we built the bitch, and we can crack her open too." He made a crude gesture with his pierced tongue to Malfesio, sending both of them into spurts of laughter.

Fitzgerald shook her head and drank. What else could she do in the midst of a conversation like this? "In that case, I have three questions for you," she said. "First, how do you two bozos propose to get in?"

Goatse grimaced. "The same way we did the first time. Through a router. Only we tricked it so the firewall we built will allow us to get in. It's virtually impenetrable to anyone else—"

Malfesio cut him off. "It will really freak out Rickey's IT chimps because we'll be invisible. They may... *may* find a breadcrumb or something, but they won't know how to trace it back."

Fitzgerald voiced her scepticism. "Invisible? Really? You two are more conspicuous than a couple of peacocks in heat. How do you know you'll be untraceable?"

Malfesio waved her off. "Stop with your nonsense. I am not worried about that shit. Those over-the-counter IT hacks working for Liquid Sky couldn't find white on rice. Anyway, we always leave ourselves a way back in... you know, in case a client tries to screw us or something. Yeah, we will walk right in even though the Liquid Sky routers sit behind the firewall."

"Of course, they do," said Goatse, pissed off that Malfesio was trying to steal his thunder. "That's obvious. Of course, they sit behind a firewall. That's just so obvious."

Goatse looked at Fitzgerald in earnest for the first time. "The thing is, doc, nobody gets through one of my firewalls." He smirked. "No way, no how. Even Rickey Dickey's IT chimps know that. I'm a god to them."

Fitzgerald shrugged. "So, what?" she asked. "Why is that important?"

Malfesio found her question beneath him but deigned to clarify nonetheless. "Because," he said dramatically, "they'll do what everyone else does. If by some miracle they detect some sort of anomaly, they'll assume some amateur tried to hack through the firewall and failed. Meanwhile we can tunnel under it and pop up right in the middle of their data any freaking time we choose. It's a beautiful thing, man."

Fitzgerald cast her eyes from one to the other several times, sizing them up before continuing. "I haven't understood a thing you've said since I got here. Honestly, I don't care. There is only one thing I want to impress upon you, so let me reiterate it. Failure is not an option here. You need to make this happen."

Goatse was grinning like king shit. "Correctamundo, doc. You came to the right place. See, that's why you're gonna pay us so much money... we're the best there is. And, on top of that, we're the best there is, *and* the best at ripping Rickey wide open. See, this is the thing, man. I don't just, like, write beautiful code. No, man, I can actually make people do and think what I want them to."

"Deception is the hallmark of his greatest work," noted Malfesio energetically. "What good is sinister code if you can't get people to do what you want? That's like... like Lucky Charms with no milk. What's the point, you know?"

"That's the art in the science," said Goatse, still pleased with all the praise. "So, this is what I'll do, right? I'll leave a few breadcrumbs around so it will look like we launched the usual type of inept attack and failed predictably. Rickey's guys will be all proud of themselves. But fear not, my lady," he added with an exaggerated bow. "We'll include in the malware package a neat little script that basically erases any information on the path we took in."

Fitzgerald was fascinated. "Really, you can do that?" she asked.

Goatse sat back, folded his arms, and nodded. "Just a little sumpin I've been cookin' up." He paused to pick something out of his teeth. "You'll be reading about it in a year or so."

Malfesio started cracking up. "If they even figure it out." He pointed to his partner in crime. "Ahhhhhhh... ahhhhhhh," he gloated in a carnivalesque voice.

Fitzgerald scratched her head. "Weren't the two of you arguing like a loathsome married couple when I walked in?"

Malfesio waved her off. "Don't go making trouble, sister. You were just witnessing brilliant minds at play."

Fitzgerald tried to keep up. "So, you're saying you can completely cover your tracks?"

Goatse wagged his finger at her. "No. You need to pay closer attention, doc. I said I can both drop a false trail so they think they found something while also completely covering my tracks. Get them to do what I want, remember?"

Fitzgerald looked at the two of them. It was hard for her to put so much trust in them. But she knew they were the best no matter what she thought about their appearance or demeanor. She knew she had no choice anyway.

"Well," she said leaning back, the tequila beginning to hit her. "I'm impressed." She shuddered a bit looking at Goatse sitting there looking so smug. "And now I feel like I need to take a shower. But I'm impressed."

"That's not all," added Malfesio enthusiastically. "Remember, if they can't find our backdoor, we can use it again in the future." He was barely able to contain his giddiness.

Goatse and Malfesio both began chuckling. Fitzgerald watched as two heads full of dreads bobbed up and down like a Rasta jellyfish.

"That's why it's called a 'blind man,'" clarified Malfesio. "What's so beautiful about it is that your slime-ball boss will actually think our firewall did the job. He'll probably send us a thank you. Maybe like a fruit basket? That would be totally num-num."

Goatse's mood changed precipitously. He backhanded his colleague in the chest. "Dude, what did I tell you about saying 'num-num'? Do you actually go out of your way to embarrass me? Why can't you just say tasty or something that doesn't make you sound like a twelve-year-old Valley girl?"

Fitzgerald was still back on breadcrumbs and blind man. "Wait," she said, amazed but cautious. "You're absolutely sure you can do all that stuff with the false trails and covering your tracks and stuff?"

Goatse snorted as if offended. "That's, like, the fiftieth time you asked me that. And, like I said, I'm sure as shit it will work. I can promise you that. It will look like a typical, inept attack. I'll lead them where I want them to go. I'll be free to do whatever I want in the Liquid Sky network."

Malfesio leaned over and whispered something in Goatse's ear. Goatse made a show of considering whatever it was Malfesio said to him. After stroking his "flava sava" a bit, he said, "My esteemed colleague has made a most excellent suggestion."

"I can only imagine," said Fitzgerald.

Malfesio rubbed his hands together and leaned in apparently for effect only, since he made no effort to lower his voice. "I've been building this nasty-ass booby trap that's kinda like a zero day."

Fitzgerald just shrugged. She had no idea what he was talking about.

"You don't know what a zero day is?" mocked Malfesio. He turned to Goatse. "She doesn't know what a zero day is. That's so funny. That's just so funny. Ahhhhhhh."

Goatse shared his partner's amusement.

"Okay, okay," said Malfesio. "I was just saying, you know... everybody knows zero."

Goatse backhanded Malfesio in the chest again.

"Right, right," stuttered Malfesio. "Sorry. Booby trap. So, I'm building this little beauty that will completely explode an entire system when triggered. With a zero day, like, you click on an attachment and, like, it's really executable for a bunch of viruses or something like that. But mine is different. I call it "Rabbit Hole." If anyone at Liquid Sky has enough brains to find our backdoor. They will have to trace our steps. It'll be like going down a rabbit hole because as soon as they climb down, so to speak, they will set off a booby trap that will, like, totally nuke not only the backdoor but everything they touched on the way to it."

Goatse stood up and raised his hands high in the air. His muffin top quivered like a new-born fawn rising to its feet for the first time. "It's beautiful," he proclaimed. "This guy has his moments."

He slapped hands with Malfesio before regaining his composure, pulling up his sagging skinny jeans, and returning to his seat.

Having recollected himself now, Goatse reassessed his lugubrious praise. "I mean it's obvious. It's an obvious thing to do. It's easy. It's so easy, you know? But they'll never see it coming, you know? So the shit's on them."

"You need to calm down," Fitzgerald ordered under her breath. "You never know who's listening, okay?"

"Anyway," said Malfesio, "by the time one of Pricky Rickey's guys triggers Rabbit Hole, we'll be long gone with your plans."

"And your money," added Goatse. "That's the most important thing." He winked at Fitzgerald. "Let's not forget the money."

Fitzgerald chewed on it for a while, allowing the tequila to continue its festive tapatio on her brain. This was exactly the sort of surreptitious darknet stuff she was hoping for when she reached out to them in the first place. In reality, though, she had no freaking idea what they were talking about, let alone whether or not they could actually pull it off. For all she knew, these two very shady bastards were setting her up.

She wondered if they were just blowing smoke up her ass? Even if they pulled it off, they would have her dead to rights for blackmail. And if she pissed them off? God only knew how easily these two could hack open every lockbox containing her personal information. Maybe they were planning to steal every penny she had? Maybe they still secretly worked for Ormand? After all, corporate espionage was a fact of life in Silicon Valley, and she wouldn't put it past Ormand to have a secret team of counter-espionage hackers on the payroll. Maybe they were going to steal Liquid-Life for themselves. Or worse... maybe they were going to set her up to take the fall?

She shook off the tequila fog. "Well," she said, having regained her composure and her guile. "There's no turning back now. It sure beats the hell out of me sneaking into Rickey's office and downloading the files onto a USB."

Malfesio laughed at the idea. "Nah, we locked out USB downloads as part of the security protocol we built. You need a special password. Anyway, that's so boring. It's, like... it's like so crumbly John McCain. That's not how we operate. We don't do stuff like break into buildings. Where's the challenge in that? I break into systems from the comfort of my own couch with, like, some Chinese and my X-Box, you know?"

Goatse and Malfesio high-fived each other again. Fitzgerald stared at them, not knowing what to think.

Goatse wagged his finger. "Like I said, doc, you're dealing with a genuine talent, not some thirty-year-old millennial living in his mother's basement."

Malfesio couldn't help himself. "Ahhhhhhh…." It was something like a high-pitched whine. "Don't be so sure about that."

Goatse tensed up like he just sat on a cucumber naked. "Shut up! It's only temporary and you know it."

Malfesio pointed at him. "Ahhhhhhh...." His high-pitched whine made Fitzgerald squirm.

Goatse didn't see the humor. "Yeah, whatever, man. I had... a bit of trouble recently," he explained to Parker Fitzgerald. "You know, investing in some crypto currencies that didn't do so well and shit," he confessed. "No big deal. It happens."

"He lost, like, all the money Ormand paid him... like a million bucks," Malfesio taunted.

Goatse banged his fist on the high-top table just loud enough to make a nearby table of rich thirty-somethings take notice. The empty glasses and silverware on the table rattled. "I did not *lose* the money. I'm only down on paper. It'll come back alright, you moron."

"Yeah, right," said Malfesio, letting loose a guffaw. "It's worth, like, thirty cents, so I guess paper is worth more." He turned to Fitzgerald. "He lives with his mommy now."

"I live with my mother for now, okay? So what? She's old. She needs me. At least my mom wasn't a stripper who abandoned me to move to, like, Florida with some dude when I was ten."

That hurt Malfesio. "You're wrong. You're so wrong. It's so obvious how wrong you are. She moved to St. Louis, alright? I could have gone with her."

Now it was Goatse's turn to laugh. "Yeah, right. She didn't even tell you she was leaving your dumb ass behind."

"You're a dumb ass," Malfesio retorted.

Goatse was quick on the comeback. "You're the dumb ass."

Fitzgerald found her hand reaching for her glass on its own the way a masochist reaches for shame. "Well," she said. "I guess that brings us to my second question. How much is this going to cost me?"

Goatse and Malfesio stopped bickering and instantly smiled. This had to be a big hit. For Goatse, in particular, as this was his big chance to move out of his mother's basement.

"Now that... that's the question, isn't it?" replied Goatse, already counting the money in his head.

Fitzgerald thought they were planning to stick it to her. She had no doubt he would play right into her hand.

Goatse glared at her. Malfesio's humiliating words were still reverberating in his head. "Considering you want us to sneak up the ass of the most famous tech company in the world and steal something right out from under Rickey Rocket's nose, that puts us in seven figures right out of the gate. But something else occured to me."

Fitzgerald knocked down half of what remained in her glass and sat back. This was going to cost her. "And what might that be?"

Goatse sniffed loudly several times. "Whatever this Liquid-Life thing is, you want it real bad. So, I'm guessing this thing has, like, tremendous market value."

"That's obvious. That's so obvious," said Malfesio. "Anybody can see that."

Goatse bit his lower lip in frustration. "I know it's obvious, you nimrod," he snarled. He returned to Fitzgerald. "Anyway, I'm, like, thinking... why don't we forget about our fee?"

Malfesio almost jumped straight out of his seat when he heard this. "What the—"

Goatse silenced him with another backhand to the chest and pushed him back down into his chair.

"I have my eyes on a bigger prize," said Goatse. "I want a piece of the action. If we're stealing this Liquid-Life thing for you, then we want half of anything you make from it. I think that's fair, don't you? Surely you think it's fair. It's fair. It's so obviously fair."

Realizing the clear value of Goatse's proposal, Malfesio changed his tune and agreed heartily. "That's obvious. It's fair. That's so obvious."

Goatse sat back and read Fitzgerald's reaction. She played it close to the vest, though. She was prepared to pay these shady sons-of-bitches a million each. This technology belonged to the world, and to the world she would gift it. But she thought... Goatse and

Malfesio didn't have to know that. As far as they were concerned, let them be all pie eyed. She was under no obligation to explain her intention to give the technology away as her gift to humanity. Fifty percent of nothing was nothing or... thirty cents less than Goatse's crypto account.

She'd already floated the bait with Liquid-Life. Both hackers smelled blood in the water. That was good. Now all she had to do was sink the hook into two more arrogant men, and God was she looking forward to sticking it to these two.

She decided to draw Goatse in a bit closer by mounting some false resistance. "You must be out of your devious little mind, my friend. You can't possibly expect me to fork over the rights to half of this technology. That would be billions when I can pay you a couple of million and be done with the both of you. Why would I do that?"

The smile quickly disappeared from Malfesio's face. Yeah, he thought, why would she do that? Suddenly, Goatse's plan didn't seem so hot. Suddenly, his partner seemed like a complete idiot who overplayed his hand.

Goatse saw that Malfesio was about to turn. He motioned for silence just as Malfesio was about to undercut the deal. He smiled sardonically and mumbled something to himself.

"Look, doc," he said. "It's like this, see? It's clear to me that you need whatever this thing is, this Liquid-Life technology. In fact, I think you need it in the worst way."

"Perhaps," she said. "Assuming I don't bag the entire plan."

Goatse continued. "Okay, so obviously we need each other, okay? Obviously, we all want to profit from this. But I must remind you that, at the same time, it seems clear that you need us if you are to profit as well, no?"

He exhaled loudly and sat back. For the first time he could remember, Goatse had given birth to humility, however grotesque the demon offspring. He felt it was completely overrated, and he didn't care for the sentiment at all.

Fitzgerald smiled. She had him right where she wanted him. Sink the hook and reel his fat ass in. She reached out and took her glass.

She held it up and nodded before draining the remains of the tequila. Uncomfortable with his vulnerability, Goatse couldn't look her in the eye, and Malfesio looked like he was going to puke any second. The hip, Afropunk revolutionary seemed rather bee-bop just then.

"I appreciate the effort," Fitzgerald said, and then sweetened it with some honey for his sore ego. "How can a woman refuse your charm? So, we have a deal. You will deliver the full file and technical specs for Liquid-Life in exchange for fifty percent of all future proceeds I receive from the technology."

Goatse held up his hand and interrupted her. "Whoa, whoa, whoa. Slow your roll there, Betty Crocker. Just remember who you're dealing with, alright? If we find out that you're holding out on us or, like, hiding a billion dollars in royalties or something like that, we'll mess with your life so bad, you won't be able to buy a free glass of water. Just remember, nowadays people are nothing more than the sum of their electronic data. In this world, I can play God. I hope we understand each other."

Fitzgerald noticed that there was a small bug crawling up Goatse's forehead. She watched it make its way into his dread locks. Goatse interpreted Fitzgerald's stare as rapt attention to him befitting the enormity of the moment. When the bug had fully disappeared into Goatse's dreads, she responded.

"Calm down," she said. "Your threats don't scare me. If I want to, I can drop a dime to the Feds any time. They would love to have you over for fifteen or twenty years. Let's not worry about nuking each other right now. Of course, this is contingent upon us not getting caught."

"Not a concern," said Malfesio smugly.

"Excellent," replied Fitzgerald. "So, you guys won't mind a one-year freeze on any payouts to you so that we are sure we're safe. And, as you said to me, if you double cross me on this, I will pay you back tenfold. I hope we understand each other on this account as well."

Goatse laughed it off. "We can disappear into thin air. In cyberspace, the air is thin, baby."

"We can disappear like that," reiterated Malfesio, snapping his ring-laden fingers.

"Maybe from me," said Fitzgerald. "Try disappearing from Rickey Ormand."

Goatse held up his hands. "Hey, hey... let's not get ourselves carried away here. We're partners, aren't we?"

"Are we?" said Fitzgerald.

"We have a deal," said Goatse.

They shook hands. Her grip was significantly stronger than his.

"Take it easy on the mouse hand, sweets," cautioned Goatse.

"Anyway, let's all calm down. Nobody will notice a thing," said Malfesio.

"Nobody will know shit," agreed Goatse.

Fitzgerald smiled as she looked at the Trump building through the large window. "There's just one last thing."

Goatse scratched his head. The bug must have tickled his scalp. "Yeah, I'm listening."

She thought about how to best position this last bit. Through Liquid-Life, Parker Fitzgerald was able to live off the earth's gravitational energy. Her bodily functions were supported by gravitational energy rather than food to generate the source of the body's electrical impulses, the very impulses triggering every human function no matter how small. She needed to drink water and take vitamins and amino acids, but food was obsolete. And the most recent research at Liquid Sky proved without a doubt that her immune system had developed new synergies with her other bodily systems to become in effect, supercharged.

During the arduous rehab period following her ordeal in Peru, Parker Fitzgerald was diagnosed with breast cancer. When her robo-prosthetic lower half was "installed," it included the Liquid-Life suite so that Ormand could capitalize on the opportunity to conduct an *in vivo* study that would otherwise be impossible. Of course, the technology was brand new, and nobody knew what to expect.

Fitzgerald's ability to survive on nothing but water, vitamins, amino acids, and gravitational energy was expected; her cancer going into complete remission was not. Her supercharged immune system, powered by Liquid-Life technology, went seek-and-destroy on her cancer cells while leaving healthy cells intact. Within one year, Parker Fitzgerald was deemed to have "no evidence of the disease" by a leading oncologist Ormand hired away from Mayo.

The implications were staggering. It meant that gravity power – harnessed by Liquid-Life technology – was one of the greatest discoveries in human history. Liquid-Life was the solution to the most pressing humanitarian crises of the new millennium. Disease, infant mortality, over-population, food scarcity, and the general depletion of natural resources necessary to support rising meat and fish consumption were soon to be relics of a fossilized era overnight. Add to that the benefits gained from Liquid-Drive, and the modern-day crises of energy, pollution, and transportation also became a thing of the past.

Ormand knew what he had. He knew that owning the intellectual-property rights to Liquid-Drive and Liquid-Life would make him the wealthiest, most powerful, and most famous man in the world overnight. When he announced Liquid-Drive and pumped it at his gala, he did so almost as a feint. He wanted everyone chasing him in that direction. He had the inside track. Every other company, including the U.S. government, had to line up for an audience with him. That's exactly what he wanted. It would keep everyone in the dark about Liquid-Life until he could finish the development.

More importantly, he could leverage those same relationships and put a stranglehold on the world when it came time to unveil Liquid-Life. The contracts for Liquid-Drive rights would surreptitiously carry over to Liquid-Life, giving Ormand a pre-established network for dissemination and exploitation. Ormand saw himself as a spider weaving a massive web that would ensnare everything. Once everything was trapped in his web, Ormand could feed off them anytime he hungered for something. Nobody would realize it because he was sitting on Liquid-Life. He was sitting on an end to hunger and disease. He was sitting on life itself... Liquid-Life.

Camille O'Keefe and Parker Fitzgerald saw things quite differently. When taken together, Liquid-Drive and Liquid-Life were poised to catapult all of humanity forward at light speed. It marked an unprecedented opportunity to level disparities among the people of the world and created genuine opportunity for all people to evolve as valuable spirits unto themselves. This more than anything else was the goal for Parker Fitzgerald, just as it was for Camille O'Keefe.

If nothing else, Parker and Camille discovered this deep connection at the gala. They also discovered that Rickey Ormand and Harry Pierson, each had their own designs on the technology. Rickey Ormand, Harry Pierson and men like them had no intention of making this life-altering technology available to all of humanity. Instead, they sought business as usual, limiting this technology to those who could afford it, the world's relatively affluent, restricting Liquid-Life to the same old tired pipeline of social inequality. Neither Camille O'Keefe nor Parker Fitzgerald could allow this to happen. Parker Fitzgerald had the power and the opportunity to stop it, in the process bringing real equilibrium to the planet.

Fitzgerald was playing this through in her head while staring off into the Chicago night and the black expanse of Lake Michigan. She was in no mood for an arrogant, patronizing lecture from a couple of dickhead hackers. And yet, she needed said dickhead hackers in order to make the world an infinitely better place. As she stared out across the endless lake into darkness, the irony did not escape her. At that moment, she felt like she was caught in a spider's web.

It wasn't until she felt Goatse's chubby index finger caressing her forearm that Parker Fitzgerald snapped out of her thoughts. She pulled her arm away in disgust. "What the hell are you doing?" she hissed.

Goatse was startled and withdrew his hand immediately. "Jeez," he said, "partners are supposed to show their affection for each other."

Malfesio laughed. "She gonna cut your dick off, man. I will keep my distance from all that, if you don't mind."

Fitzgerald was pissed. Rickey Ormand, Harry Pierson, these two schmucks, men, assholes... she'd had enough. Wasn't that why she was doing all this in the first place?

"You listen to me, you nappy-haired man pig," she fired back. "Don't ever touch me again."

Malfesio found this hilarious. "Yo, Goatse the Man Pig. Like, that's your new tag. Goatse the Man Pig."

Fitzgerald wasn't done. "I'm drawing a line here. We're business partners, and that's all. Do you understand? Don't get any illusions about being partners of any other sort. And the next time you touch me, I'm going to grab you by your stupid little nose ring until you call me mommy. Got it?"

Goatse nodded.

She glared at Malfesio. "That goes for you, too, Bill Clinton. Fries do not come with this shake. Feel me?"

Malfesio nodded. His smile evaporated.

She looked around the patio to make sure nobody was watching them. Then she removed something from her left thigh compartment.

"There's one more thing I need from you as part of this deal," she said.

Goatse snorted. He sat back in disgust and crossed his arms. "You got a lotta wants, partner."

Fitzgerald grew serious. "Ormand can't know the files have been taken. I need time. If he suspects something is up, it will completely derail my plans."

"Yeah, I got that part," said Goatse, still annoyed. "I'm just copying some files."

Fitzgerald pushed her hair to the side. "I need more than that, actually. Once he discovers Liquid-Life has been stolen and is out there for the taking, he will move aggressively to counter."

Malfesio looked confused. "But won't that be too late? Once whatever this thing is out in the open, it'll be too late."

Fitzgerald was determined to stick to her plan. "What I'm saying is that I don't want Liquid Sky to have the plans at all."

"But we can't delete them or he'll know immediately," noted Malfesio, fondling one of his technicolored dreads. "I see your dilemma."

Fitzgerald nodded. "Yeah, that's why I made this." She slid the object she took from her leg over to Goatse.

Goatse nonchalantly placed his hand over the object and drew it in. He stole a glance of it under the table. "A USB drive?" he said, quietly for a change.

Fitzgerald nodded. "It's a set of dummy files. They look a lot like the plans for Liquid-Life, but they're missing some key components. That will screw Ormand up enough to buy us a lot of time, assuming his guys can even figure out what's missing. Basically, I don't want Rickey Ormand owning this technology, and I'll do whatever I can think of to make sure he doesn't."

She caught herself just in time. She almost revealed her intention to give the technology away via open source. That would have blown the deal they just cut.

"We can make billions if we move fast enough and have enough of a head start," she said, hoping they bought it.

There was an uncomfortable silence. Goatse grimaced. "No," he said exhaling. "It won't work."

Malfesio snapped his fingers. "Damn... the audit trail."

"The audit trail?" asked Fitzgerald.

Goatse nodded. "They run Windows servers at Liquid Sky. Windows has a built-in audit-trail function. It documents every file that's deleted. I know for a fact it's a real bitch because I tweaked it myself. Only Ormand can turn it off, and I'm sure that if this Liquid-Life thing is as important as you say, he has it flagged to actually call him whenever one of the files is deleted."

"Damn," said Malfesio. "What the hell did you do that for?"

"Well," continued Goatse, "I can turn off audits for copying files. I'm pretty sure Ormand didn't think to lock that down on his own. But there's no way to delete the original files and replace them with the ones you just gave me. I'm sorry."

All three of them were silent until, without warning, Malfesio slammed his palms on the table. "Honeypot" he exclaimed. "We need something like a honeypot then."

Goatse held up his hand for silence while he thought it over. A minute or two later, he was nodding and smiling. "I got this," he said.

Fitzgerald looked around and then leaned in. "Can one of you tell me what the hell you're talking about? I've never heard of a honeypot."

Goatse held his hands out. "You're not supposed to. That's sort of the whole point."

"Okay," said Fitzgerald sceptically.

"Think Pooh," said Malfesio.

Fitzgerald winced. Just then, a group of four women sat at the table next to them. They were dressed casually in broad, flowing palazzo pants in vibrant patterns and tasteful, fitted blouses. Fitzgerald noticed that one of the women was wearing a pink and yellow head scarf. Fitzgerald could see the woman was bald and knew the tell-tale signs of chemo when she saw them. Thanks to Liquid-Life, Fitzgerald was spared the medieval treatment that killed all cells indiscriminately.

If this woman had Liquid-Life, Fitzgerald thought to herself, her cancer would be completely eradicated in under a year. This thought alone spurred her resolve, even though she had no friends and would never have a family thanks to what she was.

"Winnie the Pooh," clarified Goatse.

"He loves honey," said Malfesio. "He's always got his nose stuck into some pot of honey or some such thing. The same concept applies here."

Fitzgerald was still thinking about the woman with cancer but tried to remain focused. "So, a honeypot is something people want?"

"Exactly," said Goatse. "When you know you've got something that somebody wants real bad, it doesn't matter where you hide it. If they want it bad enough, and they're good enough, they'll find it."

"But with a honeypot," added Malfesio, "you don't really hide anything. Instead, you set up a trap. It looks like honey, but really it's a trap."

"Usually," said Goatse, "you set up a honeypot if you're trying to catch a hacker. It's like a decoy data repository."

Fitzgerald smiled. She was beginning to get the idea now. "Ah, so the honeypot lures them in so you can catch them red-handed."

Malfesio was getting really excited now. "Sometimes, yeah," he agreed, gesticulating like mad. "If you want to catch somebody and turn them over to the authorities or something like that. But you can also use a honeypot to plant information – good, bad, whatever, just information – that you actually *want* somebody to steal. Follow me?"

Fitzgerald liked the sound of this. "In which case," she said, "the cyber thief is actually doing your bidding all the while thinking they're ripping you off."

"Bingo," said Goatse, pointing both index fingers in her direction. "It's all about getting people to do things, remember? Once they take out information you want them to have and they don't know it, the sky's the limit for what you can do to them. Think about it, doc."

Fitzgerald nodded. "Believe me, I am. I totally get it. It's brilliant."

"Nah," said Malfesio. "It's pretty commonplace now."

"You think Liquid Sky has a honeypot setup?" she asked.

"Of course, they have a honeypot," said Goatse amusedly. "We built it. The bitch is deep and sticky."

Fitzgerald could hear the woman with cancer talking about her son in middle school which meant she was probably in her late thirties or early forties.

"I... I mean... like, it's a really good honeypot," added Malfesio.

Fitzgerald was a bit perplexed. "But I don't understand the application in our situation. We are the people hacking in," she said in a muffled voice. "How will that honeypot help us?"

Malfesio had the answer ready. "That's what occurred to me. The honeypot we built for Liquid Sky is irrelevant. But I have an idea. Once we hack into their server, we can build a new one. So, like, we take the fake data you put on your USB, that's the honey, right?"

"Right," said Fitzgerald, trying to follow.

"Right, right," continued Malfesio. "And, like... oh, this is great. So, we create, like a sort of honeypot inside the Liquid Sky server that has all your fake data. And then we set up a simple redirect from the real Liquid-Life files to the honeypot instead. I'm betting he's got Liquid-Life on a discreet drive of its own. I can bury it with a DWORD or something... nothing too advanced. But if we bury the real files and set up a honeypot with your fake files that looks exactly like the real thing and set it on the path they use to access the real files, they'll never know until your fake blows up when they try to actually make something. Get it?"

Fitzgerald scratched her head. "Not entirely," she said.

Goatse stepped in. "What he's proposing is like a secret file cabinet. Every time they click on one of the original files, they'll be redirected to the honeypot of fake files. And here's the best part. Every time they save one of the fake honey files, we can have it upload to the offsite backup. They use Iron Mountain. So, get this. Eventually, the offsite backup will be converted over to the fake honey files all by itself."

Fitzgerald was delighted. "Oh my God, that's perfect. I just need time. Once Liquid-Life—" she caught herself again about to reveal her intention to give it away for free. "Once Liquid-Life is ours, he'll be trying to catch up with technically invalid files."

"Exactly," said Malfesio.

She decided to put some icing on the cake. "That's all we need to make ourselves billions, boys," she lied.

Goatse and Malfesio sat back beaming. Fitzgerald stood up and pushed two white envelopes across to them. "That's for your expenses getting here, as promised," she said. "You have one week to complete your end."

"All's we need is half that," boasted Malfesio. "We keep an ammunition box of code like this around."

"Yeah, we're pretty much plug and play for something like this," said Goatse. "Only thing is, we don't play."

"Excellent," said Fitzgerald. "I expect to hear from you in the near future then."

The men nodded as they slid their envelopes off the table.

Before turning to leave, Fitzgerald took one last look at the woman in the head scarf. She was laughing between sips of Perrier. In that moment, Parker Fitzgerald reminded herself that sometimes, it took a thief to return to the people what had already been stolen from them.

It wasn't personal. She was offended by Rickey Ormand. She feared the greatest discovery in history would be wasted under his sole direction. But she harbored no vendetta. The man made her rich after all.

This was business, pure and simple. And, as Rickey Ormand taught her, in business "you gotta break eggs to make an omelette." She turned and left the London House Hotel and had no interest in ever returning.

Meanwhile, Goatse and Malfesio were still scheming.

"And... and.... I think I'll drop in a keystroke logger on his desktop computer," said Goatse, referring to a piece of malware that secretly recorded every keystroke in order to steal passwords, correspondence, and so on.

Malfesio loved it. "Ahhhhhhh... Rick the Dick in hella trouble now. Damn...."

Goatse grinned. "There won't be a single file or bank account he has that we can't empty just because we can, boy."

The two clinked glasses.

"Here we come, Rickey boy."

Chapter 25

The next few days flew by. Parker Fitzgerald went about her business as stone-faced as the finest poker player on the Vegas circuit. If push came to shove, she felt confident she could wrap Rickey around her finger (or at least her thigh) and misdirect his investigation. Her plan was to make the thing blow back on Rohit Gupta or Bai Wei, since they were running the program and had, she assumed, deep access into their respective halves of the project.

She considered what Camille said to her about intentions. She knew framing Gupta or Wei was the wrong thing to do, even if her guys blew the hack. She had no time to worry about that now. With the election over and Camille's inauguration only two months away, she had to move fast, really fast. The pressure was beginning to get to her, and it was becoming increasingly difficult to keep her cool. She decided to take a couple of days off toward the end of the week to avoid any scrutiny just in case something went wrong when the hack went down.

And so, with little more than a shrug, Parker Fitzgerald booked herself an ocean-view villa in the serene Cape Santa Maria region of the Bahamas. The flight was short, but the views were long into the never ending, crystalline-blue horizon. When the repetitive crash of the surf finally broke through the wall encircling her sense and sensibility, Parker Fitzgerald was overcome by the enormity of it all, not just with the hack but going all the way back to the quake.

More than just tectonic plates were set in motion that day in the Andes. As she stood on the balcony of her vacation villa, looking over the pristine beach, watching the sea foam dissipate atop the white sand after every wave, Fitzgerald felt torn. She enjoyed more freedom than she had in a long while. And yet, the sheer heft of everything that had gone down made her unsure of herself. That Bahamian balcony could have been the edge of the world as far as she was concerned. The crash and sizzle of those waves against the beach stirred strange thoughts in her human head. She couldn't explain why, but she kept coming back to Camille O'Keefe.

It made her smile. As smart as she was, all her degrees and whatnot "piled high and deep" as she liked to quip about her Ph.D., she still couldn't fully understand the implications of her relationship with the new vice president. All she knew was that she felt a deep connection with Camille O'Keefe. Unlike the laws of gravity that governed the waves she was watching, empirical laws that could be proven, the bond between Camille and her drew its power from somewhere outside the canon of scientific knowledge. And still, it was powerful and drew her toward Camille with no less force than the moon exerted on the sea.

Nameless, inexplicable, powerful beyond imagination, the connection between Parker Fitzgerald and Camille O'Keefe was very real. Up to that point, Fitzgerald had no idea what to do with the Liquid-Life data once her guys stole it. She fully intended to make the technology free as open source. But she had no idea how to make that happen. Where was she supposed to go? She couldn't trust Goatse or Malfesio. Standing on that balcony, allowing the energy of the time and place wash over her, she realized there was really only one option. She would relinquish the project data to Camille. It was the only way.

She reaffirmed her decision and headed back into her exquisite villa. The marble floor felt cold against her robotic feet. It made her chuckle. She wasn't feeling anything in the way that normal people felt. The warmth of the sun on her face a moment ago was real; the feeling of cold from the marble floor was simulated. The sensation of cold emanated from sensors in her robo feet that stimulated her brain in the same way the nerves in her feet would have if she actually had feet. She never considered it to be all that different.

She tied a sheer, teal wrap around her bikinied waist and picked up the phone on the end table next to the white, L-shaped couch in the living room. She could survive without food sure enough. But being a breatharian left quite a bit to be desired when it came to the sensual pleasures of fine cuisine. She seldom ate except when necessary to keep up appearances because it totally jacked up her system. Her metabolic levels thrived off gravitational energy which reduced her gut to a minimal digestive function.

From time to time, she simply had to indulge. When in the Bahamas, go with the flow. She rang room service and ordered lobster and scallop sashimi, two delicacies she'd first sampled through the creative delights of Iron Chef Mashaharu Morimoto. For that matter, she threw in a bottle of Pol Roger Churchill 2002. Her head was 100 percent human, so why not let a little bubbly have its way with her gray matter for a few hours? And if Winston Churchill could drink 42,000 bottles of champagne and still achieve all he had, what harm could one bottle do in such a lovely setting?

After ordering, she plopped down on the couch and tried to empty her mind. She sat back and ran her fingers through her blonde hair. No sooner had she taken a few deep yoga breaths than there was a knock on the door. She assumed it was room service, but how on earth did they prep her order so fast?

She was about to call out that she was coming but suddenly thought better of it. No, she thought, eyeing the door at the opposite side of the room with mounting suspicion. There was no way it could be room service. It wasn't housekeeping, either. They finished their rounds two hours ago. Her stomach contorted as she wondered if something went wrong with the hack. Her eyelids grew heavy with the weight of stress.

She stood up cautiously and worked her way to the door as if waiting for it to burst open. She wouldn't be surprised if it was Interpol or even a couple of goons Goatse and Malfesio sent to get rid of her so they could keep Liquid-Life for themselves. It could be anything, anybody. All she knew for sure was that Rickey Ormand would go ballistic if he discovered what she was up to.

As she stood staring at the door nearly in a panic, she could hear the surf running through its endless cycle of ebb and wane, a cycle as old as the earth itself. She remembered something Camille said to her at the end of the gala. In fact, it was those last words they shared before parting.

"Always remember," Camille told her, putting her arm around Fitzgerald's strong shoulders. "You are here to do something special. It's no coincidence our paths have crossed. We have been together in many lifetimes. I know you have come here this time to fulfill a special plan."

Fitzgerald remembered her first response was humor. "I don't think I saw the blueprints for that."

Fitzgerald still remembered how cool Camille was about it. "You have the blueprint in your head already," she said. "Everything you need to know is right here." She tapped her index finger on Fitzgerald's noggin.

That was when Fitzgerald knew she had to steal the plans for Liquid-Life as well as make sure that neither Rickey Ormand nor any handful of powerful men ever gained full control of gravity power in all its many manifestations. That's when she decided that Liquid-Life, with all its possibilities, belonged to the world and not some cabal of political wizards, military-industrial minions, and a CEO warlock from Silicon Valley.

"Not quite everything," Fitzgerald said to Camille, thinking seriously for the first time about hacking Liquid Sky. "There's one piece of the puzzle still missing."

Camille unwrapped her arm from Fitzgerald's shoulders and looked the scientist square in the eyes with her penetrating yet liquid eyes. "I've been around politicians like Beck and Harry Pierson enough to become too comfortable saying 'do what you have to do' to make things right. But I've also been around them enough to see it all boils down to one thing."

For a moment, the fear she was feeling was waiting for her behind the villa door left her as Camille's words played through her mind.

"Intentions," was what Camille said. "It's all about intentions. That's what I've learned from my time with Becket and Harry. I mean, I've always known this intuitively, but I saw it play out time and time again with those guys. You bring in what you put out, right? When you have the wrong intentions, it's like a giant magnet that pulls in bad energy like a huge pile of nails coming straight at you because you're holding the magnet."

"Jesus, what an analogy," was about all Fitzgerald could come up with at the time.

"Jesus knows exactly what I'm talking about," said Camille, only half joking. "But the converse is equally true. That's the point I'm trying to make, Parker. If your intentions are good, the results will be, too. Trust yourself, Parker Fitzgerald. I trust you. If you put out good, good will come back in massive waves just like the tides."

"Just like the tides." That's exactly what Camille said, and here Fitzgerald stood in the Bahamas with the waves beckoning to her. "Just like the tides."

Consistent, eternal, unseen forces always at play... just like intentions, just like gravity itself. Fitzgerald heard the waves breaking on the beach again. Her guilt rolled in and out with the tide. Standing there staring at the door to her villa, Parker Fitzgerald wondered what was waiting for her on the other side, not just the other side of the door, but the other side of life.

Fitzgerald took several tentative steps toward the door of the villa. She dropped to her hands and knees and glanced under. She couldn't make out any shifting shadows. She bit her lip and closed her eyes. The pressure was getting unbearable. All she wanted was some peace and some damned fresh fish that she didn't need to eat. She just wanted to be normal for a few days. At least that would be something.

She stood up again and spit like a baseball player. Growing up with five older brothers, each more rough-and-tumble Irish than the next, she picked up a few habits, a solid right hook and the ability to take a punch in return. A missing molar was proof of that.

"Screw it," she said, launching another thin stream between her teeth.

With little more than a twitch of her powerful robotic legs, Parker Fitzgerald vaulted herself seven feet forward. Like a famed pouncing jaguar of Patagonia Chile, she landed with deadly grace a foot from the door. She clenched her right fist and angled it to ensure her three rings would lead the way to the target, a nose preferably.

What are ya doing here, boyo? That's what her dad always said when questioning one of her brothers for some act of random idiocy.

She gripped the door knob with her left. In a bit of a crouch, she set her right leg back, knowing that with one swift kick she could shatter the leg of any man waiting to jump her. A busted nose and a shattered leg... that ought to set the tone right out of the gate. From there, all bets were off. She knew that. Once that door was open – literally and figuratively – there was no going back, no matter what was waiting for her behind that door. It was a risk she was willing to take in order to give the world Liquid-Life. Her intentions were pure.

Parker Fitzgerald flung open the door ready to lay waste to whatever might be waiting for her. The doorknob dented the sheetrock from the force. Fitzgerald shifted her weight forward ready to bury her rings into the bridge of some scumbag's nose. But there was nothing but the shrubs and bright flowers that adorned the walkway leading down to the pool area.

A hummingbird was nourishing itself on the nectar of some fragrant pink Columbines near Fitzgerald's door. Fitzgerald squinted into the bright sunshine. What the hell was going on? Someone definitely knocked on her door only seconds earlier. That much was for sure. That's when she saw it. A beautiful, black leather watch box. Fitzgerald looked around suspiciously. Was it a gift? How could it be? Nobody even knew she was here.

She kneeled down and picked up the box. She went to open it, then thought better of it. She held it up to her ear. She laughed to herself... listening to a watch box to see if it was ticking. She exhaled loudly.

"I'm losing it. I could really go for one of those Launch Pads," she mumbled.

She quickly returned inside and double-locked the door. She laid the box on the end table next to the phone. Her stomach was twisted, her heart was racing, her brain was pounding against the inside of her skull. She pressed her temples and then dialed room service. "Hi, this is... um... Mary McAvoy," she said catching herself in time to use the fake name she gave at check in. "I just ordered some sushi and champagne. Do me a favor, cancel the champagne and send up a bottle of tequila instead. Make it your best bottle of Don Julio."

She listened for a moment.

"No, I don't want salt and limes. Because I'm a woman? Really?"

She hung up the phone and made a guttural sound of disgust. "Whatever," she said, exasperated, her head ready to explode.

She realized her heart was still pounding as she picked up the watch box and plopped down again on the couch. The box said Bove and had impressive heft. Whatever chronometer was inside had to be exquisite. Fitzgerald opened the heavy box like a cliff diver opening an oyster in expectation of finding a pearl. The padded lining of the box was a beautiful, deep crimson. But there was no watch inside. Instead, there was an Apricorn Aegis encrypted flash drive sitting neatly in the concave place where a fabulous watch once sat.

The drive was a little larger than an ordinary USB stick but had a small, ten-digit alphanumeric keypad on it. A staple piece of equipment at Liquid Sky, it had military-grade, AES 256-bit CBC hardware encryption. It was a portable Fort Knox for data. That could only mean one of two things. Either it came from Rickey Ormand or it was from Goatse and Malfesio, who ordered five thousand for Liquid Sky back when Ormand brought them in to tighten up security.

Fitzgerald fingered the drive. A cold, creepy feeling ran up her spine. How the hell did anyone know where she was? She even went so far as to make the reservation under the fake name Mary McAvoy. Her eyes darted around the room. She harkened back to Lake Titicaca. Was Ormand watching her the whole time? She wouldn't put it past Goatse and Malfesio, either.

She grimaced. "Creepy-ass pervs," she muttered and opened the small note that was also in the box. It was typed, of course, but undoubtedly from Goatse.

Tricky Rickey bought me this awesome watch. Of course, he doesn't know it. His credit-card company really needs to improve their security algro. Wait, I wrote it!

She breathed a sigh of relief. So, what if they were spying on her? As far as she was concerned, it was all worth it. She held in her hand the most powerful technology the world had ever known. What she held in her hand was the end of human suffering and indignation. Her mood shifted instantly. She was overcome by the magnitude of the moment. She was going to change the world. She was about to become the most famous woman in history.

She welcomed the knock on the door this time. It was room service with her goodies. Two leaps later she was standing at the door ushering in her lobster, scallop, and tequila. The waiter laid the service tray on the table in the pastel dining room. After tipping him generously and giving him the bum's rush back out the door, Fitzgerald hastily poured herself a few fingers of Don Julio and knocked it back with ease. She poured herself a stiff second and lifted the lid off her sumptuous raw combo.

The scallops were arranged each on its shell with a wasabi drizzle of some sort. The thin slices of sweet lobster were arranged in a fan pattern around the lobster's head. The sashimi was so fresh, the antennae were still moving. The scallops quivered when Fitzgerald squeezed lemon over them.

She grunted in annoyance when there was yet another knock at the door. "Jesus," she said, raising her chopsticks into the air. "This is more work than work."

She strode quickly from the dining room to the door, feeling like she was wearing a path in the blue carpet.

"Sorry to bother you, Dr. Fitzgerald. It's room service. We forgot your white rice."

Good God, she thought, the last thing a breatharian wanted was crappy carbs. She opened the door, trying her best to contain her irritation.

The first thing she thought when she saw the huge man standing there was that he was easily 6'4". His massive arms and barrel chest were nothing like the slight islander who delivered her order the first time. Instantly thereafter, she noted the beast of a man called her by her real name even though she checked in under a fake name. Nobody at the resort knew her as Dr. Fitzgerald.

She gasped loudly. There was no time to do anything else. Before she knew what was happening, the giant man in a service tuxedo unloaded a crushing right hook, burying his ham hock of a hand squarely into her jaw.

This guy was a gorilla, a true simian caveman save for the man bun he wore as a top knot and his supple, white Bally loafers. The force of the savage blow sent Fitzgerald flying into the wall just right of the door. She crumpled to the floor. Her head felt like a spinning top. Somehow, she had the presence of mind, or the sheer strength of will, or both, to gather her deadly robotic legs under her. She gripped the door jam with her left hand and balanced herself enough to stand. It was a wonder her head didn't come clean off.

She spit out a mouthful of blood and a jagged tooth on the goon's white Swiss loafers. "That's the second tooth a guy has knocked out," she said, with disturbing calm. "But you're not my brother, Patrick, are ya, boyo?"

She let fly with a vicious side kick that landed with full robotic force on the inside of the giant's right knee. The man let out a savage scream, and Fitzgerald knew she'd blown up his leg. As he toppled to the floor, the man managed to land another brutal blow to Fitzgerald's stomach. She bent in half as the air rushed out of her. She felt like she was suffocating as she tried in vain to calm herself and catch her breath.

Bracing his busted leg in one hand, the man crawled into the foyer of the villa and pulled the door closed behind him. He and

Parker Fitzgerald were now alone behind closed doors. He dragged his destroyed leg behind him as he slid over to Fitzgerald.

"You bitch whore," he hissed trough teeth clenched, his leg searing with pain.

Fitzgerald wanted to tell him that he hit like a girl, but she still hadn't recovered from getting the wind knocked out of her. She saw the man reach into his pocket and emerge with some sort of syringe. She saw him flip the orange cap off the tip of the needle.

"I'm gonna knock you out with enough tranquilizer to drop a horse, and then I'm gonna tear up every hole you have before I take you back, you stupid bitch."

Fitzgerald began to panic now. Taking a punch was one thing. But needles, and rape, and kidnapping were way past anything she had ever imagined. Anger welled up in her as she began to catch her breath. She'd be damned if she would let this piece of shit violate her.

She did her best to ignore her aching jaw and turn fear into rage. Mounting what strength she had left, she pivoted around just as the hulk of a man sat up and raised the needle. In a desperate effort to save herself from being taken, Parker Fitzgerald scissored her powerful legs around the man's thick neck and squeezed as hard as she could.

The man started gagging. His face turned bright red and then shifted to blue. He thrust the needle into one of Fitzgerald's robotic thighs. She relished the glint of surprise in his eyes when the needle snapped in half against the metal.

"They must have forgotten to tell you that my legs are made of titanium," she said, before letting out a deep, guttural war cry. She squeezed her legs together with all her might. The force generated by the hydraulics in her legs was far more than anyone's neck could withstand, even a man this massive. Fitzgerald let out a loud grunt, and it was over. The man's neck snapped like a toothpick.

She released her legs, and his torso dropped. His Frankenstein head made a loud thud when it hit the marble. Fitzgerald rolled him over and looked at him. His eyes were still open, but they were empty now. The malice that once filled them had vanished. She now had another problem. How the hell did he find her? More importantly, was he alone, or did he have backup roaming around somewhere on the resort property?

She got her ass up and made straight for the bottle of tequila. She took a healthy swig, swished it around her mouth, and spit the dark, bloody mouthful on the dead man's white shoes. She then took another drink. This one she swallowed.

"Who's the bitch now?" she said.

She walked over to the man and checked his pockets. He had no wallet. The only thing he had was a pre-paid phone from some local tourist shop, judging from the Sun Phone logo. She scrolled through the call log. There was only one call... incoming. She recognized the number immediately.

She hit send and waited. After the third ring, someone answered.

"Is it done? I don't give a shit what you do with the bitch, but you'd better have the data she stole."

Fitzgerald said nothing.

"I said, do you have my data?" the voice demanded.

Again, Fitzgerald said nothing.

"Do you speak English, douche bag? I said, do you have my data?"

This time, Fitzgerald responded. "Well, if it isn't the Liquid Messiah Himself."

Silence from the other end now.

"Surprised to hear my voice?" she said.

More silence from the other end.

"I think this is the longest you've kept your mouth shut since I've known you, Rickey. Anyway, to answer your question... yes, I have your precious data. As a matter of fact–"

Ormand cut her off. "Where is it?"

Fitzgerald said nothing. She just fingered the encrypted USB drive and waited for Ormand to speak.

He was seething. "Listen to me, you bitch. Where is my data?"

Fitzgerald walked over to the glass dining room table, pursued her sashimi, and quickly popped a piece of raw lobster into her mouth. She'd forgotten how good fine food tasted.

She touched her jaw gingerly. In her reflection on the glass table, she could see the dark bruising already forming. She needed to ice it down as soon as possible. She had a bigger problem, though. Ormand knew where she was and what she had done. She couldn't stay there. She needed to blow the Bahamas, hit the wind, and cover her tracks. More importantly, she needed serious help. The problem was, she couldn't call the cops. They would confiscate the data, arrest her for cybercrimes, and who knew what other charges they would come up with if Rickey Ormand was pulling the strings behind the scenes. She needed Camille O'Keefe, or she was a dead woman walking. That much she knew.

"The data's safe," she said. "But I don't have it with me. I'm not stupid."

Ormand laughed ominously. "Well, that's a matter of opinion, isn't it? Look how easily I found you."

Fitzgerald gently slid a piece of scallop sashimi into her mouth and let it dissolve on her tongue, sparing her throbbing jaw the effort of chewing. The citrusy glaze gave special life to the wasabi. It helped ease the pain. Heading back to the balcony, she looked out over the sand. There was a family enjoying a day at the beach. She hadn't noticed them earlier. The kids were making a sand castle and squealing every time a rogue wave threatened to overtake their fragile construction. The parents were lying on a large, rainbow-colored blanket holding hands while they took in the sun. The entire family was sun-kissed and golden. They looked so comfortable and well-adjusted, so at ease with their environment.

Parker Fitzgerald saw the happiness the family shared. She saw the love the couple shared. And she saw that she would never share any of that with anyone because of what she was.

"Are you listening to a word I'm saying?" demanded Ormand impatiently.

"Maybe you're not as smart as you think, Rickey. So you might as well drop the attitude. You don't control me anymore. And I'm not going to let you control the world, either."

Ormand fell silent. Fitzgerald imagined the look of shock on his face, the same look he got on the few occasions someone actually stood up to him.

"Listen to me, Parker," said Rickey, in a gentler tone now. "You know I love you like a sister. I don't want anything bad to happen to you. I want to help you. So far, I have not contacted the authorities. We can keep your little indiscretion to ourselves."

Fitzgerald glanced over her shoulder at the hulk of a corpse in the foyer. "Oh, yeah?" she spat back. "Is that why you sent some prehistoric goon to kill me? Maybe I should call the police?"

Rickey was nervous. "Whoa, whoa, whoa. Nobody said anything about killing you. I sent Franco to bring you back to Liquid Sky, that's all. I wanted to talk to you... just the two of us."

"A needle full of animal tranquilizer?" she mocked. "You need to work on your social skills, Rickey. What's next? Are you going to send Bill Cosby after me, slip me a Mickey, and have your way with me?"

Ormand tried to stutter out some explanation, but Fitzgerald wasn't having any of it. "He knocked one of my goddamned teeth out and almost broke my jaw, you little shit. You want to have a one-on-one, just the two of us, Rickey? Sure. How about we meet up and I break your jaw so you know how it feels, you little nerd son-of-a-bitch?"

"Oh, really?" said Ormand, laughing. "I had a gun stuck in my mouth not too long ago. Why do you think I suddenly left town before the election? That's right, a gun... in my mouth."

Fitzgerald mocked him. "That's nothing compared to what they're going to stick in your mouth in prison after they knock all your teeth out for a better glide. Know what I'm saying?"

"Do you think you're the only person who wants what only I can create, Parker? And believe me when I tell you that I've made a new friend in the White House. Seems he wants what I have, too. You do know who I'm talking about, right smart ass?"

This revelation shocked Fitzgerald. A wave of panic spread through her again. Was she going up against Harry Pierson? Was the government after her, too?

"Yeah, yeah, whatever," she said, trying to play it off as casually as possible. "Your gargantuan friend won't be home for dinner. Just so you know. I'm not one of your chippies."

Ormand thought over his response before answering. "Look, Fitzy—"

Fitzgerald stormed in from the balcony. The sudden burst of air conditioning felt good on her aching face. All this talking was making her jaw worse.

"Don't call me that. Don't you dare call me that," she barked, her words wet with loathing.

Ormand laughed that annoying little laugh of his. Fitzgerald called it his nerd snicker. "Tell me, then. What did your two weirdo friends call you?"

The feeling of superiority left Fitzgerald like helium escaping a balloon. "What do you mean?" she said, slowly pronunciating each word.

Ormand seemed to enjoy the shift in power. "You know, those two douche bags you hired to steal my plans. Goatse and Malfesio. They actually used to work for me, but you already know that. What am I saying? Naturally, they were the first people I called when we figured out something was wrong. Franco went to round them up for me. I like to keep these things on the down low, you know? Can't have Wall Street getting word of something like that."

He started chuckling as he recalled the event. "So, get this, Fitzy. Franco brings in Goatse and Malfesio, right? You should have seen the look on their faces when Franco escorted them into my office. Honestly, I thought they were going to shit a keyboard right there on my marble floor. I kid you not. They must have thought I was onto them or something. Funny.... Anyway, they're in my office not five minutes, and you know what they start spouting off about? Come on, Fitzy. Take a wild guess."

Fitzgerald was standing in the middle of the living room staring at her reflection in the large mirror adorned with a seashell frame. She was disgusted by what she saw – half human, half robot. A freakazoid. It took all the restraint she could command to stop from hurling the cell phone at the mirror.

Sensing he had her cornered, Ormand pressed on. "No answer? Well then, let me clue you in. I brought the little shits in to hire them to find out what the hell was going on with my system. The firewall was going off like crazy. But like I said, they must have thought I was onto them because they start telling me all about your little plan and how you refused to pay them and threatened to frame them if they didn't cooperate. Then they tell me that you have...."

Ormand paused as if a bone was stuck in his throat. Fitzgerald was horrified just listening. Ormand sounded as if he was taking the whole thing personally. "They told me.... They told me that they already sent you... already sent you the Liquid-Life files. You have it all, don't you? Everything I've worked for. You simply decided to steal it, and you blackmailed these poor idiots to boot."

Fitzgerald's continued silence seemed to enrage Ormand even more. "You little bitch. You betrayed me, the one person who has given you everything. And what do I get in return? You stabbed me in the heart. Me, Rickey Ormand. Me, the man who saved your life, the man who made you eternal. Do you have any idea what this means to me, a betrayal of this magnitude?"

"Oh, get over yourself, Rickey," said Fitzgerald, disgusted by Ormand's crocodile tears.

"Get over myself?" mocked Ormand. "You've got much bigger problems than me, dear Fitzy. I have two partners who have the world at their fingertips. How do you think I found you so easily? But you have no friends, do you? You have no family. You have no husband or kids. You don't even have a vagina. Nobody will notice you're gone, just like nobody noticed that you survived the earthquake for two years before I introduced you at Burning Man. Now *that's* a nobody, okay? You're not even a person. You're a freak. You're nobody, nothing, nothing. Oh, we'll find you, Parker. If it's not me, it'll be one of Pierson's guys. If not Pierson, then one of Soros's storm troopers. You should be very afraid, Parker. Because when we find you—"

Fitzgerald let out a terrified gasp and hung up the phone. She dropped it on the floor and squashed it with her robotic foot. She threw the pieces in the toilet, grabbed her purse, passport, USB drive, and wallet, and bolted from the villa.

Chapter 26

Parker Fitzgerald scanned the immediate area for transportation. There was nothing she could use, no Vespa, not even a bicycle. As if a chariot sent by the gods, a non-descript white taxi turned into the complex and honked. Fitzgerald flagged down the car and jumped into the back seat without a second thought. The smell of old, worn vinyl seats and moldy ventilation filled her nostrils. The crackly sound of reggae music from a radio sitting on the passenger seat was the only other thing that stood out to her. Otherwise, her salvation came in the guise of a ubiquitous white taxi no different than the others she'd seen.

Fitzgerald ordered the driver to take her down the opposite end of the island, as far away from the villa as she could get without a boat or plane. The driver, a middle-aged, black islander wearing a red polo shirt, stained white shorts, and sandals, nodded. He was as commonplace on the island as his car.

"The road ends at Gordon's Settlement, ma'am," said the driver. "There's nothing there. The closest hotel is in Clarence Town a bit north of Gordon's. It's the capitol of the island."

"Good," said Fitzgerald, looking out the back window to see if anyone was following her. "Safety in numbers."

The driver smiled in the rear view. "The population of Gordon's Settlement is 86 people, miss."

"Jesus Christ," she muttered. "I'm dead meat."

She saw no other cars behind them and turned back to face the driver. "This Gordontown," she said. "How deep is the water in that area?"

"Gordon's Settlement," corrected the driver. "I'm not sure what you mean. Like for a boat?"

Fitzgerald grunted. "Yes, what's the max draw?"

The driver clucked his tongue. "Hard to say for sure. The last hurricane moved things around, you know. I do see them big yachts come and go for sure. Rich people like to go swimming and sit on the beach. Nobody bothers them down there." He laughed. "Them richies don't like us locals much. They like our beaches, though." He laughed again.

Parker seemed relieved. She sat back and considered her situation. She cursed herself for picking one of the more remote Bahamian Islands. Why didn't she just go to Nassau or Paradise Island? Why not Atlantis?

"Take your time," she instructed. At least she felt safe in the cab.

The driver smiled. "Time is money. You're American. You know that," he said. "We are on an island, but some things they don't change no matter where you are."

"I'll pay you," she replied. "Just don't drive too fast. Unfortunately," she mused, "I've got more money than there is on this island."

"Don't you worry, miss. I drive just right," said the driver. "Not fast, not slow. Just right."

"That's just great," she said sarcastically. "You're very reassuring."

"Thank you," he said.

Fitzgerald looked out at the ocean to her right. It really was a slice of heaven. But she wasn't ready to die yet. She snatched up her cell phone and dialed. She smiled when she heard Camille's voice on the other end.

"This makes two calls in, what, two weeks? People might start to think we're friends," said the vice president elect. Her chuckle was almost childlike in its innocence.

"Oh, thank God you answered," said Fitzgerald.

Camille picked up on the fear in her voice and turned serious instantly. "What's wrong, Parker? You seem out of sorts. I can sense it from here."

A trail of tears ran down Fitzgerald's cheeks as she tried to compose herself. She sniffed as she wiped them away. She could almost feel the long, narrow island getting smaller and smaller as the taxi made its way toward the end of the line.

"Tell me," beckoned Camille. "I know something's wrong." She sat down on the plush couch in her living room and crossed her legs under her long, flowing gold skirt. "I'm waiting," she said in a pleasant voice.

Fitzgerald exhaled deeply. She saw the taxi driver look at her in the rear view and smile. She felt as if he was sending her a silent message with that gesture.

"Okay, so I'm just going to tell you a bunch of stuff, and I want you to listen and not be judgmental."

Camille laughed in an attempt to lighten the mood for her friend's sake. "Me, judgemental?" She said. "That's a new one. You win the prize for most creative wrong assumption." She laughed again.

Fitzgerald smiled. The driver saw her and nodded. Fitzgerald pointed to the road ahead, reminding the driver that staying on the road was his primary job.

"Yeah... well," she said tentatively, "You might recall I told you I was going to do something pretty big, right?"

Camille sipped some hot matcha tea and nodded. "I do. The last time we spoke."

"Yeah," replied Fitzgerald. "Well, I did it. And now I'm in big trouble."

Camille tried to reassure her. "Intentions—"

Fitzgerald cut her off. "No, Camille. You don't understand. I'm in really big trouble."

Camille put her tea down and sat upright. She shot a glance into the kitchen. Now that she was vice president elect, she had a security detail assigned to her, but the two agents were in the kitchen having coffee and discussing the big Redskins-Eagles game coming up Monday night.

"Parker, what are you talking about? What happened?"

The intensity in Camille's voice surprised Fitzgerald. "Someone just tried to kill me. Well... they didn't try to kill me. They tried to incapacitate and kidnap me. Or maybe they were going to kill me later. I don't know. I'm scared, and I'm on the run."

She saw the worried look in the driver's eyes deepen as he overheard every word.

Camille stood up abruptly and moved into a corner of the room. "Wait, what? Who?" she said in a much softer voice so as not to be overheard by her security detail. "Are you alright? Where are you?"

"Too many questions," Fitzgerald shot back in an anxious frenzy.

"Sorry," replied Camille. "I didn't mean to overwhelm you. Just tell me what you can over the phone."

"Okay," said Fitzgerald, wiping sweat from her brow. "Like I said, I was attacked by some giant scumbag."

Camille was horrified. "Oh my God, Parker. Who was he? What did the police say? Did they arrest him? Are you hurt? Did you go to the hospital?"

Fitzgerald buried her face in her hand. "Too many questions. Stress. You're, like, totally stressing me out."

Camille collected herself. "Sorry, honey. Are you alright? That's the only thing that matters."

"I'm okay," replied Fitzgerald. "I guess. I mean, my jaw is pretty sore. I thought he broke it at first. He knocked out one of my teeth, the monster."

Camille's stomach hit the floor. "Oh, Parker. I'm so sorry. What did the police say?"

Fitzgerald snorted. "Police? Camille, you're not listening to me. I'm in big trouble here. This guy was sent for me. He was trying to kidnap me, or kill me, or kidnap me then kill me. How the hell should

I know? What am I going to do? Call the police? The first thing they'll ask me is why is someone after me in the first place?"

Camille was beginning to get the big picture. She shifted gears. "Parker," she said slowly, "tell me what you did."

Fitzgerald reached forward and tapped on the driver's shoulder. "Slow it down, bud. I'm in no rush, get it? Just slow your roll."

The driver seemed not to hear her, but he did slow it down.

"Parker," repeated Camille. "You need to tell me what you did. If someone is trying to kill you, it must be pretty bad."

"Rickey Ormand sent the guy after me," said Fitzgerald. "To take me back to Liquid Sky. I'm sure of it."

Camille was in disbelief. "Rickey Ormand?" She was almost whispering now. "Why on earth would he do that, Parker? You're talking around the issue. You still haven't answered my question."

Fitzgerald swallowed hard. Her jaw was really aching now. "So, I hired some guys to hack into the Liquid Sky database and steal some files. Well, steal some files and booby trap Ormand's entire system. Actually, steal some files and booby trap Ormand's entire system so I can give it away for free."

Both women were silent for a long while. Fitzgerald was staring out at the ocean while Camille was staring at a Hockney print of a serene pool nestled somewhere in the Hollywood Hills.

"It gets worse," said Fitzgerald, at last. "I spoke with Rickey after this all went down"

Camille interrupted her abruptly. "You spoke to him?"

"Yes," Fitzgerald replied, feeling a bit like she was under interrogation. "Yes, after. He said... well, he said a lot of terrible things. But what stuck out was that he had some secret meeting with the president."

"Oh, God," said Camille. "Rickey Ormand had a sit down with Harry Pierson?"

"Yes," said Fitzgerald.

"This is bad," said Camille, running her fingers through her thick hair. "This is very bad."

"It gets worse," replied Fitzgerald.

Camille braced herself. "I'm sure," she said.

Fitzgerald let it pour forth. "Ormand said that I'm in big trouble. He said that if his own people didn't get me, the president's would. He was saying that I should consider myself lucky that he found me first. And I was thinking, like, the giant scumbag who tried to tear me into pieces and, how did he put it? Oh yeah, violate every hole in my body. So, I was, like, totally nuts."

Camille couldn't believe what she was hearing. "Wait, wait.... Rickey Ormand told you that President Harry Pierson is going to send a hit squad after you?"

"Yes," said Fitzgerald. "I know, right? He said the president would be sending people after me. Oh God, Camille. What am I going to do? They'll kill me. I'm a dead woman."

"Kill you?" Camille repeated in shock. "They want to kill you? Why would they do that? What exactly did you take, Parker? What are you not telling me?"

Fitzgerald swallowed hard again. "The files my guys stole. They are for a top-secret project called Liquid-Life. Liquid-Drive and all that gravity engine stuff is just a smoke screen. Liquid-Life is the real breakthrough. Not only is it is the most amazing technology ever invented, it's the single greatest technological breakthrough in human history."

Camille was perplexed. She scratched her forehead. "I'm totally confused, Parker. I know you've been hiding something huge, but you're telling me that gravity power is not it?" "No, no," answered Fitzgerald. "Gravity power is at the heart of it all. But this whole thing about gravity engines, and Liquid-Drive, and stuff is bullshit. That's nothing. Liquid-Life catapults us a million levels above that. It actually enables people to live off gravitational energy. No food... just water. The gravitational energy is used by the body. It's amazing. It also cures diseases, including cancer. Just think, when combined with Liquid-Drive—"

Camille finished Fitzgerald's sentence. "No more energy crisis, no more environmental crisis, no more global warming, no more starvation, no more infant mortality...."

"No more corporate greed and control. Nobody really knows this, but I had cancer. Liquid-Life helped my body actually cure itself. That's why I intend to give it away. I intend to make both Liquid-Drive and Liquid-Life open source. Technology like this belongs to the world, Camille. You taught me that the first time we talked. I'm not sure if you remember."

Camille was serious and still very concerned, but she managed a soft, compassionate response. "Of course, I do, Parker," she said, peering once more toward the kitchen to make sure her security team was not privy to her conversation, which apparently involved the president of the United States. "I applaud your sense of priorities, dear. I'm just not sure about your methods. If nothing else, your life is in danger. That tells me that whatever you did doesn't sit right with the universe."

"Oh bullshit, Camille," said Parker, in a raised voice. She felt bad enough about things as it was. "You of all people should understand."

"I do understand," replied Camille calmly. "I understand more than you know. All I said was that you'll have to square things away with the powers that be."

Right now, Camille O'Keefe was about the only person Parker Fitzgerald could turn to. The last thing she needed was to get in an argument with her. She needed to stick to common ground.

"Everything you just said... it's all true," she said, pouring it on. "And I don't want to die knowing you think I did something wrong. I just want to say that my intentions were pure. When taken as a full platform, Liquid-Drive and Liquid-Life mean an end to the greatest dilemmas of our time and who knows what marvels lie ahead from there? All the problems related to energy, pollution, starvation, disease, overcrowding, poverty now... once we banish them to the past, we can write a brand new future for humanity. Something like that shouldn't be owned by a handful of greedy, violent, power-hungry men."

Having said what she wanted to say, Parker Fitzgerald reached into her mouth with her index finger and gently prodded the tender hole where her molar used to reside. Despite the pain, she was more pissed than anything else.

"And that jerk off Rickey Ormand needs a reality check," she added with hostility.

At first, Camille couldn't see Harry Pierson going after Fitzgerald for real. He was the president of the United States. But the more she thought about it, the more she believed that Pierson would do just about anything to get his hands on technology like this. It would make him the emperor of the world. And although she knew what was in store for Harry Pierson in the near future, she had to account for the very near term, time enough to take out Parker Fitzgerald.

"Just to clarify," Camille said. "You're saying that the president is involved in this, too?"

Fitzgerald laid her head back against the cracked, vinyl headrest. Even the thought of crossing the president of the United States made her temples throb. "That's what Ormand said, and I have every reason to believe him. The goon he sent really did a number on me. I can only imagine what sort of maniacs the president of the United States can send after my alloy ass."

"Where is the guy who attacked you?" asked Camille.

Fitzgerald didn't want to answer.

Camille pressed her. "Parker? What happened to the guy who attacked you?"

Fitzgerald whispered into the phone. "Let's just say he liked the Bahamas so much, he decided to stay for the rest of his life."

Camille was wobbly. She reached out and braced herself against the wall. "Oh, my God, Parker. You are in big, big trouble."

Fitzgerald was defensive. "That's what I've been trying to tell you, Camille, except you keep playing twenty questions."

The room started spinning, and Camille felt as if she might faint. "Oh, God... Oh, God. Okay...." She called on her spirit angel guides and refocused herself. "Okay, okay, we need to get you out of there like right now," she said.

"Yeah, no shit," said Fitzgerald.

She looked out the window to her right. Lining the narrow road that ran the length of the island was a long line of rocks and boulders weathered from decades of erosion. It looked like a jetty with the ocean lapping up against the rocks in some places, running shallower to expose sandbars in others. For the most part, she was surrounded by sun-burnt grass on both sides.

"The only problem is," she said, "getting here."

"Where exactly are you?" asked Camille, running her hand through her hair nervously again.

Fitzgerald shrugged. She hated not having empirical answers. "Somewhere near the bottom of this island. It's one of the smaller Bahamian islands. The road – I mean, like, the only road – is running closer and closer to the shore. But it's pretty rocky and totally shallow in places."

Camille had an instant flashback to the mission in Nigeria she helped orchestrate. That wasn't too long ago. It was terrible for Camille to have been involved with so much violence. She saw it as a necessary trade off albeit a terrible waste of human life, no matter how evil she found the Islamic terrorists. It started flooding back now... the tactics, the jargon.

"Can we get a helicopter in there?" she asked.

Fitzgerald was shocked. "A what? Who is this?"

Camille was talking as quietly as possible now. "Can we land a helicopter there?"

Fitzgerald craned her neck and looked around. "What is this, *Apocalypse Now*? How the hell do I know? I suppose so. But this is a sovereign country, Camille. You can't just send in the U.S. military, you know?" She rocked her shoulders, exasperated. She knew there wasn't much terrain left before she hit the tip of the island.

"I know that, Parker," said Camille, sternly. "But this is definitely a matter of national, if not global, security. Unfortunately, I can't go to Harry Pierson with this, not after what you told me. If what Ormand said is true, I would be leading them right to you."

"Lead them to me?" she snapped, the stress really getting to her now. "They know exactly where I am. Attacked in my villa... remember?"

Camille bit her lip. "I know that, Parker. I am just thinking out loud, okay? Cut me some slack. Five minutes ago, I was lounging around having a cup of tea. I'm doing my best here. I was thinking of maybe using a private helicopter to exfil you."

"Did you just say 'exfil'?" asked Fitzgerald, again wondering where this version of Camille O'Keefe was coming from.

"I did," replied Camille. "The problem is that word would get out. I need someone I can absolutely trust to help."

"We have no time, Camille. I am dead, do you understand? Dead... as in gone, no more, poof, vanished, no body, shark food, bye-bye Parker."

"I know that, too," replied Camille, again sternly. "You said there is good access to the water near you?"

Fitzgerald leaned forward and tapped the driver on the shoulder. "Where the hell are we... exactly?"

The driver shrugged. He pointed to a sign for Gordon's Settlement. It was only five kilometers away. "Soon, we will need a boat, miss."

The road cut closest to the shore as it had the entire trip. She had an idea. She tapped the driver on the shoulder again. "What's after Gordon's Settlement?" she asked.

The driver clucked his tongue. "There is more island, but no more road. That's as far as I go. You can walk several more kilometers. After that, you will be swimming, miss."

Fitzgerald strained to survey the area. Then she saw it... to the right just up ahead... a turn off. "There," she yelled pointing. "There. What is that?"

"That is a road," the driver said.

Fitzgerald squeezed her temples. "No shit, genius. Tell me where it leads."

The driver shrugged as if she'd just asked him to add 2 plus 2. "It runs about one kilometer almost to the water. They use it for those villas coming up on our left. Guests can access the ocean, but it is rocky. Some places are deep though. I know that."

"Jesus Christ," snapped Fitzgerald. "Now you tell me? Pull off and go down that road... hurry!" She snapped her fingers rudely.

The driver slowed and made the right-hand turn. When they came to a roundabout, he stopped. "Which way, miss?"

Fitzgerald held up her hand and signalled for the driver to pull over and await further instructions. "Camille, okay. Apparently, I am on a smaller road that takes me right up to the water."

"How deep?" Fitzgerald snapped. "How much draw?"

"It is like a bay, missus. There are shoals forming a bay. I used to dive for conch there when I was a boy. It is shallow in parts. But like I said, I see rich yachts come in for swimming, but they never come past the shoals. Too dangerous, missus."

"Yeah, well so is the wrong end of a gun," said Fitzgerald. "But sometimes it's the only perspective you have."

She returned to Camille. "Okay, Camille. The driver says there's a bay formed by natural shoals, so there's danger. Out past there, though, should be okay. He says he sees rich yachts anchor there, whatever the hell that means. I don't know. I don't have the secret military training that you seem to, so I don't have any of your weird jargon."

Camille racked her brain for a solution. "There's only one thing I can think of, Parker," she said. "Get to the water. I will call you back."

Fitzgerald was not taking it very well. "That's it? For God's sake, don't leave me here, Camille. I'm a dead woman if you do."

"You're more than a woman," said Camille. "And, you're far from dead. Now do what I tell you and wait for me to call you back."

Camille cut the call and scratched her head. It was a long shot... a very long shot. But first she had to lose her security detail for a few minutes of privacy.

"Oh, security," she sang out to her security detail. She was still feeling dizzy and out of sorts from what was going on, but she knew there was no time for any of that.

Two clean-cut agents in trim blue suits came in from the kitchen and stood side-by-side before Camille. The agent on the right was Nelson Clarke, thirty-five, about 6'4", and broad as a house. His blond hair was cropped tight but not so close as to appear too military or too militaristic. His days as a tight end for the Troy University Trojans were long gone, but he kept himself in top shape mentally as well as physically. His blue eyes were dark and somewhat foreboding. Whenever Nelson Clarke looked at Camille, she felt like he was sizing her up. She was correct. Nelson Clarke sized everyone up. His gaze could make a cashier at Chick-fil-A feel transparent and exposed. Clarke took his career seriously and considered his duty to protect the vice president elect paramount above even his wife and two young boys.

The agent on the left was a woman, Elizabeth Hamblin. She was tall, around 5'10", and a former volleyballer at Brigham Young. Raised and educated as a Mormon, Elizabeth Hamblin spent most of her life in Utah with half a million other Mormons. Her two-year missionary service proselytizing misguided Hindus in India marked the first time she'd left the United States.

Despite her lack of cultural exposure, the Agency liked Hamblin's intangibles. She was a no-nonsense woman with a real talent for grace under pressure. She consistently stood out as particularly calm, cool, and collected in rigorous training exercises that drove other agents to make mistakes in judgment. Her calm demeanor and strength of conviction made Camille feel comfortable. That was a big vote of confidence.

"Yes, ma'am?" said Hamblin.

"What can we do for you?" asked Nelson Clarke not content to simply stand there silent while his female partner directed the engagement.

Camille smiled. "I'm so sorry to bother you. It's a bit embarrassing, actually. Beth, I wonder if you would be a dear and run to the pharmacy for me. I'm afraid I am a bit... unprepared for this month."

Elizabeth Hamblin understood and nodded curtly. The vice president-elect needed tampons. "I'll be right back, ma'am," she said.

She turned to her partner and clapped him on the shoulder. She knew how competitive the former Trojan was and loved to get his goat about it. "I'd better handle this one, Clarkie."

"It's a female thing," said Camille, trying to soothe his bruised ego. "Anyway, Nelson, I wonder if you can make me a fresh cup of tea. The cup you made me earlier is cold. Better make it Earl Grey this time. I'm going to need a bit of a boost."

Nelson Clarke pursed his lips. He was thinking to himself that he might as well be wearing an apron. "Of course, ma'am," he said politely.

Elizabeth Hamblin leaned in to Clarke's ear. "Maybe you can do some laundry while you're at it."

"That's harassment," quipped Clarke, but his partner was already heading for the door.

Alone again, Camille sat down on the couch and tapped her lip with her index finger. It was definitely a long shot, she thought to herself. But what other choice was there? She had no other plan for extricating Fitzgerald. Moreover, if Fitzgerald was right about Harry Pierson getting involved as an adversary, there were very few people she could enlist for help. Having spent most of his professional life in the intelligence community, the president's reach extended nearly everywhere.

Camille racked her brain trying to devise a way out for her friend in need. That's when it hit her. Her green eyes lit up like emeralds. She needed to call Johnny Long. She needed to call him right now. She glanced toward the kitchen to make sure Clarke was out of earshot. He was busy filling the kettle and wiping down the counter around the sink. It was perfect.

She scrolled through the numbers in her cell phone until she found Johnny's. She met Johnny Long back when Beck was alive. In fact, she'd just taken up with Beck seriously at the time. Beck was giving a talk at the University of Pennsylvania, as far as she recalled, and Johnny Long introduced himself as a successful money manager with a few bright ideas revolving around Beck's comments.

Camille and Johnny Long hit it off. He was older than she, happily married, and successful in the way most people only imagine. She liked the paternal way about him. He was the guy who first put the idea of dividends in Camille's head... mandatory, minimum corporate dividends. He wasn't shy about it, either. Johnny envisioned a world in which capitalism was reenergized with lifeblood capital in the form of dividends, "the only true form of ownership through stocks." He believed that capitalism had become stagnant, with massive amounts of money pooling up among a handful of billionaire entrepreneurs, the Mark Zuckerbergs and Jeff Bezos of the world.

What intrigued Camille O'Keefe was Johnny Long's idea that in order for capitalism to work, capital had to be continually recirculated and reinvested in new technologies, new companies, new ideas, new jobs, new people, and so on. In a nutshell, surmised Johnny, companies capitalized over ten billion dollars should be required to distribute twenty-five percent of their profits in dividends. Only in this way, argued Johnny countless times in countless places, would capital truly recirculate, enabling the best economic system in the world to mature into the best socioeconomic system in the world.

That distinction made all the difference for Camille. She asked Johnny to pitch it to Beck, and Beck promised Camille he would implement it in exchange for Johnny Long's fund-raising prowess. After winning the election, Beck reneged on the deal. This didn't surprise Camille. She saw it coming. But she felt betrayed and greatly disappointed. Shortly thereafter, maybe a few years, Beck also reneged on his pact with God by putting a bullet through his head. Camille saw this coming, too, but she felt far less disappointed.

Since then, Camille and Johnny Long kept in touch. They spoke from time to time just to touch base. For the most part, they never talked shop. She kept her lurid tales of 'political intrigue' as Johnny termed them, tucked away, and he spared her the "Three-D banalities of Wall Street," as she called it. Mostly, they chatted about life and philosophy, about their assorted world travels and their assorted personal travails. They rarely met up any more since Johnny and his wife of thirty years had dinner with her in the Bahamas.

That must have been almost two years ago, figured Camille. That's what sparked the idea. "Rich yachts," the taxi driver told Fitzgerald. That's what made Camille think of Johnny Long. It was Fitzgerald's only hope. Johnny and his wife had a house and a boat in the Bahamas. What if Johnny was in the Bahamas now? After all, it was his favorite winter weekend getaway. If she remembered correctly, he kept his boat in Miami or Ft. Lauderdale or somewhere like that. Jonny loved to make the short trip aboard his Princess yacht. And if the universe was smiling on her, Camille figured Johnny would be out cruising his favorite waters right now.

Good Lord, what a blessing that would be.

Johnny bought the boat years ago but cherished it like it was just delivered shrink-wrapped and all. Christened *Southern Comfort*, the yacht was Johnny's testament to the power of capitalism and, in particular, the earnings-growth investment strategy that made him an investment powerhouse and the only retail money manager to ever win the vaunted *Battle of the Quants* global investment contest. Lavish but tasteful was Johnny's style. Costing a few million back in the day, *Southern Comfort* was Johnny's most extravagant toy by far but still demure enough to be inconspicuous among the crew-staffed, mega-yachts docked beside him in Florida or the Bahamas.

No matter how she played out the scenario in her head, Camille figured Parker Fitzgerald would be either dead or captured within two hours. Camille had been around D.C. long enough to know that a man like Rickey Ormand didn't leave loose ends. If he dispatched one man, there were certainly more lurking nearby. Even if the goal was to bring Fitzgerald back to Liquid Sky, odds were she would never be heard from again. However, if Johnny was in the Bahamas, he would be able to bring his boat in close enough to rescue Fitzgerald before another one of Ormand's boys kidnapped her or worse.

Fitzgerald's only hope was for Camille to get to her first. With this in mind, Camille drilled down quickly on Johnny's number and hit send. Time was ticking away, each passing second marking one less second in Fitzgerald's life. After several rings, she got Johnny's voice mail. She muttered something to herself and redialed. Again, Johnny's phone rang several times and then went to voice mail. Frustrated, she left Johnny a cryptic but emphatic message.

Meanwhile, Fitzgerald's cab had reached the end of the line. The side road they'd taken had run its course and brought them to a dead end close to the water.

"What now, missus?" asked the driver. "This is the end of the line."

Parker Fitzgerald lowered her head. "I know," she said. "End of the line."

Fitzgerald got out of the car and stood looking out at the crystalline water. The saline air that filled her lungs felt cleansing, antiseptic. She blew into her fist, opening her fingers intermittently as if playing a wind instrument. She acknowledged the humor of surviving an earth-wrenching quake only to succumb in a place this serene. She had achieved so much, and yet she was so alienated from every other person in the world. She started crying for the third time that day, wondering why was she such a freak, and why couldn't she just have died in Peru?

Everything depended on Camille O'Keefe. Unaware at the time, Parker Fitzgerald bought herself a bit of wiggle room by leaving Franco's lifeless body sprawled out in her room. For, as Camille assumed, Rickey Ormand had indeed sent in a back-up team. Instead of giving chase to Fitzgerald when they found Franco's body, they were preoccupied with "cleaning" the scene... removing Franco's body, sanitizing the room, erasing all signs of a struggle, and so on. If not for that, Team 2 would have been on Fitzgerald in minutes. It would be game over from there.

Not knowing exactly what Fitzgerald stole, what she had Goatse and Malfesio leave behind, and who else had a copy of the golden goose, Rickey Ormand had to play his hand very carefully. He needed Parker Fitzgerald alive and safely sequestered at Liquid Sky in order to conduct a proper assessment of the situation. This, too, bought her some valuable time. Once in his custody, however, there was little Ormand wouldn't do to her to get the information he wanted before exacting his undoubtedly excruciating revenge.

She may have inadvertently bought some time for herself, but the dark storm was about to shift her way. To make matters worse,

Ormand's Team 2 consisted of three ex-Marines who did not take kindly to Fitzgerald's killing one of their own. They may not have known Franco personally, but they considered him a brother all the same. When they discovered his body, the stakes got much higher. Snatching Fitzgerald was no longer a matter of money for them. Now, it was about their code. They lost a brother. Someone had to pay, and that someone was Parker Fitzgerald. Rickey Ormand's instructions to take Parker Fitzgerald alive and return her to Liquid Sky were no longer paramount in their minds. Their new priority was much more direct – punish Parker Fitzgerald, make her pay for killing one of their own, hurt her very badly before slicing her open from her chin to her navel.

Camille O'Keefe nearly jumped out of her skin when her phone rang. Her stomach felt like a popcorn popper when she answered. It was Johnny Long calling back.

"Thank God you called," she said, making no effort to mask the fear in her voice.

"What did you expect?" said Johnny. "Your voice mail could stir the dead. I'm worried as hell. What's going on?"

Camille stole a glance into the kitchen. The coast was clear. She walked over to one of the windows and stared out into the garden. The black soil was hard and frosted. The pavers looked old and the large rose bushes barren. The large koi pond was frozen over save for a small area around the heater, enough to allow for precious oxygen transfer to keep the dormant koi alive during their hibernation.

For the first time in a long time, she felt depressed. She placed the palm of her free hand against the window pane, allowing the cold to penetrate her flesh. "It's bad," she said. "I need a favor big time. But it might be dangerous. I shouldn't even be asking you honestly, but—"

Johnny Long put down his tonic and sat up. In the years he'd known her, he never heard her panicked like this. "What's going on, Camille? How can I help?"

Sitting in a chaise lounge next to him, his wife sensed his concern. "What?" she mouthed.

Johnny shrugged. "Camille?" he mouthed back.

A waiter wearing neat, white shorts and a red polo shirt cleared the remains of their lunch from their pool-side cabana. Johnny motioned for two more bottles of spring water.

"Please tell me you're in the Bahamas," said Camille. Pleading was evident in her voice. "Just tell me you're sitting on your boat right now somewhere in the Bahamas."

Johnny took a hand towel from the bowl of ice water on the table and wiped his forehead. Even sheltered in their cabana, the heat was intense. "I'm sorry, Camille. The wife and I are in Costa Rica."

There was silence save for a dark, little man in an electric-green banana hammock diving gracefully into the water near the waterfall and in-pool bar. His wife and kids cheered something in German.

"Camille?" said Johnny.

Certain now that something was amiss, Johnny's wife sat up, too, and put a cold towel against her cheek. "What's up?" she said.

The diver's son, clad in America-style surfer togs, shifted his Teutonic Bavarian girth in order to lift his sister into the air and toss her face-down into the pool *mit papa*. The girl shrieked like a chimpanzee and flailed, sending water flying toward Johnny and his wife.

Johnny put his index finger in his free ear and bent over. "Camille, can you speak up? Did you hear what I said? We're in Cost Rica. Where are you? What's going on? You're starting to worry me."

Johnny's wife huffed in the general direction of *die Deutschen* and pulled the drapes of the cabana closed. "That's all," she said, in a sing-song voice.

Camille was on the verge of an anxiety attack. It was very unlike her, and that, more than anything else, unnerved her the most. "Costa Rica?" she said, in disbelief. "You're not in the Bahamas?"

"No, Costa Rica." replied Johnny. "We're taking a little holiday. We're always going to the Bahamas. Like you always say, the world has so much to offer. Why not try something different for a change?"

"Yes," said Camille, struggling under the irony of her own words. "That figures."

"What's wrong, Camille? You sound completely stressed out."

Camille proceeded to give him only the details as quickly as possible. Johnny was riveted. Camille's story sounded like something out of a novel or a spy movie. Her harrowing tale stuck him as both fact and fiction, a strange combination of power politics and willful naïveté. It was exactly the sort of story that defined the modern world as he knew it.

"I think I caught most of that," said Johnny, trying hard to keep up with Camille's flurry of words so imbued with intense emotion. "I'm so sorry I can't be of assistance. But I'm sure your friend will be okay."

Camille turned from the window. Her flowy dress billowed. "No, Johnny. You don't understand, Johnny. She's not going to be okay. I have a really bad feeling. She's not making it off that island unless I do something. This is really serious."

Johnny squeezed the cold towel over his head. "I wish there was something I could do. It's not like me to sit on the sidelines when I have a friend in need. I feel terrible."

"I understand," said Camille, sadly. "But listen, Johnny. I may need to see you in the near future. It's very, very important... the best interests of the country and all that. This new technology can improve life for billions of people all over the world. If things go according to plan, I will definitely need your help making that dream a reality. But if I don't make it out of this thing alive, remember there's something huge behind the scenes that the president and Rickey Ormand are hiding. Promise me you'll take it to the press."

Johnny grimaced. "Don't say things like that. You're the one who's always saying that thoughts are things. So, don't even say it."

Camille closed her eyes. "It's true, Johnny. I'm right in the middle of something that can lift me up or drag me straight down."

They were both silent for a moment.

"Right," she said. "Talk soon, Johnny."

"Keep me posted," Johnny said, standing up. But Camille O'Keefe had already hung up.

"What the heck was all that about?" asked Johnny's wife.

"Oh, nothing much," answered Johnny Long. "Camille's in the middle of some heavy stuff."

"Funny how that keeps happening to her," his wife replied. "Someone should write a book."

Johnny nodded. "It would take a series."

Camille sat back down on the couch and stared at her phone. Panic was settling in for the long haul like arctic frost. She looked at her watch. It had been about twenty minutes since she spoke to Fitzgerald. Tossing her head back on the couch, Camille realized she had but one option left. If that failed, the world would lose Parker Fitzgerald forever.

With a sigh, she redialed her phone and waited for an answer.

"This is Camille O'Keefe. Get me the president."

Chapter 27

In the course of two frenzied minutes, Camille ran through her story. The president was not pleased. Harry Pierson's face grew a deeper shade of crimson with each new level of classified information Camille revealed. Any more of this, and he would resemble a Bing cherry.

Concerned with the delicacy of the situation but also knowing he could blow up like a volcano any second, Pierson gestured for Jennifer Daly to leave him alone in the Oval Office at once. It was okay by her, though. She'd made her peace with being pushed aside. All she had to do was facilitate the transfer of power. Truth be told, she relished the thought of leaving politics and the Beltway behind her, for a while at least... maybe forever. Who knew? She was happy to leave Big J.D. behind and walk away with some of her dignity still intact, however microscopic it was after two years of Harry Pierson trampling on it.

Whatever was wrong, Jennifer Daly knew from past experience it ran contrary to something the president wanted for himself. During their two years together, she saw Harry Pierson turn that particular shade of crimson only twice. The first time was when the Senate failed to pass his bill implementing strict limits on immigration and implementing harsh penalties for transgressors. It was a key plank in his platform for re-election, and he considered the loss nothing short of a literal slap in the face.

The second time was when Lonny Harris told Pierson that somebody leaked his plan to essentially colonize oil-rich Venezuela in the wake of the country's complete fiscal collapse. In both instances, someone dared oppose a plan Pierson devised in order to "get the world in line" with his big agenda items, as he put it. In actuality, Jennifer Daly knew there was much more going on. She knew Pierson went from scarlet to crimson on the rarest of occasions, but those occasion always shared a common denominator... ego.

Whatever was coming through that phone had to involve the one or two things upon which Harry Pierson laid the cornerstones of his self. Whatever it was – and Daly really couldn't guess – achieving it must have been supremely important to Pierson as the president of the United States, as the most powerful person in the world, and, perhaps most importantly, as a man plain and simple.

Having quickly assessed the situation, there were two things Jennifer Daly knew for sure. First, whoever was on the other end of that call was driving a stake right through the center of Pierson's ego. Second, somebody was going to pay very dearly.

Pierson motioned more emphatically a second time for Daly to get the hell out of the Oval Office. This time, she readily obliged. As she exited, she wondered how long it would be before he finally blew an aneurysm.

When the door closed, the president returned his full attention to interrogating Camille. As he contemplated the current state of affairs, he couldn't help thinking that the bitch he just signed on with was actually worse than the bitch he just sent packing. He felt his heart tighten like it was shrink wrapped. He touched his forehead, then inspected his fingertips. He was actually sweating. The sight of his glistening fingers made him even angrier.

"How did you obtain this information?" he demanded. "Do you have any idea what you're getting in the middle of, Camille? I mean...."

He waved his free hand in the air as if trying to grasp the right word among a group of nasties flying around his head.

"I mean... this whole Liquid-Drive thing is going to be the bedrock of my presidency. You do understand that, right? Explain to me, if you would, how you don't see that what's good for me is good for you? Surely, Camille, among all those spirits you commune with there must be one that has some common sense."

Camille's reticence pissed him off even more. "I'm going to ask you one more time, Camille," said the president, his bile rising. "How did you find out about my deal with Ormand to bring this Liquid-Drive thing into the government fold?"

Camille's silence was not born of resentment or any attempt to stonewall her new boss. Instead, she was listening intently, listening to the depth of his inquiry. Thus far, Pierson had only mentioned Liquid-Drive. That surprised her, for Liquid-Life was clearly the bigger opportunity by far. That's when it occurred to her that perhaps Rickey Ormand never told Pierson about Liquid-Life in the first place. Indeed, the more she thought about it, the more she was certain that Pierson had no idea Liquid-Life even existed even though it was the key to existence itself.

If that was the case... what then? Yes, she was beginning to see it now.

Pierson finally exploded into the phone. "I demand an answer, O'Keefe. This very second. Answer my damned question. How—"

Camille found the temerity to interrupt the president. "There's more," she said, in a soft, calm voice.

"No shit," Pierson spat back. "What do you think I'm trying to find out? If you know about my deal for Liquid-Drive, that means there's a leak, and his name is Rickey Ormand. And I'm going to stick my foot so far up his ass, he'll taste leather for a year. As for you–"

"No," said Camille, wavering just a bit. "There's more to it than just Liquid-Drive."

The president slammed his fist on the desk. "Stop talking in circles. Having a logical conversation with you is like trying to stab a walnut with a fork. Jesus Christ, woman. You're infuriating."

Camille checked her watch. Time was running out on Parker Fitzgerald. She collected herself. She had no time to waste arguing with an irate man. "What I mean, Harry, is that Rickey Ormand is holding out on you."

There was silent rage on Pierson's end.

The president cleared his throat. "I'm listening."

So, thought Camille, he had no idea about Liquid-Life. That was a good thing... a very good thing. She took a huge gamble calling Pierson. But now it looked like it was going to pay off.

"Harry, there's a lot more to this technology than Ormand is letting on. Did he tell you about the Liquid-Life project?"

Pierson scratched his head and figured Camille was just being her usual, dingy self. "Liquid-Drive, yes. What the hell do you think I've been talking about for God's sake?"

"No," snapped Camille brusquely. "That's not what *I'm* talking about. What *I'm* talking about is a completely different project, top secret, called *Liquid-Life.* For once in your life, Harry Pierson, please, please, please listen to what I am actually saying. This is very serious."

Harry Pierson sat back stunned. Could it be that Camille O'Keefe actually had valuable information he knew nothing about? He couldn't wrap his head around the possibility let alone the details of whatever it might be. "I... I've... never heard of it. Are you sure—"

Camille cut him off again. She had new found hope in her voice. "Listen to me, Harry. We don't have time to dance around like two roosters fighting to be cock of the walk."

Pierson focused himself and nodded. "Okay. Interesting analogy, but okay. I take it there's some sort of problem?"

Camille switched the phone to her other ear so that the RF waves would debilitate both hemispheres of her brain equally and chastised the president to the extent she knew she could get away with.

"Stop pretending you have no idea what's going on," she said. "You know damned well that Ormand's men are tracking down my source as we speak."

"I have no idea what you're talking about, Camille."

"Yeah, right," she replied tersely. "Because Ormand also told my source that you, Harry, were prepared to send in some very terrible people to clean things up if need be."

Pierson shook his head as if knocking loose the cobwebs. "Source? You have a source? Jesus, what's this world coming to? What source? Who is this source? Does everybody in my administration have people I don't know about?

"I told you we don't have time for this," urged Camille once again.

Pierson tossed his pen clear across the Oval office. "Well, shit on my stick, Ms. O'Keefe. By all means, enlighten me."

She quickly briefed the president on what was happening in the Bahamas and, in particular, Parker Fitzgerald's precarious situation. She had the president hooked from the get- go. She knew that would be easy. But now, she had to figure out a plan to move forward. That was not going to be easy. It never was with Pierson.

"It's an ugly story, Harry. It makes me nauseous just repeating it."

Pierson leaned in toward his desk. "Camille, I swear to you I have nothing to do with whatever's going down with... your source. Jesus... this son-of-a-bitch Ormand is blowing up my entire plan. I swear to you, I will shove that little turd up an elephant's ass and turn Liquid Sky into my very own toy chest."

Sensing Pierson was telling her the truth and that she had him in a position to bargain, she moved forward with haste. "Listen, Harry. We have to move on this. With Liquid-Life and Liquid-Drive together, you and I will have nothing less than a magic wand. Do you hear what I'm saying?"

"Yes," said the president. His mind was aflutter with all the possibilities that could arise from taking both Liquid-Drive and Liquid-Life in the name of national security. "That's exactly what I'm saying here."

"Good," said Camille. She felt the power rising inside her. She knew this feeling. She worried about this feeling. It always led to conflict. The intense energy rising inside her was the white-hot fire of her ego stoked by fear of losing something so dear to her as the Liquid-technology and concern for the safety of her friend Parker Fitzgerald.

Camille bit her nails before speaking. She felt an overwhelming desire to push Harry Pierson into action. The problem was that, when pushed, Harry Pierson tended to use a sledge hammer to drive a nail. She knew this. She'd enlisted his "help" before, which always amounted to her stepping aside and letting his "people" clean house. The image of Rickey Ormand's feet sticking out of an elephant's ass was more than enough to set her warning bells ringing.

Violent conflict ran counter to Camille's beliefs as well as her constitution. But what choice did she have? That's what she was pondering during this brief pause in the conversation. She felt she had no other viable options, given the mere minutes she had to work with. So, she reconciled it as a situational bind in which her ego was necessarily taking charge so that she might find the fortitude to goad Harry Pierson into action. She'd been here enough times before to know this was the moment of compromise. It was a time when she had to simply take a step in some direction, see where that path led, and re-adjust from there.

"Then the question now is simple," she said. "What are you going to do about it, Harry?"

Pierson felt the tension rising in his gut. "What I would *like* to do is gag Rickey Ormand"

"About saving my source, Harry? I don't care about Rickey Ormand right now. You can deal with him later."

The president thought about it. "First of all, let's dispense with this source shit. It's obviously Peter Piper, or Parker or whoever that robot woman is. Anyway, you said robo was on one of the Bahamian islands. It's another country's airspace, for Christ's sake. The United States can't just blow in there and pluck out your girl like tweezing chin hairs."

Camille's retort was simple yet goading. "That didn't stop Rickey Ormand from sending people in."

"But he's not the president of the United States," shouted Pierson. "There are far greater implications if I'm involved. How do you not get that? What that piss-ant does is a fart in the wind compared to something POTUS does."

Camille had been down the road of plausible deniability enough times to understand the navigational requirements of double speak. "But you don't know about any of this, Mr. President."

"Of course not," spat the president. "But now I do. That's on you, Camille. You should have gone through the State Department. Let those pencil pushing nerds take action for a change. Ever since Benghazi, all they do is sit around reminiscing about their days at Harvard."

"There's no time for that, Harry. I need you because you're at the top. This is your world. The globe is your plaything. And by the way... all due respect, Harry... sovereignty didn't bother you when you sent SEALs into Nigeria to save all those women. Where's that Harry Pierson? Where's the man who stepped in swinging his big stick like Harry S. himself? That's the guy the world needs right now. So, please find him."

"Different," said Pierson, curtly. "I know what you're trying to do. Frankly, it makes me a bit excited if you know what I mean. But this is very different."

"Grenada... Guantanamo... that thing with post-Chavez Venezuela—"

"How the hell do you know about Venezuela?" Pierson demanded. "This place has more leaks... this is starting to sound like a Trump tweet." The president was adamant now. "Listen, I had no knowledge of anything associated with that prick Chavez's death. I'll deny it till the day I die."

"I'm your vice president, Harry. I stand by your side. This is just the two of us... like Nigeria but easy peasy."

The president scoffed at the thought. "Yeah, right. There's no such thing when you send guys into an unknown situation. I can't ask a team to pull off a hot ex-fil on foreign soil and not protect themselves if the shit goes down."

"Harry," implored Camille. "This doesn't amount to much more than an Uber ride."

Pierson was still throwing counter punches. "Didn't you say there are still people chasing this woman?"

"I did," admitted Camille.

"Well then, there's the chance our guys could take some fire. Good God, woman. We can't go shooting up an island in the Bahamas. Although, I have to admit... I really like you right now. I find you very stimulating when you're advocating violence. Still, what you're asking me to do is political suicide. The Bahamas... really?"

Camille lowered her eyes. "I'm trying to save a life here, Harry. Not take one. In fact, I'm trying to save millions of lives with this technology."

Harry Pierson laughed. "There's not one without the other, Camille. You'll learn that at my side. It's like one of those balance scales. One side is life, the other death. You either maintain equilibrium or one side gets out of whack. Remember that I warned you, Red."

Camille smiled. "That means you'll help?"

The president had already made up his mind, but he felt obliged to milk it a bit more so it was clear his new V.P. owed him a big one.

"Camille, the reality of engagement remains. I can't send guys into a hot zone and ask them to—"

On the verge of desperation, Camille had no choice but to go full bore. "Harry Pierson, you're POTUS. You're the most powerful man in the world. You cut a deal with Rickey Ormand, and he held out on you. He played you for a fool. And... and... he would have gotten away with it if not for Parker Fitzgerald, and he's about to kill her to keep her from you. Parker Fitzgerald is the biggest national security crisis of the century. I don't care about myself, but this is your legacy he's destroying. So, I'll say it again, Harry. What are you going to do about it? You have minutes to make up your mind and actually do something. Otherwise, I suppose there's always a spot for you in the State Department."

She waited before dropping the final prompt.

"Assuming you can actually do something about it. Ormand might have you snookered," she said. And with that, she knew the deed was done.

Harry Pierson slammed his open palm on the desk and stood up. "Excuse me?" he barked. "Screw Rickey Ormand, screw the State Department, and screw Harvard."

"I remember what you did in Nigeria, Harry. It was an exercise of benevolent power to behold."

"Then you remember that I crushed them," Pierson continued. "And compared to *Boko Haram*, these tropical bozos in vacationland over there in the Bahamas are less than fly shit in my sugar bowl."

"Okay," said Camille. "I don't really know what that means, but okay."

"It means I wouldn't want to be them."

Camille took this as the president's acquiescence. "When?" said Camille. "We have no time."

"I don't need time," Pierson declared. "I'm the king of the world. I can move assets as quickly as moving pieces on a chessboard. What do you think, I'm some stooge in Congress who has to live by Robert's Rules of Order? Please, don't make me laugh. Nobody plays me like Ormand did, and nobody endangers people my vice president needs. Like I said, I didn't open this door with Ormand, but I'm sure as hell going to slam it shut on his fingers. I'll take care of it right now."

"Thank you, Harry. God, thank you so much," said Camille, breathing a sigh of relief but feeling somewhat dirty at the same time for manipulating someone she considered to be a spiritual child.

"Tell robo girl to sit tight right where she is. I'll have her out of there in no time. Actually, give me her cell number. We can zone in on her in seconds."

The sense of relief spreading through Camille's body was invigorating. For the first time since learning of Fitzgerald's ordeal, Camille felt like things were going to be alright.

"Thank you, Mr. President," she said, again.

"Yeah, yeah," said Pierson. "Now it's 'Mr. President.' We'll see if you say that after this thing goes down. Anyway, I'll take care of it. You don't want to know any more than that, Red. Let me do what I do best."

They signed off, and Camille quickly dialed Parker Fitzgerald.

Fitzgerald picked up on the second ring. "Jesus Christ, Camille. What took you so long? I don't think I can say the Hail Mary another fifty times."

She was looking back at her taxi driver. He was holding up his hands, wondering what the hell was going on.

"I'm doing the best I can, Parker. My first plan fell through. I had to call POTUS."

Fitzgerald almost had a conniption. "What?" she cried. "Why did you do that? He's working with Rickey. For God's sake, Camille, why don't you just go ahead and shoot me in the head while you're at it? I'm toast."

Out past the shallows, Fitzgerald saw three Brown Pelicans swirling about hunting prey. She watched as one dove sharply into the otherwise serene sea but came up empty. She wondered if she'd be as lucky as that fish. As for the fish... did it even know it was being hunted? Did it even know how close to sudden death it had come?

"Just try to stay calm," said Camille. "It seems your boss and my boss have had a sudden difference of opinion. Help is on the way."

"Is that right?" replied Parker. She laughed uncomfortably. "I feel like a fish about to get eaten by a pelican swooping in out of nowhere."

"Well," Camille said, in a serious tone. "As it turns out, that describes Rickey Ormand right about now. There's a world of hurt heading his way, and he has no idea."

This gave Parker Fitzgerald something to smile about if only in passing. "God, I like that scenario much better. What happens now?"

She turned to her driver who was calling her and pointing to his watch. He was talking on his cell phone. "Are we staying here much longer, missus? Or are you planning to move from here?"

Fitzgerald shrugged, so the driver lowered his phone and repeated himself. "I asked if you are planning on staying here, or are we moving?"

Taking it as the annoying self-interest of a local islander looking for a quick buck, Fitzgerald thought nothing of it. Instead, she rolled her eyes and waved him away. Raising his phone back to his ear, the man walked back toward his car.

"I have no idea," said Camille. "I don't ask. I don't want to know. I'll say this – you don't cross Harry Pierson and walk away whistling Dixie, that's for sure."

"Good," hissed Fitzgerald. "Screw that sinister little dork with his trendy hoodies and stupid sneakers. I hope the president shoves it—"

Camille interrupted her. "Just keep it positive, Parker. Don't get caught up in the dirty business. Do you have the data?"

Fitzgerald nodded. "Yes, I have it all. It's safe."

"We're going to get you out of there," Camille assured her. "And then you and I are going to change the world."

"Okay, so what's the plan?" asked Fitzgerald, growing more worried with every passing minute. "I'm completely hung out to dry here."

"Sit tight," said Camille. "And keep your phone on. Harry says his guys can zone in on you."

Fitzgerald snorted. "Yeah, that's easy for you to say."

Camille tried to sound as soothing as possible. "Look, Parker. Harry has a way of getting things done. I don't care for his way most of the time, but what choice do we have right now? Somebody tried to kill you or take you prisoner or whatever. We have no idea if there's another team looking for you. Getting you off that island is our number one focus right now."

"Okay, okay," said Fitzgerald. "I'll sit tight right here. I mean... I've run out of island, you know? This is it... end of the line."

"No," corrected Camille. "This is just the beginning. Trust me. I've glimpsed it. I'll see you when you get to D.C."

They said goodbye, pretending everything was okay. Fitzgerald sat on a large, black rock weathered by the sea. Looking out into the ocean she tried to imagine what was in store for her and Camille. Would they team up and really re-define the world, or was this whole thing about to run abruptly into a brick wall named Harry Pierson? Assuming she and Camille teamed up and took Liquid-Drive and

Liquid-Life to the world, was Rickey Ormand that much of a psychopath that he would hunt her down for revenge? She couldn't put it past him. Stealing his technology was like tearing out his heart.

About thirty minutes pass before Fitzgerald notices something. Her ears perk up suddenly. It's difficult to detect over the waves breaking against the wall of rocks forming that portion of the coastline, but she thinks she hears... yes, definitely. A motor, like a car or something. It's unmistakable now.

Fitzgerald scans the area nervously. She feels trouble approaching fast. Then she sees it. A silver SUV blows by up on the main road. The expensive truck stands out like a turd in a bowl of milk on the small, outlying island. Fitzgerald holds her breath hoping against hope. Then she hears the sound she's dreading... tires screeching. Fitzgerald visualizes it all in her mind like an instantaneous burst of light from a muzzle flash, the last thing she will see in this truncated lifetime. Black skids on the hot, gray asphalt, the smell of friction and burnt rubber, the occupants lurching forward from inertia as they simultaneously reach for their weapons and rack the chambers.

Now there is no doubt. It isn't a coincidence. It can't be. Not on an island that small. Whoever is in that SUV is sure as shit looking for her. She hears the sound of a vehicle ramping up and drawing closer. Her robotic legs burst into action as she sprints up to the taxi driver who is standing next to his car, door open, about to climb into the driver's seat. She can see the panic in his eyes. Whatever is running through his head, Fitzgerald assumes the worst.

She glances up at the main road and then back at her driver. Suddenly, it all makes sense. When she fled from her villa complex, the taxi driver just happened to pull in like he was waiting for her. She recalls now how the driver even honked as he pulled in like he'd been watching her the whole time. What about his cell phone? He was on a call with someone when he asked her twice if they were staying put or moving on. He was pumping her for information.

She glares at him. "You set me up, you son-of-a-bitch."

The driver has one foot already in the car when Fitzgerald grabs him by the shoulder of his red polo shirt and tries to yank his ass out of the car. He grips the steering wheel with his right hand and holds on for dear life. While Fitzgerald continues tugging, he keeps looking back toward the main road for the cavalry.

Tired of playing around, Fitzgerald flings the door fully open and takes hold of the man's other shoulder spinning him around. She raises her right leg and explodes it down onto the man's left foot which is still firmly planted on the ground. The man screams as Fitzgerald's robotic force crushes his ankle with no more effort than her snapping a twig.

"You son-of-a-bitch. You dimed me out," she screams.

The man only cries out in anguish.

Fitzgerald starts shaking the man by his shoulders again. His head thunk-thunks against the door frame a couple of times in the process.

"You little bastard. Who were you calling?" she demands. She pulls him toward her sharply, and his head thunk-thunks against the door frame again.

The man says nothing and cries out in pain again.

Fitzgerald gets right up in the driver's face now. "Tell me," she yells, her rage now reaching the point of savagery. "Tell me before I snap your other leg in half and throw you into the ocean to drown."

Her senses intensify sharply. She is acutely aware of her surroundings. She can hear seagulls squawking somewhere behind her. Spittle is running down the driver's chin as he starts babbling some nonsense about needing the money and something about his wife having cancer. It only makes Fitzgerald loathe him more, and she has no qualms whatsoever about killing him like she did Franco.

She knocks the driver's head against the car two more times. "Do you have any idea what you've done?" she yells, spraying spit in the man's face in the process. "Not just to me, but to the entire world, a world full of people just like you, you stupid shit."

The man really isn't the violent sort, nor is he particularly prone to criminal behavior. He got sucked into this whole thing because he thought he could turn a quick buck. If anything, he was guilty of naïveté, and he has a crushed ankle to show for it. Now, all he can do is wince and cower. He doesn't know anything about gravity power. He couldn't care less. All he knows is that some crazy woman is attacking him, and there is an SUV full of guys looking for her, and they pay cash.

Parker Fitzgerald looks up and sees the silver SUV speeding down the access road toward her. The truck hurtles over a sizeable bump like it is running over a squirrel. Fitzgerald realizes it's too late to flee. She contemplates snapping the driver's neck as she'd done with the guy in her room if for no other reason than sending Rickey Ormand a final Screw You, douche canoe.

That's what she decides to do – kill the miserable, sad excuse of a man she has locked in her clutches. Then she sees a picture of a black woman and two girls taped to the dash of the taxi. She assumes it's the driver's wife and kids. The woman is wearing a sort of turban scarf like a chemo hat.

"You piece of shit," she blurts out as she pushes him into the driver's seat. She wants nothing more to do with him.

The man lets out a scream as his broken ankle takes the brunt of it. Then Fitzgerald turns and runs toward the water. With her robotic legs, she can swim like a dolphin, but where would she go? She'd rather be riddled with bullets than drown. Drowning she fears more than anything else except burning to death and being buried alive.

She reaches the rocky shore. There's nowhere to hide. End of the line. She's out of island. She turns back to survey the shit show that's about to go down. The taxi driver hauls his injured leg into the cab and speeds off toward the main road. Fitzgerald focuses on the SUV. It's now facing her. To her horror, it's empty, three doors wide open. The men of Team 2 are making their move.

Three men are out in front of the truck walking cautiously toward her. They are all wearing black fatigues and black jump boots. Each man has a capture gun loaded with darts containing enough M99 etorphine to send a Bengal tiger nighty night for two days. They keep the dart guns holstered. Bringing Fitzgerald back to Liquid Sky alive was their primary directive, but that was before they found Franco dead. They have no intention of bringing Fitzgerald home unscathed if they even bring her home at all. Avenging their fallen brother, even one who wasn't part of their team, is now their top priority. Outside of that, everything else is but a contingency.

Instead of their dart guns, each of the men is gripping a far more nefarious Heckler & Koch MP-5 sub-machine gun aimed straight at Fitzgerald. Fitzgerald has no idea what kind of guns they are, but she's quite certain she's standing on the wrong side of the barrel. Seeing no other viable option but to go down swinging like a lunatic Irish woman rushing headlong to keep her lunch appointment with God, Parker Fitzgerald digs in, bends at the waist, sets her feet, and presses her arms forward like a football player practicing a form tackle. Screw it, she thinks. It's been a crazy-ass good ride.

The three men form a horizontal line a few feet apart from each other as they approach. The man in the middle seems to be the leader. "End of the line for you, sister," he says. "We're supposed to put a dart in your ass and carry you back to your boyfriend in California, but I think we're gonna stick something else in your ass instead. Oh baby, we owe you one. A life for a life. That's how it goes, sister."

The man on Fitzgerald's right switches his MP-5 to his left hand. With his right now free, he unsheathes an ominous looking blade. Fitzgerald gasps audibly. The knife, an *Ari B'Lilah* similar to those used by Israeli *Yamam*, is far more terrifying than the guns. The silver perimeter of the blade reflects the sun while the black matte finish of the blade's middle section Fitzgerald took to foreshadow an excruciating and horrific death.

The man with the knife is not the leader, but he has a strong personality nevertheless. He spits a dark stream of tobacco juice on the ground in front of him. A tiny bit of dark spittle remains on his protruding lower dip lip. "You know," he says, "my old man was a butcher. He was a good-for-nothing, drunk son-of-a-bitch, but man he taught me how to carve up everything from fish to Sasquatch. But I never butchered up a robo-bitch before. I'm just dying to see what's inside of you... especially between those legs of yours."

Certain this is her last day on earth, Fitzgerald fires right back. "You're gonna need that knife because you certainly don't have the manliness to get between these legs, you inbred, redneck, goat loving piece of crap."

The men actually laugh, the guy with the knife most of all. That isn't exactly the response Fitzgerald expected. Again, she thinks this is it, the end of the line just like that piece-of-crap cab driver said. Maybe she should have killed him after all, she wonders. At least she would have taken someone down with her, even if it was the weakling of the enemy pack. She thinks of Camille O'Keefe and what she will say. She exhales deliberately. There aren't many options to run in her head. Either she drowns five miles out, or she stands her ground and gets slaughtered like a pig. Either way, her options are heinous.

The three men continue to advance, albeit cautiously, for they don't know what the hell Fitzgerald is capable of. If dead Franco is any indication, they can't take her lightly. Quite the contrary, they intend to work her over with extreme prejudice and malicious intent. They feel it's their obligation. Fitzgerald can feel their malevolence spreading around her like mustard gas in a trench. She looks down and remembers. To help her manage the post-traumatic stress of her near-death experience in Peru, she has been seeing a psychoanalyst for a couple of years. His name is Will Derkind. Derkind is best known for his position on near-death experiences. He posits that a person never really knows how they are going to confront death until they actually come face-to-face with their own demise.

For Derkind, there's no hypothetical that survives the real deal. Death had to be nearly certain, and it had to be imminent. Only then, Derkind believed, did a person truly understand how they would react. There was no preparation for it, no training regimen or response protocol. When the only thing a person had left was the likelihood of imminent death, their response would be the true measure of who they were, a state of being beyond criticism, beyond judgement, beyond good and evil.

A Freudian – and, therefore, a Nietzschean – Dr. Derkind showed Parker Fitzgerald that the abyss is a treasure chest holding the truth about oneself. When buried under a pile of rubble high atop the world in the Andes Mountains, Fitzgerald was staring at the abyss. But she didn't crumble. Her will to remain, her will to live, outweighed her desire to disappear and simply expire. This was the moment of measure for the ineffable power of her spirit.

Derkind taught her that only someone who has been there themselves can understand that there is no passing judgment on how a person reacts on the verge of death. There is only observation. That's all there can be. Only the person standing on the threshold of their own demise can pass judgment on themselves. It is one thing to be able to live with oneself, as they say. It is quite another to be able to die with oneself. Neither requires more or less courage.

Derkind believes in the myth of the Phoenix as a metaphor for struggle and perseverance. Parker Fitzgerald believes in herself as a Phoenix and that she has arisen from the ashes a completely new life form. With this in mind, Fitzgerald steps forward, still maintaining her aggressive stance. No longer feeling the pain in her jaw, she grits her teeth and clenches her fists. If she can goad the guy with the blade into fighting her with only his knife, she might at least take him out before the other two emptied their clips into her. That, she thought to herself, would be a reasonable compromise. Yeah, if she took one down, she could check out okay with that.

"You, with the big knife and the small dick," she says. She winks at the guy.

The guy just bleats like a goat and laughs. "The goats don't seem to mind."

Fitzgerald is struck by his nonchalance. In fact, all three men terrify her precisely because they seem so carefree about killing her. She allows herself a brief moment of distracted thought. Where do people like this come from? It's that damned Y chromosome, she concludes. Then it's back to the business at hand.

She stands up straight, less threatening. "Isn't the gun a little overkill there, tough guy? Do you really need a gun to take me down? Or, are you overcompensating for your lack elsewhere?"

By this point, Parker Fitzgerald has abandoned the possibility of surviving this encounter. "Three of you against little me?" she says, laughing mechanically to piss them off. "You may think you can do what you like with a woman, but blood can be spilled on both sides." That's really all she cares about at this point. What else does she have?

"Oh, the music's playing for you, love," says the knife man.

Fitzgerald shrugs. "I'm waiting for you to ask me to dance," she says. "But you're just standing there talking into the wind."

Dark clouds roll in seemingly out of nowhere as they often do in the tropics. The incoming storm appears menacing as it dwarfs the tiny island, especially when seen from ground level. Fitzgerald suddenly feels exposed and vulnerable, the three men in black looming large like the storm clouds themselves rolling in across the ocean behind her.

The man with the knife snickers and squirts a dark stream of dip spit to his right. He forks over his MP-5 to the team leader. "Be right back."

He raises his knife higher and extends it in front of him a bit more. "Then let's dance," he says. "Bitch, I can't wait to slice you from one set of lips to the other."

He slows his pace as he approaches Fitzgerald. Now realizing the reality of her dismal situation, she takes two steps backward. The man grins. He loves to see a woman cower in fear. He gets off on it.

Fitzgerald reassesses the situation as best she can. Her legs are her best attribute. That, and she can play possum like she used to do when one of her brothers was stupid enough to get too close. She runs it out quickly in her head. If she can lure the guy in close enough to get a solid robotic kick off, she can shatter his leg at the minimum. With any luck she can plunge the knife into his throat before the other two psychos blow her away.

"I'm not going down without a fight," she says. "Sorry, Camille."

The man looks at her funny but continues to move close enough to smell Fitzgerald's perfume as a breeze blows in from the ocean behind her. He likes the fragrance. He smiles. "You smell good, baby," he says. "I like that because you're gonna shit yourself when you die. You know that, right?"

"Imagine how good my hair smells with your face buried in my neck," she responds, trying to lure him closer.

He smiles at the thought of it. "Oh, believe me, woman. I'm fixin' to sniff you all over... like a dog checking out a piece of meat."

He steps closer now, so close that Fitzgerald can see his penetrating blue eyes. The eyes seem deep, pensive, and even sensitive. She's momentarily transfixed. She's suspended in the moment long enough to give her attacker the window he's looking for. In that moment, Parker Fitzgerald knows she's made a fatal mistake.

The man is well trained, a killer by trade as well as temperament. He springs forward with the speed and dexterity of a pouncing cat. He leads with his foot, the razor-sharp blade following deftly behind in a single, fluid movement. Fitzgerald is stunned and stationary, an easy target. The blade slices through its mark precisely where the assassin planned. Fitzgerald shakes herself back into the moment and gasps loudly. She looks down. The sheer wrap she tied around her waist before she ordered room service falls to the ground. She sees a long, horizontal cut in her pink-and-white bikini bottom running from her left hip to her right.

She looks up at her assailant. He is grinning maliciously. "I'm pretty good with this thing," he says. "Thanks to daddy."

Fitzgerald's will is quickly deflating. She reaches down and pulls open the slit in her bikini. Her synthetic skin is sliced as well and has flayed open revealing exotic black composite from which her lower frame is crafted. She stares at her attacker. But this time, there's far less resolve and far more fear in her eyes.

"So, it's true," says the man. "Down there...." He gestures with the blade. "You got nothing. You must be one ice-cold bitch without no tender vittles."

Fitzgerald realizes she reacted too slowly for her plan to work and that the odds of taking this guy down are slim. He's too good with a blade. He'll slice her ass up like a butcher. Apparently, his old man taught him well. She decides to try for some sort of leg sweep or something like that and hope for the best before she is cut free from her mortal roots.

418   GRAVITY DIVIDED

The man in black tosses the knife between his hands a few times. Fitzgerald's eyes follow the blade back and forth... back and forth... back and forth... slow and certain. The man is toying with her. "High speed, low drag," he taunts. "Slow is smooth; smooth is fast."

She can see he is erect. "You're a sadistic son-of-a-bitch," she says.

"Thank you," he says.

Not knowing why and without thinking, Parker Fitzgerald sets her feet into the silty earth and hurls herself at her attacker. The man is startled enough to freeze for a moment. With the explosive power of her robotic legs, that's all Fitzgerald needs. Planting her left foot two feet in front of the man, she follows with her right. Targeting her assailant's left knee, she sweeps through with everything she has, knowing this will be her last gesture to the world.

The man attempts to dodge the kick. But he makes the mistake of stepping back with his right foot instead of his left which Fitzgerald has targeted. Fitzgerald's right instep makes full, flat contact with the outside of the man's knee. The pop is loud and unmistakable. His knee is completely destroyed.

The man crumples and screams in pain. This is the only chance Fitzgerald will get to finish him off. She needs to wrap her legs around the man's neck like she did to Franco. She glides forward like a beast of prey and slides her left leg between the ground and the man's neck. She is about to lock her right leg over the top, sealing the man's fate, when he fights back with everything he has.

He lands a savage blow with his left hand into Fitzgerald's gut. She's all human there, and she grunts and recoils as she loses her wind. The man pounds her in the stomach two more times with all his might. Fitzgerald rolls over as the involuntary portions of her brain throws her into a suffocating panic.

The man leans over and vomits from the wad of dip he swallowed when Fitzgerald blew up his knee. He wipes the vomit, snot, and saliva from his mouth with the sleeve of his black BDU's. A brutal, violent fire burns in his eyes.

He reaches for the knife and grips it firmly in his right hand. "Imma gut you now, bitch."

First, he thrusts the blade into the ground and unloads a vicious right hook that lands squarely on Fitzgerald's jaw. She drops back, out cold. The man drags himself over to her and punches her again. Bruising and swelling cover the left side of her face almost instantly.

"That's a good girl," he says with vitriol.

He rolls over onto his back and screams in both pain and fury. That's when all three men hear it... the unmistakable whump, whump, whump of a military helicopter. The pounding of the rotor blades reverberates off the water and gives all three men pause. There was no helo in their plans. Whatever's coming their way isn't friendly.

The knife man looks at Fitzgerald's unconscious body and then back at his two partners.

The leader is shaking his head. "We gotta boogie... like now."

"I'm not done gutting her yet," yelled the man, raising the knife above his shoulder.

"Hey!" yells the leader. "Did you hear what I just said? We gotta go most ricky-tick, right now."

The leader turns to the third man and points to their wounded partner. "Carry his ass to the vehicle. I'll grab robo-bitch."

The two able-bodied men carry their injured partner and the unconscious Parker Fitzgerald back to the SUV. The injured man slides gingerly into the back seat. The team leader binds Fitzgerald's hands with zip ties before tossing her roughly into the back of the truck. She smacks her head against the protruding wheel well.

"Uh, sorry about your coconut, sister," he says. With the push of a button, the large hatch closes.

The two other men roll down their windows, check their MP-5's, and prepare to repel the inbound bird. The leader is barely settled into the driver's seat when they have a visual on the helo.

"There," yells the injured man in the back seat. "Two o'clock, low to the water."

The three men look out over the coastline. The whump, whump, whump has grown much louder.

"Who the hell is that?" demands the man in the passenger seat.

"Is it Ormand?" asks the injured guy in back.

"How the hell should I know?" yells the leader as he jams the truck into gear and pins it. Dust and bits of seashells fly up behind them as they haul toward the main road. Fitzgerald's unconscious body flies against the back hatch as the truck lurches forward.

"It's coming in from the southwest. What's there?" asks the man in the passenger seat.

"Cuba" says the leader. "Guantanamo maybe?"

The truck races back to the main road, taking every rock and pothole at full bore.

"What the hell?" yells the man in back as he writhers in pain with each bump they hit. "They closed that shithole a few years ago."

The man in the passenger seat laughs as the driver turns the truck left and speeds north toward where they have their boat docked. "Nothing's ever closed," he says, "especially with this freaking Pierson guy in the White House. The guy is nasty. Black ops... it's in his blood."

"Yeah," replies the wounded man. "I hear he enjoys this kind of shit."

The leader corrects them both. "It can't be from Guantanamo, you idiots. It's too far for the range of that bird. It's probably out of Miami."

They hit another bump in the road, and the man with the shattered knee howls in pain.

The leader of Team 2 is correct. The helo is, in fact, an MH-60 Pare Hawk out of Homestead Air Reserve Base in Miami. The base is home to the 482nd wing reserve supporting the Tenth Air Force. With a cruising speed of about 185 miles an hour and external fuel tanks added for a safe margin on the inbound ride, it was a short hop to the Bahamas once Pierson gave the green light through a back channel that afforded him plausible deniability.

The gray belly of the bird stands out against the darkening, stormy sky just enough to seem ominous. Parker Fitzgerald, woozy as she is from being coldcocked twice, begins to come to in the back of the truck. She can barely move her jaw, and it aches something awful. Still, the fog of conflict is dissipating quickly. She squeezes her eyes tight. She can't believe she's actually alive. She squeezes them shut again. Looking out the back window, she thinks she sees a military helicopter closing fast from behind. She moans as she lets her head fall back down.

The SUV is no match for the helo in any way. After breaking north in pursuit of the SUV, the Pare Hawk swallows up road and overtakes the fleeing truck in seconds flat. Ormand's men strain to see the helicopter blow by over top and continue on about 100 yards ahead.

The leader slams his fist into the steering wheel several times. "Shit, shit, shit," he yells.

The Pare Hawk drops to about 5 feet off the deck and rotates counter clockwise until it is squared off facing the SUV.

Showdown time.

"Definitely not good," says the guy in the passenger seat.

The leader slows the truck.

"What are you doing?" yells the injured man in the back seat as he reaches his MP-5 out his window.

"Stand down," yells the driver.

The injured man lets loose a five-shot barrage that doesn't seem to hit anything.

"I said stand down," barks the leader as he slows the car to about twenty miles an hour. "Are you insane?"

"Screw this, man!" yells the man in back.

"You moron," replies the leader. "You're staring down the barrel of two Gatling guns, you idiot. That's 12,000 rounds a minute coming our way, so just cool your jets before I shoot you myself."

The man in the passenger seat is distressed. "Yo, I didn't sign up for this shit. That Ormand guy can kiss my ass. Let them have the robo-bitch for all I care. We'll take the half fee we already got as a retainer and call it a day."

The driver brings the SUV to a complete stop about thirty yards from the Pare Hawk. The rotor whump is deafening. Dirt and gravel are flying everywhere. The windshield is clinking repeatedly as particles and small debris hit it.

"Yeah, well," says the leader, "we gotta live to see another day. Know what I mean?"

The men drop their weapons outside the car and emerge with their hands over their heads. The injured man in the back seat does his best to prop himself against the truck in the face of the rotor wind.

The driver leans in through his open window and presses a button and returns his hands to his head. The hatch of the truck opens slowly. Out steps Parker Fitzgerald, hands bound behind her back. She's wobbly and woozy but capable of walking under her own power.

As she passes the driver, she has only one thing to say. "Tell Rickey Ormand that the Phoenix is coming for her pound of flesh."

Chapter 28

Pierson called the Saturday morning meeting trying to keep things under wraps. Jennifer Daly looked around the table. Now that the election was over, and Camille was slated to take her place as the next vice president, Daly allowed herself to imagine life after politics. Still, every time she thought about Camille O'Keefe as the new vice president, she couldn't help but pick at the scabs and reopen the sores.

In the weeks leading up to the election, Daly decided she'd had enough... enough of Harry Pierson, enough of Washington, D.C., enough of politics. More than anything else, she had her fill of the *status quo*, the *quid pro quo*, and any other fanciful *quo* terms that all amounted to the same thing – the self-serving Beltway bullshit of politics as usual.

"Frankly, I'm glad to be done with it all," she told one of her aides who handed her a steaming cup of coffee outside the Situation Room that morning. Disgusted as she was, she still wore a pressed, blue pant suit and had her hair in a tight, net bun. "Professional to the end" was her new motto.

"He's in some kind of mood this morning," warned her aide, Dana, an ambitious alumna from George Washington's Elliott School of International Affairs. "It's all I need to know. He won't even allow me in the room. Apparently, he's got some top-secret person stashed in there with him."

Jennifer Daly smoothed her blouse and blew on her coffee. "O'Keefe is in there with His Majesty and this secret guest."

"Of course," Dana whispered and rolled her eyes just enough to convey solidarity with her lame-duck boss.

Daly patted her loyal aide on the shoulder. "This town will crush your spirit, Dana. You're young and positive. Stay that way as long as you can because sooner or later, the D.C. steamroller will flatten you."

Dana sighed. "We need people like you, ma'am. We need *women* like you."

Daly smiled and shrugged. "Well, you have me for another couple of months. After that, I'm moving to Hawaii where, as God is my witness, I will never watch another political talking head pontificate."

Daly opened the door to the Situation Room and strode in. She saw Pierson and Camille, but she had no idea who the other woman was. Daly gave her a look of disapproval for her casual wardrobe – jeans, blue Lucky Brand T-shirt, and a well-worn Red Sox hat.

Daly raised her chin at the woman. "Who are you?" she asked.

Parker Fitzgerald stood up quickly. "Good morning, Vice President Daly. My name is Dr. Parker Fitzgerald."

Daly disliked the woman's raspy voice as much as she disliked her choice of attire. "Sorry, doesn't ring a bell. Should it?"

Fitzgerald squirmed a bit at Daly's brusque response. "I guess not," she said.

"Sit down, will ya," Harry Pierson barked at Fitzgerald. "You, too," he said to Jennifer Daly. He was wearing his "crisis casual" getup... dark-blue jeans, brown bomber jacket over a long-sleeve yellow Oxford, brown loafers, and blue baseball cap bearing the presidential logo.

"Parker has been through a harrowing experience," explained Pierson. "I brought her in under protective custody."

This got Daly's attention. She took a seat across from Fitzgerald. "Is that so?"

Daly picked up the file labelled *Top Secret* with the SCI code word *Liquid-Life*. She slid her pen between the covers of the folder, broke the seal, and thumbed through the pages.

"Has she read it?" this time not even gesturing toward Fitzgerald. "Did you give her top clearance out of the kindness of your heart?"

"This is classified Top Secret Presidential. You and O'Keefe are the only other people I've authorized to view this information," said Pierson.

"What about her?" said Daly, insistently, again referring to Parker Fitzgerald as if she wasn't even in the same room.

Pierson smiled. "That's the sticking point. As you'll see, she knows the entire story. The woman is the technology. The technology is the woman."

Daly looked at Fitzgerald and then returned her gaze to the president. "Interesting. Give me a minute." She continued reviewing the contents of her folder with quick efficiency, arching a brow from time to time. The silence in the room was broken only by the turning of each page in the dossier. Camille exchanged uncomfortable glances with Pierson and Fitzgerald.

When she finished reading, Jennifer Daly arranged the papers neatly and closed the file. "Well," she said flatly, "it seems I've underestimated you, Dr. Fitzgerald. It appears you are... how shall I say this... I want to say a novelty, but that would be too simplistic."

"An enigma?" said Camille.

Daly nodded. "Yes, an enigma. That you certainly are."

"And she's tough as nails," added Harry Pierson. "We could use more women like her."

Daly smiled curtly. "Apparently not in your administration."

Pierson laughed. "Now you're being patronizing," he said.

Daly sat back and crossed her legs. "Not to worry, Harry. You'll be rid of me soon enough."

The president's smile quickly turned to a quivering grimace as he started massaging his temples.

"What's wrong?" asked Camille.

Pierson waved her off. "Nothing. I've been feeling a bit dizzy the last few days. It's too much caffeine. I'm just tired. And this Rickey Ormand is a pain in my ass. I feel like there's a fifty-pound weight on my chest."

"Too much stress," Camille opined. "You need better relaxation techniques."

"What I need is no more Rickey Ormand," said Pierson. "And I'll have plenty of time to sleep when I'm dead. Until then, I'll just have to deal with the headaches."

Jennifer Daly summed up perfectly what everybody, including Harry Pierson, was thinking. "Harry, you're a hot mess."

Parker Fitzgerald was mortified. "I really apologize about all this, Mr. President. I feel like this is all my fault."

Pierson started rubbing his eyes now. "It is," he snapped. "It's entirely your fault, Dr. Fitzgerald. But, you definitely served a purpose. I'll give you that. If you kept quiet and played along, we'd never know anything about Liquid-Life."

"What the president means," clarified Daly, "is that you have something he wants. It's just that he didn't know he wanted it until you absconded with it."

Pierson underscored his nod with a firm grunt.

Parker Fitzgerald removed her Red Sox hat and ran her fingers through her hair. "What exactly do you want, Mr. President?"

Pierson's response was brisk and immediate. "You, Fitzgerald. You're what everybody's after now, aren't you?"

Jennifer Daly looked Fitzgerald over. This time, she seemed to have a much deeper appreciation for who and what was sitting before her. "My God, when Jeff finds out about you, he's going to go crazy."

"Jeff?" said Fitzgerald, cocking her head.

"Bezos," answered Daly. "Jeff Bezos. Can you imagine what he could do if he owned the intellectual-property rights to... you." She looked at Camille and then the president. "Can we even say that? Can a human being be intellectual property? Can we pull this off?"

Pierson slapped his right hand on the table but was visibly pained in doing so. "Of course, we can," he exclaimed. "Why do you think I called this emergency meeting? Listen to me, all of you. The four people sitting at this table control the future of the entire world. Just the four of us... we manage the destiny of every last person. You read the file. We can do whatever we want to now that we have her." He gestured toward Fitzgerald.

Daly snickered. "You mean Dr. Fitzgerald, of course." She turned to Fitzgerald. "It's not personal, dear. Being a man, the president was manufactured without an empathy chip. You know how it is."

"Do you see how she treats me?" said Pierson, in jest. "God, I'm gonna miss you, J.D.. I'll only have my wife to ridicule me now. What fun is that?" He poured himself a glass of water from the pitcher on the table. His hands were visibly shaky.

"Maybe you should take a few days at Camp David," said Camille, noticing the president's slight tremble and general pallor. "You could use a break."

"No time for that now," replied Pierson. "There's so much to be done. We have in our possession the greatest piece of technology in the history of the world. I could work twenty-four hours a day for the next four years and still not run out of ideas."

Jennifer Daly cleared her throat, her way of announcing she was about to get serious. "Yes, well... since we're on the topic, what are you going to do about our friend Mr. Ormand? You are going to do something about him, right Harry?"

That was the obvious question. Silence followed.

"I can tell you he'll stop at nothing," said Camille, in hope of prompting Pierson to action. "Just look at what he did to Parker."

Sensing she had the two other women on her side, Parker Fitzgerald felt comfortable in speaking her mind. "If I may, Mr. President, Rickey Ormand did try to kill me."

Pierson held up his hand. "Slow down, doc. We need to be clear about a few things. I mean, you're no angel, know what I'm saying? It's my understanding that Ormand sent some guys down to the

Bahamas to keep tabs on you after you stole proprietary information belonging to Liquid Sky."

Camille exhaled in exasperation. "Harry, really? I mean... really? Our people can spin this thing, right? Parker Fitzgerald is an American hero. We just have to position her the right way, that's all."

Jennifer Daly added her support. "Harry, it's quite clear from the After-Action Report in the file that regardless of what the guy intended, the maniacs he sent in were intent on killing Dr. Fitzgerald. And I agree completely with Camille. This is easy to manage. You can turn Dr. Fitzgerald into a superstar with the snap of your fingers."

Parker Fitzgerald leaned in, her palms flat on the shiny cherry table. "Thank you so much for stepping in, Mr. President. I owe you my life."

Pierson said nothing.

Jennifer Daly leaned in. "Returning to my question, what do you intend to do about Rickey Ormand? You can't let it go at this. The man's a renegade. This isn't like you at all, Harry. The guy's trouble. He'll be back. He'll team up with that prick Soros and will never stop pestering you."

Camille could sense the tension rising like the mercury in a thermometer on an Alabama August morning.

The president narrowed his eyes. He took off his baseball cap with the presidential seal and tossed it down on the table in front of him as if throwing down the gauntlet. "What's not like me?"

Jennifer Daly responded without hesitation. "May I be blunt?"

Camille and Parker looked at each other nervously. This was not an arena in which either of them was comfortable.

The president sat back in his high-backed leather chair and started massaging his temples again, the wind clearly gone from his sails. "If I say no, would it matter?" He managed to press out a charming grin, however artificial.

"With two months left in my term, I've earned this," said Daly, flatly. "So, then... why are you bending over for this guy?"

Pierson coughed and drank some water. Camille noticed that his hand was still shaking. "Well, that's putting it bluntly."

Daly shrugged. "Call me a duck, but I'm anything but lame. Two months from now, you'll forget my name. So why not leave my shit on the table?"

"What else are you thinking?" asked Camille.

Jennifer Daly folded her hands on top of the dossier in front of her. She was thinking. She picked up the folder, signalling an end to her ruminations. She rolled it, raised it, and held it like a sceptre. "If these two technologies... Liquid what not and Liquid who ho—"

Parker Fitzgerald managed a chuckle despite the fact that her jaw was sore as hell from being slugged not once but twice by two different men in a single day. "Liquid-Drive and Liquid-Life," she corrected.

"That's what I said," clarified Daly dryly, although a momentary smirk revealed itself. "Anyway, I haven't read the file in detail, obviously, but any idiot can see that each of these technologies will redefine life as we know it. The idea that they can be introduced together is utterly staggering. I mean...."

Daly waved her hand in search of the right words. The light danced off her gold bracelet. "Think about it. The people who control this technology control not just the energy market but every machine, business, and product that currently runs on oil, gas, electricity... whatever. Add to that the discovery of a veritable fountain of youth. Good Lord, Harry, you could probably win a third term after changing the Constitution."

Fitzgerald was feeding off Daly's exuberance. "Nothing currently runs on gravity. Everything has to be reinvented. The opportunities are endless. And just thinking that this administration can manage that fairly is the whole reason I did what I did. Mr. President, I need you to know that."

Camille scratched the nape of her neck as if trying to free up her idea. "The big reveal here is Liquid-Life. It redefines the very limits of human existence," she said. "Gravitational energy providing an essential life force is really the fountain of youth."

Parker Fitzgerald couldn't help herself. "Liquid-Life cured my cancer. I'm not talking about remission, Mr. President. It's completely gone. I am totally cancer free."

Jennifer Daly pursed her lips. It was only then that she noticed Camille's definition of "crisis casual" apparently meant black yoga pants and a mustard cowl-neck, cable-knit sweater. At least it's Lululemon, she thought to herself with a shrug. She then tossed the folder on the table as Pierson did earlier with his cap. "Anyhoo... you are right. I never thought I would say it, Camille, but your vision is perfect for the moment. We're at a crossroad, Mr. President. And Parker Fitzgerald is beyond revolutionary. She's... she's... the future. There's no other way to say it."

Parker Fitzgerald smiled humbly. She was blushing, too. "Liquid-Drive and Liquid-Life should rightly be considered taken together. That's how we designed it because that's the way to take the world by storm."

"Really?" said Camille.

Fitzgerald nodded. "Sure. Liquid-Drive is a product-driven manipulation of gravity power. But Liquid-Life? Damn, that's a whole other level. Liquid-Life is really an extension of universal energy. It's a paradigm shift. Honestly, I don't even think the term 'revolutionary' comes close. I don't think we have a word to adequately describe the size of the impact."

Camille chuckled. "I have a word for it. But it's in Light Language, so it's nonverbal... strictly telepathic."

Jennifer Daly had a sort of quizzical look on her face. "You know," she said, "the sad thing is I don't know if you're joking or being serious."

Camille just smiled. "I know," she replied. "I like that."

The president started coughing but managed to spit out his thoughts like he was hocking a loogie. "I've got a word for you ladies. Catastrophic. How about that? Any of you think about the repercussions of introducing technology that will make the entire world obsolete overnight? It's like dropping a nuke on the world."

"Oh my," said Camille. "I wouldn't put it that way."

Jennifer Daly stood up and started perusing the food table along the wall. It was covered with assorted bagels, pastries, and other breakfast fare. She picked up a butter knife and cut herself exactly one quarter of a chocolate-glazed donut with the precision of a cardiac surgeon. The others watched in fascination as Big J.D. deposited the tasty morsel into her mouth and then washed it down with just enough black coffee for a single swallow. She then placed the coffee mug on the table. It made a clink. She wiped the perimeter of her mouth with a white cloth napkin before scrunching it up and stuffing it inside the empty mug. It was remarkable. Not a bit of her lipstick found its way to that napkin.

She pivoted on her right heel with precision and returned to her chair across from Camille. She sat down and crossed her legs. "Catastrophic, huh? That's a big word, Harry. It carries a lot of weight. People don't like that word. It makes them nervous."

"Catastrophic," repeated the president. "I said it, and I meant it. The modernized world as we know it will be obsolete overnight. Boom... gone... dust. Do you have any idea what kind of chaos would ensue?"

"The economic impact alone would be inestimable," added Parker Fitzgerald.

Camille sighed. "The idea is to help people with this amazing technology, not blow them up... to use that awful analogy again."

The president just shrugged. There was no need to respond on the record.

Jennifer Daly shook her head. "I assume, Harry, you've already decided this technology constitutes a national security risk of the highest level? I mean, you're predicting major repercussions, right? Global crisis kind of stuff, right?"

Feeling a bit dizzy now, the president just nodded.

Jennifer Daly looked at Parker Fitzgerald. "So, you see, Parker. The president has the power to simply take this technology away from Rickey Ormand."

Parker Fitzgerald cocked her head and looked at Jennifer Daly quizzically. "He can do that?"

Daly pointed at the president. "The president can. If it's deemed a matter of national security, the president has full authority to assume control of the technology in the name of the American people."

Camille shook her head in dismay. "I tried to tell this to Rickey at the gala. He chose to blow me off."

"Screw him," exclaimed the president. "I mean it. Screw him. I called Ormand in to see me. None of you know that, but I did. That little shit actually sat in the Oval Office – my Oval Office – blowing smoke up my ass. He said nothing, absolutely nothing about this Liquid-Life technology. He held out on me. As Camille knows, I sent her to the gala to warn Ormand. That was fair. In return, he tried to play me. And now? He gets what he gets."

Jennifer Daly laughed. She knew it would irk Pierson to no end, and she wanted to see where it would all lead. It was sort of a last hurrah for her. "Boy, Ormand played you, huh? I bet he came in talking about how much he wanted to work together with the president of the United States... piling on all that Mark Zuckerberg humble pie bullshit, a real Silicon Valley jerk. As it turns out, he was keeping the best for himself. Go figure."

She sat back and waited for it. She knew it would come. She knew she lit his fuse. Any second now, the president was going to explode.

Harry Pierson pinched his eyes and squinted hard a few times before launching into the tirade Jennifer Daly went out of her way to provoke.

"Don't you think I know that?" he yelled. "I heard the same crap from Camille. How do you think that makes me feel?"

"Hey," protested Camille.

Pierson raised his hands. "Yeah, yeah, that came out a little wrong. But the point remains – the little bastard held out on me. And now, I'm simply gonna take away his favorite toys. Problem solved. Never mind fossil fuels. It's Liquid Sky that's going to be obsolete overnight."

Camille cleared her throat.

"Too intense for you?" Pierson asked her.

Camille shook her head. "No, but I wonder if burying all this amazing technology is the best approach?"

Pierson looked offended. "Burying it? Says who? I would never dream of anything like that."

Jennifer Daly looked at Camille... then at Pierson... then back to Camille. Ordinarily, the president would have ripped Camille a new one. He didn't. Instead, he placated her and massaged the fleshy area between his right thumb and index finger in a vain attempt to distract his brain from the ripples of pain that had grown into waves since they first sat down.

The three women looked at each other, wondering why the tiger had suddenly turned into a kitten. Jennifer Daly figured she might as well take the lead. With just a couple of months left in her term, what did she have to lose?

"So, Camille... it sounds like you have something in mind?" she said. She prompted Fitzgerald with her eyes as if to say, "Don't leave me hanging here, sister."

"Yeah," said Fitzgerald. "With something as revolutionary as this, I bet you can come up with a million amazing ways to use it to help people. It's limited only by your imagination and your intentions."

"My God, spare me," said the president, having had enough. "My head feels like it might explode in thirty seconds, and my eyeballs feel criss-crossed. Believe me, I know what you ladies are up to."

Camille locked her deep eyes on Pierson's. "What are you up to, Harry?"

The president scoffed. "Come now, Camille. Let's call a spade a spade here. You three ladies want to cut off my balls and do something ridiculous with this technology like give it away for free or something crazy like that."

Camille was about to speak when Jennifer Daly cut her off. "Just to be clear, Harry," said Daly. "Your intention is to seize the intellectual property in the name of national security and keep it within the confines of the U.S. government."

Pierson smiled and nodded. "You got that right. After trying to screw me, there's no way on God's good earth Rickey Ormand is keeping this technology. Screw him. Crossing me was the biggest mistake he ever made, and I fully intend to see he pays the ultimate price for doing so."

Camille gasped. "You're not planning to...."

Daly finished Camille's thought. "Render him harmless?" That was code for have Ormand killed.

Pierson sat back in his chair. "If I was, I certainly wouldn't discuss it."

"I can tell you one thing for sure," said Fitzgerald. "Ormand would rather be dead than have his two most prized possessions stripped from him."

"You mean three," said Camille. "I'm quite sure he considers you his most prized possession."

Fitzgerald was startled. "I... I never thought about it... about myself... in those terms."

"Yeah, well, welcome to Washington," added Jennifer Daly.

Fitzgerald was still overwhelmed by what Camille said. "This all amounts to a fate worse than death for a guy like Rickey."

"And you?" asked Camille.

Fitzgerald didn't know what to say. "To be honest, I don't really know how to feel about it."

Pierson interjected. "Well, I don't want this to turn into tea time, ladies. Dr. Fitzgerald, you've said enough. I like the sound of it." He smiled. "Yeah, I damn sure like the sound of making Rickey Ormand's worst nightmare come true. It's the least I can do."

"So, you're really just going to, like, confiscate his intellectual property?" asked Camille in amazement.

"You have a problem with that?" asked Pierson. "Your friend here just stole it. At least what I'm doing is legal."

"You mean arbitrary," Camille replied.

The president made no attempt to disguise his annoyance. "Let me tell you something, Red. That jackass Ormand is no friend of yours. And he poses a huge threat to the stability of these United States and the world as a whole. That makes it far more than arbitrary. This is a matter of national security."

Camille rested her hands on the table. Everyone in the room was sure she was going to protest. She did not. "Okay," was all she said.

Pierson was so convinced Camille was going to protest on some sort of esoteric spiritual grounds that he began his retort before realizing what she'd just said. "You don't understand— wait, what?"

All eyes were now squarely on Camille O'Keefe.

"I said okay, whatever... he has it coming. You're right. I mean... you shouldn't kill him or anything like that. But in the end, this technology is far too important to allow any one man to control it."

Jennifer Daly started laughing to herself.

"What's your problem?" asked Pierson.

"Oh, I have no problem," Daly answered. "I was just laughing because Camille's comment about one man's control can be applied to you, too, Mr. President."

"You see," exclaimed Harry Pierson as best as he could given the throbbing pain between his temples. "You're trying to cut my balls off. What's next, Camille? Some sort of U.N. soup kitchen setup where you dole out the most valuable intellectual property ever devised?"

Camille shrugged. She was about to say, "Would that be so bad," but Jennifer Daly stepped in just in time.

"Of course not, Harry," she said. She winked at Camille.

"Okay," said Pierson. "Because that would be completely un-American. You might as well put a bullet in my head right now. There's no way I would allow anything to happen like that. Give this technology away for free? You'd have to be crazy."

"That's not what I am advocating," replied Camille, a bit stressed now. She felt like things were starting to get out of control. Too many people were putting words in her mouth. She'd put a lot of thought into the thing, and she needed to unwrap it at her own pace and in her own words.

Harry Pierson gritted his teeth.

This time, it was Jennifer Daly who was concerned. "Are you okay, Harry? We can table this thing until tomorrow. We have Dr. Fitzgerald in protective custody, and Rickey Ormand isn't going anywhere."

"You can say that again. We put a deny and detain on his passport. But over my dead body do I let this thing sit," spat the president sharply. "I have to be in Brussels tomorrow to listen to some socialist bullshit about Brexit and how some bean counter in Belgium should be telling a dairy farmer in Ireland what to charge for his milk. It's enough to make my brain explode."

Camille sighed. For some time now, she had known what the future held for her and Harry Pierson. She struggled with it for days, trying to decide if she should withhold vital information she foresaw about the future in exchange for providing a greater good for the world's neediest souls. As it often was when working with Harry Pierson, Camille felt conflicted. She didn't like it, didn't like it one little bit. In fact, she hated it. For her, politics meant too much compromise; too much compromise meant too little universal good.

In the end, she opted to remain silent, withhold critical information she divined through her clairvoyance. The mold was cast. She knew Harry Pierson was about to crap out. She played the Don't Pass line. Harry Pierson was the president of the United States, the most powerful man in the world. Camille O'Keefe was the vice president-elect, already confirmed by the Electoral College, making her next in line for the presidency should something happen to Pierson.

There were two sides to every outcome. For every winner there was a loser. Every loss was a win for someone else. Camille knew this but tried to fight it all the same. "Don't talk like that, Harry."

Pierson looked at her like she had two heads. "Do I strike you as a superstitious guy, Camille?"

"It makes me uncomfortable is all," she said and lowered her head.

"Let me make this perfectly clear for you three ladies," said Pierson. He snapped his fingers, trying to recall something. "Who were those crazy women in Greek mythology who got drunk and tore men apart?"

"*Maenads*," Camille answered.

"*Maenads,* right. Nasty bunch of gals," said the president. "Perfect for politics, that bunch. It seems I have them here at the table this morning."

Parker Fitzgerald was feeling the pressure now. She wasn't used to the cynical bluntness of backchannel politics. It struck her as very negative, and she was surprised Camille was so much a part of it. She stood up suddenly and made her way over to the breakfast table. After perusing the array of offerings, she opted for the gooiest sticky bun she could find. She picked up a butter knife and stabbed the delicious spiral. In stark contrast to the way Jennifer Daly surgically removed exactly one part of one donut, Parker Fitzgerald held up the sticky bun like a lollipop and bit into the heavenly pastry. She then plopped the remainder onto a plate, thought for a moment, and added a cheese Danish, three chocolate-dipped cookies with rainbow sprinkles, and several mini pecan-pie tarts. She also grabbed a napkin before returning to her seat.

She placed the plateful of deliciously empty calories neatly next to her file folder, returned to the breakfast table, poured herself a coffee and sat back down. Three pairs of eyes were following her every move. Nobody spoke a word at first. They all watched in awe as they contemplated the immense number of calories Fitzgerald had piled before her.

It was not until Fitzgerald polished off the sticky bun that Camille spoke. "I... I thought you didn't need food to live."

"Yeah," said Jennifer Daly. "Isn't that, like, the whole point of Liquid-Life?"

Her mouth too full of cheese Danish to respond, Fitzgerald drank some hot coffee to wash it down.

"I mean, are you sure you don't want a pint of milk and a cup of sugar for your coffee?" said Daly. "It would make the perfect accompaniment to a heart attack you have on your plate."

"I don't understand," said Camille, more confused now. "Why are you eating food... if you can call it that?"

Fitzgerald swallowed the mouthful of coffee and Danish. "Oh, this?" she said, laughing nervously. "I, yeah, I don't need to eat. I mean, to answer your question, my body generates all the energy it needs from gravity which is converted with the Liquid-Life implant inside me. It's about the size of a D-cell battery. But I have to keep my stomach and other stuff in there functioning. So, I have to eat from time to time. It's like changing the oil every three-thousand miles, you know?"

Daly shrugged. "So, to be very clear before we proceed any further, you can survive fully off gravitational energy?"

Fitzgerald nodded vigorously. "Yup. I just eat to keep things moving. Sometimes I eat to keep up appearances in public. Bottom line, though, my body is very efficient. I can pretty much eat whatever I want." She gestured to her plate. "Case in point. Right now, I'm eating like this because I'm getting stressed as hell with all of this political stuff. I'm new at this. If there was a bowl of pasta in front of me right now, I would snort it. Believe me, I take stress eating to an entirely new level."

Daly grimaced. "Of course, you can."

Fitzgerald sipped some coffee. "What I mean is that I still have emotions, thoughts, feelings. I'm still a person, a woman. I'm more than just some bundle of high-tech parts and programs."

Camille nodded. Her compassion for her friend was radiant. "That's what's really important, Parker. You are a very special woman. There's nobody else like you." She puckered her lips and eyeballed Fitzgerald's plate.

Fitzgerald smiled. "Please… help yourself," she said.

Jennifer Daly cleared her throat. "I beg to differ. I see things a bit differently. Certainly, Dr. Fitzgerald is unique. And you're correct in saying there's no other woman like her. That's the whole point here. I mean, we're having this emergency meeting under the most clandestine circumstances precisely because Dr. Parker Fitzgerald is such… how do I put this?"

Camille smiled gently. "Delicacy is not your strong suit, Jennifer. Let's leave it at that. That's what I like about you most, and it's what you do best."

Jennifer Daly nodded. "Okay, then. Parker Fitzgerald is an oddity. She exists in multiple planes at one and the same time. She is more than a machine, certainly."

"Gee, thanks," said Fitzgerald, taking a healthy bite of pastry.

Daly rubbed her hands together. "Hey, I know I can be blunt. But this situation requires absolute honesty."

Camille interjected. "These times call for it. There's a role for you yet, Jennifer... after this is all said and done."

Jennifer Daly shot a glance at Camille. The two looked at each other. It seemed to Daly that Camille was setting something up here. Was it possible that Camille had some sort of plan that involved all three of the women at the table? Daly squinted as she tried to read Camille's mind on the matter.

"Like I said," Daly continued, "Dr. Fitzgerald is far more than a robot. But you are also not just a woman. If I understand things correctly, this Liquid-Life technology makes you much more than just the sum of your parts. You are... truly extraordinary in the literal sense of the word."

She looked at Pierson. "Harry, we really have no mechanisms in place for dealing with this sort of thing. The intellectual-property issues alone are mind boggling. And then, as you point out, the social, political, and economic implications of Liquid-Drive are equally ominous. Quite frankly, I don't know if the world can handle Parker Fitzgerald."

"That's been my point since we first found out about Liquid-Drive, and I dispatched Camille to Ormand's gala."

The president pointed his finger at her like she was a miscreant child. "Let me tell you something, doctor. I don't care how smart you are. There's one hell of a crisis coming down the pipeline because you and your boss feel obligated to upset the world's socioeconomic framework. Nobody asked you to do this. I didn't enlist Liquid Sky to help solve the energy crisis or discover the fountain of youth or whatever it is you have inside you. You and Rickey Ormand did this for one reason and one reason only... money."

Camille winced. She could feel Fitzgerald's pain.

"Come on, Harry. You're not trying to tell us that profit motive's a bad thing, are you?"

The president pinched the bridge of his nose. "Hell no, for God's sake. Who am I, Bernie Sanders? I'm just saying. They started this problem, and I'm going to finish it. That's all."

Still salty, the president spoke up again. "There's nothing to be nervous about, so let me reiterate my intentions. I'm taking it all. Gravity power and everything ever to be associated with it for all eternity will soon belong to the United States government. That's a good thing. It's a safe thing. It will be the cornerstone of my presidency and will put the four of us smack dab in the middle of every history book ever written from now on. Practice your best media smiles, ladies. We're going straight to the top from here."

Parker stuffed the rest of the Danish into her mouth. "That's what is making me so nervous," she mumbled between chews. "Rickey Ormand will go ballistic. Need I remind you that I barely escaped with my life, and that was before all this went down?"

Harry Pierson pounded his index finger onto the table. "If that little shit so much as looks at us wrong, it will be the last time he looks at anybody. The man is done. He needs to accept his failure. It's inevitable. Both Liquid-Drive and Liquid-Life are mine. Need I remind you, ladies, that I am the president of the United States? In the event that I want something, I have been empowered to plan it, fund it, and, yes, take it if I so desire. Rickey Ormand, Liquid Sky, Liquid-Drive, Liquid-Life... it all belongs to me in the interests of national security."

Jennifer Daly clarified the president's remarks. "You mean, of course, it all belongs to the American people in the name of national security because, well, they're the nation and it's their security you're entrusted to protect."

The president smiled glibly. "But of course, my dear J.D.. It's always about the people. I am all about the people all the time. I am simply the steward of their best interests." He smiled. "I'm simply saying that our little friend Mr. Ormand is in need of a civic's lesson."

Camille coughed nervously into her clenched hand. The others turned their attention her way. She was sweating a bit. She reached over and snatched one of the mini pecan-pies from Fitzgerald's plate. "I eat when I get nervous, too."

"How many times do I have to say it?" asked Pierson. "There's nothing to be nervous about. Quite honestly, Camille, you should be thanking me on your hands and knees."

Jennifer Daly arched a brow. "Perhaps that is not the best way to phrase that, Mr. President. You know... we women are getting all uppity about those kinds of images these days."

Pierson squeezed his temples. "Every time you speak, my headache gets worse. What I mean, Camille, is that this conflict is going to make you the first female president. Say what you want, Camille. Not all conflict is bad. You avoid conflict at all costs, but what are you sacrificing in the process? I've cleared a path for you. There will be nothing to stand in your way once I'm gone."

Camille was silent while she let the irony wash over her. "More than you know, Harry," she said. "More than you know."

"So, as I was saying before, Camille," said Jennifer Daly, still wondering if Camille had some sort of plan in mind that involved all three women. "It sounds like you have an alternative in mind?"

Camille poured herself a glass of water and took a healthy swig. "We need to get some nice herbal teas in here, Harry. Anyway, I do have something specific in mind, Jennifer. Thank you for returning to that."

Harry Pierson wiped his face in anguish. "Oh, good Lord. You ladies are dead set on making my head explode, aren't you? Now what? The three of you have been conspiring against me?" The slight wavering in his voice suggested he was only half joking.

"I assure you," said Camille. "This is the first any of you are hearing about this. There's been no collusion among us. However, there is something I've been thinking over."

That last bit got the president's attention. He was married to Camille O'Keefe professionally for better or for worse, so he figured he might as well give her a listen. It wasn't like he had much choice. She seemed intent on telling him whether he liked it or not.

Camille drank some more water, sat back, and began unpacking her plan. She ran through her entire strategy. She covered everything from the basic facts to her most abstract aspirations.

Twenty minutes later, Harry Pierson and Jennifer Daly sat staring at her in stunned silence, and Parker Fitzgerald had started in on a second sticky bun.

"I call this my plan for One World. And remember, One World is both a concept and an actual company," concluded Camille.

What shocked Pierson the most was the sheer audacity of it. "It's got some jalapeño on it, that's for sure," remarked the president. "I didn't figure you for such an aggressive maneuver, Camille."

"One World?" asked Fitzgerald. "Is that what you call it? That's a cool name."

Harry Pierson was taking it seriously. That was a good sign for Camille. "Yeah," he said. "But it sounds like you need a big banner of Stalin or something."

Camille waved her hand at Pierson. "You're stuck in a different time, Harry. The world is a different place now. People yearn for interconnection. Look at the rise of café culture, the internet, and social media. You're still thinking in terms of the Cold War. The Berlin Wall is an ancient metaphor now. Thanks to technology, we have the ability to transcend all sorts of walls... time, space, borders, you name it. We can connect and share ourselves instantaneously with people all over the world. That's what people demand nowadays. I think it's marvellous."

Jennifer Daly was also giving Camille's plan some serious thought. She wasn't sure whether she should go out on a limb for Camille. But Camille's idea was so intriguing, she had to hear more about it. She decided to take a chance. What difference did it matter now anyway?

"I have to be honest," she commented. "I think this One World idea of yours can catch on big time," she said. "You know, Harry, she's right about people using technology that makes the world a very small place indeed. Just look at the way people use social media during uprisings, revolutions, even to document their day, and everything in between."

"Which is where life happens," added Camille. "Right there in between."

The president drummed his fingers on the table. "First of all, I understand what you're saying about social media and all that stuff. At the same time, people have stopped interacting face-to-face. Call me old-fashioned, but I don't like that. More to the point, though, I'm interested in the scope of your plan. I like a grand scheme as much as the next president. But, I'm really uncomfortable with the nuts and bolts of your plan. I'm not sure if we can control it. For example, if I understand you correctly, this One World of yours would be a company that pays out 25 percent of its yearly profits in the form of a dividend? That's like…."

"Un-American," said Jennifer Daly. "I know what you're thinking, Harry. A company that pays out a 25 percent dividend? But I don't think that's exactly what Camille has in mind, is it?" She looked at Camille for clarification.

Camille nodded. "Right, right. That's not exactly what I'm advocating. At first, I thought about drafting a law requiring all big U.S. companies to pay out 25 percent of their profit every year."

Harry Pierson started choking on the words. Quite literally, he started gasping.

"Breathe, Harry," said Jennifer Daly.

"Wouldn't that be a great way to introduce your new administration," said Parker Fitzgerald.

"Are you insane? Kill me now," Pierson gurgled. "Spare me the pain and suffering."

Camille tried to laugh it off. "Of course, I knew that would never fly with you, Harry. So, I changed course. As I envision it, One World is a foundation, not a company."

"That's what I thought you said," stated Jennifer Daly nodding cautiously. "Pivoting just right can save an otherwise dead idea."

"Right," continued Camille. "So, this is how I figure it. In this foundation called One World are, say, fifty companies that will voluntarily agree to participate in this dividend plan."

"Of their own initiative?" questioned Daly, trying to position the thing so Pierson could at least contemplate it.

Pierson eyed Camille suspiciously.

"That's right," said Camille. "They join One World voluntarily and agree to pay out this huge dividend to the people who own their stock. This way, the immense profits generated by these big capitalist companies get recirculated instead of sitting in some massive bank account doing nobody any good at all, least of all the economy."

Parker Fitzgerald clapped her hands enthusiastically. "Instead of sitting in Rickey Ormand's account doing nothing, he would have to kick it back out as a dividend."

"That's exactly right," said Camille. "What good does it do anyone to have a few rich people sit on billions? We have the best system in the world. But it's bogged down right now. We have too many Rickey Ormands sitting on billions and billions in personal wealth. That money needs to circulate into new companies."

"And new technologies," said Fitzgerald, starting to get it now. "Like me." She smiled.

Pierson looked at Camille incredulously… then at Daly… then back to Camille. "You're kidding, right?"

Camille's response was dead serious. "Not at all. One World can be our World, Harry."

The president sat back in his chair. "Why does this sound familiar?"

Daly and Fitzgerald looked at Camille. What was the president referring to?

Camille smiled. "Beck."

Pierson smirked. "No crap!"

"Beck promised me he would propose this plan when he took office. My good friend Johnny Long first came up with the idea of the dividends. One World is my creation."

"And am I correct in assuming that Beck changed his mind as soon as he actually took office?" asked Pierson.

Camille looked at him. "You know the answer to that, Harry."

"And do you know why he changed his mind, Camille?" Pierson prompted.

"Because he was a lying, cheating manipulator?" said Jennifer Daly.

"Okay... okay... but no. It was because even Becket Rosemore knew when to stop short," replied Pierson boisterously. "Hands down, no question about it, who would propose something like that? A law requiring companies to shell out 25 percent of their profit? That's political suicide."

"I think you're rushing to judgment," said Jennifer Daly, surprising herself. It was like some inner voice suddenly emerged to stand up to the president. "I'm betting it's a little more complex."

Pierson rubbed his temples. He felt his lower lip tremble a bit. It was a curious feeling. He felt a bit of spittle gather on the side of his mouth as well. He wiped it away with his sleeve. "It's no more complex than wearing a Ché Guevara T-shirt and running around protesting at the WTO in the name of some radical youth brigade."

Pierson threw his hands up. "I need to be honest. Maybe the one thing he did right was run away from this program of yours, Camille."

Camille took a deep breath. "Honestly, Harry, I think there's a way to make this work."

"Why would I want to, Camille? Why?"

"My dividend plan is different," answered Camille. "We need to get money circulating. That said, I envision something like what my friend Johnny Long recommended back then with a new incentive. He's a very, very successful money manager, and he knows about this kind of thing."

"That would be an excellent plank for your second-term platform, Harry," noted Daly.

"Right," agreed Camille. "I don't know anybody who thinks we need more multi-billionaires. At the same time, we don't want to throw the baby out with the bathwater."

"So," asked Daly. "Are you saying capitalism isn't the problem?"

"Well, you don't want to know what I think about that. You won't like the answer. But, like my friend Johnny says, capitalism is the best system we have. The problem is stagnation. Too much money has piled up in too few places."

"Rickey Ormand," added Fitzgerald. "Poster child."

"Exactly," said Jennifer Daly.

Harry Pierson just grunted.

"But if we create a foundation in which a bunch of big companies pay out a good portion of their profits, large shareholders can reinvest all that money in new technologies and stuff."

"Sort of like the way I was created," said Fitzgerald. "Seed capital generated by investment profits. It's the Silicon Valley Cycle."

Daly reminded her, "You also almost died."

Fitzgerald was nonplussed. "But think about it. That's how Liquid-Life was developed. I am a living embodiment of what Camille is advocating with her dividend plan."

Camille was beaming. "You're a trope. You're a microcosm of the macrocosm."

Pierson shook his head. "I'm not seeing it, ladies. I'm sorry. Sometimes, slow change is a better course of action than radically changing course for the hell of it and causing everything to topple. And besides, why on earth would a company's board of directors want to be a part of this One World? What's in it for them? I mean you're asking them to give up 25 percent of their profits."

"No," said Jennifer Daly. "I don't think that's correct. It's *paid out* in the form of a dividend. That's completely different. That's the crux of this thing. I mean, I'm certainly no expert, but I know enough investment bankers to have learned a few rules of thumb."

"Such as?" Pierson prompted.

"Well, for one thing," answered Daly, "a dividend is real money. Institutional investors will jump at the chance to own the stock of a company paying out 25 percent of its profit in the form of a dividend. Are you kidding me? There will be a buying frenzy, Harry."

The president sat back contemplating. "Okay," he said, awaiting more details.

"Another huge benefit," said Daly, "is the way Wall Street would value that stock. Again, I'm no expert, but I remember I was having dinner with some big donor from Goldman Sachs... or maybe it was Ben Bernanke. I don't remember. Anyway, the point is that stocks that pay high dividends can be valued by their dividend-ratio method or something."

"What the hell does that mean?" asked Pierson.

Jennifer Daly shrugged. "I'm not positive, but it has something to do with raising the stock price based on the size of the dividend."

"That's right," said Camille, a lightbulb going off. "Johnny Long said that the share price of any stock in One World will skyrocket because not only will a lot of big funds and people want to buy the stock, but it will go up even more because of the way they would calculate the value based on the huge dividend."

Jennifer Daly said, "Which means institutional shareholders as well as the board of directors will be very happy indeed, Harry. That's all that really matters."

Pierson's head was spinning. He wasn't expecting any of this when he called the emergency meeting. He was expecting a tight little sit-down centered upon his intention to seize Liquid Sky in the interest of national security. He was expecting enthusiastic cooperation from a vengeful robo-gal coupled with full compliance from his transcendent vice president-elect. That's how he played it out in his mind.

Instead, he found "three women set on fighting me at every step." That's how he put it. "What's more, it appears the illustrious, tell-all Camille O'Keefe, my whimsical yet provocative vice president, has cooked up some grand plan for the redistribution of wealth rivalled only by Karl Marx himself."

Pierson threw himself back in his chair exasperated. "I guess we should just make you president, Camille. I mean, since you're making policy now."

He looked at Fitzgerald. "You, Fitzgerald. You're the thing everyone is going to be fighting over. What do you think?"

Parker Fitzgerald looked at Camille, then at Jennifer Daly, then back to Camille. Camille smiled softly and nodded. Fitzgerald was immediately relieved of the burden the president had just heaped upon her shoulders. "I think to myself what a Silicon Valley guy like Rickey Ormand would think."

"And?" Pierson prompted.

Fitzgerald cleaned her hands on a napkin before tossing it aside. "Well, he's all about the money, right? God knows he has enough. But the one thing I'll say is that he's constantly investing it in new opportunities. Like I said before, I'm living proof of that. So, I think something like One World would really interest him."

The president thought for a moment. "Thank you," he said. "But I find it hard to believe all these companies will simply line up to be a part of your fantasy, Camille. I don't see anything in it for them except giving up a huge chunk of their profits. And without the profit motive, why have a company in the first place? This kind of government intervention and control is exactly why communism and socialism fail every time."

Daly and Fitzgerald were silent. They were all but convinced Camille's fleeting endeavor had been dashed upon the rocks of Harry Pierson's infamous cynicism. But not Camille. Contrary to the look of dour disappointment Daly and Fitzgerald were sporting, Camille seemed delighted.

"I am unnerved by your grin," said Pierson. "At this point, you're supposed to be dismayed and disappointed. It's part of your initiation into politics."

Camille sat back and took in the moment. "You underestimate me, Harry. All your craggity, crunchy cynicism is interfering with your ability to dream. You wonder why on earth a company would join One World? I say to you, they will be lining up."

Pierson laughed. "And why is that?"

"Because after you seize the intellectual property for Liquid-Drive and Liquid-Life, you are going to transfer the rights to One World."

Pierson sat, mouth agape and stunned. Parker Fitzgerald and Jenifer Daly, however, were laughing riotously.

"You should see the look on your face," said Daly. "I can so totally see it on the cover of the Washington Post with the caption, 'Say What Now'?"

Daly looked at Camille. "Seriously, though, this is brilliant. I see exactly where you're going with this. It's freaking brilliant. So, One

World will control the rights to Liquid-Drive and Liquid-Life. And only companies that are part of One World –"

"And the dividend plan," interjected Camille.

Daly nodded. "And the dividend plan, of course, will be able to use it, capitalize on it, develop it, and so on"

"Oh my God," exclaimed Fitzgerald. "You're a genius, Camille. I mean... only companies in One World will have access to the most amazing technology in the history of the world. It's unbelievable."

Camille returned her focus to Harry Pierson. "So, you see, Harry, there will be the greatest possible incentive for these companies to join One World. They will have access to the technology."

Pierson thought for a moment before responding. "And what happens then? I know you too well, Camille, to think it ends there. Am I right?"

Camille felt Daly and Fitzgerald staring at her. She could hear what they were both thinking... what then, indeed?

"Ah, yes. You do know me well, Harry. So, in exchange for being part of One World and having access to the most valuable technology in the world, member companies will have to pay a royalty. Those fees will fund One World programs. This will ensure the huge leap forward in the quality of life available to the world's most downtrodden people, those poor souls who have yet to enjoy much of anything good in this world. That's all. There will be more revenue and profits generated through One World than member companies can count. If Johnny Long is right, their stock prices will soar. My only requirement it that the destitute of the world are not excluded. That's it, Harry."

Camille took a sip of water. She was done. She said what she came to say. All eyes were on Harry Pierson now. What was *he* going to say?

"Over my dead body," Pierson shouted. "Not only is it political suicide, it will bring about the complete upheaval of the world. Are you crazy? Over my dead body, O'Keefe."

After that, the President didn't say much of anything. He sat staring down at the top-secret file folder in front of him. The women sat watching him until it became evident that his torso was wavering back and forth a bit... not much, but enough to see. His skin has gone ashen, as well.

".Harry," said Jennifer Daly. "Are you alright?"

Camille knew what was happening. She had, after all, foreseen it all.

"Mr. President?" said Fitzgerald.

Camille looked at Jennifer Daly. "Jennifer?"

Daly turned her attention to Camille. The calm in Camille's voice and the way she addressed her as Jennifer unnerved her. "Yes, Camille?"

"I'm depending on you these next two months before my inauguration."

"Listen to me," said Camille, authoritatively now. "Your country needs you. The world needs you. I need you to enact this plan with an executive order. I need you to help me change the world until I am sworn in as president in January."

Parker Fitzgerald stood up. "What the hell are you talking about, Camille?"

"For the next two months, Jennifer, you will be the acting president of the United States. After my inauguration when I am sworn in as president, you will run One World."

With that, Harry Pierson's forehead came slamming down on the table. It was like a Teutonic oak falling in slow motion. The table reverberated with the impact. After his head hit the table, Pierson's body went limp, his head turned to the side. A trickle of saliva ran from his mouth. His eyes were open, and there was life in them still. But there was no consciousness.

"Oh my God," screamed Jennifer Daly, picking up the phone in the middle of the table. "This is the Sit Room," she barked into the receiver. "Lariot is down. Lariot is down."

Jennifer Daly looked up at Camille. There was panic in her eyes.

"It's a stroke," said Camille. "Massive. He will not regain consciousness."

Aghast, Daly stood up straight. "But...."

"Oh my God," said Parker Fitzgerald. "You are the president."

Daly brought her hand to her mouth. "It's true about you. You know things," said Daly, blown away by Camille's clairvoyance. "What do we do now?"

"In a few seconds the Secret Service and medical team will be here to care for Harry as best they can."

"And then what?" asked Fitzgerald.

Camille stood up, straightened her clothes and arranged her hair. "Then Jennifer Daly will be sworn in as President Daly."

Camille walked over to Harry Pierson and took his right hand in hers. She squeezed it gently. "Thank you," she whispered before walking out of the room.